PRAISE F(

The Flats

"Add this to your summer reading list
Hollywood): Beth O'Leary's debut novel, *The Flatshare*, is a twenty-
first-century rom-com that will please hopeless romantics. . . . Everyone needs to devour [it] immediately."
—*USA Today*

"A delight from start to finish. . . . A warm, enchanting love story
perfect for fans of classic rom-coms." —*Kirkus Reviews* (starred review)

"This charming debut features lovely characters being nice to one another. It's easy to root for them to get together and solve the problems
in each of their lives. Be prepared to hand-sell this one. It's a sweet
romance that will win over readers once they discover it on the shelves."
—*Library Journal* (starred review)

"*The Flatshare* is the novel equivalent of a cup of hot tea. It'll warm you
up—and heal you if you're hurting." —Refinery29

"*The Flatshare* is undeniably a romance between Tiffy and Leon; it will
give you butterflies and make you laugh. But it's also a deep dive into
the realities of relationships gone wrong, and what it truly takes to dig
oneself out of the depths. . . . An empowering look at resilience and
healthy love." —Bustle

"Clever debut. . . . O'Leary's story packs plenty of laughs and gasps;
fans of *Bridget Jones's Diary* will want to give this a look."
—*Publishers Weekly*

"Bright, feel-good, and charming." —*The Irish Times*

"It's funny and charming, but there are moments of real poignancy, too. Guaranteed to leave you with a smile on your face."

—*Good Housekeeping*

PRAISE FOR

The Switch

"*The Switch* was refreshing, engaging, and thoroughly enjoyable. This story has everything you could ask for: witty characters, strong female relationships, and a view about love that'd make anyone hopeful."

—Helena Hunting, *New York Times* bestselling
author of *Kiss My Cupcake*

"*The Switch* brilliantly encompasses all the humor and whimsy of *The Flatshare* while delving into emotional topics like grief and the importance of watching out for neighbors. Charismatic Eileen stands out as the star of this witty, joyful show, illustrating that mature women need love, too." —*Booklist* (starred review)

"A cozy, hopeful escape that will make readers laugh, cry, and feel inspired." —*Kirkus Reviews* (starred review)

"*The Switch* offers a hopeful reminder to reach out to our neighbors with an open mind. It's a cozy, lovely story about how community matters more than ever." —*BookPage* (starred review)

"*The Switch* is a heartfelt and often quite funny story that celebrates changing yourself by changing your point of view at any age."

—All About Romance

"Ingenious." —*Prima*

TITLES BY BETH O'LEARY

The Flatshare

The Switch

The Road Trip

The No-Show

The
No-Show

BETH O'LEARY

JOVE
NEW YORK

A JOVE BOOK
Published by Berkley
An imprint of Penguin Random House LLC
penguinrandomhouse.com

A JOVE BOOK, BERKLEY, and the BERKLEY & B colophon
are registered trademarks of Penguin Random House LLC.

Library of Congress Cataloging-in-Publication Data

Names: O'Leary, Beth, author.
Title: The no-show / Beth O'Leary.
Description: First Edition. | New York: Jove, 2022.
Identifiers: LCCN 2021034982 (print) | LCCN 2021034983 (ebook) |
ISBN 9780593438442 (trade paperback) | ISBN 9780593438459 (ebook)
Subjects: GSAFD: Love stories.
Classification: LCC PR6115.L424 N6 2022 (print) |
LCC PR6115.L424 (ebook) | DDC 823/.92—dc23
LC record available at https://lccn.loc.gov/2021034982
LC ebook record available at https://lccn.loc.gov/2021034983

Quercus hardcover edition / April 2022
Jove trade paperback edition / April 2022

Printed in the United States of America
7   9   10   8   6

Book design by George Towne
Interior art: © Fedorov Ivan Sergeevich / Shutterstock Images

For Bug

Siobhan

HE ISN'T HERE.

Siobhan breathes out slowly through her nose. She's aiming for calm, but it reads more *angry bull* than *zen*.

She canceled breakfast with a friend for this. She curled her hair and wore lipstick and shaved her legs (not just to the knee, all the way up, in case he fancied running a hand up her thigh under the table).

And he isn't bloody here.

"I'm not angry," she tells Fiona. They're video-calling. They always video-call—Siobhan is a big believer in the power of eye contact. Also, she'd quite like *someone* to see how fabulous she looks today, even if it is only her flatmate. "I'm resigned. He's a man, ergo, he let me down. What did I expect?"

"You're wearing sex makeup," Fiona says, squinting at the screen. "It's not even nine in the morning yet, Shiv."

Siobhan shrugs. She's sitting in one of those cafés that prides itself on its quirkiness, a quality she always finds deeply irritating in anything or anyone, and there's a half-drunk double-shot oat-milk latte on the table in front of her. If she'd known she was going to be stood up on Valentine's Day, she'd have got proper milk. Siobhan is only vegan when she's in a good mood.

"Sex is what we do," she says.

"Even on a breakfast date?"

They've never actually had a breakfast date before. But when she'd told him she was on a flying visit to London, he'd said, *Fancy having breakfast with me tomorrow morning, by any chance . . . ?* Asking for a breakfast date was definitely significant—and on V-Day, no less. Generally speaking, their dates happen in her hotel room, usually after eleven p.m.; they see each other on the first Friday of the month, plus the odd bonus day if she happens to be in London.

That's fine. That's plenty. Siobhan doesn't *want* more than that—he lives in England, she lives in Ireland; they're both busy people. Their arrangement works perfectly.

"Are you sure you don't want to give it another five?" Fiona says, lifting a dainty hand to her lips as she swallows a mouthful of cornflakes. She's sitting at their kitchen table, her hair still in its overnight plait. "He's maybe just late?"

Siobhan feels a pang of homesickness for her flat, though she's only been gone a day. She misses the familiar lemony smell of their kitchen, the peace of her walk-in wardrobe. She misses the version of herself that had not yet made the mistake of hoping her favorite hookup might actually want to be something more.

She sips her latte as airily as she can. "Oh, please. He's not coming," she says with a shrug. "I'm resigned to it."

"You don't think you're maybe writing him off be—"

"Fi. He said eight thirty. It's ten to. He's stood me up. It's better if I just . . ." She swallows. "Accept it and bounce back."

"All right," Fiona says with a sigh. "Well. Drink your coffee, remember you're excellent, get ready to kick butt today." Her American accent resurfaces when she says *kick butt*; these days she sounds as

Dublin as Siobhan for the most part. When the pair first met at the Gaiety School of Acting, aged eighteen, Fiona was all New York accent and confidence, but ten years of failed auditions have washed her out. She's unlucky, always the understudy. Siobhan fully believes this is Fiona's year, as she has every year for the last decade.

"When am I not ready to kick butt? Please."

Siobhan tosses her hair back just as a man passes behind her; he knocks her chair. The coffee wobbles in his hand, a tiny splash spilling on Siobhan's shoulder. It sinks into the telephone-box red of her dress, leaving a little stain, two droplets, like a semicolon.

It has all the makings of a meet-cute. For a split second, as she turns, Siobhan considers it—he's attractive-ish, tall, the sort of man you'd expect to have a big dog and a loud laugh. Then he says, "Christ alive, you'll put someone's eye out with all that hair!"

And Siobhan decides, no, she is in too bad a mood for large imposing men who do not immediately apologize for spilling coffee on couture dresses. An angry, righteous heat grows in her chest, and she's grateful for it, relieved, even—this is exactly what she needs.

She reaches out and touches his arm, just lightly. He slows, his eyebrows a little raised; she pauses deliberately before she speaks.

"Didn't you mean to say, I'm ever so sorry?" she asks. Her voice is sugar-sweet.

"Careful, buddy," Fiona says from the phone, which is now propped on the wonky terra-cotta plant pot in the center of the table.

He is not careful. Siobhan knew he wouldn't be.

"What exactly am I meant to be ever-so-sorry for, Rapunzel?" he asks. He follows her gaze to the coffee stain on her shoulder and huffs a warm, indulgent laugh. He pretends to squint, as if there is nothing there to see; he's trying to be cute, and if she were in a good, vegan-milk sort of mood, Siobhan might go along with it. But, unfortunately for the man with the coffee, Siobhan has just been stood up on Valentine's Day.

"This dress cost almost two thousand euro," she says. "Would you like to transfer the money, or pay in installments?"

He throws his head back and laughs. A few couples glance over.

"Very funny," he says.

"I'm not joking."

His smile drops, and then things really get started. He raises his voice first; she pulls up the dress on Net-a-Porter; he snaps and calls her a *mouthy little madam*, which is excellent, because it gives her an extra five minutes of ammo, and Fiona's laughing on her phone screen, and for a good few seconds Siobhan almost forgets that she's alone in a tediously quirky café with no date on his way.

"You're brutal, Shiv," Fiona says fondly as Siobhan settles back into her chair.

The man has stormed off, having thrown a tenner on her table *for the dry cleaning*. Everyone is staring. Siobhan flicks those shining blond argument-starting locks over her shoulder and turns her face to the window. Chin up. Tits out. Legs crossed.

With her head turned like this, only Fiona can tell she's trying not to cry.

"Did that help?" Fiona asks.

"Of course. And I'm ten quid richer, too. What shall I buy?" Siobhan sniffs and pulls up the menu from the other side of the table. She catches the time on her watch: nine a.m. Only nine a.m. and she's already having a record-breakingly bad day. "An 'Always See the Sunny Side' fry-up, perhaps? A 'Keep Smiling' kale smoothie?"

She slaps her hand down on the menu and shoves it away again; the couple at the adjacent table jump slightly and eye her with trepidation.

"Fuck me, this is categorically the worst place to be stood up on Valentine's Day," she says. The warming anger in her chest has gone, and now there's just that tightness, the lonely clutching ache of approaching tears.

"Do *not* let this get to you," Fiona says. "He's a prick if he's stood you up."

"He *is* a prick," Siobhan says fiercely, voice catching.

Fiona falls silent. Siobhan has the suspicion that she is giving her time to gather herself, which makes her even more determined not to let either of the teardrops currently teetering on her lash line roll down her cheeks.

"I know this was big for you, Shiv," Fiona says tentatively. "Have you even . . . Isn't it the first proper date since Cillian?"

Siobhan scowls, conceding defeat and dabbing at her eyes. "What, you think I haven't been on a date for three years?"

Fiona just waits patiently; they both know that she hasn't. Fiona ought to know better than to *say* it, though. Eventually Fiona sighs and says, "Are you binning him off, then?"

"Oh, he's binned. He's *done*," Siobhan says.

He's going to rue the day he stood her up. Siobhan doesn't know what ruing is, not yet, but she's going to find out. And he's not going to like it.

Miranda

THREE MINUTES PAST NINE, AND NOBODY HAS TURNED UP.

Miranda gnaws the inside of her thumbnail and leans back against her car, tapping a boot on the tire. She tightens her ponytail. She checks her bootlaces. She goes through her rucksack and makes sure everything's there: two water bottles; her climbing kit; the handsaw her parents bought her for her birthday, with her name engraved on the handle. All present and correct, no items having magically leaped from her bag at some point on the twenty-minute journey from her flat.

Seven minutes past nine and, at last, there's the sound of tires on gravel. Miranda turns as Jamie's truck pulls up, bright green, emblazoned with the J Doyle company logo. Miranda's heart is hammering at her ribs like a woodpecker, and she stands a little taller as Jamie and the rest of the crew climb out.

Jamie grins at her as they approach. "AJ, Spikes, Trey, this is Miranda Rosso," he says.

Two of the men give Miranda a look that she is familiar with: the hunted, nervous glance of boys who have been firmly instructed not to be inappropriate. Trey is short and stocky, with sullen, deep-set eyes. Spikes is a head taller than Trey and built like a rugby player, barrel-chested beneath his grubby, faded T-shirt. They each nod at her and immediately turn their attention to the tree on the corner of the plot where they're parked.

And then there's AJ. He gives Miranda a very different sort of look: the up-and-down glance of a man who hears *Don't be inappropriate with the new girl* and takes it as a challenge.

Miranda's been warned about AJ. He's got quite the reputation. *That AJ's had more women than he's climbed trees*, Miranda's old boss told her when she said she was leaving to join Jamie's team. *Face of an angel, heart of an absolutely heartless bastard.*

So Miranda is braced for the piercing green eyes, the bearded jaw, the muscled, tattooed arms. She's ready for the eyebrow quirk she gets when their eyes meet, the look that says, *I eat women like you for breakfast.*

She's not *totally* prepared for the small cockapoo puppy in his arms, however.

She double takes. AJ strokes the dog's head, implacable, as if it is perfectly normal to be carrying a tiny puppy when you arrive at a job site.

"Oh, yeah, and that's Rip," Jamie says without much enthusiasm. "New dog. Apparently he can't be left home alone, is that right, AJ?"

"Gets separation anxiety," AJ says, lifting Rip up a little higher against his broad, muscled chest.

Miranda is trying very hard not to smile. Her plan for dealing with AJ had been to completely ignore him—she's found that's usually the best strategy with cocky types. But . . . *damn*, that's a cute puppy. She's never been able to resist the ones that look a bit like teddy bears, all curly-coated and snub-nosed.

"Hey, Rip," she says, extending a hand for him to sniff. "Hey, little guy!"

Rip's tail begins to wag against AJ's side, and Miranda tries not to melt.

"He likes you," AJ says, voice like honey, gaze slick as it runs up and down Miranda's body again, and Miranda's brain puts the brakes on. The puppy may be cute, but she is directing way too much attention to the torso of the man holding him. This was not the strategy.

"Hi," she says, tearing her gaze away from Rip and directing her smile toward Trey and Spikes. "Good to meet you guys."

"Rosso's quite the climber," Jamie says, clapping Miranda on the back. "You should have seen her at the aerial rescue challenge. Never seen anyone up a tree so fast. You got your own climbing kit?"

"Mm-hmm," Miranda says, nodding to indicate her rucksack.

"I'm sending you up the big one," Jamie says. "The customer wants the crown reduced by a third." He nods at the silver birch towering over the front garden of the grand house they're parked outside. It's spindly, ducking and weaving in the wind. "Want to show these boys how it's done?"

"Always," Miranda says, already crouching to open her rucksack and pull out her harness.

THERE IS NO RUSH QUITE LIKE A CLIMB.

When Miranda was fifteen, she was walking home from school and heard men shouting in the distance. She followed the sounds to the tree surgeons training in the land management college up the road from her secondary. There was a row of pines, tall and lovely, with yellow and orange ropes hanging from their branches. The men above her were moving through the trees like Tarzan, leaping across forks to grab trunks between their knees, leaning back into their harnesses. One was even hanging upside down.

It had never occurred to Miranda that you could climb trees for a living.

The instructor had seen her watching and told her about an open day the following week when she'd get the chance to try it herself, if she fancied it. Once she'd felt the harness take her weight, once she'd reached her first branch and looked down at the ground swimming beneath her, she'd been hooked.

Ten years later and she isn't just climbing trees for a living, she's doing it *really well*. And though her parents are no closer to understanding why their eldest daughter insists on working in a profession so dangerous that she was advised to get her life insurance sorted on her first day, they have reluctantly come around to it, mainly because nobody could fail to see how passionate Miranda is about what she does.

Once she's up in the birch, with her main line anchored to the highest branch that can take her weight, Miranda forgets about Trey and Spikes and AJ. She even forgets about Carter, their lunch date, the outfit carefully folded in the bottom of her rucksack in readiness. Being forty feet up a tree is absolutely terrifying, no matter how experienced you are, and when you're doing it, there's no room for *anything* else. There's just you and the ropes and the wind and the tree, breathing around you, keeping you from falling.

AJ's pruning a hedge to the front of the property, with Rip toddling excitedly around his feet; at first Jamie stays to keep an eye on Miranda, but after half an hour or so he leaves to help AJ. The other boys are on groundwork, the heavy lifting, putting branches through the chipper. The morning goes by in a roar of chainsaws and the glitter of sawdust.

Miranda sails down the main line and lets herself land hard, heels digging into the soil beneath the tree. The rope comes down nicely for her, doesn't even catch. It's been a good morning. Her hair is coming loose from its ponytail; strands stick to her forehead as she pulls off her helmet.

"Not bad," AJ says as she walks past him to Jamie.

"Cheers," she says, and smiles at Jamie. "All good, boss?"

"Oh, I remember!" Jamie says, straightening up with an armful of hazel branches, eyes twinkling.

He's in his late forties now, no longer the fastest guy up the tree, not the one who takes the risks. But he's still got an edginess to him. A really good tree surgeon is just the right amount of adrenaline junkie. Or too much of one, and very lucky.

"You've got to be gone by half one, right? For your date?"

Miranda brushes sawdust off her chainsaw trousers. She's wearing braces—safety trousers are designed with men in mind and are always too loose around the waist. A friend she met on an aerial rescue course tipped her off that suspenders would save her from the humiliation of finding her trousers around her ankles one day.

"Yep! Lunch date," she says, unclipping the chainsaw and setting it up in the bed of Jamie's truck. "It *is* Valentine's Day, you know."

"My wife reminded me of that this morning," Jamie says, pulling a face.

"A lunch date?" AJ says behind her.

She doesn't turn around. "My boyfriend wanted to meet me right after I'd finished my first job with Jamie."

"Or he's got another woman lined up for the evening slot," AJ says.

Miranda doesn't have much of a temper. She figures anyone who's being a dick probably has a reason for it, and there's no use flying off the handle. But she also knows that tolerance can look like weakness, especially if you're a woman. She swallows.

"What are your plans for the evening, then, AJ?" she asks, glancing back at him for just long enough to catch his quick, one-sided smile at the question. "Got a hot date?"

"Depends," he says.

"On what?" Miranda pulls her hair out of its ponytail and runs her fingers through the tangles. Her hair is thick and dark, frizzy around her face, ringleted at the bottom, and almost always in knots.

"On whether Jamie'll let me ask you out for a drink this evening."

"AJ!" Jamie barks. "What did we talk about on the drive here?"

Miranda meets AJ's eyes for just a moment. He's teasing her, or maybe testing her. But there's genuine heat behind his gaze, and Miranda realizes with a jolt that he'd do it—he'd take her out for a drink, and then he'd take her home. This gorgeous, dangerous man.

Quite flattering, all things considered. Even if she does know he screws anything that moves.

"Why not? I know you're free tonight," AJ says, folding his tattooed arms across his chest. His biceps are enormous. Miranda is quite sure he crossed his arms so she'd notice.

She keeps her chin up. "Not interested," she says, and smiles. "Thanks, though." She turns back to Jamie. "Seven tomorrow morning, right? You'll message me the address?"

"Not interested!" Jamie crows. "When did you last hear that from a girl, AJ?"

AJ shrugs, bending down to pick up Rip, and Miranda can feel that his eyes are still on her as she begins to walk away.

"Been a while," he says. "But I always wear them down."

Miranda laughs at that. "Not this one," she says cheerfully over her shoulder. "I'm taken."

"By Mr. Lunch Date," AJ calls. "Lucky girl."

SHE *IS* LUCKY. MOST DAYS SHE CAN'T BELIEVE HER LUCK, actually. Carter is the sort of guy who she'd imagine would never look twice at someone like her: he's so *mature*, has a well-paid job, wears proper tailored suits. And he's gorgeous. Grown-up gorgeous, not like scruffy AJ. Carter has round glasses and a straight, manly jaw and this totally melt-you-on-the-spot smile.

The two of them met through Reg, one of the guys Miranda used to work with—he played football with Carter, and Miranda had been at the pub with Reg one day last year when half the team had come in for a drink after a kickaround. Carter had been scrubbed clean, back in his work suit because he'd forgotten to bring another change of clothes for after the match, and he'd stood out like a shiny penny. All bright smile and half-wet hair. As the rest of the lads took the piss out of his outfit, he did this sheepish little head-duck, glasses catching in the pub lights, and Miranda's stomach had swooped. That head-duck hinted at the boy underneath the broad-shouldered grown-up; it made him seem more approachable.

Miranda hadn't been able to stop staring at him, and eventually he'd noticed and offered her a small, questioning half grin, a gentler invitation than she'd expected. He must be used to women throwing themselves at him, she'd thought, but there was no expectation there. She'd asked Reg to introduce them in the end, buoyed up by three pints, giddy with the half smile Carter had thrown her way. *Rosso, Carter, Carter, Rosso*, Reg had said. *Carter, get her a drink, will you, this is a woman who deserves to be treated right.*

Now, five months later, Carter still seems to be taking Reg at his word—the restaurant he's taking her to for their Valentine's Day lunch is the sort of place with no prices on the menu and drizzled glazes around the edges of the plate. It's not far from Erstead, the Surrey commuter town where Miranda lives. She gets changed at the McDonald's around the corner, slicking on some lip balm and mascara, and feels pretty good about herself for the three-minute walk to the fancy restaurant, then immediately transitions to feeling childish and underdressed as she walks to their table in her blue pinafore dress and scuffed pumps. All the other women look really sophisticated.

Miranda lifts her bum off the chair to pull down the dress surreptitiously, under cover of the tablecloth. This is a classy restaurant, so they're only doing Valentine's Day indirectly: rose petals on tables, a general increase in candles, a vague atmosphere of smugness.

Miranda arrived a little late, so it takes her a while to clock that it's well after two and there's still no sign of Carter. He's habitually late, so this is no great surprise. But at around half past, when the waiter asks her if she wants a drink, she orders a Coke—it's getting awkward just sitting there, surrounded by loved-up couples, fiddling with her napkin and tapping her feet.

She sends Carter a text. **Where are you?! Xx**

Then another: **You're really late?**

And then: **Carter?? Hello?**

Slowly, slowly, she slips from being a woman who is waiting for her date to a woman who has been stood up. Nothing's visibly changed—she's still here, checking her phone too often, getting through her drink too fast. But everyone can see that her status is changing as each second passes, and by the time Miranda has sat at that table for forty-five minutes, without even moving a muscle she's become somebody to be pitied.

Eventually she just can't stand the stillness any longer. With each minute that's gone by, the fidgety, need-to-move feeling in her limbs has ramped up, even after a morning on the job. She tells herself she'll wait until ten past three, and makes it to five past before going up to pay for her drink at the bar.

There's no way around it: he's stood her up.

There's probably a totally reasonable explanation, she tells herself. Some really funny story. He'll tell it with all the different people's voices—he's really good at accents; he totally nails her dad's Italian one, and he's got the Liverpudlian guy in Miranda's building down to a T. They'll laugh about it. It'll become one of their stories, like, *Remember that time you stood me up on Valentine's Day?*

Right now, though, it kind of sucks. Miranda chews her lip as she waits for the card receipt to print. She knows she'll forgive Carter. She's probably forgiven him already, really, in anticipation of his excellent excuse. But for a moment, it's quite nice to imagine she's the sort of woman who wouldn't. The sort of woman who'd say, *I don't take this shit. If you stand me up, that's it. You're done.*

By the time Miranda gets home it's half four, and there's still no message from Carter. She misses her old flatmate—she could really use someone to make her a sympathetic cup of tea right now. She stands in the middle of the living room, listening to the traffic outside, wondering whether Carter decided she wasn't right for him after all.

This is pointless, Miranda Rosso, she tells herself, kicking off her pumps. *Pull yourself together.*

It's not even five yet—plenty of day left. She'll tidy up, then cook dinner and get to bed early. There's no use standing around moping. Where's that ever got anybody?

Jane

THE KEY IS HORS D'OEUVRES. AS LONG AS SHE HAS A MIN-
iature goat's cheese tart or a tiny spring roll in her mouth, then Jane
has at least three seconds of chewing time to think of a response when
she's hit with the inevitable, awful questions that arise when you're at
an engagement party and your date has stood you up.

"Still on your own-io, hen?" Keira asks. She's got a glass of bubbly
in each hand but manages to hoick her breasts up nonetheless; her
necklaces briefly disappear into the valley of cleavage at the neckline
of her ball gown.

Keira helps out at the Count Langley charity shop two days a week.
She is one of the people most determined to set Jane up with Ronnie
Langley, son of the count himself and the man who caused this whole
mess.

When Jane first started working at the shop, Ronnie took a shine
to her. Everyone who works for the Count Langley Trust is inordinately fond of Ronnie, who has one of those tragically arranged faces
that immediately inspires pity, and who is still single at thirty-five

despite being first in line to inherit a ramshackle mansion, which everyone except Jane seems to consider the height of eligibility.

It had become a charity-shop-wide mission to get Jane and Ronnie together. And so Jane had told a little lie. She'd said she had a boyfriend. Over the years the lie has grown and grown, but it has never been put to the test quite like this before.

"I'm sure he's on his way, just held up at work," Jane says weakly, checking her watch. Only a quarter past six—another hour of "drinks and mingling" before the sit-down dinner begins.

Keira eyes her, false eyelashes bobbing as she takes in Jane's outfit: the same one she wore to work today. Jane's cheeks warm. She'd thought she could get away with the pale-green cotton dress if she removed her wooly cardigan and tights, but now that she's here, it's obviously not formal enough. Behind Keira, the crowd deepens—there are *so* many guests here, more people than Constance and Martin could know by name, surely. They're in the guildhall at Winchester; the theme of the event, unsurprisingly, is Valentine's Day. There is a truly grotesque amount of pink.

"Listen, hen," Keira says, her wrinkles deepening as she scrunches her face up. "We all know you've been fibbing about having a boyfriend. You're better off just owning up, now, if . . ."

"Jane, dear, may I borrow you?" calls Mortimer.

Jane turns to Mortimer with an expression of fervent gratitude. Keira looks disgruntled as he leads Jane away from the bustle toward the edge of the room.

Mortimer Daperty is seventy years old; he wears a brown suit to work every day, has a tuna sandwich for lunch without fail and says, *Ta-ta, then, Jane! See you anon!* when he leaves at six p.m. each night. When nobody else is in the shop, he and Jane coexist in warm, mothball-scented silence, steam-ironing donated clothes and passing each other used books without exchanging so much as a word.

"You look absolutely miserable," Mortimer says kindly.

"I . . . don't do well in crowds," Jane says, trying to steady her breathing.

"And the young man who you said was coming . . . ?"

Jane is well practiced at dodging personal questions from her colleagues at the charity shop. But Mortimer usually never asks them, so this one takes her by surprise, and before she knows it, she finds herself answering.

"He was doing me a favor. We're not together, but he said he'd be my date so that I didn't have to come to this alone." She looks down at her shoes. Sensible, soft brown leather, the sort of shoes she wouldn't have been seen dead in, once. "Keira's right: I did lie about having a boyfriend."

Mortimer just nods. "A very reasonable protective measure," he says. "And this friend of yours, he's not even telephoned?"

Jane had expected some judgment from Mortimer, but his expression is kind.

"No. He's not called," she says, returning her gaze to her shoes.

Mortimer tuts, but it's not Joseph who Jane is disappointed in—it's herself. She should have known better than to rely on someone else. As a rule, she prefers plants and cats to humans these days: they're both species with a much better track record.

Every day since moving back to Winchester, Jane has gone to the Hoxton Bakehouse at opening and bought herself the low-fat yogurt pot with fruit and granola. It's an unjustifiable expense, really, but the routine is soothing, like slipping into the same worn boots each day.

When she'd first seen Joseph in the bakery just after Christmas, she'd stopped so suddenly she'd almost tripped over her own feet in the doorway. She recognized him. She couldn't say exactly where from, but he felt . . . important. Someone from her old job, maybe? She said "Oh!" out loud, and stared before she could remind herself that staring is the quickest way to draw attention to yourself, and should at all costs be avoided.

Joseph had turned and looked, but he hadn't seemed to recognize her. He'd shot her an enormous, sunny smile. Slightly perplexed, perhaps.

"Hello," he said.

For a moment Jane stood poised, frozen, eyes wide. Then— "Sorry, I thought you were . . . someone else," she mumbled, averting her gaze and scuttling to the back of the queue and out of sight. But she'd felt his eyes on her, warm and curious, as he walked out of the shop with his croissant. After that, she saw him every morning for two weeks, but still couldn't quite place him. She never made the mistake of staring at him again.

And then, just when Jane had relaxed a little: "This is a bit odd, isn't it?" Joseph said, suddenly turning on his heel to look right at her as they waited in the queue.

Jane blinked rapidly. "Pardon?" she managed, in the direction of the floor.

"Well, I know all sorts about you. I know you wear the yellow jumper on Mondays, and a pale-blue shirt on Tuesdays, and a white floaty dress on Wednesdays, and that spring-green one with a cardigan on Thursdays, and a light-pink jumper on Fridays. I know you read, because you've always got a book. And I know you like cinnamon buns, because you always give them this wistful sort of look before you order the yogurt pot. We see each other every day. But we don't talk."

Her palms sweated. Nobody else had ever noticed her outfit rotation so quickly. And she was sure she didn't eye up the cinnamon buns—or at least, not *every* morning.

At last, unable to hold off any longer, she looked up and met his gaze.

He was undeniably handsome, though if pressed on why, she would have struggled to answer. His face was very mobile and expressive; his eyebrows were a little too straight and thick and would have looked stern on a man who smiled less. His creamy white skin was flushed along his cheekbones from the warmth of the bakery, and his jaw was dusted with grainy stubble a shade darker than his hazelnut-brown hair. There was nothing in his face that explained why he was quite so engagingly good-looking, but when she met his eyes, she felt that dangerous, animal thrill that you feel in the presence of someone beautiful.

"I don't think it's all that strange," she found herself saying. "Do you talk to the person sitting beside you on the train?"

"Yes," he said promptly.

"Oh, that's awful," Jane said before she could stop herself, and he burst out laughing.

"I'm Joseph," he said. "Tell me, where are you getting all these books from?"

That's how they'd ended up in a two-person book club. As a rule, Jane does not make friends with people—or rather, people do not make friends with Jane. And yet somehow a few days later she'd found herself sitting down for a Sunday-morning coffee with him, talking about Mohsin Hamid's *Exit West*. *Books are my happy place*, he'd told her, and she'd felt herself light up, because that's *exactly* what they are to her, too.

She had, at least, ensured that there would be nothing romantic there. She had used the *I have a boyfriend* lie on Joseph, too—a protective measure, as Mortimer put it. It was only at the start of February, by which point she and Joseph were undeniably friends, that Jane had confessed she did not, in fact, have a boyfriend.

"Ah, that is good news," Joseph said. "Because I was starting to think this guy was a real prick."

"What!" Jane had always worked quite hard to make her fictional boyfriend seem like a catch.

"He's never around!" Joseph said with a laugh. "And he didn't get you anything for your birthday?"

It was true: Jane had not gone as far as buying herself a real present from her fictional boyfriend.

The ease with which Joseph took her confession made her relax, and in the last couple of weeks they've grown closer. She's given up on trying to work out where she recognizes him from—it had drawn her to him at first, perhaps, that strange, nagging sense of familiarity, but they're past that now. He's just Joseph.

And if she is sometimes a little distracted by the sunny warmth of his smile or the way his eyes turn greener in certain lights, she has mastered the art of ignoring it.

Already he knows more about Jane than anyone else who remains in her life. Not everything, of course, but still, he is shockingly unbothered by the parts of herself she regards as impossible to like: her tendency to blurt out her thoughts, her rules and routines, her indecisiveness. It's felt so good to have someone to talk to again. She had begun to find herself thinking, *What's the harm?*

Now, as Keira makes her way purposefully toward Jane with Ronnie by her side, Jane thinks, *This. This is the harm.*

"Jane," Keira says, tugging Ronnie by the arm, "Ronnie was just telling me *he* doesn't have a date this evening, either."

Ronnie is visibly quivering beside the formidable Keira. He is gripped with such intense self-consciousness that Jane can feel it radiating from beneath his suit like the warmth of an oven, even from several steps away.

"H-hello," he says. "Lovely to see you, Jane."

"Jane's date is . . ." Keira looks at her expectantly.

Under Keira's self-satisfied gaze, Jane gives up on *He's running late* or *I'm sure he'll be here any minute.*

"He can't make it," Jane says.

"Oh, poor Jane! Ever so unlucky in love!" Keira says.

Jane has no idea where Keira got this idea from, though, annoyingly, it's very accurate.

"Isn't your mother badgering you for grandkids yet? I've been on at my kids for years, and they're still dragging their feet," Keira says, sipping her drink.

Jane grits her teeth for a moment before answering. "My mother's dead," she says.

Keira recoils. Her mouth opens and closes. This is always the worst part of these conversations: the hovering silence before the other person has decided exactly which sentimental line they're going to trot out in response.

"Oh, hen, I never knew! You never said!" Keira says. She lowers her voice. "Was *that* why you left London and came here?"

The word *London* makes Jane flinch, as if someone's just grabbed her by the shoulder. Keira never lets this question go; she asks it at least once a month, in some form or other, with the blithe persistence of a truly talented gossip.

"No," Jane says, careful to keep her voice steady. "No, my mother died a long time ago. I was very young. I barely remember her."

"How utterly *tragic*," Keira says.

Ronnie is shifting uncomfortably from one foot to the other, like a child who needs the toilet. Keira pats Jane's bare arm, her hand sweaty and well intentioned; it takes all Jane's strength not to shrug it off. She never wants to be touched when she's sad. These days she's hardly touched at all, and so it feels even worse, like pulling on a prickly wool jumper when you've been wearing silk.

"Well, you've got us, hen, we'll look after you," Keira says. She offers Jane a watery, exaggerated wink. "Why doesn't Ronnie take your date's seat at dinner, hmm? Who knows! This could be the start of a new story for you!"

AS JANE STEPS INTO THE SHOP THE NEXT MORNING, SHE checks surreptitiously for lurking Keira types before making her way to the till. The engagement party was hell. She only went because Constance, who is getting married, had always been kind when they'd worked in the shop together; the event was a useful reminder that stepping outside of her comfort zone never ends well. She breathes in the musty smell of the shop and begins her usual routine on arriving at work: a spring-clean, then getting the till going, then making a start on the donation bags.

The shop floor has already been swept and there are fresh flowers in the vase on the coffee table by the bookcases, carefully placed to brighten up the space. The Count Langley charity shop is inside one of the fifteenth-century buildings to the northeast of town, down by the riverside: it's all sagging dark beams and creaking wood floors, and there's mildew creeping up behind the staff toilet like an incoming tide on sand. The Count Langley Trust owns the building; the charity supports individuals who are nearing the ends of their lives. Their funding shrinks almost as quickly as the mildew grows.

"Jane!"

She winces. It's Keira, emerging from the back room: Jane should have known when she saw the flowers. And—she turns—Constance *and* Mortimer. This is a completely unnecessary number of people to run the shop today, and shouldn't Constance be in bed with her fiancé?

"Oh, hen," Keira says, descending with her arms outstretched. "I've just been miserable all night thinking about you on your own at the party. Shall we sit down and chat about it? Wasn't Ronnie charming at dinner?"

Surely, *surely* Jane won't have to go through a whole day of this. She *can't.*

"Jane?" comes a voice behind her as the bell above the door tinkles.

She turns toward the entrance. Head ducked as he steps through the low-beamed doorway, dressed in a soft gray woolen jumper, is Joseph.

"Jane, I'm *so* sorry," he says, making his way toward them. "Hi, everyone, hi. I'm Joseph. Lovely to meet you all. I'm so sorry I couldn't be there last night for the party."

And then he rests a hand on the small of Jane's back and kisses her gently on the cheek.

It's a sweet kiss, a girlfriend-boyfriend kiss. He does it so comfortably, so easily, that Jane is all the more surprised by the shot of desire that goes through her as his lips graze her cheek.

Joseph has never touched her before. Not once. They didn't shake hands when they first met; they don't ever hug hello. He doesn't guide her by the elbow when they move through a crowd. She likes that about him: he's not tactile, and that distance, that lack of flirtation, it makes her feel safe.

But it also means she had absolutely no idea how her body would react to the feeling of Joseph's lips on her skin until this very moment. Her heart is still fluttering; she's hot; her lips are parted. All from a bare second of contact.

Mortimer is ushering Joseph through to sit down in the back of the shop. Jane's heartbeat resettles slowly; she watches the others as they all pull up chairs. Keira is staring at Joseph with her mouth open— Jane can see a little scrap of something green between two of her teeth. Constance is wide-eyed and baffled: it seems Keira filled her in on last night. Jane can't help a smile growing. It does feel lovely to surprise everyone, for once.

"I'm so sorry, Jane," Joseph says in her ear as everyone sits down in a misshapen circle among the bin bags and boxes of the back room. "I'm going to make it up to you."

His face is crumpled with concern, all furrows and quizzical lines, but it's his lips that catch Jane's attention. She's never noticed the color of them before—a matte, russet red. They're romantic lips. The sort of lips that know exactly what to do with themselves.

"That's okay," she says.

"No, it really isn't. I let you down."

He launches into the story, regaling the group. He broke his phone, then got stuck behind a cherry picker, apparently, which Jane can only assume is some sort of vehicle, then his car broke down and the driver had to help him move it to safety, and it took so long for the AA to come, and he couldn't remember Jane's number . . .

They escape to the kitchen after five minutes or so, to get him a cup of coffee. It's more of a cupboard than a kitchen, with an ancient extractor fan rattling away on the wall like a smoker with a cough, but still, it's private.

"Is any of that true?" Jane asks him. "The car, the cherry thing, the AA?"

Joseph closes his eyes for a moment and sighs. He often looks rushed off his feet whenever he arrives anywhere—he has this air to him, this slightly harried franticness, as though he's trying to be in too many places at once. But today it's more harassed than harried. He looks exhausted.

"No. Some of it, but no, not all of it."

Jane nods, looking down at her coffee. She used to drink it black, but now she has it with milk, sometimes even a splash of cream.

"I let you down. Jane. Please. Look at me."

She looks up, but her eyes snag on his lips again. She can't find room to be angry with him about last night because her brain is occupied with that kiss, that half a second where her guard dropped and she allowed Joseph to shift category in her mind.

It's not that she's *never* thought about dating Joseph. He is very attractive, after all, and as far as Jane knows, he's single—he's never mentioned a girlfriend. It's more that she has persistently ignored the impulse, knowing how completely stupid it would be, that if she lets herself see Joseph that way, she'll have to cut him out of her life altogether. And he makes it easy for her to maintain that distance: he's careful around her, as if he senses that she's flighty and might take off, deerlike, if he gets too close.

"I had a very, very bad day yesterday," he says. He looks down, scrubbing at his hair with one hand. "I wish I could . . . go back and do it all differently."

Part of the trick of not letting people into your heart is not to care when they lie to you; the trick is not to care what they say at all. This is harder than it should be, with Joseph. Jane has not been careful.

"Okay," she says after a moment.

Joseph pauses, hand still on his head, and gives her the full beam of his attention. This is the difference between Joseph-who's-just-arrived and Joseph-who-is-present. Once he settles, he listens, *really* listens, with the sort of attentiveness that most people only ever fake.

"What? Really?" he says.

"Yes, really. You were doing me a big favor, saying that you'd come to my colleague's engagement party and pretend to be my boyfriend. That was quite a strange thing for me to ask of you."

Her face heats just at the thought of it. They'd come up with the idea at their last book club; she'd opened up a little about the lie she'd told at work, how it had grown, how awkward it would be at the engagement party when they all discovered she didn't have a boyfriend at all, and he'd said, *You could always bring me. I make a great fake date. And I love an excuse to wear a tux.*

"You're . . ." He shakes his head slightly. "You should be yelling at me."

He looks so weary, now that he's not performing for her colleagues—the crow's-feet at the corners of his hazel eyes seem deeper than when she saw him a few days ago, and his skin is dry and tired. She looks more closely: there is the ghost of a bruise on the corner of his eyebrow, as if he's been punched.

"You don't look like you need to be yelled at," she says, wondering if it's rude to ask about the bruise.

"I do," he says fervently. "I deserve much, much yelling. I . . . Shit."

She looks at him inquiringly.

"I know why you're not angry with me," he says, slapping his forehead. "It's because you don't expect any better."

"Pardon?"

"I've just validated all your stuff about how people always let you down, haven't I? You're not mad because you're not even surprised."

She had been a little surprised, actually. But overnight she had chastised herself for her lapse in judgment and here she is now, safely reminded that there's a reason she gave up on ever trying to make friends.

"I asked too much of you, that's all," Jane says with a small smile. "Don't worry, though. I make a lot of mistakes, but I try not to make the same one twice."

Miranda

MIRANDA IS HALFWAY UP AN OAK TREE WHEN THE FIRST
call comes from Carter. She misses all ten of his calls, in fact, since her
phone is stuffed at the bottom of her rucksack, for the very reason that
if she has it in a pocket, she'll be so keen to read any message from
Carter she'll probably end up checking it while hanging upside down
in her harness.

She's being resolutely sunny today. She had a very large bowl of
porridge for breakfast, washed her hair, and decided there is plenty to
be cheerful about. She might have been a *bit* short with AJ when he
started asking questions about her "lunch date" (his air quotes, not
hers), but frankly, that man would try the patience of a saint. And now
she's up in the air, and the wind is blowing through the branches
around her, and it's a good day. Every day is a good day, if you look
hard enough.

Miranda is just starting on a back cut when Carter arrives at the
bottom of her tree with a large bunch of flowers.

She catches sight of him between the branches below her and loses her breath for a moment. It's just so unexpected; how can he *possibly* be here?

"Carter?" she shouts.

"Hi!" he yells up at her. "I'm so sorry! I'm here to apologize!"

"You . . ." She stares down at the ground, and then comes to her senses and realizes she's already cut halfway through the branch. "Get away from the tree, Carter!" she yells.

Where the hell are the others? She lifts her gaze and catches sight of Trey and Spikes at the chipper, and the small, incensed figure of Jamie, with AJ at his side and Rip at their feet, making his way toward the oak.

Oh, crap. She needs to get down there before they skin Carter alive for wandering on-site.

She's rushing. She's flustered. She didn't get a lot of sleep.

This is why, as Miranda turns around to position herself so she can lower back to ground, she cuts through not just her main line, but her flip line, too.

She only knows she's done it by the slightest touch of rope to her thigh. She's balanced in a V between branches, so neither of her ropes are taking her weight; she might well not have noticed it happen. But as the remains of her flip line drop around her knees, she feels the slither across her trousers, lifts her eyes to the main line and clocks it.

Her chainsaw judders in her hand. She just . . . cut through her ropes. And now . . .

Now Miranda Rosso is fifty feet up an oak tree, and there is not a single thing holding her in place.

"Miranda?" Carter calls from beneath her.

"Oh no," Miranda says mildly.

Beneath her, Jamie and AJ are shouting, presumably at Carter. She checks how much rope she has left; nowhere near enough to get her down. This wasn't an easy climb. There's no way she can get back to the ground without ropes. She would almost certainly die.

She shifts her weight slightly. Balancing on this branch felt like nothing when her main line was anchored above her, but now it feels breathtakingly dangerous.

"Rosso! Stay still! That's an order!" Jamie's voice rings up through the leaves.

Miranda freezes.

"I'm sending AJ up!" Jamie says. "Do. Not. Move!"

Even now, in a situation that could really be described as near-death, Miranda finds room to think, *Oh bloody hell, not AJ.*

"Get your arse down on the branch to take the weight out of your legs!" Jamie says.

Well, okay, Miranda thinks. *It's nice to have a plan, even if it is "Get your arse down."* She shifts little by little. One wrong move and she will fall through deadly solid branches, buffeted from rib-snapping blow to blow, until she lands like a rag doll in the debris at the bottom of the tree.

Time is stretching and pulling like an elastic band: it's never felt slower, but once she's maneuvered herself so she's straddling the branch, it all seems to be done in a moment. She breathes out, her heart slamming.

She risks a glance down, and there's AJ, throwing his main line to loop over a branch to her right. He's already not far below her. In the distance she can see Carter, with his bunch of flowers, standing beside Jamie. Next to the stolid, grubby Jamie, Carter looks like a model man in his suit, his glasses winking in the light.

"You hurt?" AJ calls.

"No, I'm fine!" says Miranda. "Just feeling like a bit of an idiot, really."

AJ says nothing to this, grunting with effort as he leaps across the fork in a branch and latches on with his thighs, already taking the slack out of his flip line. He's almost level with her now, just one branch away.

"I'm going to get my flip line around the trunk. Don't flinch."

Miranda looks insulted. "I won't flinch."

His flip line comes flying toward her, the carabiner inches from her head. She flinches. AJ acknowledges it with a twitch of a smile. He's breathless from the climb, chest rising and falling hard, but he's perfectly calm as he swings himself around to Miranda, and—so fast she doesn't have time to panic—catches her waist with his arm. His harness is clipped to hers within seconds.

The danger hasn't passed. They're both hanging off the same rope; as soon as she shifts off this branch her whole body weight will be dragging AJ down. He'll be unsteady in his harness, he'll be navigating the way for two bodies instead of one and, most importantly, she is going to have to wrap her legs and arms around him, the very thought of which is already making her hot with embarrassment.

"You know what to do" is all he says, quirking an eyebrow.

Miranda swallows. This is an emergency situation. An aerial rescue. There's absolutely nothing sexual about wrapping her body around AJ's, given that they are fifty feet in the air, wearing chainsaw trousers, and still quite likely to die.

Except . . . AJ is breathing hard, and looking at her in that steady, teasing way he has, and all the adrenaline has her buzzing. His arms are bare and muscled and covered in scratches; a long red cut intersects the tattoo of a bird in flight that sits just above his elbow. She's so close she can see the pale resin-colored flecks in his brown eyes.

It *feels* a bit sexual.

"Okay," Miranda says, a little more breathily than she would like. "I'm going to . . . grab on to you now."

"Uh-huh," AJ says, and she can hear the laughter in his voice.

"Shut up," she says, shifting her weight in his arms. He's solid and strong and his arm holds her tight. "This is awkward, okay?"

"If you say so." AJ tilts in his harness, lying back a little so she can climb onto his body.

Even through her fleece, Miranda can feel the heat of him against her chest as she wraps her arms around him and lets her harness take her weight, sliding down his frame. She turns her head so her cheek is flat against his chest. One of his arms is around her shoulders, the other easing out the rope so that they can begin their descent through the branches.

They don't speak as they make their way down; AJ's lips are pressed tightly together with the effort, and his chest rises and falls against Miranda's cheek. When they finally reach the ground, they land hard, stumbling apart in their linked harnesses.

"Thank you," Miranda says as they steady themselves. She swallows and looks up to meet his eyes. "Really. Thanks. You just . . . well, saved my life, probably."

AJ smiles as he reaches between them to unclip their harnesses. "Will you let me take you out for a drink now?" he asks.

Miranda raises her eyebrows. "My boyfriend is right there, AJ."

"Mir!" Carter calls, on cue.

"Stay where you are," AJ calls to Carter over Miranda's shoulder. "Idiot," he mutters, taking Miranda's elbow and leading her away from the tree. Rip dashes over, dancing clumsily between their feet, sniffing at AJ's shins.

Miranda frowns, shaking off his hold on her elbow. "I can walk on my own. And he's not an idiot, he just doesn't know where he's allowed to stand."

AJ shrugs away. "Whatever," he says, raising his eyebrows. "You're welcome."

She huffs. "I did say thank you."

"Miranda?" Carter calls. "Are you all right?"

She turns toward him, and at the sight of him—suit covered with chippings, hair awry, that giant bunch of flowers in his hands—any anger melts away. She is suddenly very aware that she was quite scared, up in the tree. Really scared, actually. She runs to her boyfriend and lands against him with an *oof*, burying her face in his shirt. The flowers bob in the corner of her vision as he wraps his arms around her.

"God, Miranda," he says, gripping her tightly. "I'm so sorry. I'm so sorry."

THEY MAKE THEIR WAY TO THE END OF THE GARDEN IN which the team is working today. Behind them is an enormous house with bay windows and bright-white guttering. The garden is stunning, even now in drizzly February: the lawns are pristine and the beds are carefully laid out in bark. The owner has already pruned the winter-flowering shrubs, Miranda notices with approval.

Carter sits down on a bench beneath a willow, resting his bunch of flowers across his knees and looking up at her. He's so handsome, with his brown hair mussed and those soft, worried eyes behind his glasses—it takes her a moment to remember that she's meant to be furious with him.

"Are you okay?" he says quietly, reaching for her hand. "That looked pretty bloody terrifying."

"I'm fine," Miranda says, though actually she's shaking, and her voice comes out a bit wobbly, as if she's cold. It's worth the lie, though, for the admiration in his eyes as he looks up at her from the bench.

"I can't believe you do stuff like this every day." Carter shakes his head.

"I don't tend to cut through my own ropes quite that often," Miranda says with a wry grin. She's grateful that he doesn't know enough about her job to realize quite how embarrassing that all was.

Carter squeezes her hand, then seems to remember the flowers in his lap and holds them up to her.

"These are for you," he says, and his eyes are worried again—he's blinking too fast behind his glasses. "To say how sorry I am."

"What *happened* yesterday?" she says as she takes the flowers. The adrenaline from the incident in the oak is still coursing through her; she clutches the bouquet tightly. "You stood me up!"

Carter's face twists; he looks genuinely tortured. "I know. I feel so awful. I really never ever intended that to happen, Mir, I hope you know that—I hope you never think I'd do that on purpose, or do *anything* to hurt you."

"No," she says, after a moment's thought. "But it *did* hurt me."

"Of course. Absolutely. And I know you absolutely deserve an explanation and, and, I will, I just, I can't completely sort of . . . But I *will*, and . . ."

Miranda frowns. She's never seen him like this, all emotional, his words getting tangled up. It's a little disconcerting—Carter always seems so *together*, and the rawness of his voice is so out of character that for a fleeting moment she wonders if it's put on, as if he's playing somebody else. Then he closes his eyes and Miranda notices how tired he looks, strung out and creased like he's been put through the wash. You can't fake that.

"I know I'm not always . . . that . . . open. And I want to be more open with you." He looks up at her, voice earnest. "I think things are going really well with us—I mean, they were, until I screwed it up yesterday. And you mean a lot to me. You really do, Miranda. I'm just really, really not good at the emotional stuff. And what happened yesterday was . . . It was . . . But I promise I'm going to try, and I'm going to explain, I will, I just . . ."

His Adam's apple bobs as he swallows. Miranda softens; it's uncomfortable, standing here, witnessing this, saying nothing. She's never been one to hold a grudge, and any anger she felt yesterday seems to have dissipated; right now, she just wants her and Carter to go back to how they were.

She holds her nerve a little longer, though. She's always conscious with Carter that she's punching above her weight, but she knows that doesn't mean she should concede on everything—the opposite, really.

"Could you not even message me?" she says. "Just text me back?"

"I should have. I wish I had. I'm so sorry. My head was just . . . all over the place, but that's no excuse. I'm so sorry."

Miranda's brow wrinkles. It's the mystery that's bugging her now more than anything. But he looks so miserable she feels like she can't keep pushing.

"Will you . . . will you come stay with me this weekend?" he asks.

"What?"

"No, of course you won't want to do that, I just . . ." He swallows, brushing chippings off his thighs. "It might be easier to talk to you about it there, that's all."

She can feel tears on her hand, the one he's clutching. "Carter!" she says, ducking down so they're face-to-face. "Carter, it's all right. Don't cry."

"God," he says, letting go of her hands to wipe his eyes. "I'm so sorry. I really did not want to cry. And now that massive tattooed man who rescued you from a tree has seen me sobbing on you, too," he says, looking behind Miranda. "Brilliant."

She turns and catches AJ just as he returns his attention to the hedge he's pruning.

"Oh, ignore him," she says, looking back at Carter. "He's just one of those macho types who likes to pretend to be intimidating."

Carter gives her a dry look. "You're never going to call me macho now, are you?"

She kisses him quickly on the lips. "I think you are extremely macho, thank you very much. There's nothing wrong with a man crying."

Carter's eyes flick away at that.

"Now, there *is* something wrong with a man standing a woman up in a restaurant," Miranda says, though the fight has long since gone out of her; she's set the flowers down beside her on the grass, and she twists a lily stem between her fingers, turning her gaze away from

Carter. "And I do think I deserve an explanation. But I get that you maybe don't want to talk about it here."

"I probably shouldn't have come in that case, should I?" Carter says ruefully, and Miranda laughs. "I mean, on balance."

"You *did* nearly kill me," she says, and then breathes in as he grabs her hand.

"Don't say that," he says. "Please don't say that."

"I'm teasing!" she says. "You weren't to know not to come over and say hi. It's not your fault."

"I am an idiot. A double idiot. An idiot for not being there yesterday, an idiot for being here today. I'm sorry, Miranda. I promise I will make it up to you."

She believes him. It's hard to say exactly why, but everything about this rings true to her. He seems to feel genuinely awful about it all; it would surely be hard to feign the guilty, tortured expression on his face.

"I'm still mad at you," she says, as much to remind herself as him.

"I know. Of course you are. You have every right to be."

"But I'll come stay with you for the weekend."

His shoulders sag. "Thank you. I really am going to make this up to you."

It starts to rain; she hears AJ shout an instruction to Jamie behind her, his voice ringing out across the lawn.

"I should get back to it," Miranda says apologetically as Carter removes his glasses to scrub at his reddened eyes.

"Of course, of course. Can I . . ." He looks up, popping his glasses back on, and smiles a sudden, Carter-ish grin that immediately makes Miranda feel better. "Can I help?"

"Help?"

"I've slowed you down today! Let me help." He starts shucking off his jacket. "Obviously I can't climb a tree, but is there something else you could put me to work on?"

Miranda can't decide if this is adorable or embarrassing. "Honestly, you don't have to . . ."

"Miranda," Carter says, fixing her with a very serious, grown-up glare, "I am feeling emasculated. Please help?"

That makes her snort with laughter. "All right. You can do some groundwork with Trey, I guess—Jamie'll be grateful for the extra hands. It'll ruin your suit, though. I don't think anyone has ever done groundwork in a suit before."

Carter waggles his eyebrows, and she can tell he's working hard to shed the man who was weeping on the bench just moments ago, but it's working: here's her Carter, clowning around to make her laugh, taking action, surprising her. She's already relaxing.

"If groundwork in a suit is the way to your heart, Miranda Rosso, then this is where I'll be. Now. Where do you need me?"

Miranda pulls a face. "If you could pick up the trimmings . . . under AJ's ladder . . ." She can't help laughing at Carter's expression. "You don't have to!"

He heaves a sigh. "Nobody said penance was easy," he tells her with a wink that almost distracts from the redness around his eyes. Then he sets off toward AJ with purpose, already rolling up his shirtsleeves to expose those tanned forearms, his gold watch glinting in the light.

Siobhan

ANY TRIP TO LONDON IS ALWAYS HECTIC. IN THE TWO
years she spent living by Finchley Road station after finishing drama
school, Siobhan collected at least ten friends for life, and now when
she's in the city she has to tactically back-to-back her catch-ups like
they're meetings, coordinating locations—*How about Covent Garden
instead?*—until her whole day is one long heart-to-heart. Sometimes
she just stays in a coffee shop and lets them come and go like inter-
viewees.

This time she's grateful for the constant flow of people. She ran a
Valentine's Day event at a Pilates collective, entitled *Love Yourself First:
Don't Wait for Him to Do It for You*, and spent the rest of the day with
friends nonstop. Each time she exposed the hurt—*He stood me up, can
you believe that?*—it felt a little easier.

"Isn't it interesting?" her friend Kit said, chewing an oatmeal cookie
thoughtfully. "They say it's hard to disappear these days, with social
media and everything, but I'm sure people didn't use to get ghosted in
Victorian times, did they?"

"He's a symbol of everything that's wrong with modern masculinity," Vikesh told her, sipping his green juice. "I mean, the gall! The entitlement! On which note, did I tell you about the guy who literally walked out on me mid–blow job?"

"There's only one thing for it," Marlena said, a latte mustache sitting on her upper lip. "You're going to have to hunt him down and get sweet revenge."

And now Siobhan is onstage again, and with the help of her friends, the pain of yesterday is already packaged up and neatened into a perfectly on-brand anecdote.

"You know what happened to me yesterday?" she says to the audience, crossing her legs and leaning forward. "I was stood up. On Valentine's Day."

A gasp runs through the crowd.

"Yeah. I know. And do you know what I thought about as I sat there with my cold latte, wondering whether he was going to show? I thought about embarrassment. Shall we talk about that a little? I thought about how humiliated I felt, and how everyone in that café was pitying me, and damn, I don't know about you, but I fucking *hate* to be pitied."

Plenty of nods from the audience.

"But why? Why are we so hostile to that? What if we called that *compassion*, and thought, wow, isn't it great that strangers can look at me and think, *Poor her, I hope she's okay*? Because actually, that's what *I* think if I see a woman who looks like she's been stood up. I don't think, *God, how pathetic, what a loser, nobody loves her.* Do you?"

Collective headshaking. Though there's probably the odd dickhead in there who thinks exactly that. Siobhan does truly believe her message—that people are ultimately good, and kind, and worth loving—but she also thinks that quite a lot of them are hiding it well.

"So why are we letting our *embarrassment* tell us to think the worst of the people around us? And—hang on—how has that emotion managed to get in there and tell us, *This is on you*? When, I mean, whose fault is it that I was sitting alone in that café? Was it mine? Or was it his?"

"His!" they yell, and Siobhan smiles out at them all.

"Let me tell you what I did as soon as I left that café. I blocked that guy's number and I cleared all our messages and I ghosted him, because I damn well wasn't going to wait for him to ghost me first. Am I right? You know what I'm going to say. Love yourself first. Don't wait for him to do it for you."

It's the perfect ending—her heart is thundering in time with the applause and her skin feels like it's glowing, sun-soft and vibrant with self-love, and Siobhan thinks, *This is all the love I need. The kind that's mine.*

HOTEL ROOMS ARE ASTONISHINGLY UNMEMORABLE, SIObhan finds. Now that she travels so much for work, she has stopped remembering the individual rooms and just remembers one hotel, where the bedding sometimes looks a little different from one memory to the next.

Fiona loves it when Siobhan comes back from a hotel stay. As Siobhan's success has risen, so has the caliber of the free toiletries, and it's now not unusual for her to pocket at least thirty euros' worth of miniature White Company stuff by the time she leaves.

She could, of course, buy herself White Company toiletries now. But some habits are hard to shake, and free things have never ceased to delight her.

She wraps herself up in a bathrobe (mediocre: a bit too stiff from washing, but pleasingly thick, and long enough to touch her ankles). There's a knock at the door. She frowns; her thoughts have been on free things, and for an absurd little moment she thinks, *Maybe they've sent me up some complimentary drinks.*

But it's not drinks.

It's Joseph Carter.

THE WORD SIOBHAN WOULD USE TO BEST DESCRIBE JO-seph Carter is *charismatic*. Others might say *handsome* first, but she suspects it's the charisma that gives him his good looks. He has regular features, nice hazel eyes, good bone structure; but when his face is photographed there's nothing technically remarkable about it. And yet in person he's the sort of man who turns every head. He's just *fun*—always ready to laugh, up for anything. But the charm never feels seedy: underneath all the clowning around he has this I'm-a-good-guy vibe to him, this earnestness.

If he were in an American high school drama, Joseph would be the one football player who talks to the nerds; if he were in a disaster movie, he'd be the guy who goes back for the minor character we're not even fussed about. Glasses on and he's sexy and grown-up; glasses off and you notice his charming, boyish grin, the way his quick, smart eyes catch yours and don't let them go.

When Siobhan had first met him, he had been regaling some of his colleagues with a story of a job interview in which, instead of saying, *Lovely to meet you, thank you very much*, he'd said, *Thank you to meet you, love you very much*.

Every person there had been turned toward him. Siobhan had watched him for a while—she's always appreciated someone who knows how to hold an audience. He had one of those smiles that made you feel like the only person in the world.

There's something about shiny things that appeals to Siobhan. Expensive jewelry, luxury lingerie, handsome men with perfect smiles. She knows they're probably too good to be true, but she just can't help wanting them all the same.

And that night, after she'd snagged him away from his crowd of admirers, Siobhan had discovered that sex with Joseph was absolutely, breathtakingly astonishing. He was so attentive—that same impulse that made him fit in with any crowd, that helped him hold his audience, made him an exceptional lover.

Still, she made sure it was just that, just hookups; she knew better than to let a man like Joseph anywhere near her heart. I'm-a-good-guy vibes don't fool Siobhan: in her experience, men who appear as perfect as Joseph Carter are usually absolute arseholes if you give yourself time to get to know them. She's kept matters perfectly casual, and that was clearly wise, because *look* what happened when she conceded to a breakfast date.

"I come bearing massage oil," Joseph says now, hands up in surrender in the hotel room doorway.

He is indeed clutching a bottle of—oh, her absolute favorite, vetiver and chamomile oil. Her traitorous libido gives a little hiccup. Massages are one of her weak points—she's permanently tense, and the pleasure-pain of a thumb working its way along the line of her shoulder blade always makes her lethargic with desire.

She shakes herself.

"Piss off," she says, moving to close the door in his face.

It hits his foot. "Siobhan," he says.

There's humor in his voice, and her temper flares even hotter.

"This isn't funny," she snaps. "You stood me up."

"I was late, Shiv! I'm sorry, I know it's not okay at *all*, and I owe you a huge apology, but . . . you blocked my number for being half an hour late?"

She wrenches the door open suddenly; he blinks in surprise. He looks kind of . . . ruffled. His shirt and suit trousers are creased and dusty and his hair—always inclined to messiness—is sticking up all over the place.

"It was more than half an hour," she says, pulling her bathrobe more tightly around her. Joseph is looking distractingly adorable for a man she has publicly vowed to despise. "How am I supposed to even know you showed up at all?"

He frowns and shakes his head slightly. Earnest as ever. "Why would I lie about that?"

Hmm. She examines him closely. Her curiosity gets the better of her. "What happened to *you* today?"

"Ah . . ." He runs a hand through his hair and then tries to squash it flat again. "I've been dashing between all your favorite hotels, trying to track you down."

She narrows her eyes. Her fluttering heart would very much like to believe this, but her head is much too sensible.

"Right," she says. "Well, you found me. Hi. Good-bye."

She moves to close the door again, but Joseph catches it with one hand. That gold watch of his winks under the hotel lights, drawing her eye to the firm lines of his forearm. Siobhan's never been able to resist a good forearm. Abs, pecs—she can do without those, but a man wearing a classy watch with rolled-up shirtsleeves and she's a goner.

"Siobhan," he says, voice dropping. "Come on. Please. Give me another chance."

"Nope, sorry. I don't do second chances."

His hand catches hers as she lifts it to adjust her dressing gown. She inhales sharply at the feel of his skin against hers; his eyes flare at the sound.

"Just give me one night," he whispers. "One night to make you change your mind."

She should absolutely not do this. She should kick him out and find a new guy to have great sex with—she doesn't need Joseph *specifically*, even if she is disarmingly attracted to him, and even if he does do that thing with his tongue where he . . .

"You can kick me out in the morning and I'll never call you again.

Just give me one more shot." His eyes are heavy with wanting, and she loves seeing how she does that to him, the way just their two hands touching can make him hazy with desire.

She swallows. "One night," she says, voice husky. "That's all you get."

Jane

WHEN JANE ARRIVES AT WORK ON SATURDAY, MORTIMER is hanging by two hands from a beam in the ceiling with a feather duster between his teeth.

"Oh, hello, Jane, dear," he says, voice muffled, his sensible brogues kicking a little. "I don't suppose you could be so good as to pass me that stool?"

It takes Jane a moment to react—she is not unaccustomed to strange goings-on at the Count Langley Trust charity shop, but she hasn't yet had her cup of coffee, and she's daydreaming as she steps through the door.

"Oh, Mort, what on earth . . ."

Jane rushes to right the fallen stool beneath him, and he rests his feet on it with a sigh of relief.

"You shouldn't be standing on that," Jane says as she helps Mortimer down. "I can dust up there."

"I don't like to ask it of you, dear," Mortimer says, brushing down his lapels and smoothing his gray hair back.

"I'm not royalty, Mort," Jane says.

"No, but you are an angel," he says, marching his way to the kitchen. "And I shan't have you doing the cleaning, not if I can help it."

"I am certainly not an angel," Jane says, surprised, but Mort is already out of earshot.

The coffee machine whirs in the kitchen. It's a recent gift from Mortimer's partner, Colin, who has just retired from a life of service in the Foreign Office. He has begun helping out in the shop once a week now, and when he saw the instant coffee Mortimer was handing Jane each morning, he declared himself *unspeakably horrified* and bought them a proper machine. When Mortimer tried to sell it on the shop floor, Colin told him off so resoundingly that Jane had been forced to hide behind the vintage clothing rail so they didn't hear her laughing.

There are four new donation bags today: one full of pots and pans, two filled with useless electricals they'll never be able to sell, and one stuffed with clothes.

Jane's hands still on a pretty silk blouse; she tilts it in the light, looking for stains. There's always a story to a donation bag: little ones growing up, teenagers leaving home, women declaring they'll never be a size ten again and so what if they won't. When Jane left London to come to Winchester, she took almost all the clothes she owned to a charity shop; who knows what the volunteers there made of quite so many gray suits and pencil skirts turning up on their doorstep.

Her phone buzzes in her pocket; she checks the screen and bites her lip. *Dad calling*. She's missed his last three calls—she has to answer this one.

"Hey, Pa," she says, glancing up to make sure Mortimer's still in the kitchen. "How are you?"

"Janey," he says. He sounds relieved, and her stomach twists; she's left it too long, he's worrying. "Same old, same old here. How are you?"

"Fine, good," she says, trying to muster the necessary energy for this conversation. "Just at work at the minute."

"On a Saturday?"

Jane winces.

"They work you too hard at that place," he goes on.

She can hear the creak of the armchair behind him as he sinks back, and it's as though she's there, in their little living room, with its patterned carpet and hazy warm lamplight, the stifling smell of lavender from the bunches their neighbor Judy always dropped round when she wanted an excuse to check on them both.

There's a pause. She can see him stilling in his armchair, foot hovering midway through its perpetual tapping. "Are you sure you're still having fun in London, love? You know, if you ever want to come home, there's a job waiting at the dry cleaners. You only have to ask."

She lays her hand over her eyes for a moment, pained, disgusted with herself, trying to drag up the effort she needs to stop him worrying. You'd think after all this time she'd have perfected the art of lying, but the lies get harder every time; they stick in her throat like something rancid and dry.

"No, no, really, it's great, Pa. I'm off to the pub tonight with some of the other girls from my floor. A cool new place in Clapham."

Mortimer has returned with the coffee; Jane's face heats as he places the mug down quietly beside her. He must have heard the lie.

"Good, I'm glad," Jane's father says, and that seems to have done the trick; he's settled.

"I have to go, Pa, but I'll call you soon. Maybe a video call."

"That would be wonderful. We're all really proud of you up here in Mortley, I hope you know that. I was just talking to Katie in Morrisons and she said you were a real inspiration for her son—he's applying to university this year."

The idea of being an inspiration to anybody is genuinely painful.

"That's nice," Jane says, her voice a little strangled. "I better go, Pa—speak soon."

"Look after yourself. Bye-bye, now."

Jane sets down her phone and lifts the mug of coffee to her nose. She can tell just from the smell that Mortimer has remembered to use the full-fat milk. She feels a pang of affection for this man, with his brown suit and his meticulousness, then a shot of pain as she wonders what he must think of her now, after hearing her lie.

"That was my dad," Jane begins, risking a glance at Mortimer. "I just . . . don't like him to worry. That's why I said those things. About London. He worries a lot, and I'm not . . . It's not . . ."

Mortimer looks at her with an unexpectedly sympathetic expression, and she examines the coffee in her hands so as not to meet his eyes.

"No judgment from me, dear. Colin's mother still thinks I'm a lady called Bluebell. Sometimes we can't tell a truth until we're ready."

Jane looks up at him in surprise. "Bluebell?" she says after a moment.

Mortimer smiles, eyes crinkling. "An inside joke. But yes. Bluebell is housebound, hence the lack of trips to see Colin's mum in Edinburgh. His mother is ninety-five, so can't come down here."

"Oh," Jane says, frowning slightly. "Does it hurt? Knowing Colin is lying about you?"

The question slips out—it's too personal, she shouldn't be asking it, but Mortimer is replying before she can take it back.

"It does, yes, but it hurts him more that he can't tell the truth. I think he'll get there, though. With a bit more time," he says comfortably.

If Colin's mother is ninety-five, it doesn't sound like she has a great deal more time, Jane reflects, but this is presumably a thought that has crossed Mortimer's mind already, and she manages to bite the words back before she says them out loud.

"Thank you," she says instead. "For not judging me. That was kind." She places the coffee down and picks idly at items from the donation bags: a USB cable, a teapot, a small woolen hat.

Mortimer has known Jane for a while, and now he knows two of her lies. But he says nothing else, and when she shoots him a quick, nervous glance, she's surprised to see he's still wearing that kind smile.

The front door tinkles and a middle-aged, red-haired woman enters the shop, dressed in what appear to be flannel pajamas. She's holding an umbrella, and it takes her some time to wrestle it down—one of the spokes is snapped, bending inward like a spider's limb. She swears violently. Jane blinks. The woman has a Cornish accent, broad shoulders and turned-out feet; she seems completely oblivious to Mortimer and Jane, who are watching her battle the umbrella from either end of the till counter.

"Can I help?" Jane asks eventually.

The woman's profanities escalate dramatically, and Mortimer's mouth drops open in shock. Women probably didn't say *wankstain* in his day.

"Don't worry," the woman says eventually. "Me and this umbrella are far beyond help."

The umbrella finally gives in and folds inward, and the woman gives a triumphant huff, then looks up at them with a bright smile.

"You got any clothes?" she says. "Size sixteen?"

"Sure," Jane says, rallying first.

It isn't unusual for people to turn up at the charity shop after a clothing fiasco: coffee spilled on a lapel, snagged tights, jeans ripped in unfortunate places. But a woman looking for an entire outfit, in her pajamas, is a first.

"The aim is to look like the sort of woman who doesn't lock herself out of her flat in her jimmy-jams before her first day styling a huge mansion for a new client," says the red-haired lady, following Jane through to the women's clothing section.

Jane winces in sympathy. "Oh, I'm sorry. How long have you got?"

The woman checks her watch. "An hour or so. No rush, except that I'm finding it a bit peculiar being out and about with no knickers on under these," she says, gesturing to her flannel pajama bottoms.

Jane laughs. "Don't let Mortimer hear you say *knickers,*" she says, lowering her voice and glancing toward the till. "He refers to all the underwear we get in as *unmentionables.*"

The woman lets out a hoot of laughter so loud that Jane physically jumps.

"Sorry, I get it from my dad," she says. "The laugh, I mean. Awful, isn't it?"

"It's not at all," Jane says, and she means it—the laugh is charming, the sort of laugh that makes you less self-conscious yourself, just by proxy. "I'm a little on edge."

The woman cocks her head to the side. "Bad morning?"

"Not as bad as yours," Jane says. It slips out, and she cringes, waiting for the woman to take offense, but she's rewarded with another hoot.

"That's right enough. I'm Aggie, by the way," the woman says, holding out a hand for Jane to shake.

"Jane."

They shake hands; Jane is struck by the slight absurdity of such a formal greeting when Aggie is wearing sheep-patterned pajamas.

"How do you feel about a wrap dress?" Jane says, pushing a bunch of dresses aside to reveal a dark-blue knee-length one with a tie at the waist.

"Ooh, that's nicer than what I'd got hung on the wardrobe anyway!" Aggie says, stepping back to admire it. Then she frowns. "I can't pay you, though, no cash in my pjs."

"Don't worry about that," Jane says. "We'll make a note and you can pop by tomorrow with the money. Let me just go find you some unmentionables . . ."

AGGIE LEAVES TRANSFORMED—JANE IS REALLY RATHER proud of her work. They even find her a handbag large enough to stuff the pajamas into.

The rain is coming down outside, thick and endless; the view of the street is always distorted through the old glass of the shop windows, but with the raindrops sliding down the panes, the scene looks like a painting. Jane stares out for a while, deep in thought. Aggie was nice. She hadn't made Jane feel like she was always putting her foot in it, even when she'd blurted out something blunt; Jane had relaxed with her. It had been . . . quite lovely, really.

Then the door to the charity shop slams open and Joseph Carter staggers in, his coat dripping. He steadies himself on the nearest bookcase, hands white with cold.

And just like that, Jane remembers.

A man staggering into her boss's office in a rage. Joseph.

The yelling, the slammed door. *Your fault. An accident.* More words like these, their sense lost through the wall. Then out he staggered again, face twisted. One white-knuckled hand gripping the doorframe.

He *had* worked in her old office. Their paths had crossed before, back when Jane was an entirely different person.

"Little rainy out there," Joseph says now, shaking himself off with a rueful grin. "I'm sorry. I've brought in a puddle."

"I'll fetch the mop," Mortimer says, shuffling off.

"Hi," Joseph says, smiling at Jane, who is frozen to the spot. "I don't suppose you have any umbrellas?"

Ask him, she thinks. *Tell him you remember him, that you two have met before. Ask him what happened that day when he came into the office in such a rage.*

"Umm," she says, turning toward the wicker basket where they store umbrellas.

There are three left: a Peppa Pig one, one that opens in the shape of a heart, and one branded with the words, *I've Got It Covered!*

"Your choice," Jane says after a moment.

Joseph's face shifts into an amused grin as he follows her gaze to the selection. The shoulders of his coat are shining wet; his hair is slicked back, and he looks more handsome than ever, broad-shouldered and pink-cheeked and dappled with rain.

There's a reason Jane doesn't talk about the past. She and Joseph have made it this far without discussing her time in London, and he clearly doesn't recognize her; why would she open that can of worms? What if he wants nothing to do with her once he finds out who she is? Though she swore to keep him at a distance, though she vowed to ignore the swooping sensation that had gripped her when he pressed his lips to her cheek, she can't quite bear the thought of losing him now.

This is the trouble, she thinks miserably, as Joseph opens the heart-shaped umbrella and bursts out laughing. *This is exactly why I should stick to plants and cats.*

Miranda

"DON'T OVERTHINK," ADELE SAYS, AS IF SHE HASN'T SPENT
the last hour talking Miranda through every possible worst-case scenario. "Just wait and see what he says."

They're at Waterloo station; Miranda thought it would be nice to
go shopping with her sisters on Long Acre before she got the train
down to Winchester for her weekend with Carter, but it has not been
the confidence-boosting girls' trip she had hoped for.

Adele and Frannie are *fascinated* by what exactly happened on Valentine's Day. The two of them have just turned eighteen—they're
twins, nonidentical, though they both have the same round brown eyes
and tendency to treat Miranda like their ancient and enormously embarrassing big sister. And, as of yesterday, they are living in her flat.

Adele has been nagging Miranda for months; the twins are desperate to get out of their parents' house and kick-start adulthood, but
neither of them has managed to get a job yet. When Miranda's old
flatmate moved out, it became increasingly difficult for Miranda to
find excuses not to put them up in her spare room, and after her slightly
tragic Valentine's evening, Miranda finally caved.

She should never have told them what happened with Carter, though. It's *just* the sort of gossip they love. While Miranda tries on jeans in H&M, Adele and Frannie cheerfully ruminate on the secret truths Carter might reveal to her this weekend: a second girlfriend, a criminal conviction, a harem of women living in his attic.

"I'm just excited to stay at his," Miranda says firmly, trying to cling to the attitude she'd had when she got up that morning.

She's only been to Carter's flat in Winchester a handful of times. They almost always meet at her place in Erstead, despite the fact that "her place" is a minuscule flat above a carpet shop with a bedroom blind that only ever makes it halfway down the window.

"Maybe he had to bury a body on Valentine's Day," Adele says as they enter Waterloo station. "That would explain why he wouldn't put it in a text."

"Yes," Miranda says, calling on her remaining scrap of patience, "that'll be it. Thanks, Adele."

"All I'll say on the matter," Adele continues, having said approximately one hundred things on it already, "is that he's very charming. That's often a real tell for a psychopath."

"*Carter?*" Frannie says, turning to gawp at Adele. "Miranda's boyfriend? A psychopath?"

Adele looks a little abashed. "All right, maybe I'm getting a bit carried away."

"You *like* Carter!"

"I do, I do," Adele says. She fiddles with the neon scrunchie holding her bun in place. "I remember."

"I'm sure there's some really boring, reasonable explanation for it all," Miranda says firmly as her platform flashes up on the departure boards. "Carter isn't the kind of guy to have dark secrets. He's too . . ."

"Straitlaced? All-American?" Adele offers.

"He's from Hampshire," Miranda tells her sister, trying not to sound exasperated.

"You know what I mean!" Adele says. Her eyeshadow is electric blue today, and she's wearing shiny leather trousers—it's all very Spice Girls, and *very* Adele. Beside her, Frannie always looks more muted, though without Adele for context she's pretty colorful, too: today she's in bright-red dungarees.

"He *has* got that clean-cut good-guy look," Frannie points out. "Like a brunette Captain America."

"I'm going to get on my train now," Miranda says, leaning to hug them both. "Please don't let your imaginations run away with you while I'm gone."

"Remember everyone thought Ted Bundy was really sweet!" Adele yells across the station, turning several heads. "Nobody ever suspects the nice guy!"

CARTER IS WAITING ON THE PLATFORM WHEN MIRANDA arrives in Winchester. For a moment her eyes slide over him: he's not got his glasses on and he's wearing a wooly jumper, jeans and boots, with a coat open over the top that she's not seen before. She's so accustomed to him coming to hers after work in a suit that it seems strange, like meeting a different Joseph Carter, his denim-wearing double.

His face breaks into a huge grin when he sees her, and she can't help hers doing the same. There's something so contagious about a smile from Carter, as if it's not just a sign of how he's feeling but a cue for everyone else.

"Hello," he says as she approaches him. "You look lovely." He kisses her chastely on the lips, an I'm-not-sure-if-I'm-allowed-to-kiss-you sort of kiss; Miranda resists the urge to deepen it and pull him closer. She may not think he's a serial killer, but he's still not in her good books.

As they leave the station Miranda turns left, into the car park, the way she's always gone before when visiting Carter. The pavement shines with recent rain, and Carter's coat is damp against her arm, but the sky has cleared to a beautiful tissue-paper blue.

"Ah, no," he says, reaching to touch her arm. "I've moved."

She falters mid-step. "You've moved? Since when?"

He looks uncomfortable. "Back to my mum's house," he says, nodding in the other direction, toward the center of town. "Last week."

Now we're getting to it, Miranda thinks, and her stomach hitches. Carter's family history is a little mysterious to her—he's mentioned that his dad wasn't around a lot when he was growing up, and she knows he doesn't have any siblings, but he's never told her much about his mother.

"Okay," she says. "Lead the way."

The house isn't far from the station. It's built of pale-gray brick, with a sharply pointed roof and a Gothic arch above the black door. Grand, but not especially big. It looks a little out of place on the street, which is mostly new builds; across the road there's a gym and an undertaker, and despite herself Miranda thinks of Adele's body-burying theory again and winces.

"Look, I should . . ." Carter pauses as they make their way up the steep concrete steps to the door. There is a little front garden on either side of the steps: leggy lavender that needs cutting back, a small hydrangea. "I should prepare you."

Miranda swallows. "Okay?" she says.

"You're about to meet my mother," Carter says. "And it might be a bit of . . . a shock."

Miranda's brain takes a few flying leaps. A shock *how*? Is his mother someone famous? Or is it something tragic—is she horribly injured by whatever happened on Valentine's Day?

"She's not very well," Carter says, and Miranda's heart melts.

"Oh, Carter, I'm so sorry," she says, reaching for his arm.

He turns his face away. "It's okay." His voice is a bit unsteady.

It's unsettling to see Carter emotional again. He's usually so relentlessly positive; nothing irritates him, not queue-jumpers, not people who say *btw* out loud, not even Adele. They're in new territory: Miranda's never had to look after him before, and she feels a twinge of anxiety.

"What's she . . . What is it?" Miranda asks eventually. This immediately feels like a very insensitive thing to say.

Behind them the traffic crawls by, and a bus pulls up at the nearby stop. A pair of teenage girls stare openly at them as they step off the bus.

"Let's go in, Carter," Miranda says, her hand still on his arm. She can't see his face, but the tendons in his neck are standing out like cords. "Carter?"

"Yeah," he says, moving at last.

He ducks his head as he rummages in his coat pockets for the house keys. When he finally looks at her there's no sign he's been upset, and he gives her his usual warm, reassuring smile before unlocking the door.

The hallway is dark. Post slips beneath Miranda's foot—a neutral white envelope, official-looking, addressed to *Mrs. Mary Carter.* She bends to pick it up, and when she straightens there is a woman standing right in front of her.

Miranda breathes in sharply, hand flying to her throat, post and all—she feels the envelope slice at the skin under her chin.

The woman is in her seventies perhaps, and wearing a long, loose dress that has an air of the 1920s about it: three-quarter-length sleeves, black beads at the neckline. She's very pale and thin. Her eyes are hazel, like Carter's, and her hair is bright white. For a long moment everyone is very quiet, and then Mary Carter seems to spring to life.

"Darlings!" she says, breaking into a smile that makes her relation to Carter unmistakable. It is the perfect hostess's smile. "Welcome!" She kisses her son on the cheek and Miranda hears her quietly say in his ear, "Which one is this, Joseph?"

"This is Miranda," Carter says.

"Miranda!" Mary exclaims. "Oh, how lovely, a Shakespearean name. Come on inside, darling, let's take tea in the living room."

Miranda follows Carter through. *Which one is this?* Miranda frowns; what did *that* mean?

She sets the envelope down uncertainly on a side table as they move toward the living room sofa. The room isn't at all what she expected when Mary had said they'd "take tea" in there: she'd anticipated large, patterned rugs and wallpaper, perhaps an open fireplace. Posh enough for people who *take tea*. Instead it's fusty and dated. The sofas have little beige skirts to hide their legs, and she can smell the warm fuzz of dust on the screen of the blocky old television. It's blasting out some sort of children's TV show: two grinning presenters dressed in yellow are dancing through a preternaturally bright flower field.

"Sit down, both of you," Mary says, sailing past them to straighten up a cushion on the sofa. She pays no attention to the television. "It's a terribly cold day, isn't it?"

The room is stiflingly warm—that close, dry warmth that comes from many months of radiator heat and no open windows.

"Have you eaten? Did Ania come?" Carter asks as his mother sits down in the armchair opposite the sofa, with her back to the television.

Mary Carter's eyes dart to Miranda and then to her son. Her hands begin to fuss in her lap, one thumb smoothing over the other.

"I'll go and check, and I'll make us some tea," Carter says after a beat, when his mother doesn't respond. "Miranda? Would you mind giving me a hand?"

Miranda jumps up. The urge to leave the room is almost overpowering. She's not sure what's going on, but she knows she's out of her depth here; this is adult stuff, the sort of situation in which her mother would know exactly what to do, and Miranda feels horribly young. She so badly wants to be part of Carter's life, but now that she's here, she's a little afraid of what she'll find. It's Adele's fault: all her talk of dark secrets.

"Sorry," Carter says as soon as they're out of the room. He has visibly got a grip on himself now, and he squeezes her hand comfortingly. "It's—it's dementia. She's gone really downhill this week."

Dementia. Miranda's grandfather on her father's side had the same before he died; her heart aches for Carter as she remembers how quickly her nonno had ceased to recognize her when she went to visit him.

"I'm so sorry, Carter," she says as they step through to the kitchen.

It's poky, but the ceiling is high and there's a tall window letting in a stream of wintery sunshine. The sunlight illuminates a film of dirt on the surfaces and the lino floor. Miranda instantly wants to clean; the need tugs at her like a hunger or thirst. She'd feel so much better if she could *do* something right now, scrub the hobs or wipe down the cupboards. Instead she directs her attention to the kettle, a grubby plastic thing that looks more like it belongs in her flat than the home of Mrs. Mary Carter.

"Sorry. I haven't had a chance to clean yet. What with moving in, and sorting all Mum's bank accounts . . . and then I've been out today trying to get her a security system and a panic button and a bathroom door lock where she can't lock herself in and I should have cleaned before you got here . . . but . . . I wanted to be, you know, open with you." Carter spreads his hands out. "Welcome to my mess," he says sheepishly, ducking his head, eyes seeking hers.

For a moment she doesn't know what to say.

"Are you busy thinking less of me over there?" Carter says, looking around as though he's seeing the place through her eyes.

"Thinking *less* of you?" Miranda frowns, frustrated with herself. "No! No, God, the opposite. It's amazing that you're doing all this. I'm just worried for you—this is a lot to do all on your own."

"There's my aunt, over in Braishfield, which isn't far away. She's helped a lot. And I've managed to sort carers," Carter says, running a hand through his hair. "They're supposed to send this woman Ania in twice a day to make Mum meals, but Mum says it's always someone

different coming in, and yesterday she kicked whoever it was out because she thought they were stealing her tea bags."

Miranda's turned back to the kettle; her hand is hovering over the
open box of tea bags as he says this, and she thinks for a moment that
she had better not touch them, then shakes off the thought and grabs
three. She opens head-height cupboards in search of mugs and finds
endless quantities of very expensive-looking china, gold-edged and
chintzy.

"And you're living here with her now?" Miranda says, checking for
ordinary mugs and finding none. She selects three delicate, fluted
china ones, shooting Carter a glance in case he'll tell her to put them
back, but he doesn't even blink.

"It seemed like the only solution," Carter says, opening the fridge.
"How am I meant to know if she's had any lunch?"

"Check the bin," Miranda suggests. "And . . ." She leans forward.
"There's a dirty plate in the sink."

Carter doesn't move, so she checks the bin for him. As she flips up
the grimy lid, she imagines it's her mother who can't remember
whether she's eaten lunch, and the thought is too painful to harbor
even for a moment—she shuts it down before her imagination can get
going. No point thinking like that. She's better off making herself
useful.

"There's crusts, they look recent," Miranda says. "I think she's had
a sandwich. Maybe cheese and pickle?"

"Thank you," Carter says quietly, closing the fridge door.

Miranda turns, but he's not looking at her, just staring at the closed
fridge door. She steps toward him.

"I'm so sorry you dealt with all of this on your own last week,"
she says.

He turns his face away, and there are those tendons in his neck
again, tight with emotion.

"Thank you for being open. Thanks for bringing me here," Miranda says. She's not sure if it's the right thing to say—it feels rude, maybe—but he pulls her in against his chest for a crushing hug, so she figures she's done okay.

"Miranda, I . . . There's . . ."

She waits, but he says nothing else, just holds her.

"I get it," she says tentatively. "But next time, you can't leave me sitting in some restaurant waiting for you with absolutely no idea what's really going on in your life."

He's holding her so tightly. She snuggles closer, breathing in the winter smell caught in his jumper: cold air, smokiness.

"I know this has all been a bit heavy," Carter says, his voice thick. "But I promise we'll still have a fun weekend. As soon as Mum's settled, I'm taking you out for dinner, okay? I know I have a serious amount of making up to do."

"Joseph?" Mary calls from the living room. Her voice rises. "Joseph, where is she?"

Carter loosens his grip on Miranda and steps back. "Just coming, Mum. Miranda's in here with me."

Miranda turns back to the tea bags brewing in their fancy china mugs, and busies herself finding a teaspoon as Carter goes to his mother.

"Not her," Mary says. "Not her. Where's the nice young lady you've been seeing in London?"

"Mum, sit down," Carter says calmly. "Miranda's just coming with the tea."

"Don't tell me to sit down." Mary's voice is shrill and fearful.

Miranda carries the first two cups of tea through to the living room. The television blares—some sort of nursery rhyme—and she's too hot in her roll-neck jumper. Mary is standing at the window, and Carter is on the sofa, shoulders sagging forward.

"Oh, hello, darling," Mary says with relief, turning to see Miranda. She steps toward her, reaching for the cup of tea. "You must be Siobhan."

Carter stands abruptly, moving to Miranda's side. "It's *Miranda*,

Mum," he says, and there's an edge to his voice. "I'm sorry. She's confused," he tells Miranda, voice low.

"That's okay," Miranda says, smiling at them both. "Let me fetch the other tea."

"Did I say something wrong?" Mary asks as she leaves the room. "Joseph, darling? Did I say something wrong?"

Siobhan

"YOU SLEPT WITH HIM, DIDN'T YOU?" FIONA SAYS, THE MO-ment Siobhan steps back into the flat.

Fiona got going on the tea when Siobhan's airport taxi was three minutes away. The two of them have permanent access to one another's phone locations, something they'd initially introduced as a safety measure, but that is in reality used to preempt drinks orders and snoop on the progress of one another's dates.

"I did sleep with him," Siobhan says, sighing and throwing herself down on a chair at the kitchen table. "And I've been livid with myself since he left the hotel room. But when the man's in front of me I can't think straight."

"How did you two leave things?" Fiona asks as she hands Siobhan the tea.

Siobhan remembers the morning—tangled in the sheets together, his sleepy mussed hair, his insistence that he'd go out and get them coffees from the café down the street. *Don't move*, he'd said from the doorway. *I still have a* lot *of making things up to you to do.*

"Oh, you're smiling," Fiona says, glancing over her shoulder as she wipes down the surfaces. "So can I take it that he's forgiven?"

"No! No. I should not have slept with him, obviously."

"You did say you wouldn't. A lot," Fiona says mildly. "Vows were made, I believe."

Siobhan rests her head in her hands. "Don't kick me while I'm down, Fi, my ego can't take it."

Fiona laughs, settling down opposite with her tea. "Fine, fine. So that was the last time, was it?"

"Absolutely. Last ever time. Never sleeping with him again."

This is so blatantly a lie that Fiona doesn't even comment on it. She leans back in her chair and rubs her eyes. *She's tired*, Siobhan thinks with a frown. Fiona is very beautiful, olive skinned with large eyes and dreamy long lashes, but there are the tiniest traces of wrinkles at the edges of her mouth, and a deeper one is definitely developing between her eyebrows. She has an audition the day after tomorrow, and it's important Fiona looks fresh and high-energy: she'll be up against the pretty young things just out of drama school.

What a relief to discover that Fiona needs looking after.

"Enough talking about that boy. Let's do face masks," Siobhan says brightly. "That'll cheer me up."

THE NEXT MORNING SIOBHAN HAS THREE VIRTUAL ONE-to-ones booked with employees at her main corporate client. Her brand began as a life-coaching business, and that's still much of the bread and butter of what she does. But after Cillian left, after the dark time that followed, Siobhan had thrown her whole self into work. With each new hit of success she felt surer than ever that this buzz was just what she needed, and so she fought harder, did more. She enacted the truth she so often coaxed from clients: if you want something badly enough, if you give that aim your all, the world will be yours for the taking.

Her blog traffic increased; her Instagram grew. Siobhan became more than a life coach—she became an inspiration, particularly for younger women. Requests came in for collaborations with influencers, a column on a popular women's blog, a segment on a local radio show. Now Siobhan and her talent agent have decided on "Empowerer" as her job title, though Siobhan does know that's a bit ridiculous, and when drunk refers to herself as "Emperor" instead.

The business has grown so fast it's frightening. The suddenness of her rise surely demonstrates how quickly she could fall again, and Siobhan has this constant sense of sand slipping beneath her feet as she runs, as if the ground is just waiting to trip her up.

The virtual one-to-ones are her safety net. As long as she still has those, then even if the rest goes crumbling around her, she'll be safe.

Her first session is with Bob Girl, as Siobhan thinks of her—a PA with aspirations to change careers. Siobhan's waited patiently as Bob Girl has unlocked the way her parents' low expectations held her back; she is almost ready to fly, and Siobhan can't resist a grin of satisfaction today as she hears her client say, *I think I deserve better than that.*

Siobhan has nicknamed her next client Blue Steel. His real name is Richard, and he's one of those bright-eyed silver foxes who you just know is only single because he cheated on his wife. Siobhan is absolutely convinced that Richard is holding out on her. He's a smooth talker, the sort of guy women call *slimy* but find themselves flirting with almost by accident, and she's determined to find out what makes him tick. It's partly curiosity, but it's also the only way to help him—he's been passed over for promotion twice, and she can't for the life of her figure out why. The answer is in there somewhere; she just needs him to open up.

So when he starts the session by saying, "Am I allowed to talk to you about something personal?" Siobhan has to try very hard not to look too excited.

"Absolutely. This is your time," she says.

Richard is a little pixelated on her laptop screen, sitting at the desk in his office. The shelves behind him are filled with important-looking tomes and those brown and chrome bits and bobs you'd expect to fill a bachelor's office: paperweights, globes, trophies. Siobhan wonders where they find these things—is there a shop for rich single men over the age of forty-five in which everything is made of worn brown leather?

"I believe I may have made an error of judgment today."

Siobhan waits patiently, arranging her expression to one of sympathetic interest.

"My secretary, she and I, we've—I mean, I'd say there's been a little flirtation, over the time we've been working together, but . . . we've never crossed that line." Richard meets her eyes in the camera with a suddenness that startles her; he's looking right at the lens. His eyes are a hard, pale blue that could almost be silver. "Until today."

"What happened today?" Siobhan prompts.

Richard sighs, rubbing a hand over his mouth. "She came into my office in this . . . this tiny gray dress, cinched in at the waist, tight across the arse."

Christ, thinks Siobhan, who was not expecting the word *arse* to feature in her morning one-to-ones. For a worrying moment she thinks she might laugh, but then Richard is looking right at her again, and the feeling fades.

"She came around behind the desk. Usually if she needs to pass me something she just hands it over, but . . . perhaps she saw something on my face, perhaps it was how I looked at her. She stopped just a step away from me. I was here in my chair, looking up at her, already . . ." His expression turns rueful. "Well, anyway. We kissed. And then . . ."

He's waiting for the cue from Siobhan. Despite herself, she's mesmerized. His voice is soft and deep; it's a beautiful performance.

"Go on?" Siobhan says. She keeps her tone perfectly level. Her usual polite, professional interest. She just catches his response, a slight flicker in his eyes, and she wishes they were face-to-face: she might have been able to interpret that micro-expression if he weren't just a picture on her laptop screen. It's been a while since she's seen Richard for an in-person session—when she moved back to Dublin, his company allowed her to shift to virtual sessions with those clients who were amenable. She still tries to meet them in person whenever she can, but it's been a few months.

"We had sex. On the desk," Richard says.

Siobhan tries very hard not to raise her eyebrows. This sounds too much like male sexual fantasy to be true, frankly, but Richard has never shown an inclination to tell lies before. Perhaps this is just the sort of thing that happens to men like Richard.

"You called this an error of judgment, Richard," Siobhan says after a while. "Can you expand on that?"

Richard waits for a moment before answering. "Well, isn't it?" he says. "She's my secretary."

Siobhan sits silently. It's not her job to judge—in fact, she wouldn't be doing her job if she judged. It would be robbing her clients of their own enlightenment if she were to tell them what to do.

"I'm in a position of power over her," Richard says slowly. "It was inappropriate."

He looks at her, waiting for a response. Is he looking for permission? Absolution? Is this why she's been told this story this morning? But that doesn't feel quite right; it doesn't explain the relish with which Richard recounted it all.

"Richard," Siobhan says, "what are you feeling right now?"

Richard looks away from the screen for a moment in thought.

"Young," he says finally. "I feel young and stupid. And it's fun.

Have you ever done something you shouldn't have?" Richard asks her, and then he laughs. "I'm sorry. I can't ask you that."

She smiles slightly. "No, you probably shouldn't ask me that." But she's thinking of the night with Joseph, its indolent, late-hour deliciousness, the way his skin had tasted. The way she'd smiled into her pillow when he'd gone out to fetch them coffee. The way her heart had expanded at the sight of him when he'd come back.

THE RITUAL BEFORE AN AUDITION IS THE SAME EVERY time. Siobhan runs Fiona a bath with lavender bath oil—the proper stuff that costs fifty euro a bottle. They do one run-through while the bath is filling; Siobhan tells Fiona it's the best audition she's ever seen, they'll be eating out of her hand, she'll win an Olivier before the year is out. Then Siobhan brings Fiona a honey tea in the bath. (Any sense of shame at one another's nudity evaporated years ago, around the time that Fiona picked a splinter out of Siobhan's bum after she'd engaged in a particularly ill-advised sexual adventure, and during the period when Fiona was auditioning for a show involving nudity and had spent a fortnight going topless around the flat to "acclimatize" herself.)

"No *way*. Blue Steel is sleeping with his secretary?" Fiona says, once Siobhan has filled her in.

There's a chair beside the bath to allow for these chats; Siobhan has her feet up on the side of the bath, and Fiona has her hair in a ridiculous purple shower cap that she is inordinately fond of because her grandmother bought it for her.

"Cliché, right?" Siobhan says, inspecting her nails. She needs her shellac redone.

"You should be careful, Shiv," Fiona says. "A man who sleeps with his secretary definitely has no qualms about sleeping with his life coach."

"Qualms?"

"Oh, shush," Fiona says, flicking bubbles at her. "It's a word."

"He does have that air about him, I'm not going to lie. But I think he's just the flirty type."

"Still. Watch him."

"He can't exactly seduce me via Skype, can he?"

Fiona looks at her shrewdly. "Do you fancy him?"

"What are you, ten?"

Fiona just continues to stare, eyebrows up. Siobhan rolls her eyes.

"He's hot, in a daddy-issues sort of way. But no. I don't fancy him. And I would never do anything about it even if I did. He's a client."

"Mm," Fiona says. "Wasn't Joseph a client?"

"No!" Siobhan says too loudly. "No, he was *not* a client. Yes, we met at one of my corporate assertiveness training sessions, but I never . . ." She clocks Fiona's expression. "Oh, fuck off," she says, poking Fiona's shoulder with her foot.

Fiona laughs and bobs her chin down under the bubbles to escape her.

Jane

JANE IS TWENTY MINUTES LATE TO MEET JOSEPH FOR
their evening book club session—Aggie, the pajama-wearing redhead,
dropped in right at the end of the day with a string of particularly
outlandish outfits she needed to find before morning. By the time Aggie left, Jane had the distinct impression that the visit had been about
more than acquiring over-the-top hats. Aggie drops in a lot. She's
lonely, maybe, but it's not quite that. Sometimes Jane thinks Aggie
might be checking in on her, but it seems so unlikely—why would she
bother?

Being late has made Jane flustered, and her scarf is somehow all
tangled in her hair; she battles with it as she approaches the restaurant.
She usually wears her hair in a low ponytail, but as she'd left the shop,
in a moment of vanity, she'd pulled the bobble out and run her fingers
through it, checking her reflection in the window. The dark strands fell
flat all the way to her waist, as characterless as ever. She used to despair
of her hair, how it never held a curl or stayed in a bun. Now she never
thinks of it at all. But having it loose softens her features, makes her
large eyes less buglike, her cheekbones less stark, and knowing she

would be seeing Joseph made her suddenly rather keen to look a lit-tle . . . prettier.

Joseph beams as he sees her, unfolding himself from where he's leaning against the misted windows of Piecaramba, their regular book club eatery of choice. He's wearing a wooly hat and gloves—it's a fore-boding sort of day, the sky bruised and low, already darkening. Jane's heart lifts, a sensation like the tug of a balloon. She hesitates for a moment as she reaches him. They'd never usually hug, but this time, all she wants to do is step into his arms.

After a moment he reaches forward and gently untangles her scarf from her hair. His fingers brush her neck and she breathes in sharply at the contact, even though he's wearing gloves.

"Sorry I'm late," she says as she follows him inside.

"Oh, no worries at all, you know what I'm like. This is punctual by my standards."

This is true. Until the moment Joseph reaches you he's always doing a million things at once: e-mails, calls, dropping in on so-and-so, do-ing a favor for some relation twice removed.

"How's your mum getting on?" Jane asks as they head to their table.

Piecaramba is stuffed with pop-culture memorabilia: Hulk posters on the walls, old comics, figurines balanced along the windowsill. Jane has no idea what most of the posters refer to, but she likes the atmo-sphere in here, the warmth, the sense that everybody's welcome. And Joseph likes the figurines. He has firmly instructed Jane to stop calling them "dolls," which she has duly done, so she is at least learning.

"Mum's had a good day, actually," Joseph says, busying himself pulling his chair out and removing his coat. "How are you?"

Jane smiles. It's so habitual for Joseph to turn his attention out-ward; this is part of his charm, but Jane wonders sometimes if that charisma of his is a distraction, like plumage on a bird.

"I'm well," she says. "It must get very tough, caring for her."

Joseph blinks fast behind his glasses. "Oh, you know," he says, with a bright smile, "you do what you can. I can't imagine how tough it must have been for *you*, losing your mother at such a young age. I'm very lucky to have had her with me—to still have her with me, even if she's not quite as *here* as she used to be. But you lost out on so much."

"And we're talking about me again," Jane says. It slips out, fast and cheeky; she immediately flushes with heat.

"Oh, hang on, this is rich—are you accusing *me* of being evasive, Jane Miller? Never have I met a more mysterious woman than you!"

Jane stares at him, genuinely agog. "I'm not mysterious. I'm boring. I just do the same things over and over. Wear the same things. Order the same food every time we come here. Go to work, read a book, go to bed."

"This is true," Joseph concedes, tilting his head. "In some ways. What's mysterious is *why*."

Jane shifts slightly on her seat, tucking her hair behind her ears. "I . . ." She hesitates. "I just like my routine."

"Hmm." He considers this with gratifying seriousness—she assumed he'd tease her. People tend to find her routines and habits amusing. "Have you always? Liked routine, I mean?"

Her gaze slides away. She remembers those first days in Winchester, the sheer terror of opportunity, the endless *options*. How frightened she had been.

"Yes," she says, "but . . . before I moved here, I didn't used to do things *quite* so . . ." She struggles to find the word. *I used to have more freedom*, she almost said, but that isn't true at all. "The routines are easy," she settles for. "They mean I don't have to make choices every day. I know exactly what to wear, where to go, what to eat."

"How fast to read?" Joseph says, eyebrows raised.

Jane swallows. He is referring to her one-book-per-week rule, which has always left him nonplussed, and has occasionally caused problems for their book club, too. The other week they decided to change books after trying a couple of chapters, and Jane had to explain she couldn't pick up another book until the following week. Joseph knows it's not the cost—they've met at the library café enough times for him to see she's a dedicated library user—and since then he's been nudging her to borrow a second novel when she's finished her first before the week's out.

"One book per week was a treat, when I first left London," she says. "It was a treasure I allowed myself."

"And you can't allow yourself any extras now? You get through books so fast, one a week's nowhere near enough."

Jane frowns, stiffening. "It's not . . . I can't do that."

"I understand the appeal of a routine," Joseph says gently. "I mean, I love fish-and-chip Fridays so much I get genuinely sad if I have to eat something else for my dinner, you know? But . . . isn't the one-book-only rule a bit restrictive?"

Jane's heart sinks. This is what people always say. *Restrictive. Odd. Boring.*

"It's . . . it's simple," she says, a little defensively. "That's what I needed when I arrived in Winchester. I needed simplicity."

Joseph gives her an easy, reassuring smile. "Ooh, a snippet of the truth," he says, leaning toward her. "A *clue* about who Jane Miller really is."

"Stop that," she says, but she brightens a little; it's very hard not to smile when Joseph's smiling. "Really, there's nothing to piece together—I'm just not very interesting."

"Now, I happen to know that isn't true at all," Joseph says.

Jane glances up at him through her eyelashes and then looks quickly back at the table. If he's trying to make her feel better, it's working, and she's just beginning to relax again when he cocks his head and says, "Are you ever going to tell me what happened in London?"

Jane swallows. This is her fault: she has invited the intimacy of this moment by trying to pry behind his defenses first. But . . . now they're here, this would be the perfect opening. *Actually, we used to work for*

Bray & Kembrey at the same time. You won't remember me by sight, but you've probably heard of me. She could say it. Let him in.

"Are you going to tell me exactly what happened on Valentine's Day?" she asks instead. She keeps her voice light and hopes he doesn't notice how it trembles.

Joseph frowns slightly, opening his mouth as if to speak, then closing it again. He's wearing black and it makes his eyes look greener behind his little round glasses. Jane likes the glasses. Joseph is a well-dressed, put-together sort of man, but those glasses tell her that he's not preoccupied with what other people think of him. And they're cute. Functional and earnest and sensible.

"Carter!" comes a voice from across the restaurant.

They both turn in their seats as a man in a suit pushes through the door to the pie shop. His hair is silky black, falling artfully across his forehead, and he's wearing what looks to Jane like a very expensive outfit. He has the sort of smile that you could read as cheeky if you were feeling generous, or as arrogant if you weren't.

"Scott, hey!" Joseph says, standing to hug him. "This is Jane—Jane, this is Scott."

Scott takes Jane in. Her eyes flicker to his, then back to the table. She hasn't met many of Joseph's other friends—they mostly live in London. She's heard of Scott, though, usually in the context of laddish nights out.

"A pleasure, Jane," Scott says, and she can hear the easy smile in his voice. He turns back to Joseph. "How's it going, Carter? We're definitely due a pint, aren't we?"

They chat for a while and Jane scans the menu, listening idly as they discuss when Scott's parents are next coming over from Hong Kong, and how crappy the hours are at the law firm where Joseph now works.

"And . . . how's Fifi?" Scott says.

Jane very deliberately continues to read about her dinner options—as though she won't just order the same pie she always does—but if her ears could prick up, they would have. Joseph has never mentioned a Fifi before.

"Scott . . ." Joseph says warningly, and Scott laughs.

"Okay, all right, I won't ask," Scott says, clapping Joseph on the shoulder. "Let's grab that pint next week."

"Absolutely," says Joseph, sitting back down. "Look after yourself."

"Who's Fifi?" Jane asks, as Scott heads out of the restaurant with his takeaway box.

Joseph's eyebrows shoot up. "Interesting."

"What's interesting?"

He's trying not to smile. "Tap water?" he says, pushing his chair back to go and fetch them each a glass.

"What's interesting?" Jane repeats when he returns, and this time he can't hide the smile. It seems to start at his eyes and grow from there.

"You've never asked me about women before, that's all," Joseph says.

"Yes I have!"

"No, you really haven't—ever," Joseph says, sipping his water. "Trust me, I'd remember. You *never* bring up my dating life. Or yours."

Jane is starting to feel flustered again. "You know I don't date."

"I don't know why, though," Joseph points out, one teasing eyebrow rising.

Jane swallows and reaches for her bag, pulling out *How Not to Be a Boy*. "Shall we order food? I'm ready if you are?"

"You know, as your fake boyfriend, I really think I deserve to know just a little more about your love life," Joseph says.

She blinks. "You don't have to be my fake boyfriend anymore," she says.

Joseph makes a face. "Did I just get fired?"

That pulls a smile from Jane, though her hands are clutched tightly in her lap. Something feels different with Joseph today. She seems to have given him permission to delve into the conversations he usually politely skirts around. Did she mean to do that?

"You *did* show up a day late for the job," she says, managing to keep her voice light.

He laughs, a big, expansive Joseph laugh, the sort that usually sets her at ease—only today it makes her stomach clench deliciously.

Oh God. She likes him. She *likes* him. In that moment, as Joseph laughs, Jane feels like she's just taken a step forward and found nothing underneath her, like a cartoon character walking off a cliff.

FOR THE NEXT MONTH, JANE RETREATS INTO ROUTINE. Her plan when she leaves Piecaramba is to freeze Joseph out altogether—it is the safest option—but after going through the agony of ignoring his messages for a day or two, she finds herself reaching for the phone and clicking on his name and typing, **Sorry, busy couple of days! Shall we read the latest Stephen King next?**

She is too weak, it seems. She can't help herself. So she has given up fighting the urge to see him and has compromised, doing what she does best: creating a system.

She is allowed to see Joseph once a week. One phone call; a moderate amount of messaging, leaving at least an hour between responses; no daydreaming about him. She must think of him only as a fellow booklover, someone with whom she can talk about reading. Nothing more. These are the rules.

They seem reasonable when she sets them out to herself, but now, in late March, Jane can hardly believe how often she has allowed herself to break them.

She is locking up the charity shop and thinking about Joseph kissing her on the cheek when a voice she doesn't recognize calls her name.

"Jane? Jane Miller?"

She turns. It's a gray, wet day, and the woman behind her is dressed in a large raincoat; it's only when she lowers the hood that Jane realizes who she is. Lou Savage—secretary to one of the senior partners at Bray & Kembrey.

Seeing Lou gives Jane the vertiginous sense that she has stepped back into another time. She is unchanged: gray suit under her raincoat, three-inch heels, bobbed blond hair with a thick strip of dark roots growing through at the parting. Lou had always been the one to invite Jane along to after-work drinks when she first started at Brays; they'd almost been friends.

"It is you!" Lou says, stepping forward with a smile. "Gosh, how have you been?"

"I'm—fine," Jane manages, swallowing hard, her palms beginning to sweat. Everything about this woman takes her back to that time: her neatness, the tone of her voice, the professional shine to her smile. "I'd better—I need to get home."

"Oh, sure," Lou says, smile wavering. "Right, sorry."

"No, it's not—I don't mean to be rude," Jane manages, but her breath is coming fast, and the keys to the charity shop are biting into her palm.

Lou's expression softens. "Oh, it's all right. You look like you've seen a ghost, but it probably feels a bit like you have. It's been a while, and I know when you left Bray & Kembrey it was all a bit . . ." She waves a hand in a circle, then her eyes widen. "Sorry, you probably . . . It's not that I know what happened, but . . ." She sags slightly. "You know how people talk."

Lou is more human than Jane remembers; her blustering is oddly calming. She is just a person, Jane reminds herself, not the embodiment of anything, not frightening, just a person who gets up every morning and brushes their teeth and forgets to lock the door sometimes.

"So is this where you're living these days? That's so lovely! Winchester is beautiful. What do you do now?" Lou asks, adjusting the wet hood of her coat and looking up at the charity shop windows.

"I work here," Jane says.

"Oh, full-time?"

Jane is suddenly very aware of the small badge on her chest that reads *Volunteer*. She sees the curiosity flicker on Lou's face, then the moment when she consciously wipes her expression clean.

"Well, it's great that you've found something fulfilling to do!" Lou says. She chews her lip for a moment as the silence stretches. "Listen, I always felt a bit . . . Well, I'm sorry nobody ever gave you a proper send-off. It wasn't fair of us." She fumbles in a pocket and holds out a card. "Here. Call me if you ever need anything, or if you just want to talk. Please," she says, when Jane just stares at the card. "Take it." She smiles. "If only to make me feel better."

Jane takes the card. She looks down at the little logo, the acorn. *Bray & Kembrey* in neat, official font below it. And even with the warmth of the charity shop behind her, she feels as though she's back in London, a different woman. The misery is suddenly suffocating.

"Not everyone believed his version of the story, you know," Lou says quietly as she turns to walk away. "You'd be surprised."

Siobhan

SIOBHAN'S PLAN FOR THE DAY IS DIVIDED BY THE MINUTE. She has thirteen minutes to get from the Golden Days Radio studio to the train station; the train to Limerick takes two hours and six minutes; she has five minutes to grab a coffee and a healthy snack (actually, a cookie) and then there's a car booked to take her to the business park where she'll be instructing a hundred and fifty call center employees to shape their own definitions of success. Her flight to London is at four; she times it perfectly, never having to wait for boarding to be announced, never having to run.

She does, however, fall asleep on the flight and drool on the shoulder of the elderly woman next to her.

"Don't worry, dear," the woman says, giving Siobhan's hand a pat as she unpeels herself from the woman's cardiganed shoulder. "I ate your snacks in exchange."

"I was meant to use the time to write blog posts," Siobhan says, dazed, staring at the black laptop screen in front of her as the announcements chime, telling her to prepare for landing.

"Well, looks like your body had other ideas," says the elderly woman, dabbing at her damp shoulder with a napkin.

The plane lands and Siobhan is off again, cursing herself for the wasted time. Power walking through the airport until she's overtaken everyone who got off the plane before her; slipping to the front of the taxi queue while everyone else faffs about with coffees and luggage trolleys and children. It's easy for Siobhan. She's all on her own.

The day goes by like this, in tiny, minute-shaped chunks, until it's all eaten up and she's in her room at the Thames Bank Hotel, almost dizzy with tiredness. She sits on the love seat in the window and tugs off her heels, wiggling her toes. There's a new blister; she notices it absently, knowing that she'll be too busy tomorrow to feel the pain.

She reaches for her phone on instinct and scrolls through her e-mails, then Twitter, then Instagram. These used to be the portions of the day that sprawled, but now it's part of her job, and she attacks it with the same focus that everything seems to require from her these days. She replies to as many commenters as she can, then clicks her phone screen off and closes her eyes, tilting her head against the back of the love seat.

This evening is hers, and she already knows how she's going to spend it. She and Joseph have slept together four times since she renewed her vow to Fiona that she wouldn't go anywhere near him ever again. She's been in London more than usual over the last couple of months and frankly she just can't stay away from him. It sounds so pathetically clichéd, *can't stay away*—the sort of thing weak people say to justify bad behavior. And it hardly comes close to expressing the compulsion, the *craving* Siobhan has for him, how just the thought of him makes her warm, as if she's sliding into a perfectly hot bath.

I'm in London and free if you are x

The two blue ticks appear, then Joseph is typing. Siobhan remembers she hasn't eaten, and then immediately forgets again, because he's said:

Hi! Why didn't you reply to my last message? I'm at Last Out. Could come to you afterward . . . Or you could join me for a drink? x

Last Out is one of those pretend jazz bars where the musicians play saxophone-heavy versions of songs like "Happy" and "Valerie." It's not Siobhan's sort of place—too contrived, full of people who think this is actual jazz—but it's a bar where everybody dances, even in the queue for the toilets, and she does love to dance. The idea of pressing her body up against Joseph's on a crowded floor makes her stomach clench with anticipation.

Who are you with? X

It's an old friend's birthday party. Would love to have you here x

She shouldn't go out tonight. She's exhausted; she's definitely been pushing herself too hard lately. But . . . that warm-bath feeling, that Josephness. It's so hard to resist.

Siobhan starts typing.

Be there in forty minutes. Xx

JOSEPH IS DANCING WHEN SHE ARRIVES, AND VERY DRUNK. Siobhan can see it in the way he moves: elbows a bit too loose, feet not quite in time with the music. (She was right: it's "Happy.")

His hair is sticking up on end and his shirt is clinging sweatily to his back. She can see the definition of his arms through his sleeves, the five-o'clock stubble on his jawline as he lifts his face to the ceiling, eyes closed. She heads straight for him and her body is against his before he's opened his eyes; the way they light up when they land on her face does something bad to her, something delicious deep in her chest.

"Hey, you," he says, and he kisses her deeply. They begin to dance, body to body. "I'm drunk," he says with charming candor, and she laughs.

"Yes, you are."

"I'm drunk and I'm—I'm . . ." He looks around for a moment, squinting slightly. "I'm here," he says in slight surprise. "With you."

"Uh-huh." Siobhan tries not to laugh. "You messaged me."

"Absolutely, course I did," he says, and kisses her again. "Hi. Hi."

There's a low warmth in the base of her stomach already, and as Joseph grabs her waist, tucks her closer, lifts a hand to run through her hair, it intensifies to a luxurious slow heat. There is something about Joseph. A magnetism, a drag, as if he sends the world around him spinning inward, and Siobhan's caught in the whirlpool. Now, pressed to the heat of his body, dancing hard enough to make herself breathless, she feels something quieten inside her. That rushing, driving urgency that always boils in her belly—it stills when Joseph holds her. The thought makes her nervous, and she pulls back a little, suddenly conscious that she's beginning to sweat.

"So who's the birthday boy, then?" she asks, glancing around.

Joseph points over her shoulder, grinning at someone she can't see. "The guy in the *very* questionable shirt," he says when she follows the direction of his finger. "Scott! Come meet Siobhan!"

Scott shoves his way through the crowd, half-empty glass in hand. His dark hair shines silver under the lights and someone's pinned a birthday badge to his chest. Siobhan snorts with laughter as she recognizes the "questionable" shirt as this season's Dolce & Gabbana. Joseph is so adorably clueless.

"Ah! The famous Siobhan!" Scott's drunk, too, and stares at her a bit too hard, but he's hot enough to pull it off.

"That's me. Happy birthday!" Siobhan yells over the music. "I'm going to the bar, you want anything?" She's too sober—her feet hurt. And the intensity of dancing with Joseph has thrown her.

"I'll join you," Scott says.

They move through the crowd of dancers together and stand side by side once they reach the bar. To Scott's left, a woman dressed in silver sequins weaves her hips to the music, and he glances at her with the practiced air of a man who is good at judging just how drunk and/ or single a woman is. Siobhan is pretty good at that game, too, and the woman is definitely both drunk *and* single, but to her surprise Scott turns his attention back to Siobhan.

"So what do you do, Siobhan?" he asks.

"I'm a life coach."

This gets a range of responses, normally. There's a large contingent of people who think that *life coach* is essentially another term for *scam artist*; they usually start by asking how much Siobhan charges. Then there are the people who want free therapy, who immediately launch into a litany of self-esteem issues. Finally, there are those who want to challenge Siobhan on exactly what qualifies her to advise others on their lives. These are almost always men.

Scott moves up considerably in Siobhan's estimation when he proves himself to be none of the above, and instead says, "Bet that's a tough gig, dealing with everyone else's problems all day."

"Yeah, sometimes." She smiles at him. "What do you do?"

"I'm in fundraising," he says, and she thinks, *Yes, excellent, you're exactly where you're supposed to be.*

"How do you know Joseph?" she asks as Scott orders her a glass of pinot grigio.

"We went to school together in Winchester," he says. "He used to be a total nerd, you know—we both were." He drops his voice, conspiratorial, grinning. "Don't tell him I told you that."

Siobhan laughs, and she lets Scott hold her gaze just a little too long, wondering. He's handsome, well dressed, has a sexy sort of confidence to him. For a second she entertains the thought that she could go home with him instead of Joseph, and she wonders what Joseph would do. Would he rage at her? End things? Or would he not even care?

"Can I ask you something?" Scott says.

She raises her eyebrows, as if to say, *Go on.*

"You do know he sees other women, right?"

The band has launched into an upbeat rendition of "Haven't Met You Yet." The beat vibrates through the bar under Siobhan's elbow, and she knows that if she could hear her heartbeat it would be upping its tempo, too.

"We're not exclusive," Siobhan says. This is the truth, but it doesn't explain the way she's now digging her nails into her palms.

"Good to know," Scott says with a teasing, charming smile, but the question has turned Siobhan off; she glances back toward the dance floor and Joseph is there, trying to text while he's dancing, his squinting face shining in the light of his phone.

"It was nice to meet you, Scott," she says, and moves toward Joseph, drawn his way through the crowd. Their eyes meet as he slides his phone away, and again there's that surprised, pleased look on his face, and the corresponding ache in Siobhan's chest.

Joseph stretches out his hand. "Dance with me!" he says, with one of those infectious grins.

She takes his hand. Doesn't she always?

JOSEPH IS ALREADY AWAKE WHEN SIOBHAN'S ALARM GOES off the next morning. He's lying on his back beside her, his stubble a little darker today, his hazel eyes open.

"I," he announces, "am extremely hungover."

Siobhan laughs, and Joseph turns his head. His eyes crinkle.

"Good morning," he says. "How do you look so good first thing, please?"

I only take off half my makeup when I go to bed, Siobhan thinks. *Just the eye makeup, and then I spritz the rest with setting spray.*

"It's a gift," she says, stretching, back arched.

His gaze dances down her body, as she'd hoped it would.

"Thanks for coming last night," he says, turning onto his side and running a hand down her side, breast to hip bone. She shivers, her body already waking under his touch. "It was . . . yeah. I liked having you there."

She raises an eyebrow as his fingers shift across her hip. "You liked having someone to grind against on the dance floor?"

"I liked taking you out. I liked you meeting some of my friends." He props his cheek on one hand, but the raised arm can't hide the blush that's tinged his face.

Siobhan tilts her head. That blush is quite fascinating, and his impulsive move to cover it is even more so. She remembers what Scott said last night—*He used to be a total nerd*—and thinks, *Yes, I can see that.* Joseph has the kind of looks you grow into—he would have been a gangly teenager, too broad in the shoulders, those strong, straight brows a little heavy for his face. And he's smart, she already knows that: he reads the sorts of books that get short-listed for prizes. She sees them sticking out of his coat pockets and, once, she came out of the shower to find him reading upside down on the bed, feet up on the headboard.

That blush of his makes her want things she shouldn't. It makes her want to climb into his lap and kiss him until he comes apart, until she's reached the heart of him. His hand has shifted lower now, to her upper thigh. She concentrates on the sensation. She shouldn't be thinking about who Joseph is beneath the surface. He's good in bed. That's all that's relevant.

"It was fun," she says, breathing out as Joseph's fingers shift closer to where she wants them. And then, because somehow she can't resist: "Scott's cute, too."

His hand stills. Siobhan probably should have seen that coming. Perhaps she did. It was an unequivocally stupid thing to say. That urge to push Joseph, to piss him off, it's a sure sign she's feeling things for him that she shouldn't.

"He's always popular with the ladies, yeah," Joseph says. His voice is light, but there's an unmistakable tightness there. If it was jealousy Siobhan wanted, she's found it, but all it does is make her edgy and nervous. She shifts away slightly and he lifts his hand back up to her stomach, signal read.

"So what's on today's schedule?" he asks, trying to smooth down his ruffled hair with the hand he's propped his head on.

Siobhan closes her eyes for a moment as she scans through the day ahead. "Some press, a virtual one-to-one that I rescheduled as a favor."

"You still do one-on-ones?" Joseph says.

He takes his hand from her stomach and reaches for the side table in a gesture that is almost painfully familiar to Siobhan—he is feeling around for his glasses so he can see her properly. She swallows. She could fall in love with this man so easily when he's like this, sleepy-eyed and hungover.

"When the price is right," she says, and he smiles, not fooled.

"I'm amazed you find the time," he says, putting his glasses on. "I've seen your schedules. Seven days a week, and *toilet breaks* are on there."

Her temper flares; this is a sore point. Her friends keep bringing up her busy schedule, too.

"Yeah, it's packed, but what am I supposed to do, turn down opportunities?" she says, sitting up in bed. Her clothes are strewn across the floor with comical abandon: her bra is cups-up on the table, strap dangling over, and there's a shoe impaled between the two cushions of the love seat.

Joseph takes her arm. She pulls away, but he touches her again, insistent, and she looks around at him at last.

"I was just trying to say it must be hard sometimes," he says. His expression is even more earnest than usual. "That's all. I didn't mean to criticize you. It's pretty obvious you're amazing at what you do."

It's unsettling how thoroughly he seems to understand her. The men she sleeps with usually aren't allowed to stick around long enough to garner that sort of insight. She gives him a shaky smile, but he won't settle for that—he sits up beside her, lacing his fingers through hers. His attempts to sort his hair have not been particularly successful: it's all flat on one side, sticking up on the other. His eyes blink sleepily behind his ridiculous, adorable little glasses, and the heat goes out of Siobhan's stomach, her temper subsiding like a gas flame dialed down on the hob.

"Sorry to bite your head off," she says after a moment. "I guess I'm a bit . . . strung out."

He presses her hand to his lips. "Maybe you need to take a break?"

Her temper stirs again. "I can't," she says. "It's not that simple."

"Okay," he says comfortably. "Then more massages needed, clearly."

He's far too good at deflating her when she begins to get riled up. She finds herself smiling and twisting into him for a kiss, which is breaking one of her sacrosanct hookup rules (no morning kissing until everyone has brushed their teeth) and feels dangerously lovely.

She gets up, grabbing her phone, heading for the bathroom. This thing with Joseph is getting far too deep—she ought to cut it off before somebody gets hurt.

As she runs the shower, letting it warm up, Siobhan checks her notifications. There's one from her period tracker—she's a day overdue.

Her stomach is already a little jittery after that moment with Joseph, and now it absolutely plummets. She checks the date—April seventh. The tracker is right. She's late. Her periods are regular as clockwork; she has only once been a day late, and that was because she was pregnant.

"No, no, no," she says out loud, backing up against the door. She's sickeningly cold; it feels as if something's crawling across her skin.

"Pardon?" Joseph calls from the other side of the door, and she jumps—she'd forgotten he was still back there, behind the closed door, in the part of her life in which this disaster had not yet happened.

She needs to go out and buy a pregnancy test. But the very thought makes her nauseous. She feels utterly convinced of what it'll say; she can't bear the thought of that three-minute wait, the second line slowly appearing beside the first, the horrible certainty that she's been unspeakably stupid. She and Joseph have always used contraception, but only condoms—and they're not completely effective, are they? She should have started on the pill again when sex with Joseph became more than just a once-per-month arrangement. Her hand moves to her gut and presses down hard. She's been such an *idiot*. She's let this man in and now the very worst has happened and she knows exactly how it'll go from here, she just *knows*.

"Are you all right in there?" Joseph calls.

"I'm fine! Can you just go? As in, can you leave, please?"

Suddenly it's absolutely imperative that Joseph Carter get out of her hotel room.

"What? What do you mean, go?" He's nearer the door. "Are you okay?"

The tears are so close she can feel them pulling and aching at the back of her eyes. She grits her teeth hard.

"I just want you to go."

"You want me to leave? Has something happened?"

"I'm *fine*, just get *out* of here," she says, voice rising. She can't fight the tears much longer. "*Leave*, Joseph. Go."

There is a long silence. Within it, Siobhan can hear the sound of the past repeating itself; she can hear herself cast aside, abandoned, a failure. There is an awful inevitability to it all. This isn't just about the pregnancy scare, she can sense that already: she's at some sort of tipping point, and this seems to have tumbled her over. She feels utterly mad, completely out of control. She's collapsed inward like this once before, and it's even worse now for knowing just how awful it's about to get.

"Why?" Joseph says. He sounds so concerned, as though he really cares, but he'll leave soon, he'll go, she knows he will. "Did I say something wrong, Shiv?"

Siobhan closes her eyes tightly, tears coursing down her cheeks. "No," she says thickly. "I just need you to get out. All right? Get. Out."

Another silence. Siobhan's nails bite into the skin of her palms. After a long moment, Joseph tries the doorknob, and Siobhan flinches, even though she's locked the door.

"I told you to *get out!*" she shouts.

"Okay, sorry, I'll . . . I'll go, if that's what you want," Joseph says through the door. "But will you promise to call me if you need anything?"

Siobhan doesn't reply. She's not promising him anything.

"Okay. Please look after yourself, Shiv. Please call me if I can help."

After a while she hears him walk away, hears the hotel room door shut behind him. She sinks down against the bathroom door and sobs, hearing it over and over, the sound of the door clicking shut.

Miranda

CARTER FLOPS BACK ON MIRANDA'S BED, COVERING HIS eyes with his hand to block out the spring sunlight lancing through the window.

"Gnnh," he says.

Miranda grins, perching herself beside him. She's reshuffled the room again, an exercise she engages in every few weeks, a sort of feng shui fidgeting. This room may be poky and damp around the edges, but it's *hers*, and she loves every inch of it, from the tatty broken blind to the bookshelf she built from reclaimed timber. Her current arrangement means the triangle of April sun from the window spotlights her bed in warm, lemony yellow; Miranda wants to bask in it like a cat.

"Drink too much?" she says to Carter.

He was at Scott's birthday party last night—he'd said he would be coming back to hers afterward, since his aunt was staying with his mum for the night, but she'd received a garbled text sometime around ten thirty declaring that he was too drunk and would crash at Scott's place. She wouldn't have minded him coming over drunk—she would have preferred that, actually, over him sleeping at Scott's. Miranda isn't at all sure about Scott. He's one of those people who say *Only joking, only joking* after rude remarks as though that negates them, and once, when she had her hair in two plaits, he had tugged one of them and told her she was *just too cute*.

You should see me with a chainsaw, mate, she'd said, and he'd laughed.

"Yes, very much too much," Carter says. His voice is a little hoarse. "Come here?" He pats at his chest, and Miranda shifts to lie down against him. "That's better," he says with a sigh. "Your mere presence is a balm for the soul, Miranda Rosso."

Miranda smiles. Carter smells of her shower gel—he jumped in her shower as soon as he arrived this morning. Apparently Scott spends an hour showering every morning, and Carter couldn't be bothered to wait until the bathroom was finally free.

Miranda and Carter have had a good couple of months. She's gone to Winchester every few weeks; she even accompanied him on a visit to the doctor with his mother. They are much more boyfriend-and-girlfriendy than they used to be—oddly, that strange Valentine's Day seems to have brought them closer.

"Are you suggesting I market myself as a hangover cure?" Miranda says, snuggling in.

Carter laughs. "I'm far too selfish for that. *My* hangover cure." He kisses her head. "Only you could make me laugh when I feel this disgusting."

"Is it one of those hangovers where your insides are all burny, like they're mad at you and inflicting their punishment from the inside out?"

"How graphic," Carter says, and she can hear that she's made him grin. "I'm not sure *articulating* the hangover is actually going to help?"

"Brunch!" Frannie yells through the door.

Carter makes a little whimpering sound.

"Carter is hungover!" Miranda yells back.

"Maybe we could just . . . tone down the Rosso family volume levels today?" Carter says plaintively.

Miranda laughs.

"Oh, so he doesn't want frittata?" Frannie shouts.

"Frittata? Since when do you know how to make a frittata?"

"I'm trying a new thing!" Frannie yells. "Sausage and pepper frittata!"

"Oh God. Please don't either of you say *frittata* again." Carter sits up, rubbing his eyes. "The thought of eggs . . . Gah." His phone buzzes; he checks it, face tightening, and then groans. "Damn it. I have to drop into the office."

"On a Saturday?" Miranda asks before she can stop herself.

Carter pulls a face. "Lawyers don't respect weekends."

"Boo. Okay. Are you sure you don't want any—"

"Miranda, I'm warning you," Carter says in the stern voice that always makes her laugh.

"Frittata!" she yells at him as he heads for the door with his satchel over his shoulder.

"When I am not hungover," Carter says, spinning and pointing a finger at her, "you are going to be mercilessly tickled for that."

CARTER LEFT HIS COAT BEHIND; AS MIRANDA IS PULLING on her shoes, she spots it at the bottom of her bed and smiles. She's wearing jeans and a V-neck jumper her mum bought her for her last birthday—she's off for afternoon beers with Jamie and the team, to celebrate having a particularly good month in March. Miranda picks up the coat and shrugs it on, and she grins a little giddily to herself, feeling like that girl at the party wearing her boyfriend's hoodie.

Frannie is flicking through a gossip site on her phone on the sofa when Miranda heads out of her room. The house still smells of her horrible burned frittata. Adele has gone out on some mysterious errand, which was presumably just a ruse to avoid having to eat a portion of her own.

"Oh God, I am literally obsessed with Harry and Meghan, I can't stop reading this stuff," Frannie says, looking up from her phone. "Ooh, is that a new coat?"

"It's Carter's." Miranda can't stop herself from smiling. "He left it this morning. I kind of like it."

"You look like a red marshmallow." Frannie does not seem to mean this as an insult. "Have you been through the pockets?"

Miranda blinks. "What? Why would I do that?"

"Why would you *not*?" Frannie says, already leaning over the back of the sofa and rummaging in the one nearest her. "Ooh, gum!"

"Oi, stop it!" Miranda says as Frannie gets started on the other pocket, already chewing the gum.

"A receipt!" Frannie brandishes it, then ducks as Miranda tries to snatch for it.

"We can't just . . . go through Carter's private pockets!" she says.

"They're your pockets right now," Frannie points out. "Well, it looks like your boyfriend got himself a very nice hangover breakfast this morning at Balthazar in Covent Garden! No wonder he didn't want my delicious sausage frittata!"

"Give me that," Miranda says, grabbing it back and shoving it into the pocket again.

Her heart is *tut-tut-tut*ting in her chest; when Frannie catches her expression, she sobers immediately. That's the difference between Frannie and Adele: if Frannie upsets you, she notices.

"What? Mir? What is it?"

"No, nothing."

"Your face has gone all pale and saggy. What is it?"

Miranda swallows. Scott lives in Tooting. There was absolutely no reason for Carter to be north of the river this morning. Why would he travel from Scott's flat to the center of London for a break-fast on his own, and then out to Surrey to spend his Saturday with Miranda?

With Frannie's eyes on her, Miranda checks the receipt again. It feels disgusting. Like peeling back a bandage or squeezing a spot: hor-rible but irresistible.

It looks like he only ordered one person's worth of food: banana pancakes, a coffee. Perhaps he split the bill with someone. It's probably a work meeting Carter just didn't think to mention to her.

But Carter has an Amex for work. Surely he'd use that if it was a business meeting. This receipt says he paid with a Visa debit card. And it *is* a Saturday.

"Miranda . . . ?" Frannie says, eyes round. "What are you thinking?"

"Nothing," Miranda says. "He just went for breakfast on his own in Covent Garden. That's not weird. It doesn't mean anything."

But it does suggest—just a tiny bit, if you're being extra suspicious—that he might not have stayed at Scott's last night. And if he didn't stay at Scott's last night . . .

Where was he really?

MIRANDA ARRIVES AT THE PUB SWEATY AND HYPED. FOR the whole bus journey she couldn't think about anything but that bloody receipt.

Miranda is trusting to a fault—the sort of woman you'd pick for a scam, with her sunny, guileless face and her fondness for seeing the best in people. But this is Carter, and Miranda has always felt deep down that he's too good to be true. So she can rationalize that receipt all she wants, but the doubt was already there—and now it's been fed.

"Rosso!" Jamie shouts as Miranda walks into the pub.

The smell hits her first: the comforting, reliable smell of a place where many beers have been spilled on the carpets. Then she spots the team in a booth toward the back—Jamie has an arm in the air to catch her attention, and she can tell he's already a couple of pints down. She grins as she approaches them. Pubs, blokey blokes: these are things that feel comfortable to Miranda. This is where she's at home.

"What are you drinking, Rosso? Beer, wine? One of those colorful things with ridiculous names?" Jamie says, already getting up to head to the bar.

"Whatever lager is on tap," Miranda says, "but just a half."

"A half!" Jamie pauses, recalibrating, visibly recalling that Miranda is a young woman who works for him. "Of course," he says. "Right, a half it is."

Miranda turns to AJ, Trey and Spikes. AJ is lounging—or perhaps sprawling is a better word for it. He's taking up most of the bench along one side of the table, knees wide, enormous shoulders leaning against the bench's cushioned back. Trey is hunched beside him, staring into his drink, as if auditioning for his future role as old-man-in-pub-at-ten-a.m. Spikes is on a stool that is much too small for him, and his head moves back and forth as if he's tracking the path of a bee; Miranda turns to follow his gaze and realizes he is in fact watching women go by through the pub windows.

"Well. Been another good week," she says, trying not to laugh at Spikes.

"That oak was a real bugger," Spikes says. He clocks what he's said and gets a sly look on his face. "Least nobody needed rescuing from this one, though."

AJ raises his eyebrows, watching Miranda; even Trey looks up slowly from his pint.

Miranda laughs. "It's all right. I'm over the shame," she says. "It's been almost two months since AJ had to fish me out of that oak. You can mock me. I'm ready."

"Oh, we mocked you plenty—we just made sure you couldn't hear,"

Trey says, and then, after a long moment, the corner of his down-turned mouth twitches up just slightly.

"Thanks," Miranda says dryly. She's become quite fond of Trey. He's a bit like Eeyore: mournful, morose, but somehow fun to have around nonetheless.

"Least you didn't fall out," Spikes says, sipping his Guinness with surprising delicacy for such a large man. "Trey fell out on his first day climbing."

Trey's face returns to its habitual scowl. "Did not," he says, fixing his glare on Spikes.

"What d'you call it, then?" Spikes says.

"It was a—bit of a slide," Trey says. "That went quicker than I thought it would."

"He cheese-grated the whole of the front of his body on the trunk of a sycamore," AJ tells Miranda, leaning forward. "You should have seen the state of the man's dick after that, it looked like a half-chewed stick of pepperoni."

Trey and Spikes pause in shocked silence. They *never* talk like this when Miranda's around. AJ watches her, waiting, with that particular look he has, the one that says, *I know you inside out.* Miranda meets his eyes and grins.

"If you're trying to shock me, AJ," she says lightly, taking the glass Jamie hands her as he returns to the table, "you're going to have to do better than Trey's dick. No offense, Trey."

AJ laughs. He has a deep, back-of-the-throat, gives-you-shivers sort of laugh, and Miranda is struck—as she often is—by just how easy it must be for him to pick up women. She's heard plenty of tales while she's working with the boys: stories of AJ's threesomes, his penchant for blondes, and one particularly ridiculous story about him having sex in the back of a truck while someone else was driving it cross-country.

"Salami," Trey says sulkily. "Not pepperoni. Big salami. Girthy salami."

———

WHEN AJ KNOCKS BACK THE LAST OF HIS PINT AND MOVES to go to the bar, Miranda puts a hand out to stop him.

"My round," she says. "I owe you a drink."

Their eyes meet and her face heats as she remembers the moment almost two months ago when AJ had asked her out for a drink, still breathless from their descent through the oak's branches. His eyebrows rise a little, but he doesn't say anything, he just follows her to the bar. At her questioning look, he says, "I'll help you carry—wouldn't trust those hands with five pints."

She rolls her eyes, but she's grinning. It's a relief to be mocked, frankly. When people aren't taking the piss, you really know they think you're a moron, and it's taken way too long for these guys to start ribbing her.

"So, AJ," she says as they join the gaggle of people waiting to be served. Miranda thinks twice about leaning her forearms against the bar—it's streaked with spilled drinks and almost certainly very sticky. "No early job tomorrow. What does tonight hold for you? Sex halfway up a pine tree, a foursome in the cherry picker?"

He doesn't answer, and when she turns to look at him, his expression is dark. She wonders briefly if she's offended him, but it's not quite that—he looks intense rather than angry, and his gaze is fixed on her.

"You know, if you want them to see you as one of the lads, that's fine," he says quietly, shifting ever so slightly closer. "But for what it's worth, I'll never see you that way."

Miranda's breath hitches. AJ's been pretty well behaved over the last six weeks. Sometimes there's the odd flirtatious move—not out loud, just a lingering glance, a hand on the small of her back as he moves past her—but nothing Miranda's felt she needs to tell him off for. She's almost got used to it; for AJ, as far as she can tell, flirting is his default setting.

So this—the intense look, the closeness of his body—is a little unexpected. She feels her skin going hot and turns away from him, toward the bar.

"I'm not trying to be one of the lads," she says, keeping her voice light. "I want to be part of the team. I don't see what being a woman has to do with it."

She hears him huff at that—a laugh, maybe, or a noise of surprise. He stays quiet. She catches the bartender's attention and orders their round, and when she finally looks back at AJ, he's watching her in a wondering sort of way. As if perhaps he doesn't know her inside out after all.

"Are you like this with him?" he asks, lifting two of the pints from the bar top.

"Like what with who?"

"With your boyfriend. Are you like this? Confident, sexy? Yourself?"

"AJ," Miranda warns. "That's enough."

"I can't say you're being yourself?"

"You can't tell me I'm . . . You can't flirt with me."

He smiles slightly and shakes his head as they make their way over to the table. "Miranda . . . if you don't want me to think you're sexy, you're going to need to stop telling me I can't have you. I'm no good at off-limits. It's like . . . pure temptation."

"I figured that was the appeal," Miranda says as they navigate their way from the bar across the busy pub.

"Think what you like," AJ says, brushing against her as they walk between tables. "But if I only want you because I can't have you, aren't you better off going on a date with me? Just to put the whole thing to bed?"

"Aaron Jameson, you are a shameless man-whore," Miranda says firmly. "Go flirt with one of the twenty women at the bar who are gawping in your direction."

"I don't want the twenty women at the bar," AJ says as they reach their table.

"Well, you've already slept with at least two of them, if I remember rightly," Jamie says, squinting toward the group of women who are all turned in AJ's direction. "So that's awkward."

Siobhan

SIOBHAN MANAGED TO CANCEL THE ONE-TO-ONE, BUT she couldn't bail on all the press interviews. She has no idea what she said in a single one of them. It's the evening now, and already the conversations with bloggers and small-time journalists are an absolutely impenetrable blank spot in her mind. She could well have told the news editor of *Dublin Business Journal Monthly* to go fuck herself, for all she knows.

As she walks through the darkness to the taxi rank in Dublin airport, she feels as if she is somebody else. Not abstractly—in a very real, tangible way. She is not Life Coach Siobhan; she is not Siobhan the Empowerer, the brand, the businesswoman; she is not even Siobhan, flatmate of Fiona. Ever since this morning she's just been . . . floating.

It seems astonishing that she is still walking forward, one foot in front of the other; the people around her look real, and her feet underneath her look real, but she feels a powerful, urgent need to ask someone, *Am I here? Are you sure? Is this me?*

It wasn't quite like this last time. She'd fallen apart then, but at

least she'd known who she was. Though perhaps she would have preferred not to.

"You all right there?" the taxi driver asks her as she stands beside
the car, staring at the window. Her face looks back at her. It's distorted
and strange. She digs her fingernails into her palms and it hurts, but
in a comforting sort of way, a way that brings her back to herself. She
keeps the nails there, buried in her flesh, a reminder that she's real.

"Yes," she says. "Yes, I'm fine."

She gets in the cab. The cab moves through Dublin. She watches
the faces out of the window and wills someone to turn and look at her
as she goes by.

"OH MY GOD," FIONA SAYS WHEN SHE OPENS THE FRONT
door to the flat.

Siobhan rang the doorbell; the idea of finding her keys in her bag
seemed impossibly difficult, like moving through concrete.

"Oh my God, Shiv, you look . . ."

Siobhan manages a smile. Fiona seems so like herself. As if nothing
has changed.

"I look like shit, do I?" Siobhan says.

"You do," Fiona says, firmly steering her inside the door. "You look
like beautiful shit, obviously, because it's you, but shit nonetheless. Sit
down, I'll make you a tea."

The tea is so hot that the mug burns against Siobhan's cold hands;
she can feel the marks her nails left, like pinpricks, burning a little
harder than the rest of the skin of her palms.

She starts to cry. She's cried a lot today. Any time that was not
spent with another human being was spent either staring blankly into
the beyond or curled in the fetal position, face tear-soaked, fists
clenched.

"You've run yourself into the ground," Fiona says, settling down beside Siobhan on the sofa and pulling a blanket over both their legs. "I think you're stressed, my love."

Siobhan shakes her head, gripping the hot mug. "My period's late," she chokes out, and Fiona's eyes widen.

"*Oh.*" She reaches across and grips Siobhan's wrist. "Shiv, it'll be okay. Have you taken a test?"

Siobhan shakes her head. A tear splashes into her tea. "I'm so . . ." She reaches for the right words to convey the fact that she is completely and terrifyingly adrift. "I let Joseph in," she says. Her voice is a childish whine; she hardly recognizes herself. "And now look. Look where I am. God, it was such a *mistake* to . . . to . . ."

"Fall in love with him?" Fiona says.

"No!" Siobhan says, head snapping up. Fiona's hazy and fuzzy through her tears. "No, I haven't, I haven't. I can't have."

"That's it, let it all out," Fiona says.

It's only then that Siobhan notices that her tears have turned into sobs, ragged and gulping. Her legs are suddenly aching. There's a sort of buzzing sensation in her hands and her face—it's not a tingling; that's too gentle. It's like a fierce, noisy static under her skin.

"Okay, maybe don't let it out quite that much," Fiona says, eyes widening slightly. She takes Siobhan's tea from her shaking hands. "Shiv, breathe. Breathe. Look at me."

Siobhan tries. Fiona looks like Fiona, but it's as if Siobhan's brain can't register her. All it can think is, *I'm not enough. I can't do this again. I can't live through this again.* The thought is so big it's taking up all the space and there's no room left for anything else, not even Fiona.

"In, out, in, out," Fiona tries, stroking Siobhan's back, but her breath won't do as it's told—it's coming too fast, huge great mouthfuls that hit the back of her throat like something hard.

"I . . . can't . . ." she manages. How does she stop this? How can she make it stop?

"You're hyperventilating," Fiona says. "You need to try and steady your breathing for me. Like at the start of a meditation, okay?"

It's not happening. Siobhan drops her head to her thighs, squeezing her eyes tightly shut, shoulders juddering. She thinks for a split second of the sound of the hotel door closing behind Joseph, and her breath comes even faster, and she no longer has any control over her body; she's in free fall. Her eyes will be getting so puffy, she thinks with desperation. How will she cool them down enough for her first session tomorrow? She's presenting at a school. She's going to be in front of all those people, and they'll all see her for what she is—paper-thin, inadequate.

"I have to take a test," Siobhan says into her knees.

"Okay. Let's do it, then."

"I can't. I can't do it. I can't."

"I'll be right here. I'll do it with you. Every step."

Siobhan can't lift her head from her knees. The feelings are coming in waves, each one more awful than the last, and it's as if her body is alive with loathing, as if it's streaming through her veins like ink.

"Let's just start by getting you cleaned up," Fiona says eventually. "Come on, let's get you in a bath."

Siobhan allows herself to be led, leaning on Fiona's arm; she's genuinely not sure her legs will hold her. Something awful is happening to her. She's breaking.

"We're going to do today five minutes at a time," Fiona says as she peels the sweat-soaked shirt from Siobhan's shaking body. "Like one of your work schedules, but everything on it is easy. Every single thing. The next five minutes are going to be in this bath. I will be here for every second of those five minutes. We'll talk about the new series of *RuPaul's Drag Race*. Maybe we'll wash your hair, maybe not, whatever you like."

Siobhan sobs into her wet hands, curled in the warm water with her legs against her chest.

"I'm so sorry," she manages. "You have things . . . You have stuff to do . . ."

"Siobhan," Fiona says, sprinkling lavender oil into the bath. "How many times have you looked after me?"

Yes, Siobhan thinks, *but that's different*. That's their dynamic—Siobhan's the fixer, the one who sweeps in and sorts things out for everybody else. She never lets anybody see her *weak* like this, not even Fiona.

"You've never been this much of a fucking mess," Siobhan says, balling her fists against her eyes. She's digging her nails into her palms again, chasing that feeling she found outside the taxi, the brief satisfaction that came from a shot of quiet pain.

"Stop that," Fiona says sharply, reaching for one of Siobhan's hands. "Shiv. Stop it."

Siobhan lets Fiona prise her hand open. There are four curved little cuts running across her palm, the imprints of her fake nails, bluish and swollen. Two have begun to bleed; Siobhan watches the blood grow with a detached sort of pleasure.

Fiona reaches for a sponge and gently cleans one hand, then the other.

"Please don't do that again," she says quietly.

Siobhan looks up at her friend. She feels tiny and lost. Completely undone.

"Shiv, promise me. Next time you want to hurt yourself like that, you come and find me, wherever you are."

"I wasn't hurting myself," Siobhan says, blinking.

Fiona raises her eyebrows at the blood beading in Siobhan's left palm.

"Okay," she says. "Well, whatever you call this."

"Oh, I . . ." Siobhan begins as Fiona wipes the fresh blood away. "I'm sorry. It just felt . . . better. I didn't mean to make it bleed."

"There are better ways to feel better," Fiona says. "And we're going to find them. First, though, shall we wash your hair?"

Siobhan lets herself be laid back in the water. She closes her eyes. Five minutes at a time. She can do that. Surely.

"Fi," she says suddenly, opening her eyes and lifting her head from the water. "Fiona, am I real? Am I really here?"

Fiona smooths shampoo into the roots of Siobhan's hair. "You're real, Siobhan Kelly. If you were a figment of someone's imagination, you would probably be less sweary, and you wouldn't borrow my shoes so much."

Siobhan laughs wetly at that. She and Fiona look at each other in surprise—neither of them thought she had the capacity to laugh, apparently. Fiona smiles, and leans forward to work the shampoo into Siobhan's scalp.

"How about we make a deal?" she says. "If you don't exist, I'll tell you. Okay? I'll be the first person to let you know if you're not really there."

Siobhan closes her eyes again, and nods slightly before sliding down into the water.

Jane

AS SPRING UNFURLS INTO SUMMER, JANE BEGINS TO RE-
lax again. Lou's business card is tucked safely behind a jam jar of dried
flowers on the mantelpiece. Jane continues calling her father and telling white lies, she walks to the Hoxton Bakehouse for breakfast, she
slips into her worn brown shoes and patches up the elbows on her
Thursday cardigan when it starts to wear thin. One book per week.
One splash of cream in her coffee. Beautiful, careful simplicity—that
is the life Jane has built for herself.

And then there's Joseph. Certainly beautiful, not at all simple.

Jane has tried to see Joseph as a friend again, but it's as if she's
turned on a light and now can't find the off switch. There's no dim-
ming it. Her feelings for him are brightening with every week that
passes, and she feels sometimes that he must be able to see it glowing
in her chest, the great fierce ball of love that's growing there.

He has done nothing to help the situation. He is kind and clever
and charming; he listens, he remembers the things that matter to her.
He never crosses a line or says anything even slightly flirtatious.

And he brings her books.

It starts in May: an extra library book on her doorstep. No note, nothing, but she knows it's from him. She brings it inside, and the temptation is too great—it's not clear cut what the rules are when someone *else* has brought the book into her flat, after all, and she finishes their book club thriller by Wednesday, and her Thursday evening feels so long and empty.

He leaves them for her every week. There is no particular moment when Jane confronts him about this, or when Joseph confesses, but one day he asks her what she thought of *Oroonoko*, and she messages him when she reaches *that* moment in *Gone Girl*, and just like that, the doorstep books have become part of Jane's routine.

Through June and July, she and Joseph race each other through everything from gritty literary crime to bodice-ripping romances—Joseph has given them the challenge of setting aside genre snobbery and trying *everything*. It's mid-July when they meet to discuss *Seducing the Dashing Duke*, and Jane's wearing her favorite dress, her Saturday one; she lies back on the lawn of the cathedral grounds and lets the cream skirt flare out around her legs, its silk barely bending the blades of grass. The sun is a warm, foggy glow behind her sunglasses. She sets the book open on her stomach as she waits for Joseph, feeling the jitters there beneath its pages, the butterfly excitement of knowing he'll soon be lying on the grass beside her.

"I'm late! Again!" Joseph says cheerfully as he plonks himself down. "But I have an excellent excuse."

Jane smiles, eyes still closed behind her sunglasses, saving up the moment she gets to open her eyes and see him. "You always do."

Joseph lets out a happy groan as he stretches himself out beside her.

"Is there anything better than sun on your face?" he asks.

The way you smile when you clock me across the street, Jane thinks. *The feeling when our hands brush. The smell of you, cedarwood and lemon.*

"I love summer," she says idly, "but I prefer spring. All that hope, everything waiting to come to life."

With her eyes closed like this, she can imagine his body is only a hair's breadth from hers, that she could roll over and straight into his arms. The sun shifts behind a cloud and reappears, its lazy heat sliding across her skin.

"Let me guess. You prefer Christmas Eve to Christmas, too?" Joseph says, and she can hear the smile in his voice.

Jane presses her lips together. The last few Christmases have been awful, stilted affairs—she and her father go to her aunt's family for the day, but her dad hates the holiday season, and Jane hates having to tell so many lies. *Yes, London's great, yes, job's going well* . . .

"What was your excuse for being late?" Jane asks Joseph, not particularly keen to talk about Christmas. Though, yes, she's always loved the anticipation of Christmas Eve, and she prefers Fridays to Saturdays, and sometimes running her thumb down the uncracked spine of a brand-new novel is so delightful it's *almost* enough to hold her back from starting chapter one.

"I was getting us appropriate book club snacks."

Jane hears the rustling of paper bags. She turns onto her side, letting *Seducing the Dashing Duke* slide to the grass, and opens her eyes as Joseph begins to empty out the bags. His stubble is darker today, as if he was running late and didn't have time to shave; it changes his face, giving that good-guy sweetness a new edge. He's dressed in shorts and a white T-shirt, and the V at the neck shows a little chest hair, something she had never imagined she'd find attractive, but can't seem to look away from.

"Victoria sandwich," he says solemnly, "since it features in that scene with the queen. And phallic sausage rolls, in honor of the Duke's penis"—Jane has begun to laugh now, and he grins at her, delighted—"and some of these round iced buns with glacé cherries in the middle for what I hope are obvious reasons." He sets them down in pairs and beams. "I made you laugh!"

"You did," she says, propping herself up on her elbow.

"No easy task," he says, taking a large mouthful of a sausage roll. "Mm. Just as good as the fair maiden said. So, what did you think of the book? Great, wasn't it?"

His shamelessness is infectious, though she does wonder if he came armed with phallic pastry jokes as a means of breaking the ice. They've never discussed a book with quite so many sex scenes before; it would be very like Joseph to consider this and try to find a way to make things more comfortable.

"It was *really* good," she admits, reaching for an iced bun. It feels a bit scandalous to go straight for the glacé cherry, but she does it anyway. "I read it in a day. I thought the duke would be awful, but he was commanding and dukey without being a total . . ."

"Prick?" Joseph supplies, finishing off his sausage roll. "Absolutely. It wasn't what I expected at all. Sex scenes are usually so cringey in books, aren't they? All that talk of what's going where, or they go in the other direction and it's all a simile about the moving of the tides or something, and you can't figure out what they're up to. But . . ." He picks up his copy and thumbs through to a page he's turned down. "Here. The way he describes touching her after all that time dreaming of it, when it says he *ran his hands across the silk-soft skin of her stomach and barely breathed. It was too much, like the taste of the richest honey, almost too sweet to be borne, and as he lowered his lips to the swell of her breasts, their . . .*"

He clears his throat, still looking down at the book. Jane's heart is thumping, and there's a corresponding ache low in her belly, because she knows how that scene goes on and just the *thought* of Joseph mentioning a fictional duke kissing a fictional maid's nipples is apparently enough to make her hot with desire. She keeps her face carefully blank, but surely he can feel the tension in the air between them, its thick heat, as if the sun has turned a fierce beam on them both.

"Yes, well," Joseph says, and there is a sweet pink blush staining his cheekbones now, which is not helping all the feelings blossoming in Jane's belly. "I thought it made complete sense. I knew exactly what he meant. As in, I could imagine it. As in, it was very evocative." He looks up sheepishly. "God, no wonder it's hard to write a good sex scene, I can't even talk about one."

Jane smiles. "I know what you mean. The wait is part of what makes it so—so hot, isn't it?" She looks down as she says *hot*—it's not a very Jane thing to say, but she can't think of another word for it. "All the time they spend not touching, it means that when they do . . ."

"Yeah," Joseph says, clearing his throat. He reaches for the Victoria sponge and begins to unwrap it. "Some people are worth waiting for, I guess."

She thinks about this comment endlessly once they've parted, each taking their share of the pastries and cake. Whenever her mind wanders, instead of taking her back to places she doesn't want to go, it brings her to that sweet, hot moment on the grass, and Joseph saying, *Some people are worth waiting for*, and she never tires of playing it.

THE PHRASE COMES BACK TO HER AGAIN A FEW WEEKS later, on one of those baking early August days that make England feel like it's transplanted itself to somewhere nearer the equator. She and Colin are sunning themselves on foldout chairs outside the charity shop; it's been two hours since the last visitor (looking for sun cream, which they do not sell), and Colin is a much more lenient substitute manager than his partner. *Donation bags can wait*, he said, shooing Jane out into the sunshine. *This weather won't.*

"So, Jane," Colin says, adjusting his cap. He is completely bald, and

Mortimer is very insistent that he wear a hat when it's sunny; Colin obeys, but maintains that Mortimer has no say in the *type* of hat. Today he is wearing a wide-rimmed black cap that says *I give no fucks* in large letters across the front. "I am thinking of asking Mort to marry me."

Jane turns to stare at him behind her sunglasses. They're drinking iced tea—she made some the other day, and Colin has now declared himself *obsessed* and insists that she make it whenever he's in the shop. Jane's heart had hitched when she saw a net of lemons on the side in the kitchen, labeled *For our Jane's special iced tea!! DO NOT TOUCH!*

"That's wonderful," she says.

"I always thought he'd ask me. He said he would, once, years ago, that he wanted to be the one to do it. I think he's waiting for something, but I don't know what." Colin sips his iced tea. "And I fully believe it'll be worth waiting for—of course *he's* worth waiting for—but I do wonder if I shouldn't take the bull by the horns and ask myself."

Jane bites her lip and thinks of the moment when she asked Mortimer if he minded that Colin had lied about him to his mother. *I think he'll get there, though*, Mortimer had said. *With a bit more time.*

"Would you want a big wedding? With all your family there?" Jane says.

"Big, certainly," Colin says with a chuckle. "I'm sure Mort would want his lot there, but it's just my mum now, and she—well, she wouldn't be able to come anyway, unless we married in Edinburgh."

Jane doesn't *know* that Colin's mother is the last thing Mortimer is waiting for before asking Colin to marry him, but . . . There was something in Mortimer's voice when they spoke about "Bluebell." A faux lightness, rather unconvincing. Jane thinks briefly of the last conversation with her father—she'd pretended to be standing in Regent's Park—and closes her eyes in pain.

"Would you want her there? Your mum? Do you . . . think Mortimer might?" Jane says, speaking carefully.

Colin is too wise for this; he looks sharply at her. "Has he said something to you?"

Jane shouldn't get involved. It's not her business, and she actually has a relatively good relationship with these people now; she doesn't want to ruin it by meddling. But there is a wounded edge to Colin's voice, a wariness to his posture, and for a strange moment she wants to reach across and lay her hand on his arm, an impulse she hasn't had in a very long time.

"He just told me she doesn't know about the two of you," she says gently. "He was making me feel better, actually, for lying to my father. I haven't told my dad I left London. I just can't bring myself to let him down." She tightens her ponytail, eyes averted. "What I mean to say is, we sometimes tell lies to the people we love, I understand that. But I do wonder if that might be the missing piece, the last thing Mortimer's waiting for?"

Colin looks down at his drink, cap shading his face.

"You know," he says, in a rather small voice, "I think I already knew that, really."

Jane sits quietly. The street is busy, packed with pedestrians with shopping bags piled up their arms, but nobody comes toward the charity shop; she and Colin are sitting in their own little sunlit world, iced teas in hand.

"Thank you, Jane," he says.

Jane's phone buzzes loudly on the rickety table between them. Colin jumps, clutching his chest.

"Lord. I hate those confounded things," he says, eyeing it with distaste.

Jane smiles, flicking open the e-mail. It's a Paperless Post invitation. *Martin Wang & Constance Hobbs, along with their families, invite you to attend their wedding ceremony . . .*

Her heart sinks—down it goes into her belly, stone-like, awful. She'll have to go. It would be rude not to, especially after she went to the engagement party back in February. But what will she wear? Who will she talk to? What if she's left all alone in the crowd, or, worse, expected to make interesting small talk with strangers? She mutters a *Just a moment* to Colin and heads back into the cool of the charity shop; the dry, hot sun is suddenly too much for her.

There is nobody inside, and as Jane stands there in the quiet, she is hit by a sudden compulsion to *do* something. She allows herself one delightful moment of childish petulance and throws her mobile phone at the gigantic stuffed polar bear that lives beside the till. The phone bounces between its ears, down through its outstretched front legs and lands in its lap.

"Ridiculous to put the poor thing sitting up on its arse like that," comes a voice from the shelves to the right of the till.

Jane jumps and turns to see a woman emerging with an enormous pile of paperbacks. On closer inspection, it's Aggie, the pajama wearer.

"Been here awhile," Aggie says, setting the paperbacks down by the till with a groan. "Sorry if I startled you. I don't know about you, but I've never seen a polar bear sitting like that. Not that I've seen a great many polar bears. Anyway, what I mean to say is, I can see why you'd want to put the poor thing out of its misery."

Jane collects her phone rather sheepishly from the polar bear's lap.

"I just . . . received an e-mail about something I'd rather not have to do," Jane says, slipping her phone into her pocket.

"Seems I have a habit of crashing in on your bad days," Aggie says with a grin. "Here, shall we have a tea and you can tell me all about it?"

Jane blinks. She's just preparing her usual answer to this sort of question—*That's kind of you, but I'm too busy to stop*—when Aggie starts speaking again.

"I've got a better idea, actually. Can your boss spare you for a few minutes?"

"Oh, I'm not the boss of anybody," Colin says airily, appearing from outside. He still has his *I give no fucks* cap on; Jane catches Aggie's admiring glance. "Jane, do take a break if you'd like to."

"I'm fine," Jane says quickly. "Thank you. I need to sort through the . . ."

"Five minutes," Aggie says. She's looking at Jane shrewdly. "Three, if you want. Anyone can spare three minutes."

This is difficult to argue with. And there's something about Aggie. She reminds Jane of Joseph, ridiculous as that seems—but she has that same focus, that engaging sense that she is actually listening to you instead of just thinking about what she wants to say next.

"If I can't improve your morning, I swear, I'll leave you alone forevermore," Aggie says, holding her hand to her heart. "But I bet if you give me three minutes, I can make you smile."

Why are you bothering? Jane wants to ask her. *Why are you even trying?* Silence stretches out between them; Jane can't figure out what to say. Aggie sighs.

"Look, Jane, I just feel like we could be friends, basically," Aggie says after a moment, with some exasperation. "I don't think I've asked anybody to be my friend since I was twelve and needed someone to sit with on the bus, but you don't seem to be getting the hints, so I'm just going to be up-front."

Jane blinks. "Oh," she says, taken aback. "Really?"

"I wasn't a very cool twelve-year-old," Aggie says dryly.

"No, I mean . . ." Jane trails off.

"Is it so hard to believe that someone wants to be friends with you?" Aggie says. She's joking, but she sobers when she sees Jane's expression. "Oh. *Right.* Well, come on, then. I'm not taking no for an answer."

Aggie leads Jane out of the shop, leaving her tower of paperbacks behind on the counter.

"I'm like a dog with a bone," Aggie says cheerfully, turning left out of the shop and heading to the houses down by the river. "I wouldn't have let up until you said yes, you know. Here, this is me." She unlocks the front door of a small block of flats, redbrick and tidy, with geraniums in blue pots on either side of the door.

They head up the stairs and into flat 4. The room beyond is bright and decorated by somebody who clearly has an artistic eye. Jane steps through into the living area, where a long, ochre sofa is decorated with peacock-patterned cushions; the skirting board is painted jet black, and the floorboards have been varnished to shine. Jane turns to take it all in and then laughs suddenly, catching sight of the enormous artwork taking up the back wall.

It's a bright-pink canvas, the color so dense it seems almost to glow. Across the painted surface a phrase has been written in what looks like black permanent marker.

Most people are shit, it reads. *What are you going to do about it?*

"Like it?" Aggie asks, slinging her bag down on the sofa. She checks her watch. "Don't answer that, we're already a minute and a half down. Come on."

She leads Jane onto the balcony. It's not a particularly inspiring view. Below them is a car park lined with garages, their steel doors pulled down like sad, closed eyes.

"Here," Aggie says, and places something heavy and soft in Jane's hands.

It's a water balloon. There is a whole bucket of them in the corner of the balcony, different colors and sizes, all neatly tied at their necks.

Jane stares at the viscous, slippery, childish thing in her hands, then looks up at Aggie.

"I'll demonstrate," Aggie says, and then, with a dramatic overarm maneuver in the manner of a bowling cricketer, she throws the balloon off the balcony to the tarmac below.

It lands with a crack, exploding in a bright shower of water.

"Your turn," Aggie says.

"You want me to . . . Throw water balloons off your balcony? At the ground?"

"Yes," Aggie says patiently. "Go on."

"What about the mess?" Jane asks.

"I'll clean it up later. I do it all the time. Just have a go."

The balloon wobbles and slides in Jane's palms. She shifts it into her right hand and looks down from the balcony. The remains of Aggie's balloon lie limply below, a bright-green rubber splatter on the tarmac.

Jane throws her balloon. She does it quite a lot harder than she means to—once her arm starts moving, the force just grows, and suddenly she wants to *break* it, to see this globular jellyfish of a thing in her hand explode.

When it bursts, it feels like letting something go.

Before Jane can turn to look at Aggie, she's passed her another balloon, this one a dark, vibrant red, and a little larger. Jane leans forward over the balcony and lifts it up high, then drops it. And another balloon. And another. It's immensely satisfying, and she's laughing now, and Aggie's throwing balloons, too, and someone has opened a window down the way and leaned out, curious, retreating at the sight of two adult women whooping and chucking water balloons over the edge of their balcony.

When all the balloons are gone, Jane is breathless. She turns to Aggie, who is grinning at her, a strand of red hair sticking to her forehead.

Her *friend* Aggie.

And why not? Jane has believed for so long that nobody could possibly want to be her friend—her time in London taught her that lesson.

But here is a woman who *asked* to be friends with her, and just down the road is a net of lemons reserved for *our Jane*, and sitting on her phone is a text from Joseph telling her how much her last message made him smile.

Perhaps I am not so hard to like, Jane thinks fiercely as she meets Aggie's eyes. *Perhaps I am not so peculiar, so awkward, so difficult. Perhaps he was wrong about all that, too.*

"Good, eh?" Aggie says.

"Yes," Jane says, and she smiles. To her immense surprise, she's happy.

It's one of those feelings, happiness. One of the ones you don't really notice is gone until it comes back.

"ASK HIM TO BE YOUR DATE, THEN," AGGIE SAYS, REACHING for the wine bottle.

She is stretched out on the ochre sofa; Jane is sitting in the armchair, holding one of the peacock cushions against her chest. She can still hardly believe this has happened. On Aggie's encouragement, she messaged Colin asking if he minded her not coming back to the shop; he had rung her to reply (*I haven't got the thumbs for typing on these things*, he said) and pointed out that they had sold zero items in the last four hours, so she probably wasn't required, but he'd call her if there was a sudden rush of enthusiastic charity shoppers.

And now it is ten p.m. and Jane is still in Aggie's flat.

"I can't ask him to be my date," Jane says.

It has been so long since she has spent this amount of time in another person's company, just talking. She feels both drained and exhilarated.

"Course you can," Aggie says. "You asked him to be your date before, didn't you?"

"It was different back then. Now . . ."

Now she tries to read meanings into the books he leaves on her doorstep, losing hours to the question of why he gave her *Sense and Sensibility*, why he chose *The Fault in Our Stars*. Now when they're apart she longs for him to appear in his usual whirl of last-minute energy, to hear him laugh, to meet his warm, hazel gaze and feel that flip-flop sensation in her belly as their eyes connect. Now she is falling in love with him.

"Why not just ask him out?" Aggie says. Her makeup has run a little into the creases below her eyes, and her skirt has bunched up to a crumpled mess under her thighs, but Jane already knows Aggie well enough to know that she gives no shits about either of these things.

"I can't." Jane fiddles with the edge of the cushion in her lap, heart thumping. "I don't date well."

"You don't . . . date . . . well?"

"I'm not a good girlfriend," Jane says.

There is a long pause.

"That's a really weird thing to say," Aggie says after a while. Her tone holds no judgment, just curiosity.

Jane looks up at her. "Oh, I just meant I'm not good at relationships—men just . . . they go off me after a while. I always get it wrong." She lifts one shoulder. "And I'm intense. When I fall for someone, when I'm with them, I lose . . ." *Myself,* she thinks. "I lose perspective," she says instead.

"Hmm," Aggie says, cocking her head. "Can I just say that *I'm not a good girlfriend* sounds like a thought someone else has put in your head? *I'm intense*? *I always get it wrong*? Who told you those things about yourself, Jane?"

Jane stares at Aggie. They sit like this, in silence, Aggie's face open, Jane's shocked.

"Oh," she says. "Umm."

"Nasty ex?" Aggie says with sympathy. "Do a number on you, did he?"

Jane's heartbeat seems to be pulsing in her cheeks, red hot.

"Would it help to point out that *I* think you're great? I've basically chased you down for half a year until you've conceded to be friends with me," Aggie points out, swigging her glass of wine. "And everyone at that charity shop talks about you like you're their beloved grand-daughter. People love you, Jane. Whatever you've been told."

Jane doesn't know what to say. It's as if Aggie has poured some-thing cool over the boiling, wretched sadness that always burns in her chest, dousing it in one great gush. *People love you, Jane.*

To Jane's shame, she is beginning to tear up. She stares down at the cushion in her lap. She doesn't know what to say.

"Thank you," she whispers. "You're very kind."

Aggie makes a *pfft* sound. "Eh, I'm honest," she says. "And, hon-estly, you're clearly half in love with this Joseph chap, and you deserve to be happy, and you should ask him out on a date. Then at least he'll know how you feel—surely it's much more painful this way, with you in love with him and him not even knowing?"

"It's more painful, yes," Jane says, swallowing back the tears. "But it's much safer."

FIVE DAYS LATER, SITTING ACROSS FROM JOSEPH AT THEIR favorite table at Josie's Café, Jane finds herself saying: "You know when you asked whether I'd fired you as my fake boyfriend . . . ?"

"Yes?" Joseph says, cleaning his glasses on his T-shirt. He's bright eyed and energized today—he's just played football, and his hair is still wet from showering. He beamed at her when she arrived at the café, and he said, *Jane, you look lovely today*, and she had thought, *Marry me marry me marry me*, then, *Stop that, Jane, just* stop *it*.

"Well, I wondered if you would accept your old position back. Come back to the firm for one last job, as it were."

She was trying to lighten things, but now she wishes she hadn't said *the firm*. Joseph still doesn't know that Jane used to work at Bray &

Kembrey, and she flinched a little as she said the word, and now he's giving her his head-tilted, eyes-curious face.

"You need a date again?" he asks after a moment.

Jane looks down at the menu. Why, why has she begun this conversation? Why is it not possible to snatch words in midair and take them back?

"It's Constance's wedding at the end of September. I have to go, but I hate those sorts of big events, and I would really . . . I would love you to come with me."

"As your fake boyfriend," Joseph says.

"Oh, ignore me, it's so stupid. I shouldn't have asked," Jane says, pressing her hands to her face.

"It's okay," Joseph says after a beat. "I just wanted to be clear."

Of course he does. There is probably some lovely, beautiful woman out there who he's been chatting with on a dating app or something; he might even have a girlfriend for all Jane knows. They've not talked about his love life for a long time—not since that comment Scott made, that mention of a woman named Fi, or Fifi, maybe. Joseph has never said a name like that again, has never spoken of a girlfriend; but then, Jane has never asked.

"Let's just pretend I never said that," Jane says, looking down at the menu again, though they've already ordered. "I really . . . I so hate turning up at those things on my own. But I just need to be braver. It will be a good challenge for me."

She doesn't mean this. She is already plotting her excuse for missing the event: could she contract food poisoning? She'd rather not lie—she's doing so much of that already. But perhaps she could just undercook some chicken, or drink some curdling milk?

"I'm happy to do it, if you want me to. If you need someone there with you," Joseph says.

"Oh, no," Jane says. "That's okay."

She can feel him seeking her gaze, dipping his head to try to catch her eye. Her heartbeat seems so big and loud she's sure he can hear it, like there's a raw, hot drumbeat pulsing through the café.

"Jane," Joseph says eventually. "It's fine. If you need me, I'll be there." There's a pause. "That's what friends are for," he says, and Jane thinks she might cry.

"Right," she says. "That's what friends are for."

Miranda

IT'S AUGUST 25: MIRANDA'S BIRTHDAY, AND HER ABSOLUTE favorite day of the year.

She knows she should probably prefer Christmas, or some other day that involves celebrating goodwill and family and, well, other people. But she's just never lost the childhood excitement of waking up on a day where you get to do everything you want *all* day. Everyone has to be nice to you; you get loads of texts from friends; and there are surprises, like this one: Carter turning up at her flat with a large plate of maple-syrup-soaked pancakes.

"Brought all the way from Winchester," he says proudly, setting them down on the kitchen counter.

They're from Josie's Café, Carter's favorite brunch place. Miranda beams at him.

"You brought them here on the train?"

"Of course. Only the best for you." He kisses her, bending her backward in her pink patterned pajamas, and she nearly falls. When Adele walks into the room they're tangled, kissing, on the arm of the sofa.

"Gross," Adele says through a yawn. "Happy b-day, Mir. Are these for sharing?"

She's already produced a fork from somewhere and is advancing on the pancakes with obvious intent.

"They're for Miranda only," Carter says before Miranda can open her mouth to snap at her sister. "Birthday privileges: no sharing required."

"Thank you," Miranda whispers in his ear as they straighten up, adjusting their clothes.

"Morning," Frannie says, padding in wearing Miranda's slippers and an outfit that could only be described as a negligee. "So what are we doing today, before the party starts?"

"*We* are having a day out in London," Miranda says, snatching at the fork Frannie has just produced from the drawer. "No pancakes! Make your own breakfast!"

Frannie pouts. "Birthday diva. So we're not invited?"

"No, you're not," Miranda says. "You can get the spare room tidied before everyone arrives for the party tonight."

"Why does our room need to be tidy?" Adele asks, eating a handful of cornflakes straight from the box. "Nobody is going to be going in there, right? I've got valuables."

"What? No, you haven't," Miranda says. "And someone might go in there, it's a party. Just tidy it, would you?"

"You used to be fun," Frannie says.

"No, I didn't," Miranda says cheerfully.

"It's true," Adele says. "You were born sensible."

Carter laughs at that, then shoots Miranda an apologetic look, to see if she minds. She smiles at him, though in truth she would rather he didn't hear this sort of thing—Adele and Frannie always make her sound like such a *loser*. She can take any amount of teasing from the lads at work, but somehow her sisters' needling always manages to find a nerve.

Miranda's phone buzzes: a video call from her parents. They're on holiday in a camper van in Austria—since the twins moved out, they've embarked on various adventures that Miranda can't help thinking are better suited to backpacking teenagers, especially since they insist on taking her grandmother with them when they go.

Miranda grabs the pancakes and the fork and makes her way to her bedroom, answering as she settles herself down against the bed's headboard. Her mother, father and nonna bob into view, and then out again—it seems her mum is in charge of holding the phone, and, as per usual, can't get the hang of pointing it at their faces. Undeterred, they launch into a cacophonous rendition of "Happy Birthday."

"Miranda! My baby girl!" her mother says, speaking much louder than necessary. "All grown up! Oh, I remember when you were just a tiny thing, all fists and little feet, screaming blue murder when they first placed you in my arms . . ."

It's the classic birthday conversation, which is essentially a monologue, delivered by Miranda's mother, about Miranda's life thus far; her nonna and Miranda's father contribute occasionally, but Miranda's mum likes to remain center stage, so they don't get much of a look-in. By the end, Penny Rosso isn't even pretending to try to get her husband and her mother-in-law in shot.

When they say good-bye, Miranda's cheeks hurt from beaming, and she's finished the whole box of pancakes, which she's pretty sure were intended for two people. When she returns to the kitchen, Adele is lounging on the sofa watching a video on her phone with the sound up, and Carter is hunched over writing something at the kitchen table. He looks up and then hides it on his lap. Miranda smiles. His Christmas card had been a hand-drawn illustration of her up a Christmas tree, complete with tiny sketched chainsaw. He's no good at drawing, and it couldn't have looked less like her, but it didn't matter: it was the fact he'd tried.

It's adorable that he's hand-drawing her a birthday card, too. Though it might be a teeny bit more adorable if he'd done it ahead of time, instead of while she was getting ready for their day out. Carter's lateness, his last-minute-ness, it's charming—but it's also a little grating for Miranda, who has never really understood how people can be consistently late. Why don't they just realize they always need to factor in more time?

"Give me two minutes, birthday girl," he says sheepishly, covering the paper with his hand. "And then I'm taking you off on an adventure."

MIRANDA CAN FEEL HERSELF MAKING MEMORIES TODAY. She just knows that these moments with Carter will come back to her as she curls up in bed, or as she takes this same train into Central London one day, and she won't be able to help herself smiling.

Things have been a bit . . . quiet with Carter, of late. It's not helped by her two younger sisters constantly rattling around the flat with their loud music and their hair straighteners and their endless high-volume chatter (*Why are they never in the same room as one another when they talk?* Miranda wonders). But as she and Carter walk hand in hand through Kew Gardens in the summer drizzle, and as Carter lets her ramble on excitedly about the trees and shrubs they find as they explore . . . things feel perfect again.

On the train home he recounts a particularly ridiculous exchange between his aunt and his mum, complete with an excellent impression of his aunt's prim Scottish tones, and makes Miranda laugh so hard she snorts, startling the elderly man snoozing across the aisle. Hearing Carter able to speak so openly—and even lightly—about his mother's illness makes her heart bloom. As she wipes her eyes and squeezes his hand, she feels like she's got her old Carter back, resilient, always laughing, always making *her* laugh.

They get back to the flat a little later than planned—the guests are arriving at half seven, and it's already well past six. Frannie is still wearing her negligee and Adele is wiping down the kitchen with the wrong cloth, leaving wet arcs across the surfaces that may actually make it look worse than it did when it was dirty.

"D'you want me to do your makeup?" Adele offers kindly as Miranda emerges from her bedroom in her party outfit at half past seven.

"What?" She glances in the mirror that leans against the living room wall. "I've got makeup on!"

Frannie and Adele exchange a glance. It's not one of those twin secret-language glances—it is completely transparent to all parties. It says, *She is beyond help.*

It is only after observing these glances that Miranda realizes Trey, AJ and Spikes are standing in the doorway of her flat, with Carter closing the door behind them; she straightens, suddenly blushing. It's strange seeing them all here, as if her two lives are overlaid on top of one another and it's making the scene blur.

"I think your makeup looks great," Carter says, just as AJ says, "You're beautiful."

Everyone goes very still. In the silence, Frannie drops a bottle top on the kitchen floor and lets out a little *eep* as she makes herself jump. AJ doesn't cringe or bluster or even look at Carter. He just smiles at Miranda.

"AJ, isn't it?" Carter says stiffly. He's wearing chinos and a shirt, and he looks gorgeous: fresh, smart, the sort of man you can't help but fall for.

AJ shakes his hand. He's made an effort for tonight—he's in an oversized hoodie and one of his rare pairs of jeans that isn't ripped or stained. AJ doesn't really do "presentable"—this is as smart as he goes.

"Ambrose," Spikes says, as he shakes Carter's hand.

"What!" says Miranda, coming to life again. "*Ambrose?*"

Spikes looks bashful. "What?" he says. "I didn't choose it."

"I genuinely thought you were born Spikes," Miranda says wonderingly, accepting the six-pack of beer Spikes is holding in her general direction. "Thanks, I'll get these in the fridge."

"So," Carter says, following her through to the kitchen. He leans in to mutter in her ear as she opens the fridge. "You didn't tell me the massive tattooed man from work was in love with you?"

"Oh, shush," Miranda says steadily, shifting some of Adele's many half-finished yogurt pots to make room for the beers. "AJ just likes to stir up trouble."

"Mm," Carter says. "Do I need to go all caveman on his ass?"

"Did you just say *ass*?" Miranda asks, turning to face him.

"Yes," Carter says, straight-faced. "It was very threatening."

Miranda laughs and kisses him, arms laced around his neck. "Don't do anything to anyone's ass, please."

"It's good to have boundaries, Rosso," says Trey as he wanders past with a plastic cup full of red wine.

Miranda leans her forehead on Carter's shoulder and half sighs, half laughs. "I'm sorry," she says. "My colleagues are a bit . . . different from yours."

"Hey," Carter says, shrugging his shoulder so she'll lift her head again. "If you like them, I like them."

"Miranda, some more of your middle-aged men are here!" Adele shouts.

It's her old boss and one of the climbers from her last job. She beams at the two of them, disentangling herself from Carter to dash over for hugs and hellos.

"Does *everyone* who is coming to this party think that an oversized T-shirt with jeans is a look?" Frannie asks as Miranda returns to the kitchen, laden with bottles.

"Yep," Miranda says happily. "Absolutely."

IT'S A LONG, DRUNKEN PARTY, THE SORT OF NIGHT THAT staggers and weaves its way onward until it's almost dawn and you're so giddy with tiredness you can't tell if it's the booze or exhaustion that's making you dizzy. Miranda ends up falling asleep on Adele, on the sofa, at around five in the morning.

AJ left with Trey at some point before midnight, probably off to a nightclub or something. Miranda ignored AJ all evening—when he ambled over to speak to her at around half eleven, she said, *You're in the doghouse*, handed him the bottle opener, and went off to find Carter.

Miranda wakes at half eight—horribly early given the time she fell asleep the night before. She limps toward the kitchen (Spikes stood on her toe last night during a heated game of beer pong, after which there was a lengthy discussion of whether she would need to go to Accident and Emergency, the conclusion being no, it's only a toe, what are they even for?).

"Hey," Carter whispers, emerging from Miranda's bedroom.

She rubs her eyes. "You slept in my bed?"

He smiles, looping an arm around her waist, pressing a kiss to her forehead. "Someone had to. Now. What is your post-birthday-party-hangover breakfast of choice?"

It sparks something. The post-birthday-party-hangover-breakfast thing. Over the last few months, Miranda has genuinely set aside that crumpled receipt for banana pancakes in Covent Garden; she's never asked Carter about it because she trusts him, and she hardly ever thinks about it now.

But as she looks up at his sleepy eyes and mussed hair, she does think about it. Just for a moment. Long enough to make her say, "Balthazar in Covent Garden is yours, right?"

He frowns, pulling back to look at her properly. "Hey?" he says.

"Your favorite place for a post-party breakfast."

He doesn't say anything, just stares at her.

"After Scott's birthday party, when you were really hungover. That's where you went before you came here, isn't it?" Miranda swallows. She feels a bit sick now; the hangover is settling into her pores, thick and clinging.

Carter's frown deepens. He searches her face.

"Was it?" he says eventually. "Did I say that?"

It strikes her as an odd thing to say, though she's not precisely sure why. Her body buzzes with that disgusting fuzzy feeling that comes from dehydration and too much booze.

"You must have done," she says lightly. "Where else would I have got that idea from?"

If Carter is trying to cover his surprise, he's not doing a particularly good job. He's still frowning at her, with his hand on her waist, when Frannie emerges from the spare room and declares she's going for a run.

Miranda winces, breaking eye contact with Carter. "A *run*?"

Frannie's long, dark hair is pulled up in a perky ponytail, and she's wearing ridiculously tiny shorts.

"Uh-huh," she says, as if Miranda is being very slow today. "I woke up a little bit hungover, actually, and just thought, a run will sort me out."

"She doesn't know what a hangover is yet," Carter says with foreboding as they watch her bounce out of the door. He looks down at Miranda and smiles. "So—fry-up? The café on the corner?"

"Yeah, definitely," she says with relief, leaning into his chest. *Thank God that's over*, she thinks. She's not sure how she wanted that conversation to go, but it definitely wasn't like that.

Siobhan

"I THINK," SIOBHAN SAYS, FLOATING PAST HER FRIEND Marlena, who is bobbing around on an inflatable flamingo, "I just need to work out the meaning of life. That's all."

They're in Greece, just outside Athens. Fiona chose the hotel, and it's ridiculous: a gorgeous five-star palace filled with staff who scurry dutifully out of your way and approach you with deferential drinks on trays if you're lying by the pool.

When Siobhan found out she wasn't pregnant, back in April, it didn't fix her the way she'd expected it would. She'd stayed broken. She'd remained unsure of whether she was really there at all, in fact, and even now she's chased by an awful, anxious sadness, a sense of her absolute and total inadequacy.

She took an extended leave of absence from work. Left social media, stopped work on her blog, passed her one-to-one clients on to another life coach. Slowly, painfully, through endless heart-to-hearts with her friends and an intensive bout of therapy, she's spent her summer figuring out how to piece herself back together again.

"The meaning of life?" Marlena asks, adjusting her black one-piece.

Her legs are wrapped around the neck of the inflatable, and there are several men on the edge of the pool who are looking at her in a way that suggests they are very envious of the flamingo.

Marlena is the sort of woman you'd never describe as pretty, always beautiful. She's Fiona and Siobhan's closest friend from their days at acting school, and moved back to Dublin in July, which means at last Siobhan and Fiona are seeing her as much as they'd like to. She models full-time now, and usually has a stunning girlfriend on her arm, though never for long enough that Siobhan ever really gets to know them. Marlena is a great friend, but a terrible woman to date.

"Yes, that," Siobhan says, tipping onto her back. "I think if I can just figure out the meaning of life, then I can work out what to do."

The sky is a deep, cloudless blue, and the water is deliciously cool in the heat. They've been here for a week now; Siobhan ought to feel more relaxed than she does. It's been five months since that pregnancy scare sent her spiraling inexplicably into madness. Eight weeks since Joseph finally gave up trying to contact her.

At first she'd treated him the way she always treats guys when she's ghosting them. She ignored his messages—though in truth, in the early stages of her mental health crisis, a single text from him sent her spinning into sobbing spells that seemed to make time stretch and squeeze, until she'd wasted hours on the sofa, wracked with self-doubt. But he didn't do what most men do: he didn't get angry, or self-righteous, or disappear after a week or two. He kept messaging—not so often it was a pressure, just often enough to show he was still thinking of her and wanted to know if she was okay.

Until, eventually, he didn't. **It's been three months,** he wrote. **So I figure I'd better take you at your word that you want me to leave you be. Really hope you're all right, Shiv, and that maybe our paths will cross again one day xx**

"Work out what to do about . . . ?" Marlena asks, tipping her sunglasses down her nose.

"About . . . all of it," Siobhan says, waving a vague hand up at the sky. "Work. Men. Money." She thinks *children* but can't bring herself to say it. The thought alone makes her ache. This topic has bobbed up repeatedly in the endless conversations she's had about her breakdown, and she still hasn't found a way to approach it that doesn't feel painful. "All the important things," she adds instead.

"Well, for what it's worth, I think it's sex," Marlena says. She stretches, arching her back, and gives an expansive sigh. One of her poolside admirers looks rather faint.

"What's sex?" Fiona asks, swimming over in her favorite purple shower cap.

"The meaning of life," Marlena says.

"Oh God!" Fiona says, looking horrified as she treads water. "That's so bleak! If it's sex, what am I living for?"

"Frankly," Marlena says, "I've been wondering that about you for a while."

Fiona splashes her, and Marlena shrieks, hand flying to her sunglasses, but she can't keep steady and the flamingo throws her—she goes crashing into the water. Several men perk up on their sun loungers, presumably hoping that she will require rescuing, but she bobs up again a few seconds later, spluttering, as the inflatable flamingo blithely swans off to the other side of the pool.

As Fiona and Marlena undertake a very uncivilized splash war, Siobhan paddles to where her bag lies beside the pool and fishes out her phone. No new messages. She flicks open her chat with Joseph and stares at his last message. The urge to reply strikes her as terrifyingly similar to the compulsion to hurt herself: a deep, raw tug that takes visceral strength to ignore.

A new message pops up as she's holding the phone—it's Richard, Blue Steel, her one-to-one client. She blinks in surprise.

Hope you're enjoying your holiday. Looking forward to our session when you get back. It's not the same without you x

"Siobhan Kelly!" Fiona barks.

Siobhan turns. Fiona's not usually the barking type, but her expression is suddenly extremely stern.

"What are you looking at, young lady?" Fiona says.

"Oh no." Marlena breaststrokes her way over from the corner of the pool to which she had fled from Fiona. "She wasn't, was she?"

"I wasn't on e-mail!" Siobhan protests, laughing. "I promise."

Siobhan has found it a *little* difficult to let go of her work life during this period of recovery.

"You were frowning. It was a very Siobhan-at-work frown," Fiona says sternly.

"It wasn't. Honestly. I was . . ." She growls slightly under her breath. "If you must know, I was looking at Joseph's messages."

"*Oh*," says Fiona.

"But I'm not going to message him," Siobhan says quickly.

"And remind me . . . why not . . . ?" Marlena asks, gripping the edge of the pool.

"We were getting too close. It was getting *relationshippy*. I don't want that."

"And you don't want that because . . . ?" Marlena says in the same tone. "I mean, you know I'm all for the single life, personally, but you seemed pretty happy with this man when you were seeing each other."

"Relationships are stressful and they tie you down and they're—they're just—not worth it."

Fiona and Marlena are wearing identical expressions: eyes narrowed, heads tilted.

"I'm going to say something and you're not going to like it," Marlena says. "Your ex treated you really badly, Shiv."

"I don't want to talk about Cillian," Siobhan says, backing up a little, treading water.

"I know you don't. You never do. But the fact is he left you high and dry, and you were—you were *pregnant*, Shiv . . ."

"Stop it," Siobhan snaps, face flaring with heat. They never mention that. *Never.* Fiona stares wide-eyed at Marlena, as if she can hardly believe Marlena had the nerve.

"I wouldn't be surprised if some of what you've gone through this year is about processing that trauma," Marlena says, unwavering.

"Yes, well, we all figured that out," Siobhan says curtly. "Pregnancy scare brought back memories, blah blah. Well done."

"It's not just about the pregnancy. It's about Joseph, too," Marlena says. "Cillian hurt you. And now you push people away so they can't push you away first."

Siobhan recoils, hurt. The sun is too hot on her shoulders, even here in the water.

"No, I don't," she says.

"Yes, you do," Marlena says firmly.

"Christ! Is this an intervention? You cannot do an intervention in swimwear! Come on. Let's just relax. Isn't that what this holiday is supposed to be about?"

"It's supposed to be about looking after ourselves," Fiona says. She's uncomfortable; she hates tense conversations, and she hates when Siobhan's temper gets the better of her. But she's soldiering on, bottom lip caught between her teeth.

"We want to help," Marlena says. "But you have to let us in. This business with Joseph . . . I mean, he genuinely seemed *nice.* He made you happy when you were with him. Those messages he sent you were good-guy messages. I worry that you're sabotaging yourself. You won't let yourself be happy. You push yourself so hard with work, like you've got something to prove about how full and meaningful your life is, and . . ."

"Enough!" Siobhan hisses, throwing her hands up in a spray of pool water. "I did not come all the way out here to Athens to be told that my life can't be full and meaningful unless I've got a boyfriend!"

They both stare at her, obstinate, resolved. Nobody is backing down.

"You know we don't mean that," Fiona says eventually.

Siobhan huffs and turns to climb out of the pool. "I'm going to cool off," she says. "See you later for *fun* cocktails. Any mention of trauma and I'm out of there, all right?"

Fiona and Marlena stick to Siobhan's rules for the rest of the holiday. No mention of trauma. But the tension hangs over them, and Siobhan can't shake what they said to her. *You push people away.*

Is that true? It seems absurd. Why on earth would she do that, when the very last thing Siobhan wants is to be left alone?

Jane

"I LOOK SO ... DIFFERENT," JANE SAYS, TURNING BACK AND
forth in front of the mirror.

Aggie beams at her reflection, perched on the bed behind her with
the bag of online shopping on her knees.

"You look like you," Aggie assures her, "just all dressed up."

Jane can hardly believe she's doing this. When she moved to Winchester, she was so bruised, so fragile; the sudden plethora of life
choices in front of her had been completely overwhelming. Once she
left London behind, there was nobody to tell her what to eat, where to
go, what to wear. The choices had seemed exhausting.

So she had bought seven outfits, one for each day of the week, all
carefully layered so they would serve for every season. It was much
simpler—it freed her to make other decisions, ones that mattered.

But the other day Aggie had said, *Why not wear something other than
the pale-green dress on a Thursday? And for that matter, why not let yourself
have a cinnamon bun for breakfast instead of the yogurt?* And Jane had
thought, *I can't. I can't.*

It had struck her then, lightning-sudden: *This isn't freedom.* Her systems might have calmed her once, but now they'd become another trap. Having two books per week is just *better*, and why shouldn't Jane be allowed better?

So here she is, shopping.

The dress is vibrant scarlet; it reaches the floor, and the skirt slits open right up to her thigh, revealing what feels like *acres* of leg whenever she walks. Jane hasn't revealed her legs like this in quite some time, and they seem somehow childish in their exposure, knobbly-kneed and awkward. Her cat, Theodore, watches her from the warm spot by the radiator, a gray fluffball of disapproval.

"You don't think the red is a bit too . . . noticeable?" Jane says.

"There's nothing wrong with getting noticed," Aggie tells her.

There is if you have something to hide, Jane thinks, stomach flipping as she turns to examine herself from the back. The fabric clings to her bum, which is rather wobblier than it was when she last looked at it. Her hair is loose—she tends to wear it down now—and it's less straggly since Aggie gave the ends a trim.

"I shouldn't keep it," Jane says, suddenly fretful. "I don't need it. I can just wear . . ."

"Jane," Aggie says sternly. "Why shouldn't you keep this dress?"

"Because . . ." *I don't deserve it.* That's what pops into Jane's head.

Aggie gives her a knowing look. "You're punishing yourself for *something*, no matter what you say," she tells Jane. "Whoever made you believe you don't deserve things is a prick, all right? You haven't let yourself have a single new item of clothing in years. This dress is made of recycled plastic bottles, for God's sake, woman—this is as guilt free as it comes. And you look stunning. Seriously. Joseph isn't going to know what's hit him."

THE NEXT DAY, JOSEPH IS EARLY FOR THE WEDDING—THIS is a genuine first. He waits for Jane outside the church, his jacket over his arm, the usual warm, ready smile on his face. He's dressed in a dark-blue suit with a burgundy wool tie, and he's wearing his glasses; he looks so at ease, so effortlessly handsome. Jane is a tangle of nerves, as if her insides are a ball of yarn. Has he always been so tall? In a suit he is suddenly a little intimidating, an alternative version of the soft-eyed man she usually sees in wooly jumpers.

Joseph's eyes widen as she approaches. "You look amazing," he says, kissing her on the cheek. "Wow. Red?"

Jane stares down at his shoes. "It was Aggie's idea," she says. Her voice comes out even more quietly than usual, and Joseph ducks his head to catch her words. "I am regretting it a bit."

"No, it's lovely," Joseph says, offering his arm. "Now. Are you ready to be my girlfriend?"

It's awful, the leap her heart takes. As if she's just gone flying over a speed bump.

"I'm ready," she says, and her voice only shakes a little. "Thank you for doing this. Again."

"No problem," Joseph says lightly. "Though this time around we'd better get our story straight. Your colleague Keira had a lot of questions the morning after the engagement party, and I can hardly remember what I told her. We met . . ."

"At the Hoxton Bakehouse," Jane says as they make their way toward the church's entrance. It's a bright, clear September day; it rained first thing, but now the sun is out and the puddles between the cobbles are glinting gold. "We kept that story the same. Though I think you said you . . ."

"Started going to the bakery just to see you," Joseph says. "Yeah. I stumbled upon you once, and thought how beautiful you were, and then I started dropping in at the same time every day, in the hope of seeing you."

It's too much; it's painful. But it's a delicious, good-bad pain, like the sugar burn at the back of your throat when you've taken a great, jammy bite of doughnut.

"And our first date?" she says. Her voice is too breathy; Joseph can surely tell that something is wrong.

"I think we say we met as friends first," he replies after a moment. "Perhaps just keep it simple and say that one night after book club . . ."

He's waiting for her to step in now and finish the sentence, but she can't, she can't.

"Things shifted," he continues quietly as they reach the church doors. "And we realized our feelings had changed from friendship to something much deeper."

They move inside the church. There are already at least a hundred people here. Jane breathes in the smell—cool stone, a hint of incense, the slightly damp musk of a building that can't afford to fix its leaking roof.

They file into their seats just before the music starts. When Constance appears, walking down the aisle on her son's arm, Jane feels a surge of pure, undiluted envy. The bride looks radiant with delight. Jane snaps a photo of the signing of the registry to send to her dad later—proof she's done something with friends this weekend.

After the ceremony, they walk to the reception at a nearby pub. Inside it's rammed and sweaty, too full; the bar staff look stressed and there aren't anywhere near enough tables. Jane and Joseph squeeze their way through to a pillar with just enough of a ledge around it to balance a glass. For ten minutes or so Joseph is gone, fetching them drinks from the bar, and Jane stands alone, desperately exuding unapproachability. This, of course, is when Keira descends.

"Jane! Look at you!" says Keira, running her gaze up and down the length of Jane's body. "Good for you, trying to dress up a bit! It's very flattering."

Colin appears behind Keira, dressed in a pale-pink suit and hat, with Mortimer beside him, wearing a particularly fetching variation on his usual brown three-piece.

"You're a vision," Colin says, and Mortimer nods firmly.

"Lovely, Jane, dear," he says.

"Thank you," Jane says, relaxing slightly.

"And you've got that gorgeous man in tow again! I'm *so* pleased, though I don't suppose he's a count, is he? Like Ronnie?" says Keira, just as—at last—Joseph wriggles his way between two groups of middle-aged men, a glass in each hand. He's sweating slightly and the pub lights catch on his forehead and upper lip. Jane finds it quite charming, which feels like a new depth to sink to—even sweating in his suit, she can't resist him.

"Though perhaps you don't need a count, hen," Keira goes on, giving her a nudge. "You know we're all dying to find out where you get all that money of yours from."

Joseph's gaze flicks to Jane as he hands her a glass of white wine and greets Colin and Mortimer. Her stomach swoops. *No, no, no,* Jane thinks, gripping her glass. *Not today, please.*

"So, Joseph!" Keira says, rounding on him, to Jane's relief. "Will you two be next?"

"Next to what, sorry?" Joseph asks politely.

"Next down the aisle!" Keira crows, reaching across to pat Jane on the cheek.

"*Oh,*" Jane says, flinching away from the hand and shooting a fearful look at Joseph, who—to her relief—seems to be trying not to laugh.

"We're not in any rush," he says diplomatically.

"How old are you again, hen?" Keira asks Jane.

"Thirty," Jane says.

"Ooh, well, clock's ticking!" Keira says.

Jane's already tense after the comment about the money. She has meekly, silently endured so many snide remarks from Keira over the years. Quite suddenly, she thinks, *Why do I put up with this?*

"You mean that my childbearing years are numbered, so I'd better hurry up and get married?" Jane says. "That's a bit insensitive, Keira."

She just can't resist it, and actually, it feels *good* to let herself say the thought out loud without cringing at her own bluntness. She's angry, and why shouldn't she be? She might not even *want* children. As it happens, she does, very much, when the time is right—but what does Keira know?

"Well, I was only being honest!" Keira blusters.

Jane has to bite back a wicked little smile as Keira's cheeks redden. She's feeling better already.

"How are your childbearing credentials?" Jane asks, turning to Joseph. "Fertile, are you?"

He lets out one of those appreciative laughs she loves, the ones that mean she's surprised him. "You know, I don't often get asked that?" he says.

"Really?" Jane says, side-eyeing Keira. "That must be nice."

"Something I won't ever take for granted again," Joseph says solemnly, and behind him Colin is chortling. "Now, if you'll excuse us, Keira, Colin, Mortimer . . ."

He leads Jane away through the melee. Despite the crowd, she's feeling quite triumphant for finally standing up to Keira. But as they move deeper into the throng, she has to grab on to Joseph's sleeve as somebody shoves her, and suddenly all the bodies, their closeness—it's stifling. The triumph seeps away and her grip on Joseph's sleeve tightens.

"Where are we going?" she calls, just as the door to the pub garden comes into sight.

"I thought you might like some air," Joseph says. "I know crowds aren't your favorite."

Jane takes a deep breath as they step through the doors into the garden, glancing back inside. "Thank you. Oh, I shouldn't have spoken to Keira like that," she says, suddenly fretful.

"It was brilliant!" Joseph says, and his eyes crinkle at the corners. "I've never seen you like that before. I like sharp-tongued Jane."

She catches his warm gaze for a moment and tries not to smile. "Oh, well. She doesn't come out often—at least, not on purpose."

"Can I ask . . ." Joseph says as they shift out of the way of a couple moving past them. "What Keira says, about money? What did she mean? Is your work at the charity shop not paid?"

Jane closes her eyes for one pained moment. She'd so hoped he'd let it drop. She twists her wineglass back and forth by the stem, watching the liquid catch the low light as the shame warms her skin.

"No," she says, eyes still on her wine. "No, I volunteer there."

"Oh, wow," Joseph says, frowning slightly. "Oh, okay."

He is too polite to ask the question—*Where do you get your money from, then?* But it hangs in the air as though it's been said.

Jane takes another deep breath. The silence thickens, darkens between them. She is going to have to lie to him.

"When I left my old job, I got a . . . sort of . . . payout from my boss. I'm eking it out." She swallows a gulp of wine as the shame burns hotter.

"Oh, right, like a redundancy package?"

"Mm," Jane says into her glass.

"What is it you used to do again?" Joseph asks.

This is becoming nightmarish. Jane reaches for a way to wriggle out of this conversation but finds nothing; the soft jersey fabric of her dress suddenly feels corset tight. Being grilled on her life choices by Keira would be preferable to this.

"I worked at a large law firm," she says eventually. Not a lie, but certainly an evasion.

"No way," Joseph says, starting a little. "You know what I do, right?"

"Yes, I know," Jane says, and she looks around, growing desperate. "Are you getting chilly?"

"No," Joseph says firmly. "Why didn't you mention that you worked in law, too? I probably know the firm's IT team—I might even have worked there, I've moved around a fair bit."

"Yes," she says, and now her voice sounds horribly strangled and high. "Yes, maybe."

He sighs. "Jane . . ."

Jane closes her eyes for a moment. "Why are you pushing me?"

"I'm sorry," he says after a pause. "I just don't get why this is . . . difficult. You keep so much hidden. Why can't I just know this small thing about you?"

"I thought you understood. I mean . . . why can't I know what happened on Valentine's Day?" Jane says, opening her eyes to meet his. "Isn't that the same?"

His expression is shocked, as though she's slapped him.

"Oh," he says. "I . . . That's different." A muscle jumps in his jaw. He's usually so expressive, but now his face is set.

"Why?" Jane asks.

"Because that's . . ." He deflates suddenly. "Oh God, I don't know. I'm sorry. I don't mean to push you to talk about your secrets if you don't want to. I guess I just can't help wanting to *know* you." He looks at his empty glass. "Shit," he says. "That would be the double vodka talking."

Two young children dressed in formal wear come dashing between them, and Jane steadies herself on the pub wall.

"Let me get you another drink," Jane says, reaching for his glass with one shaking hand. "Same again?"

"So we're . . . so we're done talking?"

"What do you want me to say?"

"I want you to tell me things you don't tell other people," Joseph says with sudden intensity, and he's closer to her, though she's not sure which of them moved. Both their hands are on his empty glass, held between them like they're on pause. "I want you to let me in. I shouldn't want that, I know I shouldn't, but I do."

Jane stares fixedly at his throat. She can't bear to lift her gaze to his face. Instead she examines the grainy dots of his stubble, like dark sand on his skin.

"Why did you ask me to come today?" he asks quietly.

He touches her. Just a finger against her finger, against the warming glass in their hands. A shot of sensation fires the moment his skin brushes hers, and for a split second she genuinely wonders if he's given her an electric shock.

"I wanted . . ." Her throat is so dry. Someone is laughing too loudly nearby. "I wanted you. Here, I mean. I didn't want to do it without you."

"So you just needed a friend. That was it."

For a brief moment, Jane lifts her gaze to his. His pupils are dilated, inky pools. There is something new and raw and yearning in his gaze. Desire forks through her as their eyes meet—and then they're stepping apart, flustered, awkward, because here is Keira again, batting her enormous fake eyelashes and offering Joseph some kind of half apology for being rude, and Joseph's let go of the glass they were holding, and his eyes are as warm and affable as always, and it's over, it's gone, as if the moment never was.

"I'll get you another," Jane says, already slipping away with the glass in her hand.

THEY'RE CALLED TO THE MEAL SHORTLY AFTER THEIR conversation with Keira, and Jane is dismayed to see that the couples on each table have been seated apart, presumably to encourage mingling, which happens to be one of her least favorite activities. The woman next to her is the girlfriend of someone at the top table. She keeps rearranging her hair on her shoulders and talking to Jane about reality television programs she's never heard of; it is all intensely stressful.

Jane escapes to the toilets and her phone buzzes as she waits in the queue. A text from Aggie.

Have you told him how you feel about him?! xxx

Jane chews her lip for a moment, then steps out of the queue and heads for the garden, already ringing Aggie's number.

"I *can't* tell him," Jane whispers, perching on a bench with its back against the wall of the pub. "Aggie, I can't. Even if I thought I could . . . even if I wanted to. He asked me about London."

"Oh," Aggie says, unperturbed. "That's a good sign."

"A good sign?"

"That's the difference between a friend and a lover, Jane. A friend doesn't need the whole of you. If you don't want to tell me about your life before we met, I don't give a toss—I'm in it for the Jane that's here and now, aren't I? I take you as you come. But if I loved you, I'd want everything. Wouldn't I? Don't you want all of him? All his secrets? All the versions of Joseph that exist out there, all the people he is when he's at work and with his mother and with the lads at the pub?"

"Yes," Jane says wretchedly. She wants to know why mentioning Valentine's Day hit him like a blow; she wants to hold his hand as he manages his mother's dementia; she wants to peel off every layer of him until she finds his core, the kernel of Josephness, the man he is when he's alone. She is so far gone now—bitterly, painfully in love.

"But you don't want to talk to him about what happened in London?" Aggie prompts.

Jane bites her lip, hesitating. "It's not just that. We used to work together."

Aggie inhales between her teeth. "Oh, you're joking. You met Joseph in London?"

"No," Jane says, smoothing her red dress over her thighs. "I met him in Winchester. But I recognized him from my old job. I just . . . I didn't think he'd ever realize that I used to work at the same place, since he hadn't clocked it right away, and I didn't . . . think it would . . . come up."

There is a brief silence on the line.

"Hello?" Jane says, checking her signal.

"I'm still here," Aggie says. "Just wondering if what you've said is true, that's all."

Jane pauses, a little affronted. "What do you mean?"

"Well. You've not told me precisely what happened in London, so I'm guessing a bit here. But from what I can tell, you haven't let a guy speak to you for more than five minutes for a seriously long time. So why him?"

"You think I was—you think I made friends with Joseph because he worked at Bray & Kembrey?" Jane shakes her head. "No, it's not that. It definitely wasn't."

"Maybe it wasn't," Aggie says. "But I think you knew it was a risk. I think you knew it would come up. And that's interesting. Maybe you are ready to talk about it?"

Jane stares out at the picnic benches with their branded sunshades, debris waiting to be cleared beneath the umbrellas. Half-drunk pints, crisp packets, ashtrays. There's a silk scarf abandoned under a bench; for a moment in the darkness it looks like a little crouched animal.

"Hermiting yourself away and sticking to your routines was never intended as a life change, was it?" Aggie asks gently. "Just a coping mechanism, right? I wonder if you needed some time to process some stuff, and you needed quiet for that, but now maybe you don't need quiet anymore. Maybe you're at a point with your process where you need to talk."

Jane sits silently, testing the thought, the way you might swill a mouthful of wine. She has never really imagined herself as having a *process*. She is a before-and-after: she was one person, and then she gave away her belongings, got on a train, and became someone else. The idea that she is still in evolution is genuinely quite shocking to her. She shifts uncomfortably, wishing she hadn't left her jacket inside; the air is cooling as the day slides into evening, and the bare skin of her legs is pimpling with cold.

"Or not," Aggie says with amusement, faced with Jane's long silence.

"No, no, I hear you," Jane says, clearing her throat. "It's just quite a . . . big thought."

"Well, park it for tonight, then," Aggie says comfortably. "But trust your gut. If you want to open up to Joseph, do it, I say. What's the harm? You know this man pretty well, right? You know that you can trust him?"

Jane hesitates. *Does* she trust him? Though it's completely hypocritical of her to hold Joseph's secrets against him, the first thought that comes into her head is: *He won't tell me what happened on Valentine's Day.* Does that make him untrustworthy?

It shouldn't. But that secret feels important. Jane can't help feeling that until she knows it, she won't truly know Joseph.

THE DAY HASN'T GONE EXACTLY AS JANE HAD IMAGINED, but the moment after the first dance when Joseph takes her hand and leads her onto the dance floor is every bit as beautiful as she'd day-dreamed it to be.

"You okay?" Joseph murmurs into her hair.

She nods, scrunching her eyes tight for a moment as she sways in his arms. The song is John Legend's "All of Me," and the words are so perfect it hurts. For the first time in a very long time, Jane aches to give herself away, every part of herself, all her struggles and contradictions.

"Jane," Joseph whispers, and his hand shifts on her lower back, pulling her a touch closer.

The warmth of his body makes her weak. She can't bring herself to open her eyes. They sway, feet barely moving, and Jane can feel his breath on her hair, featherlight, intoxicating.

"Jane, I'm sorry I pushed you earlier. I understand that you just need a friend."

Another electric shock passes through her as his right hand shifts its grip on hers. The barest contact with him feels overwhelming. What would it be like to kiss him, all lust and tongue and rough stubble, bodies pressed tight?

"That wasn't why I asked you here."

She says it in a rush; it comes from somewhere dark and impulsive, the part of herself that might stand on the train platform and—for a split second—imagine stepping forward onto the tracks. In the silence that follows, she is genuinely shocked at herself.

"No?" Joseph says after a moment, bringing his face closer to hers as they dance. Around them, couples circle slowly, lazily, as the music shifts to a different song.

Jane pulls back to look at his face. He meets her eyes and it's like stepping into the sun's heat—she feels it everywhere, over every inch of her.

"What is this?" he asks, voice husky. "What are we doing here?"

"I don't know," Jane says. They're barely moving now, and Jane's face is tipped up to his. It is difficult to say what's harder: fighting the urge to kiss him or taking the leap.

She lifts her chin. It's a tiny motion, so small, but Joseph's pupils dilate and his jaw tightens and she knows he can feel it, too, the breath of air between their lips, the decision that's waiting to be made.

When it comes, the kiss is electric. It's the barest whisper of a thing, a touching, but it burns through Jane's body like something searing. Their lips brush once more, a little deeper, and the heat blazes through Jane and it's all she can do not to fall against him, to let her knees give way.

Then suddenly he's pulling back, his hands on her shoulders, his head dropped. She falters, almost losing her footing.

"I'm sorry," Joseph says, voice catching. "I can't."

It takes her a moment to understand the words. She can still feel the ghost of his lips against hers, as though the kiss, like Jane, is one step behind.

He holds her at arm's length, hands gripping her shoulders tightly. His breath is ragged and his gaze is still fixed on the floor. Their stillness feels wrong, as though they've stepped out of time, frozen while the rest of the dancers move on around them.

What does he mean, he can't?

The horror rises slowly, crawling across her skin like a shiver.

"I'm sorry, Jane. I shouldn't have . . . I'm so sorry."

There's someone else, then. Some lovely, beautiful woman who gets to kiss him like it's nothing.

"You should have told me you were seeing someone," Jane says. She is startled by the calmness of her voice. "Why didn't you say something earlier?"

He takes so long to answer she wonders if he heard her.

"I'm sorry," he says eventually, lifting his head. There's desperation in his eyes, and exhaustion, and maybe something a little like wildness. "It's hard to explain. I'm . . . I'm a bit of a fuckup, really, Jane, but I'm trying. I'm trying to be a better man."

She shouldn't have raised her chin. If she hadn't made that tiny motion, if she'd held still, she wouldn't be feeling this gaping pain in her chest. She always gets it wrong, *always*.

"I'm sorry. I should never have . . . I should have been clearer. But I do want to be a friend to you, if you'll have me," he says. "If you'll still have me."

No, she thinks. *No, no, no. I want all of you, every piece, or nothing. This hurts too much.*

But it doesn't hurt enough to say good-bye.

So she lays her head against his chest and says, "Of course. Of course we're friends."

Miranda

OCTOBER PASSES, AND THE AUTUMN CLOSES IN: RAIN SNEAKING down the neck of Miranda's waterproofs, great heaps of papery bright leaves, endless acorns and winged sycamore seeds. She is already wishing for spring. The shorter the days get, the less herself she feels.

The one blessing in among all the dampness and chill is that things with Carter seem to be blossoming. Something shifted in him toward the end of the summer: he was more present all of a sudden, more engaged, though until that shift happened she'd never quite put her finger on the sense that she didn't have the whole of him.

It's the Friday after Halloween, and Scott is throwing a party—something he tends to do at the slightest provocation. Carter comes straight to Miranda's flat from work so they can get ready together; he's loosening his tie as she answers the door. She loves that move, the tilt of his head as he does it, the way it signifies that he's play-Carter now, not work-Carter.

He bends to kiss her and breathes in her freshly washed hair. "Hey. You smell of summertime," he says.

"I wish." The flat is bitterly cold, partly because there aren't enough radiators, partly because Miranda always forgets to put the heating on until it's too late. "Is that your costume?"

She points to the carrier bag in his hand, and he grimaces.

"Yes," he says. "A friend picked it out for me. I don't know why I let her help."

Miranda is always so sure that she has no suspicions about Carter anymore, until the moment when he does something like this— mentioning a woman, but not by name. And then *voom*, here they come again. Valentine's Day, the receipt, the strangeness of Mary Carter asking *which one* Miranda was when she first visited the house.

"Oh?" she says, as casually as she can manage. "Who was it?"

"Oh my God," Carter says, stopping stock-still in the center of the room and then bursting out laughing.

Adele and Frannie have just exited the spare bedroom in their Halloween costume.

"I cannot *believe* I let you talk me into this," Frannie says.

Frannie is the back end of the cat. Adele is the front. The front is definitely the better of the two options.

"Are you two going to stay stuck to one another all evening?" Miranda says. "What if one of you needs a wee?"

"Forget weeing. What if one of us meets a hot guy?" Frannie says.

"There will be no hot guys!" Miranda says, suddenly feeling like taking Frannie and Adele to an adult party was a huge, huge mistake, whether they're eighteen or not.

"Don't worry," Adele tells her. "Frannie's never going to pull dressed as a cat's arse, is she? And it unzips, look."

She twists, attempting to demonstrate how she might unzip the cat's body, thus freeing Frannie from an evening of following Adele around dutifully, but she can't reach. Frannie swats at Adele's hands.

"Here, I'll do it." She unzips them with some difficulty. The cat splits in half; Carter looks slightly horrified, and there *is* something a bit grotesque about it. As unrealistic as the costume is, nobody wants to see a cat cut in two.

"There!" Adele says. "Perfect."

"Now Frannie is just a cat without a face," Carter points out.

"And that's, like, the Halloweeniest thing ever, no?" Adele says breezily.

She has come off rather well here, even if she does have half of a cat's body flopping down the back of her legs. The front of the cat costume is actually decidedly low cut, Miranda notes with a frown. Poor Frannie's costume is just black felt right up to the neck, and *her* half of the cat's body sticks out of her front, giving the impression that she might well be dressed as a pregnant nun.

"Hurry up, get ready!" Adele says, ushering Carter and Miranda toward Miranda's bedroom. "Fran, we need to go get some beers."

"Dressed like *this*?" Frannie says as Miranda closes the door to her bedroom.

Carter breathes out a laugh. "Your sisters . . ."

"I know," Miranda says, rolling her eyes but grinning. "We are definitely going to regret taking them with us. Let's see this costume of yours, then—oh, I *love* it!"

It's a cowboy costume, complete with hat and boots.

"I'm going to look like a twat," Carter says, scrubbing at his hair and looking down at the costume on Miranda's bed.

"You're going to look sexy," she tells him, trying on his hat. "Oh my God, I wish you'd said. I would have gone for a cowgirl thing!"

His eyes widen slightly. "I *do* wish I'd told you," he says, shifting closer, taking her by the waist. "That hat looks far too good on you."

His hands shift against her, snagging on her T-shirt, finding skin. She tilts her head up at him and he kisses her softly, but with intent: one of those skillful Carter kisses, the kind that make her wobbly at the knees.

Miranda glances toward the door. "There's definitely not time," she whispers. "Those two will kill us."

"How long does it *really* take you to get ready?" Carter asks, beginning to kiss his way up her neck.

This has changed lately, too. He was always a sexual guy—there was always a sense that he'd be up for it whenever she was. But over the last couple of months it's become more intense; he seems to want her more, and it thrills her, this new hunger in him, the way he can't keep his hands off her.

Outside, the front door slams as the twins head out. Carter's eyebrows rise.

"The corner shop is only three minutes' walk away," Miranda says regretfully, her hands sliding up Carter's chest. He's still in his suit jacket, still wearing his loosened tie.

"But in half a cat costume . . ."

"Slower," Miranda concedes. "Five minutes."

"And choosing beers . . ."

"Adele *is* very choosy." Miranda chucks off the hat and lifts her T-shirt over her head.

"Plus, you know," Carter says, hands sliding to the clasp on Miranda's bra, "that pedestrian crossing on your road, the lights are really slow."

Miranda's laughing now, breathless and hot as he slides her bra down over her shoulders.

"You really know how to talk dirty to me, don't you?" she says, then gasps as her bare skin touches the fabric of his suit.

Carter laughs against her lips. "I haven't even got to how overcrowded it can get on the pavement outside the pub," he says.

EVEN WITH MIRANDA GETTING READY AT SUPER-SPEED, they're late; she kicks Carter out of the room to stall Frannie and Adele when they get back from the corner shop, and gives all her attention to trying to dampen down her disordered hair. She hardly needs to go near a bed and she gets bed hair; it's very unfair. Carter looked perfectly civilized when he stepped out of the bedroom door, shooting her a wink behind him, now dressed in full cowboy gear.

"Mir, is my phone in there?" Carter calls a few minutes later, by which point Miranda is looking slightly less flustered and a bit more like Alice in Wonderland.

Miranda looks around. Carter's phone is lying on the bed.

"Uh-huh," she calls, then looks down at herself. She's in knickers and white tights only; she'd planned on finishing her makeup before putting on the dress. "Umm . . ."

"Just check the event," Carter calls. "We're looking for the address so Adele can book us an Uber."

This is Adele's way of trying to get Miranda to hurry up. Miranda rolls her eyes and flicks open Carter's calendar.

It's open on today, and there's the event: *Halloween at Scott's*. But it's another event beneath it that's caught Miranda's eye.

My night;)

That winking face. It's not the sort of thing Carter would write, particularly on a note only meant for himself. It's something a woman would write. And *she* certainly hasn't put this in his diary.

She hesitates for just a fraction of a second before she clicks on the event. Where you would usually enter the location, it says, *First Friday of the month is MINE, Joseph Carter, and don't you forget it x*. The event is set to repeat every month.

"Mir?" Carter calls.

She swallows. Her heart is beating heavy and hard. She scrolls backward through the months—September, August, July—looking for traces of herself in Carter's diary. *Dinner with Mir. Stay at Miranda's. Mir to Winchester.*

She has never spent the first Friday of the month with Carter.

They've been together on the days either side in August and July; they were together the following Friday in September; but never the first Friday of the month. She keeps scrolling: June, May, April. The first Friday in April fell on Scott's birthday: April sixth. It was Saturday, April seventh, when Miranda found that receipt showing Carter had just had breakfast in Central London.

Was that where he was when he said he was at Scott's party? Was he with some other woman?

The door clicks open. "You okay?"

Miranda looks up at him, and he must be able to read it on her face. He turns serious immediately, slipping into the room and shutting the door behind him.

"What is it?"

He glances down at the phone in her hand and his face tightens.

"You asked me to check it," Miranda blurts.

"I meant on Facebook," he says woodenly.

He reaches for the phone. She hands it to him, the screen still lit up on the first Friday in April. *My night;)* is right there, clashing with the diary entry for Scott's birthday party, the two events sitting side by side.

Carter looks down at the phone screen for a while, and for once, his emotions aren't there on his face, ready to be read. In fact, right now Miranda can't make sense of his expression at all.

"There was an entry for today." Miranda's throat feels very dry. "I . . . I scrolled back."

He takes so long to look up. Miranda bites her lip. She is too deeply entangled to know whether what she's done is paranoid or reasonable. All she can feel is the pounding of her heart and the sweat prickling the back of her neck. She's still topless, wearing nothing but tights, and the realization makes her fold her arms across her breasts.

"Miranda," Carter says after an engulfing, awful silence. "This isn't what it looks like."

That's what they always say, isn't it? When someone confronts a cheater on television, they say, *This isn't what it looks like.*

"What is it, then?" Miranda asks, and she means it—she's desperate to hear a reason that makes absolute, perfect sense. Her skin is buzzing with that urgent need to *move* that always strikes when she's feeling panicked. She wants to run, to scale a tree, to feel her muscles burning.

Carter doesn't say anything. He swallows. As she watches him, Miranda knows he is trying to come up with a lie, and suddenly she's terrified he won't find a good one, that she'll have to strip out of these Alice in Wonderland tights and get into her pajamas and cry in her bed because they've broken up.

"Was it an ex?" she blurts. "Is it an ex-girlfriend who put that in, you know, as a repeat event?"

Carter's tongue flicks out to lick his bottom lip. He glances up at her at last.

"Yeah," he says. He tries a smile, and that makes it worse, because it's so *fake*. It's not his proper smile. His face is too pale; he looks tired and a little shocked. "Yeah, it's that. I'm sorry. I should have deleted it."

"Why haven't you?" Miranda's voice seems to be shrinking. She wishes she was wearing something.

"I don't know." He rubs a hand across his mouth. "I guess I just didn't think of it."

"Every month when it came up, you didn't think of deleting it?"

Carter winces. "Sorry. I thought I had, but maybe . . . Maybe I just deleted a single event rather than the series?"

Now she knows he's lying. She's been back as far as April and every date night event was still there.

"I'll delete the event series. I'll do it now." He does it with a delib-erateness that Miranda finds slightly painful; it's as if he is having to demonstrate it to her, as if she's being unreasonable.

"You know we've never seen each other on the first Friday of the month?"

Carter reels back slightly, looking down at her with those glassy, un-Carter-ish eyes.

"Haven't we?" He gathers himself. "Ever? I'm sure we must have."

"Well, not for the last six months. I haven't checked before that."

"It's a coincidence, Miranda."

Miranda looks down at her feet. Carter touches her then, just very gently, on her right shoulder. She thinks about flinching or shrugging away, but it feels so natural to have his hand on her, and by the time she's considered the gesture it's too late.

"Miranda? What are you thinking?"

"Where were you on Friday the sixth of April?"

Meeting his eyes feels impossible now that she's looked away.

"What—what do you mean? I'd need to check my diary, Mir, I can't just . . ." He pauses. "Oh, hang on, that's Scott's birthday. I was at his birthday party," he says. His voice has dropped slightly—it's ir-ritated him that she's asked, and that makes Miranda's steady temper stir at last.

"Well, what am I meant to think?" she says, and her gaze snaps up to his. "You had breakfast in the middle of London the next morning. You had a date night with someone in the diary that evening."

"I also had Scott's birthday party in the diary that evening," Carter points out. "And today, I had that—that event series thing in there, but I'm here, aren't I? I'm not off on a date with somebody. We're going to a Halloween party together."

"Right," Miranda says, because, annoyingly, this is quite a good point. "Okay. Well . . . Okay. So an ex just put it in and you hadn't got around to deleting it and it's a total coincidence that you've never hung out with me on a day when that's in the diary."

"We're hanging out now, aren't we?"

"Are you actually being mad at me about this?" The heat is beating high in Miranda's cheeks. "Are you *actually* raising your voice at me when you've got a *date night* in your diary with *another woman*?"

"Miranda," Carter says with an exasperated sigh. "That event has been in my diary for a long time, okay? I promise you, I'm . . . I'm not seeing that person anymore."

Miranda notes the careful absence of a name. "Well, you've deleted it now, haven't you, so there's no way of knowing when it was first put in the diary," she points out. She grits her teeth. They stare at each other, silent for a while.

Carter bends to the bed and passes her the dress. "Here," he says, and somehow that annoys her, too, as if she's being told she ought to cover herself up.

"I haven't finished doing the makeup," she snaps. "I have to do that before I put the dress on."

Carter raises his hands in that universal male gesture, the one that says, *Jeez, okay, don't bite my head off.* There goes a little more of his Perfect-Carter shine.

"What are you two doing in there? It better not be any funny business!" Adele shouts through the door.

Miranda meets Carter's eyes for a moment. Just twenty minutes earlier he'd been inside her, her back against that door, his hands gripping the backs of her thighs. It feels like an impossibly intimate thing to have done with this stranger of a man.

She closes her eyes and tries to clear her head. His explanation does make sense—though he's still never given a reasonable answer for why he had breakfast in Central London on April seventh if he really was at Scott's birthday party the night before. But she *knows* he lied to her.

She just knows it. She wishes she hadn't offered him up the solution of an ex, because now she'll never know if he only agreed because she'd given him an out.

"You and this woman. How long were you two together?"

"Miranda . . . do you really want to talk about this now?"

She doesn't. It's painful to think of him with someone else, more painful than ever when part of her is convinced that *my night* wasn't from an *ex*-girlfriend at all. Who leaves plans from an old relationship in their diary?

Carter sighs, and his shoulders soften.

"Miranda," he says gently. "If I was seeing someone else, don't you think you'd be able to tell? Look at me. I'm completely committed to you, I promise. There's only you. There's only *you*."

He lifts a hand to her jaw, tilting her head so she's looking up at him, and the gesture makes her bottom lip quiver with sudden emotion.

She doesn't think he's lying now. His eyes are clear and he's holding her gaze.

He presses a gentle kiss to her lips. "I'm sorry that I left that in my diary. You know how cluttered my life can get. You know how disorganized I am. But it's gone now. And if you want, you can have every Friday ever after. All the Fridays. They're all yours."

"Hello?" Adele yells through the door. "Hel-*lo*?"

"We're coming!" Miranda shouts, turning away from Carter, back to the mirror. "God, I've got no time to sort this makeup now. I'll have to just fudge the rest."

"You look great," Carter says, and Miranda resists the urge to laugh. She's half-dressed, for God's sake, with one eye done and the other completely makeup free.

"Are we okay?" he says tentatively, coming up behind her. They look so good together in the mirror, even with Miranda's face half-made-up. She fits just under his chin; his shoulders are so broad, wrapping around her, and he's in that sexy cowboy outfit. He looks like something straight out of a fantasy.

Miranda's anger seeps away as she looks at their reflection. It goes like water down a drain, and all she's left with is tiredness.

"Yeah," she says, because she doesn't know what else to say, and they have to get to this party. "For now. We're all good for now."

Siobhan

BY EARLY NOVEMBER, SIOBHAN FEELS LIKE A CHINA CUP that's been smashed and glued back together. She's painfully aware of all her new joins, the places where she cracked—but she would tentatively describe herself as whole again.

She's only been to London a couple of times since her mental health crisis; even after all these months of recovery, it still feels foreign and strange here, like a hostile land that requires her to be somebody else. She's dressed in heeled boots and skinny jeans: this is power-dressing à la Siobhan. Her coat is enormous—fake fur with a giant, draping hood. She looks like the sort of woman who'd be stopped by a roaming photographer for a *Vogue* column on London street style, and as she catches sight of herself in a shop window she has a little flutter of that feeling that she now knows is called *disassociation*, that sense that she is observing herself from a distance, that she can't tell if she's real.

She's heading to the office space she rents when she's in London, to restart her one-to-ones with Richard and an assortment of other clients: Bob Girl, Forehead, Tie Guy. She's gradually picking up her duties again, or the ones that are still there to be picked up.

Richard arrives first, just as she's getting herself set up. This office building is one of those places with AstroTurf in the corridors and vending machines full of fruit and smoothies; Siobhan has never been able to decide if she finds it refreshingly cool or tediously quirky.

It's been months since Siobhan has seen Richard in person; she's reminded that he is a bit less svelte than he seems when sitting behind a desk on a screen. But when he smiles he is as charming as ever, stretching out a hand to shake Siobhan's and then leaning in to kiss her on the cheek.

"How have you been, Richard?" Siobhan says, pulling her notepad onto her lap. She finds the notepad calms more traditional people; it makes things feel official. It also, helpfully, gives her something to do with her hands.

"It's been an . . . interesting few months," Richard says, resettling his tie against his shirt. He leans back in his chair, crossing one ankle over his knee, smoothing a finger across his top lip. "Businesswise, I'm very much on track."

When Siobhan first started coaching Richard, he came to their meetings with a bullet-pointed agenda of exactly what he wanted to get from life coaching. A promotion; a few specific business issues he needed advice on handling; and he wanted to talk to her about making men like him better. *I get on well with women*, he'd said, with a slightly embarrassed smile, *but men tend not to like me*.

"And you?" Richard says, with the practiced eye contact of a man who knows how to look engaging. "You're well?"

"I'm fine," Siobhan says. "I hope my sabbatical gave you a chance to explore a different approach with Eko?"

"I must say, it wasn't quite the same."

Siobhan smiles politely and says nothing to this. Richard looks mildly surprised at the lack of response—Siobhan is usually more obliging with him—but continues.

"In terms of my personal life . . . My secretary and I . . . Things have continued to, ah, develop. We struggle to keep our hands off each other, if I can be frank. Her body, the things she does to me . . . I mean, Christ, I'm like a teenage boy again. Hormones raging. We had sex in my office chair just this morning, for crying out loud."

He looks up at Siobhan as he says this, and suddenly she knows. It's something about being in the room with him. It makes it completely obvious in a way that Skype just couldn't.

It's a kind of exhibitionism. Telling Siobhan about this fantastical secretarial seduction, the sex in the chair, the raging hormones. It's nothing to do with needing to talk the emotions through; he wants *her* to hear it.

Siobhan hates it when Fiona's right.

As Richard continues to talk about his sexy secretary, as he shifts in his chair and sits with his legs spread wide, Siobhan wonders what exactly she's supposed to do here. He's not actually said or done anything specifically inappropriate. She could withdraw from the agreement she's just renewed with Richard's company's HR team, but that would mean losing *all* her one-on-one clients, and the corporate assertiveness courses she runs there, which earn her a lot of money. She could potentially address the concern with Richard directly, but . . . he's so slippery. Her instinct is that it wouldn't end well.

Somehow, though, she needs to extricate herself from Richard Wilson's life. Siobhan curls a hand into a fist, but her nails are too short to really bite the skin of her palm. All her other self-harming tics—gnawing the skin of her wrist, tugging at her hair—have eased as she's worked at her mental health, but this last one lingers, a habit she just can't shake when she's feeling stressed.

And this is most definitely stressful. Siobhan may not have the best track record when it comes to men, but she's been around the block enough times to spot a really bad egg. And, more worryingly, she knows that when she's at her weakest, when she's feeling her most inadequate, men like Richard are just her type.

———

SOMEHOW, TODAY, ALONE IN A HOTEL BAR WITH THE thick, misty chill of November pressing against the windows, one large glass of pinot noir is enough to break Siobhan's resolve.

She's going to call Joseph. She knows she is. It's humming through her bloodstream, tingling in her fingers. At some point between ordering the glass of red and finishing it off, it becomes an inevitable, unassailable truth, even as she sits here telling herself she won't do it.

Maybe Fiona and Marlena are right, she thinks. *Maybe I can't let a man in because of Cillian.* She stares morosely at her glass. It's so galling to think that such a weak man has had such a long-lasting impact on her. She'd loved Cillian, but she *shouldn't* have—he really wasn't all that. *And even he rejected me*, she finds herself thinking, and winces.

She misses Joseph so much she *aches* when she thinks of him. She's lost count of how often she's opened their chat and read all the messages he sent that she never replied to; the other night she even dreamed about him. There was a llama there as well, and a man with a pot of jam balanced on his head, but still. This is not how it usually goes when she calls time on hooking up with someone.

Today with Richard has reminded her why she keeps men at a distance—most of them are arseholes—but it has also made her think of the ways that Joseph is different. How he didn't just make her feel sexy and wanted, he made her feel secure. Happy.

Joseph picks up after the third ring. More than two hundred days of abstinence gone in less than five seconds.

"Siobhan?" he says.

She closes her eyes, fingers clasping tightly around the stem of her wineglass. Behind her in the bar a woman barks out the punch line to a joke and the rest of her table laughs. The hubbub of everyone else's lives continues, and Siobhan's here, alone, hunched over a table, holding Joseph's voice to her ear.

"Yes, hi," she says, then screws up her face in a wince. Why wait *months* to make a call and then start it with, *Yes, hi?*

"You called," Joseph says, sounding shell-shocked.

"You answered," Siobhan points out, and she feels slightly better about that one, even if it is just stating the obvious.

"I didn't think . . . It's been a while."

Siobhan shifts the glass back and forth. There's a tiny amount of wine remaining in the base, not enough to drink.

"But you saved my number," Joseph continues slowly, and she wonders if she can hear a smile in his voice.

I shouldn't have called you, she thinks. She has been thinking it ever since he said her name, because, honestly, the moment he did that, she was done for. She can't resist the sound of her name in Joseph Carter's mouth.

"Are you in London right now?" Siobhan's voice is husky.

"I'm actually just traveling back to Winchester," Joseph says after a moment. "I was at a party, but . . . Yeah. I left."

She checks the time. Half eleven. She'd gone out for Italian food with Kit, and then had dessert and a catch-up with Vikesh and Kalvin back at their flat before returning to the hotel bar for a nightcap, and . . . it got late.

This is not an appropriate time to ring a man unless you are ringing him for sex.

Well? Siobhan thinks as she toys with her wineglass, looking at her stubby little fingernails, cut short like she's a kid who won't stop scratching. *What* are *you ringing this man for, Siobhan Kelly?*

"I could . . . I could come to you," Siobhan says. "Just to talk. I mean. It *is* the first Friday of the month. Mine, right?" she adds softly.

The silence is excruciating. She can't decide which part of that sentence was more humiliating: the fact that, after all this time, she is coming out to commuterville for him in the middle of the night, or the fact that she's pretending it's *just to talk.*

"I'd like that," Joseph says as she opens her mouth to try to take it all back. "I'd really like that, Siobhan."

There he goes again, saying her name. She closes her eyes for a moment and knows that she will be wracked with terror and doubt about this decision for every minute of that train journey to Winchester.

"See you soon," she says, and hangs up.

IN THE MOMENT WHEN THE TRAIN STOPS AT BASING-stoke, she comes so close to chickening out that she stands to get off. She could just head back into London and make it all a funny anecdote that ultimately ends with her being an independent woman who certainly doesn't travel an hour for a hookup with a guy she used to sleep with. Or maybe she could just kick around in Basingstoke for the night—doesn't she know someone in Basingstoke? A woman she met while doing her Level 3 Certificate in Counseling Studies? Or was it Kit's ex, the short one with all the hair?

But she just stands in the aisle as if paralyzed, her handbag tight against her side, and then the doors are beeping and shutting and the train is moving off again and here she still is, on her way to Winchester at one in the morning. And it's terrifying. She's putting herself out there. With a man. This is not comfortable territory.

There is nobody waiting on the platform when she gets off the train at Winchester. The night air is bitingly cold; a drunk man staggers past her, singing "You'll Never Walk Alone," and a woman in six-inch heels tells him to shut up, but she's grinning, scampering after him as best she can in her shoes. Siobhan has so many people in her life; she has almost never felt lonely. But in that moment, watching the man wait for his girlfriend to catch up in her heels, with a big drunken grin on his face, it pierces her like something sharp. She wants a person who will wait for her.

"Siobhan?"

He's coming down the steps from the other platform, hands in the pockets of his coat. He looks just the same—glasses on, rumpled brown hair, big smile. Seeing him sends a wash of relief through her, sweet and warm, like the moment when you hear the good news you've been waiting for. She wonders how they'll greet each other, but he just kisses her simply on the cheek and then pulls her into a quick hug.

He doesn't take her back to his place.

"Too far from the station," he says, but he's not quite meeting her eye, and the sense that he's lying chases away that warm feeling that came over her when she saw him; for a moment she thinks about pulling away and heading back to the station. Then Joseph tucks her tighter against him, and the smell of him, the feel of his body against hers after so many months apart, is enough to keep her there.

They check into a cute little hotel a couple of minutes' walk from the station. She is grateful that it isn't just a Travelodge, as if somehow that makes this feel less seedy. The owner seems to know Joseph, and she's just wondering whether he brings other women here, her heart sinking, when Joseph surprises her by saying, "Shall we get a drink in the bar before they close?"

She had assumed they'd go straight to the room.

"Sure," she says, and he's already making his way to a table in the window, shrugging his coat off. She asks for a glass of pinot noir without thinking—another hotel bar, same glass of red wine.

"So." Joseph smiles at her, but his eyes are slightly wary, or maybe even hurt. "You wanted to talk."

This whole situation has become increasingly bizarre. Siobhan and Joseph don't talk. They don't meet each other at stations. They don't sit across tables from one another with drinks.

"Well. You said in quite a few of your messages that you missed me," Siobhan says, raising an eyebrow to make it sound arch rather than needy.

Joseph looks down at his pint with a smile that's almost rueful;

Siobhan's hands flex in her lap. She has a bad feeling. He looks tired; she wonders for the first time why he left his party so early and was already heading home at half eleven.

"I did miss you," he says, and the bad feeling blooms. "I do miss you. But . . ."

Oh God, Siobhan thinks, fists clenched. *Oh God, he doesn't want me anymore.* This is the nightmare scenario, the one she played over and over on the train down here, and she's already opening her mouth to say she's not interested in him either when he continues, "Look. It hurt a lot when you froze me out this summer." He meets her gaze and holds it. "I was . . . Things seemed to be going well with us, and then you completely ghosted me. I couldn't figure out why."

"Yes," Siobhan says, fiddling with her wineglass. "I get that that was . . . confusing."

This is why it's important to actually draw a line when you decide you're going to draw one. Not draw a line and then bloody ring them again and turn up in their hometown at one in the morning.

"You were upset about something, that day in April," Joseph says. "And I left you alone, because you said you wanted that, but it . . . didn't feel right. I thought all day about going back to check on you. I think I should have."

Siobhan breathes out slowly. "I would probably just have kicked you out again."

Joseph presses his lips together in thought. "Do you know why?"

It's an odd way to ask the question—it's something she might say to a client in a session—and it hits a nerve, because Siobhan isn't sure she *does* know why. Or rather, she has her suspicions, and she doesn't want to confront them.

"I just don't like to be—you know. I don't like to be left behind." She grimaces. This is *not* what she wants to be doing right now, digging over her own miserable personal life. She spends so much time digging over other people's, you'd think she'd have the knack, but she's never liked going inward like this. "And sometimes when I feel like that's happening, I think I can sort of, well, leave the other person behind first."

"To stop yourself getting hurt," he says.

"To stay in control," she corrects him quickly. "To make sure I'm in charge."

"Right," he says, smiling slightly. "I get it."

"But I'm sorry," she says after a long silence. "If I hurt you. Or, no." She lifts a hand. "That's one of those politician non-apologies. I'm sorry *that* I hurt you."

She gets a proper smile from him then, a Joseph smile, and it's like sipping something hot. Her own smile grows in response. Just like that, seeing that look on his face makes it worth groveling, worth swallowing her pride. *I'm beyond help*, she thinks, panic stirring, but all the while she's still grinning at him, like her face hasn't caught up with the rest of her.

"Honestly, when you cut me out of your life it was a bit of a wake-up call. I've been trying to be a better guy. Settle down a bit, drink less. And no more . . . nonexclusive relationships." Joseph looks away.

"Is that why we're downstairs talking instead of upstairs in bed together?" Siobhan says lightly, but her heart is thumping; she doesn't know what she'll do if he turns her down.

"Yeah, partly," Joseph says, sliding her a look that makes her shiver. "And partly because I think maybe we didn't do enough of the talking-downstairs stuff last time around."

Last time around perhaps suggests there will be another time around. Siobhan sits up straighter, crossing her legs, letting her foot brush his shin. He shoots her a little chastising eyebrow twitch. She looks back, all insolence, no shame.

"Siobhan," he says, and her gaze slides away at his tone. "I can't. Not anymore. I'm . . . seeing someone else."

Oof. She withdraws her foot, hands clutched tightly in her lap. *Okay.* She tries to rally. It's bad, but it's not as bad as it might be: it's not that he doesn't want her, merely that he's found someone else in the meantime.

"Is it serious?" she asks, swallowing. Of course he's been snapped up. Just look at him. It is painfully obvious, now, quite how deeply she feels for this man. When they'd been seeing each other, she had been so insistent that she and Joseph remain casual and nonexclusive, but now the idea of him in someone else's arms makes her want to break somebody's nose.

Joseph toys with his pint glass. "I'm not sure. Maybe."

"Is it like it is with me? Is it as intense as it is between us?"

He flushes. She so loves that blush; it's like a glimpse at the boy underneath the polished, handsome man.

"Siobhan . . ."

"All right, all right, I shouldn't ask that. Fine."

Siobhan chews her lip. She can be hard-hearted, even unscrupulous if needed, but Siobhan would not steal someone else's man. Girl Code is important to her, perhaps one of the most important things: there's very little she wouldn't do for the women in her life.

Which means, if Joseph's taken, she has to accept it.

What a fool she's been. All these months without him, and for what?

"Friends, then?" she says.

He looks relieved, those broad shoulders sagging. "Absolutely. I'd really like that."

"Well, I'm in London again the weekend before Christmas. If you're around, perhaps we could see each other. As friends."

He narrows his eyes slightly. She raises her eyebrows back at him.

"I mean it," she says. "Just friends. I've no interest in stepping on someone else's toes."

But. Nor is she quite ready to completely let him go.

Jane

JANE'S THUMB HOVERS OVER JOSEPH CARTER'S NAME.

They've communicated a couple of times since the wedding, but they haven't seen each other for the last month and a half. It's just innocuous texting, the sort that Jane hates—conversation with no substance. *How are you? Doing good thanks, how's things with you?*

They may have said they were friends, but is this really friendship, this *how-are-you*-ing? If it is, she doesn't want it. She wants the whole of him, the smell of him, his arms around her as they dance. She has given up on fighting this feeling now. The pain of that wedding dance in September showed quite how futile it was to try not to love Joseph Carter; accepting the agony of it all has been a peculiar kind of relief. *Being a human is messy, Jane*, Aggie told her the other day. *No amount of rules can fix that. Sometimes you just need to let yourself feel something, even if it's ugly.*

Slowly, deliberately, Jane taps Joseph's name. The message she's drafted is waiting there: **Are you still on for dinner this evening? x**

They'd made the plan long before the wedding—they'd been talking about cooking after reading *To Lahore, With Love*, and Jane had mentioned her special chicken curry, the one she makes when she needs comfort food. He'd jumped on it. *You have to make it for me,* he'd said. *I'm inviting myself round for dinner, here, hand me your phone.* She'd laughed at his enthusiasm, told him it wasn't *that* special; he'd picked a date months ahead, so she had plenty of time to practice, he'd said. She'd relaxed—November was so far away. Cooking Joseph dinner would break all the rules she'd built to keep him at a distance, but she had plenty of time to find an excuse to wriggle out of it.

Perhaps he knew that she'd only accept if he picked a long-distant date. Far enough away that it felt safe. Jane has changed so much since *Comfort curry for Joseph* went into her diary—now the thought of *not* having that dinner is much more awful than the idea of cooking for him.

With a sudden intake of breath, Jane shifts her thumb across the screen and taps send.

She's so preoccupied staring down at her phone that when the bell tinkles above the door of the charity shop, Jane takes at least five seconds to look up and notice her old colleague Lou standing there, rolling onto the sides of her feet, looking uncomfortable.

"Hi," Lou says apologetically. "I didn't know how to get in touch with you except by turning up here, and . . . we need to talk."

"Oh," Jane says, glancing toward the back of the shop, where Mortimer is sorting piles of tatty paperbacks. "Sorry, you . . . you came all the way from London? To see me?"

Lou nods, pressing her lips together. "Would you like to go somewhere private?"

"I'm okay here," Jane says, suddenly a little afraid. Mortimer is a rather reassuring presence, and he's out of earshot anyway.

Lou twists her lip, glancing around. "Okay. I just . . . wanted to warn you. I wasn't sure you knew anyone else at Brays anymore, or that there'd be anyone to tell you. There's a rumor going round the firm. It's brought up—it's got people talking about . . . your departure. Again."

Please, just say it, Jane thinks, heart beating so hard she can feel it down her arms, down her legs.

"He's looking for you," Lou whispers. "I'm sorry. I thought you'd want to know."

The fear comes curling in like smoke. Jane grips the edge of the till so hard her fingers ache.

"Okay," she says shakily. "Okay. Thank you for telling me."

"You could come to London? Face him on your own terms? I'd have your back, you know, if that helps. Sorry, I know you hardly know me, so that probably doesn't mean much."

It actually means more than Jane can comprehend right now.

"Thanks," she says, her voice very small. "But I'll just stay here. I'll deal with it if it happens."

"I think that's what I came here to say, really," Lou says, pulling an apologetic face. "You're sort of . . . *at* the dealing-with-it moment, I think? I mean, won't he be able to find you here? You're not far from London."

Jane winces. That's not even the worst of it. Anyone who knows her well knows that Winchester is where she was born, and is the place where her mother died. It's why she came back here when it would have been far more sensible to go somewhere further afield if she really wanted to run away. She's just always felt a pull to this place.

She doesn't remember her early life here—all she knows is the village near Preston where she grew up with her father. He never speaks about Winchester; there is something illicit about this beautiful city, for Jane, and when she discovered that the Count Langley Trust had a charity shop here, it felt like fate. One of the very few pieces of Jane's mother's life that she knows about is that the Count Langley Trust helped her to plan her end-of-life care when she knew she was dying. Jane found the paperwork once, as a teenager, tucked away with the funeral order of service. She'd stolen the order of service—it was covered in photographs of her mother that she had never seen before, and she'd stared at them for hours, soaking in her mother's smiling face, her soft brown eyes so like Jane's own.

Jane could flee again. Leave Winchester. Go somewhere he wouldn't find her.

"No," Jane says aloud, her voice strangled now. "I can't leave here yet. Not yet."

There's Joseph, the dinner they had planned. And oh, Aggie; Jane's little flat; the taste of Josie's Café pancakes and the warmth of Pie-caramba . . . She can hardly bear the thought of leaving it all behind. She clenches her eyes shut. If she has to go, she'll go. But not yet.

BY THE TIME JOSEPH ARRIVES–PREDICTABLY LATE–THE flat is filled with the fragrant smell of slow-cooked spices and Jane is dressed in her silky cream Saturday dress, her feet bare, her hand wrapped around a chilled glass of tonic water.

"Hey, you," Joseph says, kissing her on the cheek.

She manages, through serious effort, not to swoon.

"Hi," she says instead, clinging to the sideboard. "Hello."

"I'm so sorry I'm late," Joseph says, bending to greet Theodore. "My mum was struggling with the bathroom door, and then I got a call from work about a USB port, I think someone's kid had stuck gum in it if I'm honest, but there was no convincing the managing partner of that, but, oh God, you didn't need to know that, I'm sorry, I'm a lit-tle . . ." He straightens up and leans his shoulder against her fridge. It groans slightly in protest; like most things in Jane's flat, it is old and rubbish, but in a charming sort of way. "Nervous. Things are feeling a bit weird between us, aren't they?"

"Well, yes, a bit," Jane says, fluffing the rice with a fork and avoid-ing his gaze. It's not like Joseph to babble; she finds it painfully en-dearing.

"That's my fault," he says, rubbing the back of his neck. His watch flashes gold under the kitchen lights. "I'm sorry. I should have been clearer with you from the start about what—what I was able to give."

"You never said to me that we'd ever be anything more than friends," Jane says after a careful pause.

She takes her nicest bowls out of the cupboard, and they clink in her trembling hands. It is excruciating to be talking about this. She wants to curl inward, can't bear to look at him. She runs her thumb across a chip on the edge of her bowl.

"I mean, when we met, you told me you had a boyfriend," Joseph says. There's something strange in his voice. "So, you know."

"I know. You never saw me that way. I understand."

"No, Jane, no, that's—that's not what I'm saying." His voice drops, and he reaches out a hand as if to touch her arm, then lets it drop. "I find it hard being just friends, too."

Her skin flushes hot. She risks a glance at him through her eyelashes as she begins serving their meal; his face is serious, and there's a bloom of heat traced across his cheekbones, a sure sign he's feeling something he's not saying.

"But that's all you have to give," Jane says slowly.

"Yeah. It's all I have to give."

The idea that some other woman holds the rest of him—it makes Jane feel desperate, wild, hateful. At least he's not told her a name. She knows, if he does, she won't be able to prevent herself from trawling through social media until she can track down the woman he loves more than her.

"Is that . . . okay? It's really up to you, Jane. If it's too much . . . you know, us hanging out together, being friends . . ."

"It's not too much." She smiles quickly. For a moment she considers a teasing, *Please, you're not totally irresistible, you know*, but she's really trying to stop lying where she can, and so she swallows it back. "I'm glad to see you."

"Are you sure?"

She can feel he's doing the head-duck, trying to catch her eye, and it makes her heart squeeze.

"I'm sure," she says. "Would you mind setting the table?"

She makes it through dinner without behaving oddly; she tears up once when fetching them both seconds, but her back is turned to Joseph, and if he clocks it, he doesn't say. But her emotions are all over the place after seeing Lou.

"Jane?" Joseph says tentatively as they finish the last mouthfuls of dessert.

It's a chocolate mousse; Jane's never made one before and she's not *totally* confident it won't poison them—all that raw egg white—but it tastes delicious, and frankly, death by chocolate sounds relatively appealing right now.

"Are you all right?"

Oh God, she thinks, the tears rising again. *Don't ask me that.*

She takes a sip of water; her hand is shaking so much that she spills a little on her plate.

"What is it?"

His voice is gentle. It makes it so much worse. *Why can't you just be awful?* she thinks. *Why can't you just be some awful, lying, womanizing cheat who never told me about his girlfriend, who let me think I was the only one?*

She'd take that. Right now, for a split second, she thinks, *I'd be your other woman. You wouldn't even have to lie to me.*

She pushes away from the table and stands as the tears return. Because this is who she really is: a woman who loves so hard she loses all her morals in an instant.

"Excuse me," she says, heading for the bathroom.

Joseph follows her, but to his credit, he doesn't try to reach out and touch her. When she closes the bathroom door behind her, she hears him lean his back against it and slide down to floor level. She echoes the gesture, dipping her head down between her knees and staring at the bathroom tiles. They're already spotted with fresh tears. She's crying hard but silently, the well-practiced sobs of someone who knows how to stay unheard.

"Jane, I'm so, so sorry," Joseph says, voice muffled through the door. "I didn't know how hard you'd . . ."

"It's not you," Jane calls out, though it is, it *is* him, she feels like it always will be. "There's some—there's some other things happening. It's all just become a little much, that's all." She reaches for the loo roll and blows her nose. "I'll be all right in a moment, really," she says, trying for a shaky smile.

There's a long silence on the other side of the door. "I really am so sorry," Joseph says.

The silence stretches on. The useless bathroom fan whirs on the opposite wall, a strand of cobweb caught in its teeth.

"I wasn't lying about going to the Hoxton Bakehouse to see you," Joseph says.

Jane goes still, tissue balled in her left hand.

"The story we cooked up, for how we got together? When I said I used to come at the same time every day because I hoped to see you there, because I thought you were beautiful?"

Jane presses her balled fist to her chest. There's a real pain there, as if her heart is truly breaking, and some absurd part of her brain tells her she needs to hold her chest in tight to stop it falling open.

"I wasn't lying. I wish I had been, really, because I'm not proud of that, but I wasn't lying."

"Is that why . . . is that why you started speaking to me?" Jane manages. Her voice is thick with tears. "Because you thought I was beautiful?"

"I thought you were . . . fascinating, really. I'd told myself there was no harm in looking. And then it just seemed like there was no harm in making polite conversation, either, and then it was such a relief when you said you had a boyfriend, because of course that meant you were off-limits, and I didn't have to worry about being tempted. And then by the time you told me the truth about the boyfriend . . . we were friends, then, and I thought it would just stay that way. I was so *pleased* with myself." His voice catches. "I thought I'd done it. I thought I'd made friends with a beautiful, smart, funny woman, and I hadn't tried to take her to bed."

The thought alone is enough to make Jane shiver.

"But here I am," Joseph says. "And all I want to do is open this door and take you in my arms and kiss you."

She hears a thud—his fist on the floor, maybe—and jumps, jolting the back of her head against the door. She closes her eyes and stays there, face lifted to the ceiling, head pressed back against the cool wood. She wants to save it all: the feeling of the tiles beneath her, cold against her dress; the tight wetness of drying tears on her cheeks; the sound of Joseph telling her he wants her.

"I made a promise to myself, Jane," he says, and she wonders if he's crying too: his voice is thick and low. "And, God, I want to break it for you. Why is this so *hard*?"

"I made a promise to myself, too," Jane says. She's trembling all over now, head to toe. "And I've already broken it. I said I wouldn't fall in love again, Joseph, and you've—you're . . . I can't *do* this. I can't do things by halves. I can't have you and not have you. I can't share you with someone else."

"Jane, don't." He's definitely crying now.

Jane thinks for a moment about opening the door. Letting him take her in his arms and hold her, see what their willpower could withstand.

"What are we meant to do?" Jane says quietly. "What do we do now? Can we be friends?"

"We're not doing too well at it right now," Joseph says, and that makes Jane laugh. "But I want to. I really want to."

She tries to imagine it. Book club meetups the way they used to be, coffees at Josie's Café, the messages she would wait one hour to respond to. She's been Joseph's friend and in love with Joseph for months. Why does that have to change now?

But it does have to, because she's told him now; he knows. They can't undo that tiny little fraction of a moment in September, the kiss that so nearly wasn't.

"I don't think I can be your friend, Joseph," Jane says, opening her eyes. "I can't do it. I'm sorry. If I did, I'd just be fooling us both. I'm not going to stop loving you."

He's silent for so long that Jane suddenly feels very alone here on the bathroom floor. As if she's just talking to herself, and Joseph was never really there.

"Okay," he says eventually. "Okay."

He takes a deep breath, and she hears him move. She turns compulsively toward the door, but she doesn't open it—she has to let him go or she won't let him go at all.

"Bye, Jane," he says. "I hope you know I . . ." He takes another breath. "I hope we'll meet again sometime, maybe. When we're both in a different place. When it's a better time."

Jane says nothing. They won't. Because she's leaving tomorrow. She decided somewhere between *I don't think I can be your friend, Joseph* and *I'm not going to stop loving you.*

The Outer Hebrides, maybe, or somewhere remote in rural Wales. A place where there is absolutely nobody, because then by definition there will be nobody with whom Jane might conceivably fall in love.

Miranda

MIRANDA'S NOVEMBER SLIDES BY IN A HAZE, AS IF THE weeks are happening to someone else. It's hard for the team to work with the bad weather; she's at home more than she'd like to be, rattling around the flat and trying to keep herself busy. Carter is resolutely cheerful, maybe even more charming than usual. He's making an effort. She still has those flashes of can't-believe-my-luck as she looks at him across a pub table or leans her head against his bare chest in bed, but they're rarer. The shine has rubbed off him a little, like the gold on cheap jewelry.

It's December now, bitterly cold, and there are Christmas lights strung haphazardly between the sycamores lining her road. She's filled the flat with too many decorations, determined to bring some cheer. Home late one afternoon from a day of Christmas shopping, while she's downing a pint of water in the kitchen, a garish reindeer falls off the fridge door and stabs her in the foot with its merry, sparkly horns.

"Oh . . . fuck! Bugger. Fuck fuck fuck!"

"Miranda!" Frannie says, popping her head up on the sofa. "Did you just swear?"

Miranda jumps. She didn't notice Frannie was there. "No," she says guiltily, and then pulls a face, still hopping on one leg. "Maybe. I spend all day with men who swear a lot, okay?"

Frannie grins. "Doesn't bother me, you're the goody-two-shoes."

That rankles, somehow. Maybe it's the winter chill sitting under the neck of her shirt, or the fact that she hasn't exercised all day, or the stinging pain in her right foot. But something snaps.

"Do you know what, Fran, I'm actually not a goody-two-shoes. Nobody over the age of twelve is, to be honest with you, but that's beside the point, what I'm saying is—I'm actually pretty badass. I live on my own, or I did before you two turned up uninvited, and I have a *great* job, which I love, which by the way involves doing really scary and brave stuff every day, and I have a lovely boyfriend." Her voice catches on *boyfriend*. She plows on. "I'm not the person I was when we lived together at Mum and Dad's, okay? I have a life of my own now. And you're eighteen, Fran. Maybe you should be looking to get one of those, too, instead of following Adele around and slobbing around at my place rent free."

Frannie's eyes widen with alarm. They look at each other in silence for a moment.

"Sorry," Frannie says in a very small voice.

Miranda sags, still balancing on one leg. "No, I'm sorry. I'm being horrible. It's this weather. It makes me Scroogey."

Frannie pulls herself up and twists to face Miranda properly, hugging a cushion against her chest. "Do you want us to move out?"

"No! No. I'm sorry. I just . . . Sometimes I feel like you guys can be a bit oblivious, and you talk to me like I'm some sort of . . ." She waves a hand, dropping her foot to the floor. "I don't know, a total loser?"

Frannie's eyes get even wider. "We don't think you're a loser. We don't think that at all! You should hear Adele telling people about your job. 'She's the only female tree surgeon in the county.' She's always showing off about you!"

Miranda gawps at her sister. "Are you serious?" She pauses, absorb-ing. "Also, that's not true, by the way."

"Oh my God, shall we like, clean more?" Frannie looks posi-tively panicked now. "Or cook dinner? Or . . ."—with growing horror—"pay rent?"

Miranda tries very hard not to laugh. She joins Frannie on the sofa.

"Maybe clean a bit?" she says, examining her sore foot. No blood—how disappointing. "And just appreciate that this is my space, and I sometimes want to have dinner with my boyfriend without being in-terrupted."

"Dinner," Frannie says with a significant look. "Got it. You guys do have dinner a lot, don't you?"

Miranda whacks Frannie with a pillow. "Eww," she says. "Surely you're way too young to know about dinner. In my head you're still twelve, Fran."

"I wish someone wanted to have dinner with *me*," Frannie says, earning herself another whack with the pillow.

They end up gossiping and belly-laughing late into the evening, and Miranda goes to bed more cheerful than she's been in weeks. It had felt good to yell at Frannie a bit, frankly. And it had also felt good to do something *nice* together, even if it was just chatting on the sofa with tea and biscuits and an increasingly large heap of blankets on their legs.

She gets into bed at eleven, wearing a hat and wooly jumper to withstand the chill. This is a late night by her standards, and they'll be starting early tomorrow, but she can't sleep. She stares up at the black-ness, thinking, thinking, thinking, not getting anywhere.

This happens far too often now. Miranda Rosso is a doer. She cracks on, she tackles things, she gets stuff done. She doesn't lie around *wondering*. But this business with Joseph just feels . . . untackleable. As in, there's nothing to tackle—there's nothing there, it's resolved, and yet she keeps coming back to that receipt. The unexplained breakfast. *My night;)* in the diary.

She scrunches her eyes shut, willing herself to sleep, but she's not even close to tired, and lying in bed seems to be making her less sleepy, not more. It's as if lately there's something electrical that starts sparking in her belly as soon as she turns off the light. Suddenly staying still is intolerable.

She gets up and clicks the light on, squinting at the brightness of the bare bulb. Her phone is plugged in on the floor by the bed, and she crouches down to flick through her apps absently. Her WhatsApp opens onto her chat with Trey; he's online, and she frowns, checking the time. After three in the morning.

She hesitates and then begins typing.

What are you doing up? Xx

Trey has become a solid friend these last few months. He's a reliable, comfortable sort of person; Miranda finds his pessimism rather charming, like the belligerence of a small, self-important terrier. When one of the groundworkers who dips in and out of the team called Miranda a *stupid bint*, Trey came to find her while she was eating her lunch and asked her if she was all right; when he wanted to work on his climbing, he came to her, not to AJ, and she was touched.

Doing stupid shit with AJ, of course x

Miranda smiles.

What sort of stupid shit?

He sends a photo in response. It's almost impossible to see what's going on, the image is so dark, but after examining the screen for a few seconds Miranda realizes she's looking down from the basket of a cherry picker in pitch blackness. The boom is extended, the way it would be if they were working right at the top of a tree.

?! Where are you guys?

Outside my mate Reedie's house.

And you're up in the cherry picker because . . . ?

Because Reedie wanted to see over the hedge into his neighbor's garden.

Miranda snorts.

In the dark??

Can't be doing it in the day can we? Someone would see us.

Another picture follows: this time the scene is lit by the bright beam of at least one headtorch. She can make out the top of a thick privet hedge and the line of what she suspects is AJ's leg on the bottom left corner of the photograph.

You okay? x

Miranda hesitates before replying.

Overthinking stuff. Can't sleep.

Need cheering up?

This is not a particularly Trey-ish thing to say, and Miranda stares at the message in surprise.

Yeah, that'd be nice.

Hold up then. With you in twenty.

What??

But he's gone. Miranda scrolls back up to reread the exchange but, yes, it still sounds like he's planning on turning up at her flat at three in the morning. She considers getting dressed, but instead she eats up the time by going back through the messages she and Carter exchanged around the time of Scott's birthday, when he went for that mysterious Central London breakfast. She starts to feel sick again, overhyped and trapped in her little bedroom.

A new message appears at the top of her screen, from Trey.

Open your curtains.

She gets up, realization dawning, and by the time she draws the curtains back she's already laughing. There they are, AJ and Trey, standing in the basket of the cherry picker, Trey clutching a beer, AJ glancing up from the operating panel. He's parked the vehicle in the road and extended its arm up so they're right outside her window.

"Oh my God," Miranda says in a low voice, shoving the window open. The broken blind clatters against the frame and she pushes it aside as she leans out to speak to them. "What are you two *doing*?"

"What does it look like?" AJ says. He's wearing jeans and a leather jacket, his spare hand tucked in his pocket, and even with only the light from her bedroom and the streetlights below, Miranda can see the amusement in his eyes. "Want a beer? Or a ride?"

"I . . ." Miranda looks down at herself. She really should have dressed. She's wearing a wooly hat, fuzzy pajama bottoms and a threadbare jumper with a thermal underneath. "Hang on," she says, ducking back inside to grab a hoodie and a coat.

Climbing out of her bedroom window is a lot harder than teenagers make it look in films. It doesn't help that Miranda's muscles hurt most of the time—a fact of life that she has long since come to accept—and this requires a fair amount of flexibility. She wriggles through, grabbing the bars of the boom lift's basket, and climbs up.

It's snugger than she expected with the three of them in here. She realizes, too late, that she left her phone inside, but actually it's quite pleasant to be out here in the nighttime fresh air without it. It's like leaving real life behind.

"Hi," she says, looking from AJ to Trey. "Where are we going?"

AJ shrugs and opens her a beer with his teeth. "Where do you need to go?"

She meets his gaze. He's wearing the expression he often wears when he looks at Miranda: something halfway between curiosity and devilishness.

"I need to clear my head," she says.

AJ nods once. "All right," he says, turning back to the platform controls. The boom begins to retract, and Miranda bumps into AJ as she steadies herself. The contact makes her skin hum. This tends to happen when AJ is nearby. She's learned to ignore it, to pack it away, but tonight for one rebellious moment she thinks about leaning into him. Deliberately, provocatively.

He would let her. He'd take the opportunity to lace an arm around her waist, perhaps, or press close to her body. She knows he would.

"What's with the nighttime adventure?" Miranda asks, shifting away from AJ as best she can in the space available. The wind is tugging at her hair; she tucks it more tightly under her hat.

"AJ needed cheering up, too," Trey says, and Miranda's eyebrows shoot up.

"*You* did?"

"What, you think pretty boys don't have feelings?" Trey says, and AJ shoves him.

The cherry picker is trundling along the street now. Miranda is pretty sure they shouldn't be driving an articulated boom lift here without some sort of special license, and besides, it's stupid for them all to be up in the basket like this—Jamie would always make sure they had a harness secured at the restraint point if they were up here. But as she swigs her beer, she's surprised to notice that she doesn't care. Miranda's buzzy and alive again, and it feels *good*.

She considers Trey's question. "I think he has feelings," she says, glancing toward AJ. "I just think they're usually the horny kind."

AJ snorts. "You think you've got me all figured out, don't you?"

"Pretty much," Miranda says, sipping her beer, letting the hops hit the back of her tongue and feeling her shoulders relax. There's something about a cold lager—it has all the best associations. Pub nights, heart-to-hearts, the times when she is most herself.

"Well, maybe I've got layers," he says, raising his eyebrows at her as he operates the controls. "What's the matter with you, anyway? Why couldn't you sleep?"

She teeters on the edge of telling him, but in the end, she can't quite bear to share it. If she tells them about the receipt, the diary entry, then she won't be able to pretend it's not happening any longer. And deep down she knows exactly what it'll sound like if she says it out loud.

"Just one of those days," she says, tilting her head to look up at the fairy lights as they trundle slowly through suburban Erstead. She could almost reach up and snag them, they're so close. Behind them the sky is deep, inky black—she can't see a single star.

"That man of yours?" AJ asks quietly.

She looks at him. With the streetlights to either side of them, and the soft glow of the Christmas decorations, he's golden. The tattoo on his neck catches under the lights: a branch working its way from his chest, its leaves just touching his collarbone. For a moment as they move through the glow of the Christmas decorations above them, that tattoo almost seems to be growing across the skin, tendrils reaching.

"You've gone quiet these last couple of months," AJ says. His head is tilted to the side; his eyes, as always, hold hers for a little longer than they should. "You're not being . . . Miranda."

"That's true," Trey says, staring out at the houses as they trundle past the sign that thanks them for driving carefully in Erstead. "You're mopey."

"Am I?" Miranda stares at them both; Trey keeps his eyes averted. She's genuinely surprised: she's been a bit down, that's true, but not so much they would notice, surely?

"Feels a bit like you're, you know . . . " Trey gestures with his hands, as if he's pushing something down. "Squashed," he finishes. "You're a bit squashed."

"Squashed?"

"Yes," he says firmly. "Yeah. That's it."

"Right," Miranda says faintly.

The houses are farther apart now, the detached type that sit back from the road, with long drives and those pointy metal spear fences that are a tree surgeon's worst nightmare. The wind bites Miranda's cheeks as she grips the ice-cold bars of the basket.

"I don't like it," AJ says.

There's a softness in his voice that makes it impossible not to look at him; Miranda's stomach flips. It's harder to ignore it now, the stomach-flipping, the eye contact, the way she looks forward to the bigger felling projects because it means working with him. She's been so careful—she's never let him in. And she won't. Not even now.

It's just getting harder, that's all.

"So me and Carter are having a bit of a rough patch," Miranda says with a shrug. "Everyone has those." She tries a grin. "If either of you had ever been in a serious relationship, you'd know that."

Neither of them laughs. AJ's gaze is fixed on the platform controls.

"I've had a serious relationship," he says eventually.

Miranda blinks. "Oh. Really?"

"He used to be totally whipped," Trey says, leaning back against the bars as the basket bounces. They're raising their voices slightly over the wind. "When we were at school, it was all about him and Mini. They were together until she went to uni. She left him because—"

"Trey," AJ says quietly.

Trey shuts up. Miranda looks between them; it's too hard to read their expressions in the darkness.

"Why did she leave you?" Miranda asks.

AJ huffs, a sort of sigh, a half growl. He looks out at the fields that are beginning to open up beyond the last of the streetlights. There's no other traffic—nobody else who's dumb enough to be driving around rural Surrey at almost four in the morning.

"She wanted some smart, rich guy. She thought she'd find that sort of bloke at uni." AJ shrugs a shoulder. "Married a banker in the end, so I guess she got what she was after."

Miranda stares at the back of AJ's head, thinking of how he plays up the rough, tough-guy thing: always in dirty jeans, always flexing those biceps, always checking out women.

"Then what happened?" she asks.

"Then I realized there was a whole world out there," AJ says, shooting her a smirk over his shoulder.

But Miranda knows him better now. She knows that smirk is his favorite tool when he's deflecting.

"Did she break your heart?" she asks.

Trey shifts between them. The silence stretches out, shaky, unsound, the sort of quiet that almost makes you wince. She shouldn't have asked the question, it's too personal—they don't have this sort of friendship. She's made sure of it.

"You might say that, yeah."

Miranda's not sure what she's more surprised about: the idea of AJ having a broken heart, or AJ telling her about it.

"I'm sorry," she says. She swallows. "Is that why you sleep around so much?"

"Miranda," AJ says, and there's an edge to his voice now. "I haven't slept with a woman for almost a year."

This stuns her into momentary silence.

"What?" she says.

AJ takes a corner too abruptly; the three of them are thrown together, Trey's elbow in her gut, AJ's back against her side. By the time they've moved apart again, AJ has arranged his expression into one of blank indifference.

"Why have you never . . . You always . . ." She looks back at Trey. "Everyone says you're a total womanizer!"

AJ snorts. "Trouble with *everyone* is they don't check in too often for updates. I slept around a lot in my early twenties, yeah. But not now. I'm done with that."

"But . . . but you're always hitting on me!" Miranda says.

"Yeah," AJ says, and his lip twitches. "I know."

"So what, that's . . . just . . . teasing?"

Trey leans back with a groan, looking up at the night sky. "I'm not drunk enough to witness this conversation."

Miranda looks between him and AJ, nonplussed. AJ rolls his eyes slightly.

"No, Miranda, that isn't just teasing."

"So you—so, sorry, you do want to sleep with me, or you don't?"

AJ starts to laugh. Miranda watches him, the dark trees behind him bobbing a little in her vision as the basket bounces.

"I want to take you out for a drink," AJ says, swiping the back of his hand across his mouth. He catches her gaze and holds it. Completely obvious and flirtatious. But maybe . . . *not* something he does with everyone? "I've never asked for anything other than a date, have I?"

Miranda opens and closes her mouth, gripping the bars of the basket behind her. Trey is still staring up at the sky, pretending to be somewhere else, presumably, and she feels like kicking him into action, asking, *Are you seeing this? Are you hearing this?*

The cherry picker begins to slow. On autopilot, the three of them brace themselves to one side as the basket weaves in the air and AJ parks them up on the side of the road. As he kills the headlights, they're plunged into full-on, thick-as-velvet darkness. The stars are visible now they're away from the streetlights: endless silver pinpricks, like shining poppy seeds scattered across the sky. The cold wind catches at the back of her throat as if she's swallowed ice. Trey and AJ are just shadows now; she could almost pretend they weren't there at all, and that she was floating here in the sky.

"All right?" AJ says.

He's touching her; just a hand on her elbow. Two fingers at most. But it feels decadent, delicious, and it takes all of Miranda's willpower not to lean into his touch. She's not floating now. She's *here*.

"Yeah, all good." She doesn't lean in, but she doesn't move away—it's AJ who drops his hand. "Where are we? What are we doing here?"

"Night climbing," AJ says. "I've got spare kit you can borrow."

"That's all kinds of bad idea," Miranda says, but her heart's already beating faster at the thought. She's never climbed at night. "What about tie-in points? Setting lines?"

Trey turns on his headtorch and Miranda flinches at the sudden light, shielding her eyes with an arm.

"Oops," Trey says. "Sorry."

He turns to examine the trees beside them, his beam dashing against the bare, wet branches. It's windy, too; the leaves are rustling like wrapping paper. Not a great day for climbing even if in the light.

"We brought the cherry picker so we could check it all out before we go up," Trey says, nodding his headtorch toward the branches. "It's all very health-and-safety."

Miranda snorts, but she's flexing her hands already, rolling her shoulders. Suddenly she wants a climb more than anything. This may be stupid, but it's *exciting*. It's been a long time since she's felt properly excited.

"Here." AJ hands her a headtorch. "Just take a look. You decide if you want to climb. If you do, you'll be in my helmet."

Their hands touch as she takes the headtorch.

"What about you?" she asks.

"Famously hardheaded," he says, flashing her a quick smile that Trey's torchlight catches head-on. "I'm all for risk-taking, but I like that brain of yours."

He lifts a hand and touches her hair underneath her hat, just by her ear. His hand is gone in an instant, but still, her body buzzes.

IN THE END, MIRANDA BORROWS TREY'S KIT—AFTER IN-sisting on going first, then making six failed attempts to get his main line round one of the lower branches in the dark, he declared himself *too drunk for all this business* and clambered out of his harness in an ungainly fashion, passing it to Miranda. He's now settled in the cherry picker's basket, using his headtorch to track their movements and give them a little more guidance when they need it.

She and AJ climb the same tree, each taking opposite sides. Miranda goes slowly, painfully so. It's been a while since she's done a climb without the weight of the chainsaw on her hip, and for the first ten minutes or so she's off balance as well as half-blind. She's had a beer, too—only one, but still, it's numbing her edges, and her reactions are definitely a little slower than they should be. That said, though, without that beer she would probably be too sensible ever to attempt climbing in the dark.

The problem is the tie-in points. It's hard enough getting a rope clean over a branch in the daylight, let alone when the branches above are a mass of gray-blackness against the sky. Everything takes at least five times longer than it would normally. But it's fascinating how it changes the climb: she feels everything more, the bark against her knees, the rope burning on her palm, and she's listening to the tree, its heaves and groans, its closeness. She is completely focused. No thinking, no wondering, no obsessing about Carter. Just climbing.

"Stop here?"

AJ is closer than she expected. They're both near the trunk, and she's lost all sense of how high she's climbed, but it feels as if the tree is thinning out, nearing its canopy. It's later than she thought, or earlier, rather—between the branches, behind AJ's shoulders, there's a sliver of pink on the horizon.

"Yeah." She's breathless, chest heaving. It's only now she feels the sting of all the grazes on her arms and legs. Her pajama trousers are ruched inside her harness and one arm of her hoodie has slid up; her headtorch beam catches blood on the sleeve from one of the deeper cuts on her forearm. She maneuvers over toward AJ, who's shifted himself into a seated position on a branch that's almost horizontal, and then fixes her main line so it's taking a little of her weight. With her flip line around the tree's trunk, she's as secure as she can be. She breathes out, reaches up, and turns off her headtorch.

AJ's is already off, and the effect is instantaneous. Out blinks the light, and for a moment there's just dizzying blackness, an absence; she reaches out blindly to grip the tree trunk beside her as if she's falling in the sudden darkness. Then her eyes begin to adjust and reality creeps in as the world comes back into focus. It's not nearly as dark as she'd thought it was. Between the black twigs scratching across the sky, the horizon is a soft streak, and the woods around them are charcoal gray, lightening by the moment.

"We should get down, get to work," Miranda says. Her voice is a little rough from calling to AJ as they climbed. "At least the adrenaline'll mean we're not tired."

AJ smiles. She can see him, just about: the shape of his bearded jaw, the shine of his eyes.

"Always looking on the bright side," he says. "We've had no sleep?"

Miranda laughs. She should be worrying—she's *never* turned up to work after no sleep; that would be madness, and it certainly isn't safe. But she is full of the buzz of the climb, and up here in the oak she feels more at ease than she has in weeks.

"Jamie's going to kill us," she says.

"Bet this is nothing on the stunts he pulled in his day. Besides. I back you. Coffee on the way over there and you'll be as on-form as ever."

She watches him as he stares out toward the approaching dawn. It's strange to think that comments like these—*I back you, as on-form as ever*—might not just be flattery after all.

"I thought I was just a game to you," Miranda says eventually, turning back to the horizon. Already the sky is shifting from pale gray to a light, wintery blue, and that thin pink streak across the horizon is deepening to magenta. "All the flirting and stuff. I thought you just liked the challenge."

"Maybe at first," AJ concedes after a moment. "But maybe not. Maybe not even then. I knew you were someone special the moment I met you, to be honest. You're just like . . . you're not even capable of being fake. You're completely yourself. Also gorgeous, obviously, which helps."

Miranda's breathing faster again. She rubs her palm lightly against the tree bark beneath her, letting it rasp against her skin.

"I get it, though." He glances sideways at her for a moment. The dim light turns the green of his eyes misty and grayish, like lichen. "I guess I don't know how else to be. I don't do . . . serious chats with women."

"You're doing one right now," Miranda points out.

"Maybe I've got to be sixty feet in the air, then."

Sixty feet? Miranda glances down, but she can't make out the ground beneath them. No matter how experienced a climber you are, you never quite get used to that feeling of looking down, the sudden shift of perspective, the moment when your brain is told, *This is dangerous.*

"Can't be that," Miranda manages, fixing her gaze on the horizon again. "You've talked shit at sixty feet plenty of times."

AJ laughs.

"I don't know whether it's all that much better, you know," Miranda goes on. "That you actually liked me when you were hitting on me. I have a boyfriend. The nice-guy thing to do would be to realize I'm off-limits and behave yourself."

"Yeah, well," AJ says. "I never claimed to be a nice guy."

"Don't do that."

He looks at her inquiringly.

"The whole 'I'm just a bad guy' cop-out thing. Take responsibility, AJ. You *are* a good guy, you know you shouldn't flirt with me when I'm not single."

He pauses, thinking. "Maybe," he concedes. "Maybe I know that. But I don't think I crossed a line."

Miranda's eyebrows go up. "You don't? So you'd flirt like that with another woman if we were together?"

"No," AJ says immediately, and then winces. "Uh. Well. I'm not sure that's the same, but fine, all right. It's just that man of yours doesn't make you happy, and I *would*."

Miranda tightens her grip on the branch beneath her, letting the bark bite her palms.

"AJ," she begins, though she doesn't quite have the energy to stop him.

"Tell me." He shifts a little closer to her, and she can feel the heat of his body beside her. "Does he love you as you are, or does he want you to be somebody else?"

The word *love* throws her; it's like being winded. AJ isn't saying he loves her, of course he isn't, but . . . just the word in his mouth feels significant. She's always imagined he would sleep with her and then ditch her. Whenever she's imagined anything, which is as little as she possibly can. She shoots a glance at his profile; it's light enough now that she can see the scruff of his beard.

"I actually think Carter does . . . like me as I am," Miranda says eventually. After all, she and Carter have never said *love*. "I don't think he necessarily *gets* me, but he doesn't try to change me." She breathes in deeply; the air smells faintly smoky, that wintery morning smell. "I think it's me, really. Maybe I don't take *him* as he is as much as I should, you know, maybe I have too clear an idea of how he should be in my head. My grown-up guy who's got his life all sorted. And really he's . . . human, I guess."

She glances down. It's definitely borderline morning now. And she definitely needs to stop talking before it all comes spilling out, the way she just can't trust Carter anymore, the fact that she doesn't know how she can ever get that trust back.

"We have to go, AJ," she says. "We need to get down and get to work."

"We do," he says comfortably, making no movement. "I kind of want to stay here, though. Don't you?"

Miranda pauses for a long time before she answers. She hasn't ever encouraged AJ. Not once. Not a word, not a look, nothing. Right now, sitting here as the sun rises over the woods, with the real world below them, with AJ beside her, she so desperately wants to.

But Miranda Rosso isn't that woman. She's committed to Carter, for all the trust issues, and she likes AJ too much to string him along.

"Look, AJ," she says. "You need to know that nothing will ever happen between us." She swallows. "I'm sorry. I just don't want you hanging around waiting for me when I'm never going to show up, you know?"

"Right," AJ says quietly after a moment. "Well. That's that, then."

It's the right thing to do. Miranda's sure of it.

It just doesn't completely *feel* like the right thing to do, that's all.

WORK IS *HORRENDOUS*. JAMIE TAKES ONE LOOK AT THE three of them when they arrive ten minutes late—pretty impressive, considering—and his face goes thundery.

"Water, all of you," he says. "A pint each and whoever throws theirs up does the worst of the heavy lifting."

They all hold their water, thankfully, though Trey looks like he might well have thrown up a little in his mouth. He definitely fares the worst—he'd been steadily drinking while AJ and Miranda were climbing. At one point he drops a log perilously close to Miranda's foot and Jamie lays into him so loudly the client comes out of her house in her nightie to see what all the commotion is about.

When it's finally over and Miranda gets back to the flat, there are flowers waiting for her on the doorstep. Red carnations, rose hips and eucalyptus leaves, all bound in scarlet ribbon. The note reads, *To bring some brightness to your week! With love, Carter x*

She carries them inside and puts them in a pint glass, and then, very suddenly, as she places the bouquet in the middle of the table, she starts to cry.

"Mir!" Adele says, poking her head around the bedroom door. "Oh my God, are you *crying*?"

She's even more shocked than Frannie was when she caught Miranda swearing.

Miranda wipes at her face hurriedly. "No, no, I'm fine," she says, but her voice is thick and it's *so* obvious.

Adele comes up behind her and closes her arms around Miranda's waist in a backward hug. Miranda pauses, one hand on Adele's wrist, touched by the gesture; it makes her eyes prick again, and she breathes out in a frustrated groan, breaking away from Adele to reach for the kitchen roll so that she can wipe her face.

"Where's Fran?" Miranda asks. Having *both* her sisters seeing her crying feels like too much humiliation for one day.

"She's at a job interview," Adele says, and Miranda spins to look at her. Something in her expression makes Adele burst out laughing. "Don't be *so* shocked," she says, heading for the kettle. "Frannie's always been the go-getter of the two of us, hasn't she?"

"No?" Miranda says, and Adele sniggers. "Oh, you were joking."

"Yeah, I'm teasing, but I am proud of her. She just went and did it all on her own!"

Something in Adele's voice makes Miranda wonder if the joke went a little deeper than that. If you're always the twin who does everything first, it must feel strange to see your sister head off and do something you've never done yourself.

"Why the crying?" Adele says. "I assume you want a tea?"

Miranda shoots her an of-course-I-do look and makes for the sofa. She collapses back on it with a sigh. Has she ever been this tired before? The backs of her eyes feel like sandpaper and there's a dull ache in her limbs, as if she's got the flu.

"It's been a very long day," Miranda says.

"You can talk to me, you know," Adele says.

Miranda props herself up on one arm so she can see her sister. Adele's busying herself making tea, but there's something contained about the casualness of it all, like she's putting it on a little. Miranda wonders if she and Frannie had a chat about Miranda's meltdown post-reindeer-to-the-foot yesterday.

"Thanks," Miranda says, lying back, and then she thinks about how good it felt to laugh with Frannie. "If I tell you something," she says, "will you promise not to tell anyone? Other than Fran, obviously, and you'd have to swear her to secrecy, too."

"Of course," Adele says. "Totally. I'm really good at keeping secrets now."

Miranda smiles wryly up at the ceiling. The *now* is in reference to the fact that when they were children, Adele was responsible for tattling on everyone, even Dad when he snuck a cigarette on the back step.

"I really like Carter," Miranda says after a moment. Adele places their teas down on the table and nudges Miranda's feet up so she can slip in under them, pulling Miranda's legs onto her lap once she's sitting down.

"Right, okay?" Adele says. "That's good?"

Miranda has her concerns about whether this heart-to-heart is going to work out. She closes her eyes for a moment and it almost hurts, how good it feels, but she doesn't want to sleep. If she goes to bed her mind will start racing again.

"You really like Carter, but . . . ?" Adele says.

"But," Miranda says. "But . . ."

"But," Adele says, very seriously, and suddenly Miranda starts to laugh. They've said the word too many times now; it's sounding ridiculous.

"What! What! I'm listening!" Adele protests. "I didn't mean, like . . . *butt*, I just meant but!"

Miranda pulls her feet up into her chest, belly-laughing now, tears in her eyes. Adele whacks her on the shin.

"Concentrate! Tell me what upset you! Come on, I'm going to be super helpful."

Miranda sobers and lays her feet back in Adele's lap.

"I really like Carter, and he's perfect for me on paper."

"On *paper*," Adele says, and Miranda pulls a face.

"I didn't mean to go all *Love Island*," she says.

"No, no, you're speaking my language," Adele says. "I like it. Go on."

"But I'm scared. I feel like . . . I had in my head that our relationship was perfect. And it isn't." Miranda breathes out. "Even saying that feels awful. He's such a nice guy." *Is he? He is, isn't he?*

"But . . . ?" Adele looks at Miranda disapprovingly as a smile grows on Miranda's face. "No laughing! I'm serious. *He's such a nice guy* is not a whole sentence? Or, like, it's not a reason to be crying when he gives you flowers?"

"He's such a nice guy *but* I sort of feel like I don't really know him." Miranda presses a hand to her forehead, smile gone. "God, that's so ridiculous. We've been together for so long. Obviously I know him. But it's like there's this . . . locked door. And sometimes he shuts down. And with AJ . . ." She bites her lip.

"With *AJ*," Adele repeats, with great significance. "Pass the tea."

Miranda shifts with a groan to reach for their teas one by one.

"AJ from your birthday party? The tattooed sexy lumberjack?"

"We're not lumberjacks here in the UK, Adele, we're—"

"I *know*," Adele says with a slurp of tea. "I know what your job's called. Please. I just think he *is* a lumberjack. I mean, the man was basically wearing flannel."

Miranda opens her mouth to ask what *basically flannel* constitutes, and then thinks better of it.

"Well, yes," she says. "That AJ."

"He has none of these mysterious locked doors," Adele prompts. "Is that what you mean?"

Miranda thinks about this. That's not quite it. There are definitely unplumbed depths to Aaron Jameson.

"It's more like, with AJ . . . I know he'd give me the key."

Adele pauses, taking another gulp of tea. "That is so profound," she says. "So, like, Carter shuts you out?"

"Yeah," she says. "Yeah, that's exactly it. He's *actively* holding stuff back. Withholding stuff."

"Lying?" Adele asks.

"Yeah," Miranda says slowly. "I think so. Maybe. But . . . I can't work out why. I don't think he's cheating on me. I really don't think that."

"Right," Adele says, a little uncertainly.

"Okay, I think that *sometimes*," Miranda concedes. "But it doesn't . . . *feel* true."

"But a few things have made you *think* it might be true?"

The receipt. The diary entry. Mary Carter insisting that Miranda isn't really Carter's girlfriend; she means *the other one*.

"Yeah," Miranda says. "There are a few things. They're getting in my head. I've done so well at keeping AJ at arm's length. But now all the doubts about Carter have weaseled their way in and it's getting so much harder."

"Well," Adele says, cupping her hands around her tea mug. "Then you need to dig."

"Dig?"

"Get some more intel. Do some spying."

"On *Carter*? I can't spy on my boyfriend."

"Course you can. You need to take matters into your own hands, Mir. That's what's bothering you, that's what I reckon. You hate letting stuff happen to you. You need to *do something.*"

Adele sits smugly in the silence as Miranda stares at her, open-mouthed. That's *exactly* it. How did Adele know?

"I'm a genius," Adele says. "You're welcome. You can make me another tea if you like."

Siobhan

"TOO SLUTTY."

Siobhan chucks the boots behind her and reaches for another pair.

"Too try-hard."

"These?"

"Too *Oh, I just stepped off my boat.*"

"Specific. Okay. These?"

"Too young for you."

Siobhan gasps in mock outrage, pressing a hand to her heart. Marlena sniggers.

"Are you having fun?" Siobhan says, reaching for her favorite pair of brown boots with the three-inch heels. There's a reason she always ends up in these.

"Yes?" Marlena says. "Was that not clear?"

Fiona enters, blaring "All I Want for Christmas Is You" on her phone and holding a tray of steaming mugs. Her signature Baileys hot chocolate. Siobhan closes her eyes as she breathes in the smell; nothing says Christmas more than a Fiona hot chocolate. Siobhan always tries to replicate it at her parents' house on Christmas Day, but it never comes out the same. There's some magic Fiona-ness in there, some essence of best friend.

"Still packing?" Fiona says, gawping at the mess of clothes on Siobhan's bed. "You *can't* be taking all that."

Fiona packs infamously lightly—she is one of those people who decant shampoo into special small travel bottles instead of buying new toiletries, and by the end of a holiday she will have worn everything she's brought at least twice. Siobhan likes choice. And she does not rewear, that's a given.

"I need a lot of outfits," Siobhan says, settling down on the end of the bed with her mug of hot chocolate. "I don't have a clue what this trip to London is going to involve. I need a possible meeting-his-friends outfit, I need a first-almost-proper-date-night outfit . . ."

"Do you?" Fiona says. "Isn't this a specifically *not*-dating event?"

"Well, it is as far as I know, if this other woman is still in the picture," Siobhan says, sifting through dresses piled on the bed. "But it's best to be prepared."

"That's the spirit," Marlena says, hips starting to waggle to the music. "You go get your man, Shiv."

"Marl, careful, you'll spill it," Fiona says.

Marlena gives her a withering look. She once jumped in a pool while holding a glass of champagne and didn't spill a drop.

"I think it's great you're giving him another chance," Marlena says, sipping her hot chocolate mid–dance move. "You've not had a proper relationship since Cillian, and that's weird. You are a relationship person."

"Thanks, Marl," Siobhan says dryly. "Though this is strictly friends, please remember. I am *not* 'giving him another chance.' Fiona's not had sex in about seven years—can't you start on her?"

"Oh, believe me," Marlena says through a mouthful of hot chocolate, "she's next in my crosshairs."

———

BEING WITH JOSEPH CARTER IN THE DAYTIME, OUTDOORS, is quite surreal. Like going into a nightclub with all its lights up or seeing a photo of a dog in the driving seat of a car.

As they approach the enormous Christmas tree in Covent Garden, they're pushed together by two groups of passing tourists, and Siobhan's hand brushes Joseph's. She's touched this man countless times, in countless ways, but somehow the contact of their gloved hands here in this crowded square is just as intimate as anything they've done in bed. Siobhan shivers.

"Totally overrated," she says, clearing her throat and looking up at him. They're discussing their relative opinions on New Year's Eve, which, in all her twenty-eight years, Siobhan has found to be absolutely, reliably crap.

"No!" Joseph says with horror, as they dodge a small procession of children on a school trip, all wearing neon rucksacks. "Who doesn't like New Year's Eve?"

"Umm, everyone?" Siobhan says. The cold is making her cheeks ache; she's probably horribly pink and blotchy, and she's wearing far too light a foundation for this, but she really doesn't care.

It's been such a wonderful day. Christmas shopping and hot, strong coffees from cool cafés; people-watching on benches and pausing to listen to buskers singing Christmas songs.

"What do you do to celebrate? Maybe that's where you're going wrong," Joseph says.

"I've tried everything," Siobhan says as they step into the covered market. A waft of cinnamon and apple emanates from a fancy cosmetics shop, and the window of the shop next door is filled with stacks of macarons in every pastel shade. "Dinner party with close friends, massive rave, fireworks on the rooftop, house party . . ."

"Massive rave?" Joseph repeats, examining Siobhan with mild surprise.

"Sure. I rave." She raises an eyebrow at him, and he laughs.

"I'd love to see that," he says, and she snorts, as if to say, *You'd be so lucky.*

"So where will you be spending New Year's?" she asks him. It feels absurdly good to walk beside him like this, to have a whole day of him. It's pure indulgence—chocolate ice cream, expensive red wine.

"Scott and I are going to a party organized by the charity he works for—it's this massive gala thing at the Grange, near Winchester," Joseph says. They idle along, shifting through the crowd, window-shopping. It's the least focused activity Siobhan has taken part in for quite some time, and she doesn't even mind the lack of purpose—it feels good just to roam with him. "It looks like some kind of Greek temple, this place, but once you get inside, it's all bare plaster and boards. It's really amazing—a friend of mine got married there last summer."

We are talking about weddings! goes some part of Siobhan's brain, the way it always does when a man mentions this topic, and she cannot silence it, no matter how much she tells herself she doesn't even believe in the institution of marriage. That particular social norm is just in too deep. She blames the beloved romantic comedies of her childhood.

"Sounds incredible," Siobhan says.

There is a pause. A gaggle of teenagers push past, mid–heated discussion about Kanye West; a toddler wails, hands in the air, and is scooped up into his dad's arms. "Jingle Bells" blares out from a boutique selling handbags a few paces ahead of them. The absence of an invitation to this amazing New Year's Eve party is deafening, louder than all of these things, and Siobhan smiles wryly down at her feet. A useful reminder not to get too carried away. After all, they're just friends.

———

THEY GO OUT FOR DINNER THAT NIGHT, TO A DINGY, EX-pensive restaurant in Soho. The waiting staff are overly jovial for Siobhan's taste, but the food is great. Joseph seems different—he's laughing a bit too loudly, talking a bit too much—and after a while Siobhan comes to the heart-melting conclusion that he's actually a little nervous.

Siobhan is finding the opposite. Somehow the removal of sex from the equation has actually made this infinitely more relaxing. It hadn't occurred to her that she could just hang out with a man she has feelings for, without the pressure of romance. She figured hookups were the smartest way to make a relationship work because it takes the good bit (sex) and leaves all the fuss (the rest). Today has been a revelation.

"So come on," Siobhan says, a glass and a half of wine down. "Since we're just friends, we can be honest, right?"

"I was honest before," Joseph says mildly, and Siobhan laughs.

"No, you weren't. Nobody is when they want to sleep with someone."

Joseph blinks at her through his ridiculous round glasses. It is a sign of how truly smitten Siobhan is that she doesn't even want to take him shopping to replace them. The fact that such a handsome man wears such poorly chosen glasses is a great mystery, and undeniably endearing.

"I'll start. I pretend to take all my makeup off at bedtime, but if you're there I leave my eyebrows on."

After a surprised pause, Joseph laughs. "Your eyebrows?"

"Yes." She waves a hand at her face. "These are a carefully constructed act of deception. I am actually almost eyebrowless. Horrendous overplucking in the early noughties. I blame Britney Spears."

"I feel like I understood less than fifty percent of what you just said," Joseph says. "But your eyebrows look great to me."

Siobhan rolls her eyes, sipping her wine. "That is my point exactly, but sure. You go."

"Well. Umm. I definitely pretended to be less into you than I was, I guess."

Siobhan wasn't expecting that one. She holds Joseph's gaze over the rim of her glass, watching the tantalizing flush of his cheeks, that sign that he's not quite in control of himself. It makes her want to lean across the table and kiss him slowly, the sort of kiss that would be scandalous in a place like this.

"Why the hell would you do that?" she asks instead.

Joseph fiddles with the menu. "You made it very clear you wanted something casual. I didn't want to come on too strong and scare you off."

Siobhan bristles. "I don't scare easily."

Joseph looks up at her with a slight smile and waits. She rolls her eyes again.

"Fine, I scare a little."

"You did ghost me for months just when things started getting really good," he points out, and the charm is back in his eyes, that vulnerability tucked away again.

That wasn't because you liked me too much, Siobhan thinks. *It was because I was starting to really like you.*

"All right, moving on. What are your pet peeves in relationships? What really gets your goat?"

Joseph pauses in thought. "Noisy eating," he says. He shakes his head. "It's like nails down a blackboard for me."

"Noted," Siobhan says, wishing she hadn't just ordered spaghetti.

"This one might sound odd, but . . ." He presses his lips together, thinking. "I find women have this tendency to put me in a box."

Siobhan sets down her glass and watches him, head tilted. Now, *this* is interesting.

"What sort of box?" she prompts when he doesn't continue.

"I don't know, exactly. I think I come across as . . . I don't know, how *do* I come across?" He looks up at her, grinning sheepishly. "You're an expert on reading people."

Siobhan does like to be referred to as an expert.

"You come across as very polished, someone who has their life together," she says, tilting her head the other way. "Like a good guy. A good, solid, reliable guy."

"Wow," Joseph says, laughing. "Nothing sexier than solid and reliable."

"No, no, it *is* sexy," Siobhan insists. "Honestly, women love that shit. It's a nest of vipers out there. I'm sure there's some primeval stuff going on about wanting a guy who won't walk out of our cave as soon as they've impregnated us, or whatever." She winces slightly. "And anyway, girl or guy, people like to feel protected by their partner, don't they? They want someone who makes them feel safe, like nothing bad will ever happen to them when that person's around."

Their food comes, and for a while that takes their attention, but Siobhan is not to be so easily sidetracked.

"So the being-put-in-a-box thing, it's a pet peeve of yours?" she says, twisting her spaghetti around her fork.

"Oh, I don't know," Joseph says, looking down at his pizza. "I guess I just always feel like women want me to be something I'm not sure I can be. I'm really not perfect, you know?"

"Is that so?" Siobhan says.

"Do *you* think I'm perfect?" he says, and his gaze flicks up to catch hers for half a second before returning to his plate.

Siobhan thinks about his big, easy smile, the way he makes everybody comfortable, the way he's everything to everyone.

"Definitely not," she says. "And honestly, I think you should probably stop spending so much time trying to be."

His smile startles her. She'd expected that to rile him.

"That's what I like about you, Siobhan Kelly," he says. "You give it to me straight."

———

SIOBHAN AND JOSEPH END UP MEETING UP AGAIN ON Sunday for a brunch that slides into a lunch that slides into an afternoon tea. It is a genuine surprise to discover that they get on well. Siobhan has always regarded Joseph as a charismatic guy, the sort you can't help but enjoy spending time with—he presumably makes everybody feel that way. But it's not just that, she's sure of it. They *click*. He makes her forget herself, makes her laugh until she cries mascara down her cheeks, makes her feel like the world is infinitely brighter than she thought it was. The hours slip by and all the while she's wishing them back, wishing she could just have another few minutes with him, like a kid who doesn't want Christmas to end.

Now that he's gone and this fact has sunk in, it has of course terrified Siobhan, particularly given that she cannot have this man who was hers for the taking eight months ago.

"Fiona," she hisses into her phone, pacing back and forth on the strip of carpet between the bed and the television in her hotel room. "Fiona, it was *so nice*."

"That's great," Fiona says. There's a beat. "Isn't it?"

It's Monday morning and definitely too early to ring someone; Fiona sounds half-asleep.

"No!" Siobhan says, pressing a hand to her forehead. "I'm all . . ."

"A-fluster?" Fiona offers mildly.

"Eww, no," says Siobhan, a woman who does not do flustered. "I'm just . . ."

"Weak at the knees?"

"Will you stop that? I'm just *freaked out*. I let him in, Fi. Way in."

"All right, Siobhan, I don't need the graphic details," Fiona says, and Siobhan can hear she's trying not to laugh.

"Argh! Not like that!" Siobhan says. "Friends only now, remember?" This comes out somewhat bitterly. "But I think he knows I like him as more than that. I'm way too invested. I shouldn't have spent all weekend with him. He's got the upper hand now, hasn't he? And he's got a girlfriend, and I'm going to be friend-zoned forevermore, following him around like a puppy until he kicks me to the curb . . ."

"And then?" Fiona prompts. "And then you'll be sad?"

"No," Siobhan snaps. "Then I'll be angry."

"You seem angry already," Fiona says. "If you don't mind me saying."

"You are not helping!"

"That's because you're not making sense, Shiv," Fiona says gently. "Your plan was to just get to know him as a friend, right, and then if it ever developed into more . . . ?"

"Shh!" Siobhan says, because she has not specifically *articulated* this plan, and hearing it out loud makes her feel like a very bad person. "I don't want to steal him off someone or anything. I've not got a plan. There's no plan."

There is silence on the other end of the line.

"Hello?" Siobhan says. "Are you still there?"

"Yes," Fiona says carefully. "I'm just wondering why you *are* trying to be friends with this man you're in love with if you're not trying to . . ."

"Shh!" Siobhan says again, clapping a hand to her forehead. "Oh, fuck, I'm a planner, aren't I?"

"It's in your nature," Fiona says sympathetically. "I don't blame you."

"Right, well, this has been a disaster." Siobhan sits herself down on the bed. "I feel like I'm going to do something mad. It's sort of bubbling up in my belly."

"Don't," Fiona says. "Really, Siobhan. Just go to bed, get a few more hours' sleep before your flight. Don't self-sabotage, *please.*"

Siobhan bites her lip. Fiona has done so much looking after her this year. It didn't use to be that way: a year ago Siobhan would never have let anyone see her in the state Fiona's seen her, no matter how close a friend they were. Siobhan is the one who does the looking after. She's got too comfortable leaning on other people since her breakdown; she needs to toughen up again.

Her phone buzzes. She glances at the message.

Siobhan, it's Richard Wilson. I hope you don't mind me contacting you, I know we don't have a session booked in today but I could really use one. I don't suppose you have time to slot me in? Apologies for contacting you at short notice x

Richard, Blue Steel, of sex-on-the-desk. A client. Off-limits. And just the sort of callous, hard-hearted man Siobhan would usually take to bed, before she met Joseph. Shiny, polished, bad news.

Her body thrums. There's panic sliding under her skin, that horribly familiar sensation like lava running through her; she's primed to make a very bad decision.

She absolutely shouldn't reply to Richard right now. It's imperative that she retain complete professional boundaries with him, given her suspicions that he sees her as more than just a life coach. If she were at home, with Fiona in the next room, she wouldn't even consider it. But she's here, in a hotel room in London, and Joseph Carter belongs to somebody else.

I'm actually in London at the moment. I could meet you for break-fast? Best, Siobhan

RICHARD LOOKS A LITTLE SLIMMER THAN WHEN SIOBHAN saw him last, and it suits him—in his tailored blue coat and checked scarf, he is the quintessential silver fox. Siobhan stands and shakes his hand when he arrives; he leans in to kiss her on the cheek. He smells of overcomplicated, expensive cologne. The moment she feels his lips on her skin, Siobhan wishes she had not texted him back. This was categorically a terrible idea—she doesn't even want to see him. Why has she done this? Why does she do these things?

"It's good to see you," Richard says, and his hand lingers on her hip as they step apart.

She chose a neutral café close to the hotel: not at all romantic, very impersonal. But now that he's here, this does not feel like a usual session. She swallows.

"So how are you doing?" Siobhan says, sipping her tap water.

This morning has slid away from her, and there is a quiet pulse in her belly now, a knot of growing panic. She glances at her phone, faceup next to her knife and fork: there's a message from Fiona, a screengrab of the flights from Dublin to London on New Year's Eve. **How about it?! xxx** the message reads. The thought of Fiona makes that fearful sensation pulse a little louder in Siobhan's stomach; Fiona will be so disappointed in her. She wonders briefly if she could just get up and leave now—she's proven whatever point she needed to make to herself, hasn't she? She's shown that Joseph doesn't own her.

"Oh, Siobhan," Richard says. "There's a situation at work. And I really need to talk it through."

Siobhan relaxes slightly. This is comfortable ground. "Go ahead," she says.

"Remember we spoke about my secretary?"

"The one you're sleeping with?" Siobhan asks politely, gesturing a waiter over as she does so. She needs to make sure this is a coffee, not a breakfast.

"Yes. Her. Well, she . . . Look, she gave me this form, it's to do with issue proceedings, I won't bore you with the details, but the fact is it needs to be signed and filed by a very particular date. But we got a little, ah, a little distracted. And I did sign it, but if I'm totally honest with you, I didn't put it in the post tray for her to send it off. So it didn't get filed in time."

"So you're in some trouble?" Siobhan asks. "Flat white, please," she tells the waiter. It is not an oat milk day.

"Ah. Well, I *would* have been. I would have been. But I shredded it. The form, that is. And I told her she never gave it to me."

Siobhan stares at him, trying to formulate a suitably neutral, life coach response to this completely unacceptable pronouncement.

"Look, she won't lose her job, I'll make sure of that," Richard continues, saving Siobhan the effort. "And in some ways, it's sensible, isn't it, to have something she owes me for, you know? In case things between me and her ever get more complicated? An insurance policy."

Siobhan's patience, always thin, has worn away completely; this is her job at its worst. This man just proves himself to be more and more of a prick every time she meets him. He's set up the woman he's sleeping with so he has ammunition if he ever wants to get her fired? And he's here for, what, a bit of positive female attention now his secretary is presumably mad at him?

If she's doing her job properly, Richard will come to the realization that he has been a twat of his own accord—Siobhan fully believes this is the only meaningful way for Richard to effect change in his own life. But also, she'd *really* like to tell him he's an arsehole. For a moment she wishes she'd not insisted on absolute confidentiality with each client when she set up this contract; she'd been thinking of protecting the individuals she coached, making sure she wouldn't be required to "report back" to their employer. But now there's some poor woman whose job is at risk and she can't report Richard to his HR team without breaching her own bloody contract. She shifts uncomfortably in her seat.

"How are you feeling about that decision, Richard?" she asks eventually.

"Well," Richard says, and his tone is slightly wounded, as though the answer should be obvious. He tries to hold her gaze in that practiced way of his, the behavior of a man who has read *How to Win*

Friends and Influence People too many times. "It's complicated, obviously. I'm not saying I did the right thing. I came to you because I thought you'd listen, and we've had . . ."

Siobhan has that sense that a bad thing is coming, something looming and unpleasant that she won't be able to dodge.

"We've had a connection, haven't we? You and I?" Richard says, looking her right in the eye with a slight smile.

There it is. She swallows.

"I believe it was a mistake for us to meet outside of my office like this, Richard," Siobhan says. "I think in the future it's really important that we keep our sessions to the pre-agreed times and locations, okay? It needs to be clear that our relationship is an entirely professional one."

Richard frowns. "Come on, now."

"If you overstep any further, I'm going to have to say we don't meet in any capacity at all, Richard."

He looks at her appraisingly. She doesn't like that look. It's slow, calculating, the way a cat looks at something it would like to catch.

"All right, Siobhan," he says, in the tone of somebody humoring a child. It's a voice he's never used on her before. "Let's call time on today. But I look forward to seeing you again soon. After all, you know my secret now." He smiles slightly. "All the more reason for us to continue our sessions together, I'd say. I can't see myself with anyone but you."

CHRISTMAS PASSES IN A SOMEWHAT PAINFUL BLUR OF family gatherings and forced chatter. It's not that Siobhan doesn't get on with her family; it's more that they simply don't understand each other enough to be close. Her parents try their best to feign interest in what she does, but they're numbers people, mathematicians, and deep down she knows they think life coaching is a load of bullshit. They'd never say it, of course, but that's almost worse. Siobhan would prefer a nice healthy confrontation.

Her brother is ten years older than her, and they've never been particularly fond of each other; she spends Stephen's Day at his house, his children clinging to her limbs and demanding piggyback rides, making her heart ache with their little hands and their beaming smiles. She escapes so early it's definitely going to be considered rude. It will no doubt pass into the great family history as another example of Siobhan being flaky and getting too big for her boots.

She's back in her beautiful flat in Dublin for the day after Stephen's Day, which just so happens to be her birthday. Siobhan hates birthdays. She is not a fan of aging generally, and a celebration designed specifically to acknowledge the fact that she's one year closer to thirty—and, in fact, only one year away from thirty—is not something she enjoys. She's tried throwing enormous parties to distract herself in the past, but these days she prefers wine and ice cream with Fiona and Marlena.

"Ladies," she says to them as she and Fiona settle on the sofa and Marlena stretches herself out on the carpet, glass of wine beside her. "I have been doing some thinking over the Christmas period and I believe I may have a self-destructive streak."

"No!" says Marlena in mock surprise.

"Shut up," Siobhan says. "The question is, what do I do about Joseph? I've royally ballsed that whole thing up."

She gnaws at her lip, wrapping her hands around her wineglass to resist the urge to dig her nails into her palms. Her mental health is wobbling; she can feel the dread and self-disgust tugging at her edges.

She can hardly believe she met with Richard outside of working hours. It was so monumentally, intentionally stupid. And she didn't even *want* to see him. But it's been the wake-up call she needed. No wonder she broke down in April: her need for control, her inability to let people in, her tendency to act out if she's panicking . . . There was no way that could all continue to rumble on without it wrecking her.

She breathes in and out slowly. It's not too late to make a change. Hopefully.

"Look, Shiv, you've just got to decide how much you care about him being with someone else, basically," Marlena says. "If it were me and I really loved this guy, I'd at least have a shot at telling him, especially if he said things with this other woman were only *maybe* serious."

"Don't you think it's wrong?" Siobhan says. "I know we don't know her, but she's still a woman. She doesn't deserve that."

"If he's meant to be with you, he's meant to be with you," Fiona says after a moment. "You're not trying to seduce him. You're just telling him how you feel so he has the information to make a choice."

"As far as he knows, you guys were just hooking up, right? And he thinks you never liked him as much as he liked you." Marlena shrugs. "I think it's worth a shot, Shiv."

Siobhan reaches for the tub of ice cream on the coffee table, swapping it for her wineglass, and digs a spoon into the gooey softness at the edges of the pot. She can feel herself caving; perhaps she always knew she would. It is just so excruciating to think of Joseph out there settling for someone else, never knowing how she feels.

"Well . . . what about the New Year's Eve party?" She told Fiona and Marlena about Joseph's New Year's plan, partly because it sounded epic—that half-falling-down Grecian mansion—and partly because he really did seem to enjoy New Year's Eve, something she finds fascinating. "We were planning on being in London anyway, and it's not that far from there. I could surprise him. A grand gesture."

"And you'll tell him you . . . ?" Fiona asks.

"Love him?" Marlena finishes.

"Oh, fuck, do I?" Siobhan says with genuine panic, clutching her ice cream spoon tightly. "Shit. Shit, do I?"

The other two are trying not to laugh. Siobhan groans, leaning her head back against the sofa arm.

"I suppose I do." The thought makes her sweat. "That's terrifying.

Christ. But I'm so done with pushing good people away, I really am."
She sits back up and swallows a freezing mouthful of ice cream. "New
Year's resolution: don't fuck up my own life."

"Cheers to that," says Marlena, lifting her glass. "So are we coming
with you? To this party?"

"To pick up the pieces if he's in love with another woman, you
mean?" Siobhan says wryly.

"Umm, no. To celebrate the joyful moment when you win your
man back," Marlena corrects her.

Jane

JANE HOLDS HER PHONE UP TO THE BARE WHITE SKY, squinting against its brightness.

"Hello?" she calls. "Can you hear me now?"

The signal bar appears, disappears, appears again. Aggie's voice is tinny and stutters on the other end of the line, and the phone shakes in Jane's hands—she's freezing. Calls can only be taken on the hill above the cottage where she's staying in rural Powys; there's no signal anywhere else within walking distance, and she hasn't got the Wi-Fi sorted yet.

"I can sort of hear you," comes Aggie's voice.

She's yelling, as if that'll help with the signal problems. It's moments like these when their age difference really shows, Jane reflects with a smile.

"You sound a bit like a Dalek!" Aggie shouts.

Jane laughs. These conversations have been the highlight of every day this last month since she moved here, even though her toes are numb with cold in her boots and her cheeks are stinging in the wind. Jane has never been more grateful to have such a good friend. Christmas was bleak and lonely—she'd told her dad she was renting a cottage in Wales with friends, unable to bear the thought of lying about her life again for three days at her aunt's house in Preston, but she regretted it bitterly. On Christmas Day she missed her father in a new, visceral way, almost as if she'd lost him, too.

But Aggie's Christmas present had brightened the day a little, and now it hangs above the old metal bedframe in Rhosyn Cottage: a painting of Winchester, stylized in pink oil paint.

"Promise me you'll think about coming down for tomorrow night?" Aggie yells. "It'll be fun! Honest!"

The wind rips in Jane's ears. Her hair is tied as tightly as she can get it at the nape of her neck, but strands have worked their way loose nonetheless, and they whip her forehead and cheeks, trail into her squinting eyes.

"I'll think about it," Jane promises. "Bye, Aggie."

"Love you lots," Aggie yells. "Stay warm!"

Jane stays in the cold after Aggie hangs up. She is staring at her phone, the weather forgotten. Her eyes sting. Aggie has never said *love you* before.

JANE GLANCES OVER HER SHOULDER. THE YOUNG MAN behind the till looks away very quickly and blushes so scarlet that Jane can't help but continue to look at him, watching the color bloom on his skin and turn him an entirely different shade. It makes her think of that paint-stroke flush on Joseph's cheekbones, how it transforms his face from polished perfection to something even better.

Someone beside her chortles. It's an elderly lady who she's seen in the village shop a couple of times before: she has a fierce, pointed nose and ferocious frown, all somewhat undermined by the Winnie-the-Pooh-patterned glasses hanging on a chain around her neck.

"Just ask her out to dinner, Malcolm, go on, would you?" the woman calls to the man behind the till.

Malcolm turns an even more virulent shade of red.

"Oh dear," Jane says quietly, lowering a bunch of carrots into her basket. "Umm . . ."

"Gladys!" Malcolm barks. "Please! I don't . . . want to . . . bother . . . the nice lady." He looks as though he profoundly wishes he could unsay *the nice lady*, or perhaps just cease to exist altogether.

"It's Jane," Jane says, raising a hand. "Hello, Malcolm."

"Come on, New Year's Eve tomorrow!" Gladys says, lifting her glasses painstakingly slowly and then examining Jane more closely. "Hmm," she says. "Perfect night for a romantic dinner! You don't have plans, do you? You're staying up at Rhosyn Cottage on your own, aren't you—nothing to do up there except watch the red kites. Come down for dinner at Malcolm's. Go on, he's a lovely boy, I've known him since he was in nappies."

"Gladys!" Malcolm says again, gripping the edge of the till. "Please don't! I'm a . . . I'm a grown man! I can ask out women myself! I'm so sorry," he says to Jane, who is trying very hard not to smile.

"That's quite all right," she says.

"Well?" Gladys says to Malcolm, waving an arm. "Ask her, then!"

Malcolm is beginning to sweat. Jane takes pity.

"I'm afraid I have plans," she says. "I'm seeing a friend of mine."

Gladys narrows her eyes. Jane steps back slightly under the force of the elderly lady's glare.

"A male friend?"

"No, no," Jane says, though it occurs to her now that it would have been a better lie—she had just imagined Aggie as she said it. It's been a while since she's had to pretend to have a boyfriend; she's out of the habit. "A female friend. As in, just a friend."

"Coming here, is she?" Gladys says disbelievingly.

Jane pauses. Gladys seems very well aware of the fact that Jane is living alone at Rhosyn Cottage; Jane has a feeling that the absence of a second car at the property may not go unnoticed.

"Actually," Jane says, "I'm going to a party with her."

The sentence sounds ridiculous, and she feels in some vague way that they can tell this—that Malcolm and Gladys know Jane doesn't voluntarily go to parties—so she commits the cardinal sin of liars everywhere and keeps going.

"She does the styling for an event at a beautiful historic house in Hampshire. It's Grecian revival." Jane winces slightly. Gladys's face remains unmoved by the architectural credentials of the Grange; Malcolm, meanwhile, is slowly transforming from ruby red to white again. "Anyway, she gets free tickets as part of her payment, and apparently it's an amazing event, so I'll be going to that with her." She tries a smile. "I'm not usually one for parties, but you know how it is. I don't want to let down my friend."

Her stomach twinges as she says this. Here, it seems, is some truth. She *doesn't* want to let Aggie down, and Aggie sounded so proud when she talked about the indoor trees, the purple and blue uplighting on the rugged, tumbledown mansion, the sparkling ivy she had already hung for tomorrow's event.

Aggie has always been there for Jane. As she approaches Malcolm at the till, basket in hand, it occurs to Jane that being a good friend comes with responsibilities. She wants to show Aggie that she supports her. She wants to be there for her.

She loathes parties. All those people, all that noise, the fake laughter, the showiness. But. But.

She loves Aggie.

TRAVELING BACK TO WINCHESTER FEELS A LITTLE LIKE driving back in time. It's been five and a half weeks since she packed a suitcase, coaxed Theodore into his travel crate and said good-bye to the team at the Count Langley Trust charity shop. Mortimer hadn't seemed surprised that she was leaving with little notice, but he had teared up when he hugged her good-bye.

Back aching from the drive, Jane eventually parks up in front of Aggie's garage, in the car park they once bombarded with water balloons. Aggie's already standing in the doorway to the building as Jane climbs out of the car; she must have spotted her out of the window. Seeing her familiar, beaming face, her scatty red hair—it is almost painfully heartwarming.

"You *came*," Aggie says, ushering her inside.

Even just the smell of Aggie's flat, the combination of sharp, lime-bright perfume and the smell of recent vacuuming . . . it makes Jane's stomach clench. Oh, she misses Winchester. She misses home.

"Did you pack something to wear?" Aggie asks, already busy making Jane a cup of coffee.

She gets a little pot of cream out of the fridge, and Jane reaches for her friend's arm, stopping her mid-step.

"What?" Aggie says, looking down in surprise.

"You remembered," Jane says, looking at the cream.

Aggie grins. "What, how you take your coffee? Course I did, you ninny. It's only been five weeks. You thought I'd forget everything about you while you were gone, did you?"

It's more that Jane never imagined someone would care enough to notice those details in the first place. She lets go of Aggie's arm with a rather wobbly smile, and heads to her favorite spot on the ochre sofa.

"No, I didn't pack anything special to wear," Jane says. "Everything I took to Wales was quite . . . practical."

Thermals and wooly socks and fleeces. Not exactly appropriate for an enormous gala event at a falling-down mansion house. Jane's stomach flutters; now she's here, she's nervous, and not for the reasons she imagined. She thought she'd feel under threat, back in Winchester, given what Lou told her before she left. But whatever logic tells her, she feels safe here—Aggie's flat is somehow, in Jane's mind, an unassailable castle.

No, the nerves aren't about her London life catching up with her. They're about going to a *party*.

"Good," Aggie says. "I popped in to see Mortimer and Colin and they rustled up the perfect outfit for you yesterday. Colin was *very* insistent that I pass on the message of how much he and Mortimer are missing you, and he also said, hang on, let me get this right . . ." She purses her lips as she stirs the coffees. *"Don't say no to the push-up bra until you've tried it on with the dress."*

"Oh no," Jane says, taking the coffee from Aggie and pulling a face. "I don't think that sounds very . . ."

Aggie holds up a finger. "Colin has spoken!" she says. "Are you going to defy Colin?"

Jane hangs her head. "No, of course not."

They catch up over their cups of coffee. Jane doesn't have much to tell—not a great deal happens at Rhosyn Cottage, bar the odd mishap with the central heating. But Aggie does enjoy the story of Gladys and Malcolm.

"So that's what convinced you to come!" Aggie crows.

"It wasn't quite like that," Jane says, frowning—this feels important. "It was more they . . . they made me realize I *should* come. I want to see you, and support you, and . . ." Jane's chin wobbles again; she can't understand where all these emotions are coming from. "I'm sorry. I'm just very grateful to you."

"Oh, shut up," Aggie says. She pats Jane's leg. "Come on. Finish your drink and let me fairy-godmother you. And then, Jane Miller, you shall go to the ball."

THE DRESS IS A RICH GREEN SILK, TYING BEHIND JANE'S neck and ending just below the knee. It exposes a dizzying amount of skin: her arms, her shoulders, a great sweeping triangle of her chest. Colin was right—the effect of the push-up bra is slightly astonishing. It's been so long since Jane has worn actual lingerie, and it feels like total decadence, even if the bra is secondhand.

Aggie hands her some strappy shoes with a small heel; clearly Colin and Mortimer had a realistic idea of how competently Jane would manage to walk in high heels. She slips them on as Aggie rummages disparagingly through Jane's makeup bag.

"Most of this stuff is so ancient it's caked up," she says, holding a pot of foundation up to the light. "And you can't borrow my cover-up, it's so pale you'll look like you've come down with something. Good thing you have a natural glow, eh? At least you can borrow my mascara."

Jane manages to poke herself in both eyes and draw a black line on the left side of her nose in the process of applying said mascara, much to Aggie's amusement. In the end, Aggie takes over.

"Right. I think you're done. Finish up with a clear gloss on the lips?" she says, handing Jane a pearly pink tube. "There, you look beautiful."

Jane risks a glance in the mirror. Her reflection stares back with wide, serious eyes. She so rarely looks at herself, and when she does, she doesn't look like this. Aggie's right. She feels beautiful. Her eyes begin to fill with tears again and she breathes out in frustration, lifting her gaze to the ceiling.

"No crying!" Aggie says sternly. "Come on, think happy thoughts. Ponies. Puppies. Theodore shitting himself in pure abject terror when he sees a spider."

That makes Jane laugh.

"Better!" says Aggie. "Now, we should go. I need to be there early for finishing touches."

JANE SWALLOWS AS THEY MAKE THEIR WAY UP THE SWEEP-ing gravel drive toward the Grange. It's truly magnificent, like something out of a Greek myth; behind its pillars, the night sky is swirling black. It's a clear evening, and cold enough to make her eyes water.

Staff buzz around the mansion. Only five hours until this year becomes the next one. Aside from the dreadful obligation to go to parties, Jane has always rather liked the concept of New Year's Eve. Newness, a fresh start—these things appeal to her. For the first time in a long time, Jane is struck by the thought that she might not want to entirely leave this year behind.

"Don't be nervous," Aggie says firmly, raising a hand in a wave to a group of staff fiddling with the lights beneath the pillars. "You look gorgeous, you'll have me the whole time, we'll have fun."

"I don't want you to have to look after me," Jane says fretfully, smoothing down her dress. She didn't have a coat that went with her outfit, so she's gone without one; it's freezing, but she's had good training with all her hilltop phone calls to Aggie.

"I like looking after you," Aggie says matter-of-factly. "Why do you think I hounded you down until you became my friend? I'm a childless single woman in need of a project. Without you I'd have to take up knitting."

Jane snorts as Aggie shoots her a grin before turning to chat to the security man on the door. Jane happens to know that Aggie is profoundly happy with the life she's made herself, for all her jokes about knitting. It's part of what Jane admires about her. Jane finds the idea of being happily single quite amazing. She's only ever achieved lonely and heartbroken, really.

"This isn't enough of a project for you?" Jane says as they pass through into the mansion. "Oh, Aggie," she breathes.

It's like walking into a dark fairy tale. The building looked pristine from the outside, but inside it's been left tumbledown and artfully neglected. The plaster is half torn from the walls, exposing red brick; the ceiling is open to the floor above, its edges jagged, showing the broken ends of the beams that once held the second story in place. A fireplace is decorated in heavy wreathes of ivy and yew, and there are trees positioned around the space as if they've always been there, growing in the wreckage.

"It's stunning," Jane says, turning to her friend.

Aggie shrugs, but she's smiling. "It's easy when you work with a canvas like this. I hardly had to do anything."

She puts Jane to work shifting things infinitesimally back or forward, lighting candles, rearranging foliage. People are beginning to arrive when Aggie suddenly launches into one of her characteristically inventive swearing sessions.

"Titwank! Titwank!" she says, winding down. "The bloody sponsor banners!"

She dashes off deeper into the building. Jane follows, slightly perplexed. Along the back wall of one of the rooms, hidden in shadow, are three folded silver-white banners.

"Come on, we need to hang these somewhere. They ruin the décor but I've got to do it, they've paid for it, after all. Maybe in the armchair area, so they don't ruin the effect when people first walk in. I wonder if I can get away with that," Aggie muses as she unfurls the top banner.

Jane goes still. She feels as if someone has run icy liquid down her back, over her shoulders, slipping beneath the fabric of her dress. It's horror. Familiar and awful.

Bray & Kembrey, says the banner, in bold navy type, beneath the icon of an acorn. *Generous sponsor of tonight's fundraiser.*

"Aggie," she says, backing away. "I can't be here."

"What?" Aggie looks harassed, her hair jumping out of its bun. "Would you carry the other banners, please, just those ones there?"

But Jane is already turning. She's already running.

"Jane!" Aggie shouts.

"I can't," Jane calls, voice catching in her throat. "I'm so sorry."

She flies back through the party, between bodies; there are already so many more people here than there were ten minutes ago. Heads turn toward her. Everyone's uplit in Aggie's purple and blue lighting—they look horrible, nightmarish, looming at her through the dark.

She forces herself to slow. Her heart is like a fist pounding on her chest. She's not come to the front entrance, she's made a wrong turn—but there's a door, and she begins to run again once she's through it, down an enormous, endless flight of stone steps.

Jane is too busy watching her feet; she doesn't notice that there's someone climbing the steps ahead of her until it's too late. They collide. She glances off his chest and loses her breath. He staggers back under her weight and then takes hold of her upper arms in firm hands, steadying her.

She can see his polished shoes, the bottoms of his suit trousers. As she tries to move on past, murmuring an apology, she keeps her eyes downturned, but his grip tightens. Her heart batters and batters at her rib cage as if it won't be kept in.

"Jane Miller," the man says. His voice is soft and rich, like expensive whisky. "I don't believe it. I trawl the United Kingdom for you, and here you are. Falling right into my arms."

Miranda

"I CAN'T *BELIEVE* YOU'VE FINALLY LET US DO THIS," FRAN-
nie says, brandishing a makeup brush with genuine glee. "Do you have
any idea how long we've wanted to give you a makeover?"

"Not a makeover!" Miranda protests, glancing at her watch. It's
already almost eight—they're at Carter's mum's house, where Carter's
still living, and he's waiting for them downstairs. He doesn't seem all
that excited about this party, for some reason, and so Miranda's feeling
edgy, the way she always does when Carter's acting strangely. "We
don't have time for a makeover! I just said put a bit of makeup on me,
that's all."

"Sure, sure," Frannie says, waving this away. "Adele? You're on
dress?"

"Hang on, I've *got* a dress," Miranda protests, trying to stand.

Frannie pushes her down again with surprising strength.

"Sit," she says, moving to stand in front of Miranda. "Close your
eyes. Relax."

"This is not relaxing! I don't trust you two."

Frannie gasps, wounded, and then swats Miranda around the head when she opens her eyes.

"Shut!" she says.

"Aren't you meant to be the nice twin?" Miranda says.

"I've brought a few options, Mir," Adele says, rummaging in the ridiculously oversized bag she packed for a one-night trip down to Winchester. "I assume you're happy with getting your boobs and legs out?"

"See? I *am* the nice twin," Frannie says smugly, getting to work on Miranda's face.

MIRANDA HAS TO BEGRUDGINGLY ADMIT THAT THEY'VE scrubbed her up well. After some tension, and a certain amount of yelling, Adele conceded on the outfit and let Miranda wear something that she felt comfortable in, rather than one of Adele's clubbing outfits, which Miranda had not seen before and has now insisted her sister never wear again. So Miranda is dressed in a high-waisted skirt with a tucked-in silky top and her favorite pumps. It's a little casual for such a swanky party, but formal wear makes Miranda sweat. It's always so tight and uncomfortable and you have to think about which bits of you are going to show every time you sit down.

She idly browses through the clutter on Carter's desk while Adele and Frannie argue about which clutch she should take. They're *thrilled* to be invited to this New Year's Eve party—it was so sweet of Carter to say they could come—and they are demonstrating their excitement by being even louder than usual.

There's a pile of books at the back of the desk—he's clearly run out of space on the bookshelves. All Carter's books are ratty and badly looked after. Unsurprising, given they're usually jammed in his coat pockets. There's a copy of *Manage Your Mind* on the desk with a ripped spine and a train ticket as a bookmark; *Exit West* is unusually tidy, but the book beneath it has a spine so creased that it takes her a moment to read the title. *Finding a Better You.* As she picks it up to read the subtitle—*Moving Through Grief, Addiction or Trauma*—she reveals a card under the pile of books.

Her skin goes hot-cold. The name on the envelope is *Siobhan.*

You must be Siobhan, Mary Carter had said when she first met Miranda. The name has stayed with Miranda ever since; Carter has never mentioned it, not once.

She glances back at Adele and Frannie, who are now yelling loudly enough that even Miranda—well accustomed to the volume of a Rosso argument—can't help but wince. She slowly sets down *Finding a Better You* and picks up the envelope.

She shouldn't open it, clearly. But she thinks of what Adele told her, how she needs to dig, take matters into her own hands, and she knows she's going to do it. As Miranda slides her finger under the seal, she feels as if she's slipping, her feet giving way beneath her.

It's a card. One of Joseph's hand-drawn ones. It shows a man and woman standing in front of a gigantic Christmas tree in a square labeled as Covent Garden; they're looking at one another, but not touching. Inside is a message in Joseph's messy script:

Dear Siobhan,

Happy birthday! I don't doubt that you'll be celebrating in style.

I've thought a lot about our Christmas weekend together. And I'm umming and ahhing about whether to send this to you and tell you . . . I don't know. It felt like more than friends to me. And more than what we had before, too—more than the springtime hookups, more than the sex. And I really want to know if it felt that way to you.

Anyway, enjoy your wine and ice cream. I bet the year ahead holds wonderful things for you, Siobhan Kelly. xxx

"Mir?" Frannie says. "You all right?"

It feels so *wrong* to see these words in Carter's handwriting. Like seeing him holding someone else's hand. She thinks of that moment she caught him writing her birthday card on the morning before their trip to Kew Gardens, and can hardly believe that there's someone else in his life that he writes these cards for, too, with their hand-drawn covers and their messy, wonky, boyish handwriting. It's so . . . *intimate*. It makes her feel sick.

"Mir?"

Adele and Frannie come up behind her. One of them puts a hand on her shoulder, but she twists to keep her back to them, examining the Christmas tree on the front of the card. Carter was in London the weekend before Christmas. Was that when he was with Siobhan? Oh *God*, Miranda's furious, she's rageful, she's so deeply *sad*. All the nastiest emotions, unfurling in her belly as if they've been waiting there all along.

Carter is making his way up the stairs; she can hear his footfalls on the carpet.

"What's wrong?" Frannie and Adele chorus.

Miranda shrugs off their hands and shoves the card back under the book on the desk. There's a soft knock at the door.

Miranda stares at the pile of books. She can feel Adele and Frannie trying to catch her eye, exchanging puzzled glances with one another.

"Hello? Can I come in?" Carter calls.

"Can he?" Frannie whispers, putting an arm around Miranda. "What's going on, Miranda? What was on that card?"

"Oh my God," Miranda says. She clears her throat and snaps her gaze from the desk to the door. "Yes. Yes. Come in."

"Are you guys okay?" Carter says as he opens the door. "Wow, Miranda, you look great."

She looks at him. Her smart, suit-wearing, book-reading boyfriend with his neat, adorable glasses, his big open smile. The good guy. The one you trust.

Miranda may swear from time to time now, but it still takes a lot to bring a bad word to her mind. But as she looks at Carter, she's thinking, *You absolute fucking bastard.*

She knew he was a liar. She'd *known.* She should have followed her gut. Carter meets her eyes and his expression shifts a little; he's wary, maybe, or guarded. He glances toward the desk.

"Mir? Are you all right?" Frannie says with uncharacteristic timidity, and Miranda looks away from Carter with effort.

She wants to scream at him. She wants to tear into the books, throw them at him, scrunch that carefully drawn card into a ball and hurl it at his head. She wants to shove past him and run out into the freezing December street and keep running until the burn in her muscles eases the raging adrenaline blooming under her skin.

But her sisters are here. They're excited for their New Year's Eve party. She can't just lose it in front of Adele and Frannie—she's meant to be the adult.

So she grits her teeth and swallows it down. She even smiles. It's amazing, really. She would never have thought she had it in her. She thinks of what AJ said about her, how she's *not even capable of being fake*, and for a moment she wishes with her whole heart that she was in her work gear and halfway up a tree with a man who sees her as the person she would really like to be.

The cab is waiting outside the house. Mary Carter waves them off from the window, her silver hair perfectly smoothed, her expression a little worried, as if perhaps she's forgotten where her son is going. Or who he's going with.

Carter squeezes Miranda's knee and it's all she can do not to slap his hand away.

"What's going on?" he says in a low voice.

Adele and Frannie are sitting opposite them, their feet tapping in rhythm to the song playing on the taxi's radio.

"Later," Miranda says. She can feel Carter's worried frown. She knows him so well. Or at least, she thought she did.

THE PARTY IS LIKE NOTHING MIRANDA HAS EVER SEEN BE-fore. For starters, it's in this insane country house that looks like a ruined palace inside. There are actual trees in pots, ten-foot olive trees and birches, reaching up through the gaping, open ceiling to the floors above. Everything is lit in purple and blue and twinkling silver fairy lights, and there are trailing branches of yew and holly over every available surface; it feels like something out of a film.

When they arrive, Carter is swallowed up in a crowd of friends, or maybe colleagues—she can't really figure out how he knows these people, and he's not explaining. He disappears for a while, something about dealing with an issue with the sponsors: this is a fundraiser for the human rights charity Scott works for, another fact that Carter failed to mention.

To his credit, though, when he's back, even though he looks a bit stressed and rattled, he does introduce her to everyone. *My girlfriend, Miranda*, he says over and over, a hand hovering on her upper back. But then, it sounds like he's *just friends* with this Siobhan woman for now, so perhaps he sees no harm in putting all his eggs in one basket. Now that he and Siobhan are not currently engaging in *springtime hookups*.

"Miranda!"

She turns. It's Scott. She hugs him in greeting and reintroduces her sisters, who he met briefly at his Halloween party; Frannie is looking at Scott with far too much interest for someone ten years younger than him, and Miranda scowls at her until she rolls her eyes and flounces off with Adele to get drinks.

"Almost midnight!" Scott yells in her ear, over the music. "You ready for 2019?"

Miranda is watching Frannie and Adele disappear through the

crowd with some anxiety. They *are* adults, obviously, it's just . . . they're also children, and she feels responsible.

"Hey?" Miranda says, turning back to Scott. He repeats himself, mouth closer to her ear; his words fuzz below all the noise of the party, but this time she catches them. "Oh, yeah," she says grimly. "I am very ready for a new year."

"Yeah?" He looks at her with interest. He's drinking a lager from the bottle and wearing a silver-blue shirt that should look hideously 1990s but actually looks excellent. "Did 2018 not go as planned?"

"Do you know who Siobhan is?"

Miranda really has no idea she is going to ask this question until it's left her mouth. Scott's eyes widen.

"Ah," he says. "So . . . Carter's told you about her?"

"Not yet. But he's about to."

She glances over at where Carter stands in a gaggle of people, ducking his head to speak to a curvy blond woman in spindly high heels. When she looks at him she feels a wave of something akin to hatred; it's disgusting, like swallowing something rotten. Miranda doesn't do hate. She's turning into someone else, and he's done that— Carter's done that to her.

"Look, what you have to understand is . . ." Scott is trying to choose his words. "Siobhan will always have this hold over him. He just can't ever quite let her go."

"Oh, poor him," Miranda spits. "I'm sure it's all Siobhan's fault."

Scott pulls a face, taking a mouthful of beer.

"Okay, I'm staying out of this," he says, moving to leave.

"Did Carter come to your birthday party this year?" she asks.

He stops. His eyes flick toward Carter. "Umm, yeah?" he says. "Yeah, he did."

"And did he stay at yours afterward?"

"Yes?" Scott says.

Miranda's not at all convinced. He's probably just covering for his friend. She grits her teeth as the rage pounds through her. She's only got angrier from the moment when she put that birthday card back on the desk. Or before, maybe—maybe it's been building up for months, like calcium in a kettle, lining her insides, turning her hard.

"Hey, my two favorite people!" Carter says, coming up behind them, clapping one hand on Scott's shoulder and looping the other around Miranda's waist. She shrugs him off and he looks at her with a frown.

"I'm off," Scott says, tipping his beer to Carter. "Good luck."

Carter tries to take Miranda's hand. She dodges.

"Miranda? What's going on? You've been angry with me all night."

She moves away. The sound of the band blaring out a cover of Katy Perry's "Firework" quietens a little as she heads outside. It's almost midnight; there's already a crowd on the lawn in front of the manor house. There's a rumor of fireworks and the choice of pre-midnight song is making the surprise a little obvious.

"Talk to me," Carter says, catching up to her.

She spins. He recoils slightly at her expression. They're standing under the pillars by the entrance, and he's half-lit by the light streaming out from the party inside, half-dark.

"I know about Siobhan," Miranda says.

For such a momentous sentence, it sounds very small.

Carter goes still. The band is wrapping up Katy Perry, drumbeat throbbing, and Miranda catches the sound of glass breaking, someone shrieking in surprise. Carter's chest rises and falls quickly, as if he can't catch his breath.

"What's Scott been saying to you?" Carter asks eventually. His voice isn't what she expected. She thought he'd be defensive. Instead, he sounds afraid.

"Oh, nothing. You don't need to worry about your friend, he's kept your secrets. I found her birthday card, waiting to be sent. On your desk."

He passes a hand over his face. "God," he says.

"Aren't you going to *say* anything?" Her voice rises as inside the party the singer announces that it's one minute to midnight. "Aren't you going to grovel, to tell me how sorry you are, tell me that I mean more to you than she does?"

Carter recoils again. "What?"

"What do you mean, *what*? Aren't you sorry for what you've done to me?"

"What I've . . . Miranda." Carter rubs a hand across his face. "I'm sorry I didn't tell you, okay? Is that what you want me to say?"

"*Is that what I want you to say?*" Miranda's shouting now, voice cracking as the crowds inside scream and the band starts a low, thrumming drumbeat, building anticipation, getting them ready for the countdown.

Carter takes her hands and he doesn't let go as she tugs. His face is twisted with emotion, that ugly, clenched mask that men wear when they're afraid to cry.

"What do you want from me, Miranda?"

"I want you to own up. To *apologize* for disrespecting me and lying to me and *cheating on me*."

His grip on her hands falters; she yanks hers free.

"What are you talking about?"

She can hardly hear Carter over the noise of the band now, but it doesn't matter. She's already walking away beneath the pillars, leaving him behind her.

"Shall we say good-bye to 2018?" yells the singer, dragging out every syllable, and the cheer grows even louder.

"I never cheated on you, Miranda," Carter shouts at her back. "God. I never cheated on you."

She turns on her heels, fists clenched at her sides. For a moment she really thinks about hitting him, just marching over and punching him in the face.

"So how do you explain the diary entry? The birthday card? The mysterious breakfast in Central London, right by Covent Garden, where you spent that weekend with Siobhan?"

His face is almost demonic, twisting in the effort to hold back tears. It's so obvious. *Why doesn't he just cry, for God's sake?* she thinks bitterly, watching him try to compose himself as the lights flash through the doorway behind him.

"I can't talk about this, Miranda," Carter manages eventually.

"Are you *kidding* me? You *can't* talk about this?"

He's backing up now, away from her, toward the faceless crowd inside the party.

"Stay where you are, you spineless son-of-a-bitch," Miranda yells, and she doesn't even recognize her voice—she'd *never* normally say a thing like that. She takes a deep breath, fighting back a sob. "Do you still have feelings for Siobhan?" she asks, and this time her voice is querulous.

Carter's face seems almost angry now, still masklike, still awful. He's turned his gaze away from her. After a long, strange moment, he regains his composure and looks back to meet her eyes.

"Yes, I still have feelings for Siobhan," Carter says bitterly. "I've tried to move on, but . . . yes. I do."

Even though she's been expecting it—goading him for it—it still somehow catches Miranda unawares with its sharpness, digging deeper than she thought it could. She presses a disbelieving hand to her face, and she thinks, *Is this really happening? Is this really happening?*

The countdown begins inside, to the roaring appreciation of the crowd, and still that drumbeat pulses behind it all. *Ten. Nine. Eight.*

"But, Miranda. You've got it wrong. I didn't cheat on you with Siobhan."

Six. Five. Four.

"Yes, she put those dates in my diary. Yes, I wrote her that card for her birthday."

Three. Two. Carter moves at last, striding toward her, grabbing at her arm as she tries to walk away from him.

"But, Miranda. Miranda, listen."

One. The crowd erupts, and the gunshot pop of fireworks almost drowns out the words Joseph Carter says next.

"That was a long time ago. All of it. Siobhan and I . . . That was more than two years ago now."

Siobhan

"HELLO, 2016!" THE LEAD SINGER SHOUTS, AND THE NOISE blossoms until it's so loud it's just one sound, one thumping, straining roar.

Siobhan throws her head back and screams along with the crowd. She's never been readier to step into a new year. There's no denying it: 2015 was *messy*. The Siobhan of 2016 is going to be happy and healthy and determined not to get in her own way.

"You okay?" Fiona yells in her ear. "Will we get some air?"

Siobhan wants to stay here, at the very center of the dance floor, swirling and spinning on her stilettoes, but one look at Fiona's face tells her that her friend is flagging.

"Sure," she says, following Fiona away from the band and out onto the lawn outside. The pillars of the Grange are lit up in all their grandeur—Joseph wasn't wrong about this party. It's truly epic.

"So? Have you found him yet?" Fiona says, lifting her hair from her neck to cool off. It's drizzling slightly, the sort of rain that you can barely feel on your skin.

"No," Siobhan says, looking back toward the mansion. "I haven't seen him anywhere in there."

"Maybe he changed his plans," Fiona says, her eyes on Siobhan's face. She's wearing eyeliner, a small concession to the fact that this is a party.

"He made it sound like he always came to this," Siobhan says.

Stepping out of the party seems to have taken some of the energy out of her; she's suddenly aware of the sharp pain where her shoes cut into her skin. She swallows and lifts her chin. So Joseph's not here. It doesn't actually matter. There's nothing magical about New Year's Eve—if it's a few more days before she tells him how she feels, so what?

"It's just that you've barely thought about anything else for the last three days, right?" Fiona says when Siobhan makes this point.

Siobhan scowls at her. "Have, too." She absolutely hasn't. "We've had a good night, haven't we?"

Fiona keeps her expression politely positive.

"Oh no, you're hating it," Siobhan says, pulling Fiona in for a hug. "You just want to go home and watch Christmas films, don't you?"

"No! I love parties! Parties are great!" Fiona tries, arms closing around Siobhan's waist. "Okay, fine, I don't love massive parties like this, where you can't hear anything and everyone's wasted and getting off with each other at midnight. But . . . I do love you? So . . ."

"And I love you, so . . . we're going," Siobhan says, pulling away from Fiona. "Come on. Let's peel Marlena off whichever beautiful woman she's currently shifting."

"Shifting?" says Fiona, tucking her arm into Siobhan's as they head back toward the building. "Really?"

"I'm predicting a 2016 comeback," Siobhan says. "Just you wait. By 2017, no one will say *kissing* anymore—everyone will be saying *shifting* again."

Fiona laughs. "What else is going to happen in 2016?"

"Hmm. I think 2016 is going to be the year we sort everything out. Peace and goodwill and understanding. We'll all be more tolerant and compassionate, and we'll stop wearing jumpsuits because we'll all realize, hello, what about when you need to pee? And . . ."

Siobhan trails off. Fiona's still walking, still giggling, and it takes her a moment to clock where Siobhan's looking. As soon as she does, her expression transforms from amusement to fascinated incredulity.

"Are those people on *horseback*?" she says.

There are indeed two people approaching the Grange on the opposite gravel track, on large white horses—or *steeds*, Siobhan thinks. These horses are steeds. They're enormous and very maney and they pick their feet up a lot as they walk, as if the ground isn't good enough for them.

What catches Siobhan's attention so completely, however, is the fact that one of these men is Joseph Carter.

He's not a particularly competent rider—not that Siobhan is any judge, but he seems to be bouncing around a lot. But nonetheless, there is something about a handsome man on a white horse that just . . . *works*.

"That's Joseph," she hisses to Fiona. "And his friend Scott, I think. Oh my God."

Her stomach clenches, because if Joseph's here then it's *happening*, it's time, she has no choice but to do what she vowed she'd do: she has to tell this man she loves him. She is so preoccupied with the enormity of this idea that it takes her a moment to really compute the other key facts.

"What are they *doing* on those horses?"

"I have no idea," Fiona says. "Does Joseph ride horses?"

"No?" Siobhan says as the two men on horseback bounce their way toward them. "Not generally?" They are approaching faster than she thought; her stomach clenches. "Shit. Okay. This is it. Oh my God. Will you deal with Scott?"

"Deal with him?" Fiona says, eyeing the horses. "Deal with him how, exactly?"

"I don't know, you're a resourceful woman," Siobhan says as Joseph comes into focus, his hazelnut-brown hair flying in the wind, his cheeks pink with exertion. He's so broad shouldered. He looks so good on horseback. *Oh, fucking hell*, Siobhan thinks, *I'm a lost cause. Shouldn't I be looking at this man and thinking,* Why is that twat on a horse?

The men are nearly upon them now. Joseph is laughing at something Scott's saying, gripping the reins a little too high against his chest. Scott whoops; there's already a small crowd of interested onlookers forming underneath the pillared entrance to the Grange.

"Shiv, I am not good at thinking on the spot!" Fiona hisses. "You know this!"

"Yes, you are! You are brilliant at improv!" Siobhan says, hitching her dress up and checking her hair. Her heart is racing. It's not exactly the way she imagined this moment—more livestock, for instance—but here's her chance to tell Joseph how she really feels about him, and she is absolutely, mind-blank, hands-shaking terrified.

"I'm not! You just think I am! I knew your ridiculous faith in my abilities would come back to bite us in the ass one day! Oh, hi," Fiona says rather desperately as Scott and Joseph trot by. "Can I hitch a ride?"

Siobhan stares at her askance for a moment before returning her attention to Joseph. He does a literal double take when he sees her, pulling so hard on the reins that the horse comes to an abrupt halt and rears, lifting its front feet a good half a meter from the ground. Miraculously, Joseph manages to cling on, but Siobhan shrieks despite herself.

"Bloody hell," Joseph says breathlessly, clinging to the front of the saddle with one hand and the horse's mane with the other. "That just happened."

Meanwhile Fiona seems to be boarding Scott's horse. She shoots

Siobhan a what-the-fuck-is-happening look as Scott hauls her up to sit in front of him.

"Ow!" Fiona says. "They make this look much more comfortable on television. Right. Onward to the party! Don't wait for these two, they need to chat. Scott, was it? Hi, I'm Fiona. Or Fi, if you prefer. Normally I don't do quite this much straddling when I first meet a man, but this was an emergency."

Her voice fades as the two of them trot away. Joseph and Siobhan stare at each other for a while, her neck craning back, his face flushed.

"Hi," Siobhan says, relieved to hear that her voice isn't shaking as much as the rest of her. "Nice horse."

"Scott's idea," Joseph says, still clinging on. "They belong to a woman in Stockbridge who offered a ride as part of the charity raffle and then said we could borrow them to get people excited about the prize and . . . well, it's a long story, all very Scott. Did we miss midnight?"

Siobhan laughs. "Yeah, by some way."

"Damn. Horses are not as fast as you'd think," he says, flashing a quick, daft grin, the sort he always wears when he's clowning around. "Do you want to . . . come up here?"

"Not really," Siobhan says, looking the horse up and down.

It surveys her with an expression that suggests it is not particularly keen to have her, either.

"I'll head down, then," Joseph says, eyeing the ground with some trepidation. "Hmm. The ground is quite a way away, isn't it?"

Siobhan looks around, shaking her head slightly, but smiling despite herself. It is so Joseph to have ended up so late to the New Year's Eve party he missed the countdown altogether, and to have *such* an elaborate excuse. How does he get into these situations? And why does she find it adorable?

"Over there," she says, pointing to a long flight of steps to the left of the main entrance, leading to a different wing of the mansion. It's edged with low walls—one of those will be easier to dismount onto, she figures.

"Right," Joseph says, digging in his heels slightly. "Off we—*oof.*"

Siobhan walks along beside Joseph and his horse and wonders quite how she has ended up here. Her frightened pulse flutters at her throat; she steadies her breathing, flexing her hands at her sides. Once they reach the wall, Joseph dismounts extremely ungracefully, and then winces, turning his back briefly to do some rearranging.

"So," Siobhan says, when he spins back around and lunges for the horse's reins as it tries to wander off for some tastier-looking grass. She's smiling despite the nerves—Joseph just looks so adorably all over the place. "Am I going to get a bit more explanation of how you ended up with this new pet?"

"First up, surely—what are you doing here?" he asks, blinking at her. "I didn't . . ."

"Invite me?" she says brightly, feeling the bruise on her ego blooming.

He flushes. "I mean . . ."

"It's all right. I came with friends, we were heading to London for New Year's Eve anyway, and there were tickets still on sale for this, and we figured it was only a small detour." She presses her lips together, resisting the urge to stop here, play it cool. She takes a deep breath. "But I did come to see you."

Something flickers in his face—hope, maybe? Or is that wishful thinking from Siobhan?

Steeling herself, swallowing hard, she steps toward him across the lawn, until she and Joseph are close enough to touch. The horse wickers behind Joseph and he startles.

"I can't . . . Sorry," Joseph says eventually. He smooths down his hair with his spare hand. "I'm trying not to jump to conclusions, but this feels a bit too good to be true, so can I just check exactly why you've come to see me? In case it's because you want to return something of mine, or had to tell me some bad news in person, instead of the reason I am really hoping you're here, which is . . . well . . . the reason I would have showed up in Dublin to see *you* if I'd had the nerve?"

The vulnerability in his voice gives Siobhan the courage she needs, and before she can second-guess herself, before she can get in her own way, she opens her mouth and says, "I came to tell you I love you."

They stare at each other, perfectly still.

Siobhan can hardly believe she's said it. She has never said those words to any man except for Cillian, who ultimately let her down so profoundly it seems to have taken her half a decade to recover.

"Oh God," she says into the silence. "Fuck."

"No!" Joseph says, reaching out and taking her hand. "No, no, I'm . . ."

"Horrified? Appalled?"

"Really happy," Joseph says, and his face breaks into one of his finest enormous smiles, and Siobhan is beaming back at him, and she can't even feel the cold, doesn't even mind that it's begun to drizzle and her hair will be ruined.

"God, really? You really love me?" Joseph says.

"Why?" Siobhan says through her smile, stepping closer to him. "Do you love me, too?" Her tone is teasing, arch, but she wants the answer so much it's hard to breathe.

"Oh, absolutely," Joseph says. "I've known ever since that awful morning in April when I left you in that hotel bathroom. I tried to get over you all year, I tried committing to other people, but the moment I saw you in Winchester I knew I was still a goner. I just never thought you'd love me. You never really *seemed* to."

Siobhan laughs, dropping her head to rest it on his shoulder. The happiness is growing and growing, fizzing in her fingertips, dancing down to her half-frozen toes.

"I'm an actress by training, remember?" she says, lifting her face up to his. She sobers a little when she sees his expression; he's not quite as assured as his voice makes him sound. "And I'm sorry, you're right, I should have opened up to you about how I felt. I was afraid, I pushed you away, I . . ." She smooths a hand along the flush that touches his cheekbone, down to the stubble of his jawline, relishing it, *glorying* in the feeling of her skin against his. "I do love you. I love you."

Joseph beams at her, all white teeth and wind-scuffed cheeks and gorgeous hazel eyes. Being this close without kissing him is becoming unbearable, so Siobhan stands on tiptoe and lifts her face to his. It's so decadently wonderful to just *kiss* him, not holding anything back. She lets her body melt into his; it's hard to believe that she did this without thought so many times. Her skin hums with desire, the way it always does when she's within a meter or so of Joseph Carter.

"Oh shit," she says suddenly, breaking away from him. "The other woman?"

He blinks down at her, hazy-eyed. "Sorry?"

"You said there was someone else," Siobhan says impatiently. "Another woman you were seeing?"

"Oh, no, no," Joseph says, leaning to kiss her again.

Siobhan pulls back, not satisfied with this explanation.

"No, I mean, there was, but then we had that weekend in London before Christmas and it was so obvious I wasn't over you. I called it off with Lola. I actually wrote you a birthday card telling you I thought we were much more than friends, basically, but . . ." He looks sheepish. "I lost it. And I thought it was maybe a sign I shouldn't tell you."

Siobhan rolls her eyes. "It was a sign you need to be more organized," she tells him, and he smiles as she presses her lips to his again. The kiss deepens and heat pools low in her belly as she remembers how Joseph's body just gets hers, how she finally relaxes when his arms take her weight.

"God, I'm so glad I came here," she says, her mouth still against his.

"Never would have met Nighthawk, otherwise," Joseph says, pulling her close. She can feel how hard his heart is beating through his coat.

"Nighthawk?" she says into his chest.

The horse whinnies on cue.

"Oh, he's called Nighthawk?" Siobhan says, laughing, tipping her chin back again to look at Joseph.

"Of course. My favorite comics when I was a kid," Joseph says, stealing another deep kiss, his tongue touching hers.

"Joseph Carter," Siobhan says when they part, linking her hands around his waist. "Are you a massive nerd hiding in the body of a hot jock?"

He beams down at her. "Absolutely. And you said you love me. There's no taking it back now."

"You've not said it, you know," Siobhan says, then winces at herself. "Sorry. I'm actually horribly needy, you will realize this. I have thus far hidden it well."

"Not needy," Joseph says, pressing his lips to her cheek. "And you've not hidden it that well, Shiv."

"What!"

"I just mean, someone hurt you," he says, more quietly now. "I could tell that the first time we met. You keep your heart guarded."

Siobhan's unsettled; this is all such uncharted territory, and in among the joy that fear is still there, too. Joseph smooths a cold hand over her cheek and smiles down at her.

"I love you," he says. "I love you, Siobhan Kelly. I've loved you for absolutely ages. I can't shake you, in fact. Just ask Scott. He's sick of me going on about you."

"He's probably comparing notes with poor Fiona," Siobhan says, pressing her forehead to Joseph's chest. "She's sick of me droning on about you."

She realizes with sudden surprise how freezing cold she is, and just as abruptly decides that she doesn't care. She never wants to go back inside. She wants to stay here, in Joseph's arms, with Nighthawk the incongruous white horse grazing behind them. Being present is something Siobhan struggles with, but right now she has never felt more *in* a moment in her life.

"God, do we get to just . . . be together now?" Joseph says with something like wonder. "Are you my girlfriend?"

"I think so," Siobhan says, smiling up at him. "It does feel a bit straightforward for us, doesn't it?"

"No, no, no. Don't start overthinking," Joseph says quickly, widening his eyes in mock panic.

"Kiss me, then," Siobhan says, dropping her gaze to his lips. "It's a surefire cure."

"I'll remember that," Joseph says as he leans in and takes her mouth in one of those deep, luscious, tingling kisses, the kind that feel too good to be true.

Jane

ONE LOOK AT HIS FACE AND IT'S AS IF SHE'S FALLEN
through time. She's the Jane she was back then: overawed, smitten, so
easily swayed. He's a little grayer at the temples than when she saw
him last, and a bit puffier, as if he's lost weight, then gained it again.
But his eyes are still that arresting, wry, sparkling blue, and they're
locked on her.

Richard Wilson is very good at eye contact. When Jane worked at
Bray & Kembrey, when she was Richard's secretary, it was that charming eye contact that made her fall for him so completely.

"We need to talk," he says. His hands are still gripping her arms,
dry and warm; she tries to wriggle free, but he's holding tight. They're
halfway down the steps, and for a wild moment Jane thinks about
pushing him. Letting him tumble down the stone steps and out of her
life for good.

"Richard, let me go," she says, trying to sidestep him.

"Not this time," he says firmly, but he shifts so he's only holding her
right arm, and begins to walk her down the steps like she's a criminal

being chaperoned to a police van. "Come on. You hate these sorts of parties. I'll drive you home."

She mustn't get in a car with him. Her skin is crawling. His hand on her arm feels wrong. Indecent.

"Let go of me, Richard, or I'll make a scene," she says as calmly as she can.

He seems surprised by her recalcitrance. There go those engaging eyes—now he's all brows and fixed jaw. She remembers that look well, too. He collects himself with visible effort and tries a smile, coming to a standstill beside her. Jane looks down pointedly at the hand on her arm, and after a reluctant moment he loosens his grip and shoves his hands in his pockets.

"All right," he says. "I'm sorry. I suppose I'm coming on a little strong. But I've been looking for you for a very long time, Jane."

"Really?" she says. She's collected herself, too; her voice is more measured now. "I've not been far away. If you really wanted to find me, you could have."

At first, she'd longed for it. She'd imagined he'd come and beg her forgiveness, sweep her up, take her back to the life where she belonged to him. It had been so terrifying leaving London to start over—she hadn't realized how accustomed she had become to living life according to Richard's edicts until she was alone and had only her own rules to abide by.

Richard stretches his arms out. They're now standing on the lawn; a group of smokers nearby talk in low voices, and a couple walk hand in hand toward the river, the light of the party playing across their dipped heads.

"Well, ah, you've got me. The situation has changed a little, Jane. I thought we needed to check in. It's been too long."

Check in. As if this is a work meeting. Those lines were always so blurred between them. His insistence that she wear gray suit dresses every day—was that the request of her boss or a controlling boyfriend? The way he always chose what they ate for every meal he had her order to the office—wasn't that just reasonable, given he was her superior? When he told her she was better off skipping the after-work drinks with the other secretaries because she was too indiscreet, was he just looking out for her professionally?

Jane takes a deep breath. These are old thoughts, out-of-date ones. She has proven him wrong: it may have taken her a while, but she *has* made friends, and she has begun to discover the Jane those friends see in her. And if he was wrong when he told her that she *just didn't gel with people*, that she was *odd, peculiar*, that *people would never get her the way he did*—then maybe he was wrong about everything else, too.

Jane no longer believes that she is a woman who is impossible to love. This is even more of an achievement, she realizes, given that Joseph Carter does not love her. She lifts her chin slightly and meets Richard's gaze.

"What do you want to speak to me about?" she asks.

"Don't you want to go somewhere warmer? Here." Richard shrugs out of his jacket.

Jane steps back. She's shivering, but even just the smell of Richard's jacket makes her stomach turn.

"No, thank you," she says. "Let's just make this quick."

His eyebrows go up. The Jane he knew would have taken the jacket—she'd have done whatever he asked of her.

"What did you expect?" she asks quietly. "Did you think nothing would have changed?"

"Not exactly," Richard concedes, but he did, that much is clear. "I just want to talk a few things through. There's been a bit of a mix-up at work, and there's a chance someone might want to get in touch with you and ask about our . . . working relationship, when you were at Bray & Kembrey. I just want to make sure you and I are still on the same page."

"A mix-up?" Jane says, voice quiet. "Is it like the *mix-up* before you fired me?"

His eyes narrow slightly; he's not quite following. "I didn't fire you, Jane, I had no choice but to let you go. You already had a warning on your record, and you made a mistake that cost the firm an awful lot of money, if you remember."

"I haven't forgotten," Jane says steadily.

The warning had come shortly before he'd revealed Jane's mistake with the issue proceedings form. She'd messed up his diary, apparently, and he'd missed an important meeting. She'd accepted the disciplinary action at the time, despite her confusion—she was *sure* she'd put the meeting in on the right day—but lately Jane has begun to wonder. Richard might not have been able to get rid of her for the mistake with the issue proceedings form alone. He'd needed something else.

And by that point it had been clear for some months that he wanted rid of her. His interest in sex had dimmed; the office rumors about the two of them had started; someone had caught them in the conference room after hours.

"Is there another harassment complaint against you?" Jane says. "Is that why HR are asking questions?"

Richard's chin snaps up, eyes sharp. "There was never a complaint."

"Oh," Jane says diffidently. "So you managed to make that go away, did you?"

"There was never a complaint," he says again, stepping closer to her.

Jane flinches despite herself, stepping back, unable to hold her ground. She looks down at her shoes, confidence slipping. But there *had* been a complaint. She'd seen the paperwork when she'd packed up her desk, tears coursing down her cheeks, the door to Richard's office firmly closed.

"Can I count on you to tell the truth, Jane?" Richard asks.

"Which truth would that be?" Jane says. It's the sort of blunt remark he'd have chided her for if she'd dared to let it slip when they were together. He liked his Jane sweet and mild mannered.

"It would be much simpler to focus on our professional relationship. There's no need to dwell on the personal one. It'll only complicate things for me."

She stares at him then. "You were my boyfriend," she says. "You . . . you were my *everything*."

He sighs, lifting his eyes for a moment. "Let's not be melodramatic."

Jane thinks of the times he'd told her they were *made for each other*. How he'd cuddled her into his lap, stroking her hair, reassuring her when she'd said something silly in a team meeting or gotten panicky at a big corporate event.

Richard sighs again when Jane says nothing. "Look, I didn't want to have to bring this up, Jane. But you owe me. You know you do."

Oh God. The money. The money.

Had she known even then that it was meant to keep her quiet? That it was another way to own her? She likes to think that she didn't—by the time Richard broke up with her, Jane had become so accustomed to him paying for things. It had started with a small loan when she'd struggled to pay rent a few months after arriving in London; then it had been dinners and gifts; then a regular monthly payment so she could live the lifestyle he wanted her to live. Pretty clothes, an apartment he preferred to the boxy little place she'd rented when she first got to London.

He had been so kind when he'd told her the relationship was over, holding her hand as she sobbed, telling her that he'd still look after her. He had to let her go from Bray & Kembrey—the mistake with the form just couldn't be overlooked—but he knew it would be hard for her to cope on her own, and he'd make sure she was okay.

When the lump sum had appeared in her bank account, she'd felt a flash of hope. If he was giving her all that money, he must still care. If a corner of Jane's mind had wondered why the conversation about the money had occurred in the same conversation in which he'd told her she would turn down the exit interview with HR, if a part of her saw that harassment complaint on the desk and wondered what HR would think if she told them she'd been sleeping with Richard in secret for more than a year . . . That part of her was so worn down by then. Silenced by months of Richard asserting that Jane always got these things wrong. She shouldn't get involved in his business. She wouldn't understand.

"That money has been serving you well, by the looks of it." Richard drags his gaze down her body.

"This dress was from a charity shop," Jane says stiffly, but the excuse is empty and she knows it. He's right. She's lived off that money. It's allowed her to work at the charity shop for free, to rent her beautiful white flat in Winchester and her cottage in Wales. She felt so ill-equipped for real work when she got to Winchester. How could she possibly work in an office? She was terrible at office politics; nobody ever liked her; she'd only mess things up. *I can't cope on my own*, she'd thought, over and over, like a mantra.

"If you're running low, Jane, I can help," Richard says, his voice suddenly softer. He tilts his head. "Are you struggling?"

Something in Jane's chest pulls. An old, dormant impulse surfaces for a moment. *Yes*, she wants to say. *Everything is harder without you.*

Then she thinks of Aggie, hair flying in the wind as she hands Jane another water balloon. She thinks of Keira's face as Jane stood up for herself at Constance's wedding reception. She thinks of Colin, drinking his iced tea, saying, *Thank you, Jane.*

Jane is running out of money. But Aggie has already said she would be welcome to help her out on some of the bigger projects on a free-lance basis, and with her experience at the charity shop, she can probably find a job in retail. She is perfectly capable. She'll cope.

So no. She doesn't want to take Richard's money ever again.

But she *does* want to know just how desperate he is.

"How much?" she says. She unfolds her arms, knotting her hands behind her back instead. Not exactly a power pose, but the best she can manage. "How much to keep me quiet?"

He looks at her appraisingly.

"I hardly know you anymore," he says. "Where's my sweet little Jane?"

"Long gone," Jane says with a slight smile. Imagine if Richard knew that Jane was now a woman who wore red dresses with thigh-high splits; imagine if he knew she was brave enough to kiss the man she loved, even if it would break her heart. "Say what you want to say."

The party rolls on through the silence between them, loud and raucous, full of people waiting for their fresh start.

"Twenty thousand," Richard says eventually. "We'd have to be careful with the paper trail, so you might not get it all at once."

Jane nods thoughtfully. "Give me your card," she says. She knows he'll have one in his inside pocket—he never goes anywhere without one. "And I'll call you when I'm ready to talk."

THERE IS A MOMENT, WHEN SHE'S TURNED HER BACK ON Richard Wilson and walked toward the building, when she thinks about fleeing. The last thing she wants right now is a heaving crowd of bodies, the *thump-thump* of pop music, the sweat, the lights. But she left Aggie in there without a word, and Aggie doesn't deserve that.

Jane's trembling. Seeing Richard again wasn't at all like she had expected it to be. It was almost . . . exhilarating. She has never felt the difference between her present and former selves so acutely: standing there in front of the man who dominated her life in London, she had felt like an entirely different woman.

As she walks across the lawn, away from him, she spots a painfully familiar figure leaning up against one of the enormous pillars of the Grange. He's backlit in flashing lights, his hair a little mussed, his shoulders broad. Her stomach jerks; she stops dead.

He's watching her. Right away she knows something's wrong. His posture isn't normal. He's not relaxed and easy, exuding charm. He's stiff, arms folded. When he eventually moves toward her, his fists are clenched at his sides.

"Joseph?" she says, voice small. It's been so long since she's seen him, and even through the disquiet at how tense and angry he seems, she feels a thrill of joy just for his nearness.

"Why were you talking to Richard Wilson?" Joseph says, voice clipped. He seems to take her in, to really see her at last, and his face softens slightly. "Are you all right?"

Her heart thunders in her ears. "I'm fine. I didn't know you'd . . . Why are you here?"

"I come to this party with Scott every year. How do you know Richard?"

He's standing too far away from her, angry, wary; she hates it. But she knew this would happen—why else did she keep it from him that she worked at Bray & Kembrey at the same time as him? She's only once seen Joseph like this, and it was years ago, the day he stormed into Richard's office, when she was just the secretary sitting behind her computer screen.

She could lie to him. She considers it—she wants to, frankly. But there's nothing to lose now. She's lost Joseph already. He has a girl-friend; he didn't choose Jane. And all of a sudden, the idea of lying feels absolutely exhausting. It's a new year. She would very much like to begin it with the truth, for once.

"I was Richard's secretary. I worked at Bray & Kembrey before I came to Winchester. I left sort of . . . in disgrace, really. Everyone knew I was being let go because he was dumping me." The shame feels too enormous—it seems to radiate from her, hot and red. "I didn't want you to know. I didn't want you to see me as that woman."

Joseph's eyes widen. He looks genuinely staggered.

"You were Richard's . . ."

This is all he says, but it's enough to break her. She doesn't know exactly how he'll end that sentence, but she has an idea. *Slut, whore, plaything.* She heard enough of the rumors that went round the firm before she left—the things she let Richard do to her, the places they did them. Some completely fanciful, others excruciatingly true.

She pushes past Joseph and runs, heading inside to the anonymity of the party, the possibility of finding Aggie.

"Jane, wait!" Joseph calls behind her, but she's already inside, pushing through the noise, the bodies, head down, beginning to sob.

"Hey," someone says, grabbing her arm.

She flinches at the contact and staggers aside, looking up. It's Joseph's friend Scott.

"Jane, isn't it?" he calls, shifting sideways between couples to get closer. "Hey!"

She glances behind her. She's a good way from the doors now, a dense crowd between her and Joseph.

"Are you all right?" Scott asks.

"I'm fine," Jane says, still looking back toward the door.

She should go. Find Aggie. But Scott is right here, and there is something she so badly wants to know.

"Scott. Is Joseph here with his girlfriend?" she blurts.

Scott pulls back, forehead puckering. "Umm? He doesn't have a girlfriend. Actually, I kind of thought you were his girlfriend, to be honest."

She stares at him. The lights shift across his face. She was a little wary of Scott when she first met him earlier in the year, but right now his gaze is gentle, and he's been careful to stay out of her personal space since she flinched when he touched her, despite the difficulty hearing each other.

"I don't understand," Jane says, and she's beginning to feel foggy; the noise of the party is so hideously loud, the music pounding like a headache, the screeching voices and laughter rising vulture-like above it. "He told me . . . He said . . ."

"Jane?"

It's Aggie. Jane turns blindly toward her friend's voice. Aggie reaches a hand out to steady her. Her hair is even scattier than usual; one red strand is standing straight up, bobbing gently in the breeze coming through the door.

"Let's get you some air," she says.

"Can't go back outside," Jane manages. "Can we go—somewhere . . ."

"I'll take you out back to the catering tent. No, don't worry, I've got her," she tells Scott as she guides Jane through the crowds. "What's going on? Why did you run off?"

Jane stumbles after her and then takes a deep breath of the fresh winter air as they step out at the back of the mansion, into the complex of tents and generators keeping the party running. She closes her eyes as Aggie leads her into a warm nook between two canvas tents, the noise of the staff and the kitchens whirring away around them.

Aggie is kind. She has seen so much of Jane, her strangeness, her weakness, and yet she still seems to love her. She is the sort of friend that Richard made sure Jane would never have in London. With a friend like Aggie, Jane's stronger, more *Jane*.

"Aggie," Jane says, voice trembling. "Can I talk to you about what happened in London?"

Miranda

"I BROKE UP WITH CARTER," MIRANDA SAYS.

It's seven in the morning on New Year's Day. She's sitting with Adele and Frannie on the living room floor—somehow they've all gravitated down there, cups of black coffee in their hands, legs outstretched, feet touching. A triangle of Rossos. Instead of staying the night at Carter's mum's house, Miranda marched them both into a cab to the station and got the train back to Erstead at God-knows-what-time, on one of those postmidnight stopping trains that pulls into stations called things like Betly-in-the-Hedges and Bottom's Wallop. The twins slept through it all while Miranda just stared out into the darkness, reliving the party over and over.

"You *what?*" Adele yells, spilling her coffee down her arm in her consternation. "Shit," she says, licking herself clean, catlike. "But seriously, you what?"

Miranda drops her head into her hand. It was awful. Nightmarish. After Carter had said that he wasn't dating Siobhan anymore, and hadn't seen her for years, he completely shut down on the issue and wouldn't talk about it at *all*.

What about Valentine's Day? She had yelled at him. *What about that breakfast after Scott's birthday party? Why do you still write this woman a birthday card? You've literally just told me you still have feelings for her, for God's sake!*

I don't want to talk about Siobhan, was all Carter would say, and it was like his face was made of stone. *I don't want to talk about her.*

You talk about her, or I walk, right now, Miranda had said.

"Oh no," Adele says as Miranda relays the conversation. "An ultimatum."

"They always end really well," Frannie says, pulling a face.

"Yes, well, you two were inside getting *way too drunk*, so you were not there to advise me on what a bad idea it was to offer Carter an ultimatum," Miranda says.

The twins had been in the middle of an extremely high-stakes dance-off when she'd found them. When Frannie had forward-rolled through a scattering of broken glass, Miranda had decided it was well past time to step in and take her little sisters home.

"So what did he say?" asks Adele, leaning her head back against the sofa cushion.

"He went really quiet. And then he said, *You know what, the fact that I can't talk to you about this . . . it just shows we're not right for each other. This isn't right. You want me to be this perfect guy and I'm just not.* Or something crappy to that effect. And then he kind of backed away and ran."

"Ran?"

"Maybe walked," Miranda concedes. "But it was very much in the spirit of running. A running-away walk."

"So what now?" Frannie says.

Miranda groans and finishes her coffee. "Now I go to work," she says. "And try not to feel too sorry for myself."

"How *do* you feel?" Adele asks after a moment as Miranda gets to her feet.

"I don't even know. Hungover. Confused. A bit annoyed?"

"Not sad?"

"Oh, yeah, definitely sad," Miranda begins, and then she pauses. Is that true? She almost feels . . .

"Do you feel relieved?" Frannie says.

It's not exactly that. Not quite. But she's been angry with Carter for so long. For all the wrong reasons, it now seems, but . . . whether or not he cheated on her, he's definitely been hiding things. For the last few months, she's had this awful niggling feeling that Joseph Carter isn't the man he seems to be.

There's a sense of something lifting now that the tension is out in the open at last. It feels good to have taken action instead of just letting it fester, even if the consequences have been drastic.

Miranda stares down at her sisters' upturned faces. She thinks of what Trey said, that night in the cherry picker, how he told her she was *squashed*.

"Oh God," she says. "What have I been *doing* these last few months?"

It's as if a heavy fog is clearing. Those sleepless nights, the obsessing. The amazing evenings with Carter, curled up together, laughing until she ached, then the moment when he walked out of the door the next morning and the doubt resettled like dust. If Miranda was the sort of woman who talked about things being a *headfuck*, she would definitely say this last six months or so had absolutely been one of those.

"It's all been extremely not-Miranda," Adele says, brown eyes suddenly rather serious. "So much *drama*."

"So much angsting," Frannie adds.

"And not enough smiling," Adele says.

"No," Frannie says. "The Miranda of 2018 was very frowny."

"And a frown really ages you, Mir," Adele says, still wearing her most serious eyes. "You *know* we need to talk about your skincare regime as it is."

Miranda reaches for a cushion from the sofa and chucks it at Adele, more to break the tension than anything. She can't think about all this right now—it's too much. Why is everything so complicated? When did everything get this way?

Thank God she's working today. Miranda Rosso needs to get up a tree, and pronto.

JAMIE ISN'T TOO HARD ON THEM TODAY—HE KNOWS HE'S asking a lot, getting them to work on New Year's Day. He is also paying them double, which is some consolation to Miranda as she traipses through a muddy meadow, dragging a bag full of twigs and small branches behind her. No climbing today—she's on groundwork.

Never overfill the bag, that's the rule. Little and often. And yet, *every* time, she fills the bag too much, and then it's horrendous dragging it all the way to the chipper, and . . .

"Here," says AJ, appearing beside her and taking the handle. "I'll do it."

"I can do it," Miranda says automatically, trying to grab it back. Rip dances between her feet, tail wagging. He's so grown-up now, but definitely still a puppy at heart. Also still largely incontinent, which isn't surprising given that AJ has made no effort to train him.

"You've done eighty percent of it already—I know you can," AJ says, nodding back at the distance she's already covered. "But your hangover looks worse than mine, so I'm doing a good deed. Okay?"

She smiles. There are dark circles under his eyes, but he looks happy.

"How was your New Year's Eve?" she asks, walking beside him as they approach the chipper.

"It was good, actually," AJ says. His muscles are straining as he pulls the bag, and Miranda feels a little thrill as she remembers that actually, she's allowed to look. She's single.

"AJ *met someone*," Spikes says, standing up from where he was bending behind the chipper, an enormous grin on his face.

Miranda's stomach swoops. "Yeah?" she says, as lightly as she can. She ducks down to scratch Rip's chin; his tail thumps through the grass.

AJ scowls at Spikes.

"A *girl*," Spikes says, stepping back quickly as AJ dumps the bag of debris dangerously near his toes. "And do you know what they did all night long?"

I don't want to know I don't want to know I don't want to—

"What did they do all night?" Miranda finds herself saying, eyes on Rip's earnest wet nose.

"They *talked*," Spikes says.

AJ thumps him on the arm, and Spikes twists with an *oof*. Miranda's heart is hammering. She looks at AJ—he's trying to hold back a grin, but it's tugging at the corner of his lips, and quite suddenly Miranda feels like the biggest fool in all the world.

It's just wounded pride, she tells herself as she heads back across the meadow with AJ walking silently beside her and Rip trotting along between them. *It's natural that you're a bit disappointed he's over you.*

"So this girl," she says, glancing sideways at him. "You really like her?"

"I think so," he says, rubbing the back of his neck. "I think I might. I dunno. It's just . . . good to be open to it again."

He looks at her for a moment; she doesn't let herself catch his gaze.

"You said it yourself," AJ says. "I have to move on."

MIRANDA STANDS IN THE SHOWER, HEAD TILTED BACK, eyes closed, and lets the water sluice off the layers of grit and sawdust. What a day. If she's going by the last twenty-four hours, 2019 is going to be monumentally rubbish.

"Are you done in there?" yells Frannie.

"No! That's why the shower is still running and I'm still in it!" Miranda shouts back.

She can *hear* the flounce through the door. She rolls her eyes and reaches for the shower gel. This shouldn't feel nearly as miserable as it does—and she shouldn't care at *all* about the AJ thing, obviously. But she's mopey and grouchy. She keeps replaying it all, the moment when Carter walked away, the grin tugging at AJ's lips when he talked about the woman he'd met the night before.

She turns the shower off and climbs out, wrapping herself in her towel. Frannie is waiting on the other side of the bathroom door when she opens it. Miranda jumps.

Frannie looks like she's about to launch into a tirade about the length of Miranda's shower, but then she catches Miranda's expression and thinks better of it. "Want me to make some hot chocolate?" she says instead.

"Yes," Miranda says, shoulders sagging. "Urgently, please."

Siobhan

ON THE DAY IN JANUARY WHEN JOSEPH TAKES SIOBHAN
to meet Mary Carter, she tells him about the baby she lost.

It's an enormous moment, monumentally significant for both of
them. Joseph has never brought a woman home before, though his
mother has apparently been dying for him to do so since he took Sharon
to prom aged sixteen. (Siobhan was bemused to find herself feeling quite
jealous of Sharon—her feelings for Joseph constantly take her by surprise
with their intensity, but envying a sixteen-year-old in a pomegranate-
colored ruffled gown feels like a new low.)

Mary embraces Siobhan in the hallway of her Gothic little house
near Winchester station. It's dingy, and there's a vagueness to Mary, a
sort of weary glamour. Siobhan is sickeningly nervous; her stomach
churned for the entire journey from Dublin to this hallway. But Mary
is the consummate host and makes it easy. As she ushers Siobhan
through to the living room, Siobhan spots an episode of *Ambition*
muted on her television—it's a BBC Three show filmed in Dublin, and
the lead went to drama school with Siobhan. Before long the two
women are comparing notes on the various plot twists of the series so

far and Joseph is beaming at them from the doorway as he returns with china cups filled with tea. Too milky—he always makes it too milky. Joseph will forever be the man who volunteers to make the drinks, but he's never been very good at precision.

After lunch, Mary does the quintessential mum thing and fetches the photo album. Joseph is her only son and she is extremely proud of him. Siobhan flicks through the photos of his childhood, this beaming, messy-haired, red-cheeked boy, and can't help smiling, though really she's not the sort of woman who cares much for childhood photos. She'd *never* let anyone see any of hers. She was not a cute child. All scowl and stickiness.

Joseph's father features for the first few years of the photo album—blond head bowed over the baby in his arms, a large hand with a smaller one tucked inside. He's gone by the time Joseph's two or so. He met someone else, Joseph told Siobhan on one of their nightly phone calls, the calls that sprawl into the slurring, dozy, early hours.

Joseph and his father are still in touch, though Joseph's dad is a little absentminded—forgets birthdays every three years or so, can never keep track of Joseph's girlfriends. Siobhan has quiet suspicions that Joseph's deep-seated people-pleasing tendencies stem from this absent father figure of his, though she's yet to broach this.

"Oh, look at me!" Mary says, ducking down to pick up a photograph that has slipped from the back of the album. "I was so proud of that little bump."

Siobhan takes the photograph and her throat tightens. It shows a young and very beautiful Mary, side on. Her hands are cupped around her newly curved belly, eyes downturned, mouth smiling. She's wearing a sunflower-yellow dress and exudes happiness.

Siobhan never got to the point of having a baby bump, just first-trimester bloating, but in the couple of weeks before her miscarriage she would have to leave the top button of her jeans undone, and every time she pulled up the zip she felt a thrill of joy.

"Excuse me." She stands and makes her way out to the hall. "Which way is the bathroom, please?" she manages.

"I'll show you," Joseph says, jumping up and following her. "Here, upstairs."

She walks quietly up the staircase, body pounding with remembered pain.

"Are you okay?" Joseph whispers.

"Mm-hmm." It's all she can manage. Her fists are clenched, and Joseph reaches out and pries one open, sliding his hand into hers.

They reach the upstairs hall and neither of them makes any move toward the bathroom visible through its open door. Siobhan looks down at their joined hands and concentrates on not crying.

"I was pregnant, once," she whispers. "When Cillian left me, actually. But I lost my baby a week after he walked out."

"Oh, Siobhan." Joseph pulls her into him, crushing her close, and she burrows into the warmth of his jumper, pressing her face to his chest so hard it almost hurts. "Oh God."

Siobhan gives up on not crying. Her shoulders heave, her sobs muffled in Joseph's chest.

"I'm so sorry," Joseph whispers, pressing his lips to the top of her head. "I can't even imagine how a person gets through losing so much all at once."

"Cillian said he wanted the baby," Siobhan says, pulling back slightly, doing her best to dab at her ruined makeup, checking whether she's got it all over Joseph's jumper. "But I guess he didn't. And then the baby was gone, too." She shrugs, trying to regain some composure. "It got hard to trust people, after that."

"Shiv, I can't pretend to understand what you went through, I just . . . I'm so sad that happened." Joseph shifts back, and she can see it on his face: it's like he's feeling it with her. Her hands clutch at his back, and she turns her gaze away; she can't bear seeing her pain reflected in him like that.

She sniffs. "It's okay. I'm okay. That photo just really got me."

"Of course." He winces, pressing his lips together. "I'm sorry. And I'm really . . . I'm honored you trusted me enough to tell me."

She'd not thought about it much, actually. It had seemed so natural. This only now strikes her as remarkable—she's never even allowed Fiona to bring up the topic, and here she is, in Joseph's arms, telling him everything.

And it feels good. Having that truth that she always carries in her belly out in the open. As she shifts her gaze back to meet Joseph's eyes, she wonders how brave she can be.

"Can I ask you a question?" she says, forcing her own hand.

"Of course," he says. "Anything."

She takes a deep breath.

"Do you want children?" Her voice is shaking slightly. "I do. A lot. It's kind of a big deal for me."

Joseph smiles easily. "Absolutely," he says, lifting a hand to her cheek. "I absolutely do."

Siobhan sags against him. She'd not realized how much she'd been holding that question in, but the ease with which he answers fills her with a rolling, flooding sort of joy, so sweet it's almost overwhelming. She's a mess of tears and smiles, sobbing again, laughing, too. He holds her tight.

"Well. Good," she says into his jumper eventually, as she manages to pull herself together. "Okay. Right." She sniffs, shifting to run her fingers under her eyes and catch the streaks of mascara. "Shall we go back down before the tea gets cold?"

"Give yourself a minute," Joseph says, pressing his lips to her forehead. "There's no rush." He pauses, wearing a slightly worried frown, watching her fix her face. "You know," he says, "you really don't have to have it together all the time. I would say now is a key time when you can just . . ." He waves a hand at her face. "Have a bit of that eye makeup on your nose and it's fine?"

"Oh God, my nose?" Siobhan says, already scrubbing.

Joseph laughs and dives in to kiss her, and she doesn't even stop him, though her face is a mess and still wet with tears. She lets him pull her close and hold her, and lets the emotions roil, the joy and the sadness. As it all begins to settle to a low hum, she presses her cheek to his chest and feels something else blooming: the peace that comes with letting someone else take a little of the burden.

TELLING JOSEPH ABOUT THE MISCARRIAGE CHANGES EV-erything. Something in Siobhan comes loose; over the next couple of weeks she unspools, sharing more and more, faster and faster, as if she's pulled a door ajar and it's now swung open.

She doesn't always feel sure of him—often she is breathtakingly convinced he'll leave her. Occasionally she snaps at him, bracing herself to push him away, but he comes to her and holds her and just like that the fear spirals away.

There's one day in January when she tells him quite how bad April 2015 was for her. He takes her hands in his, palm up, and presses his lips to the place where her nails would bite. She can hardly bear the sensation, the tenderness of it.

"I get scared," she whispers. "That those awful feelings will come for me again, and I'll go back to that place."

"You won't. You've come so far since then. And if you do," he says, lips against her hand, "I'll be here."

It's the best thing he can say to her, and he knows it. *I'll be here.* He says it all the time—he seems to have an endless supply of reassurance now he knows it's what's needed. At first Siobhan is prickly about it, doesn't like him handing it out like that just because he knows she wants to hear it, but eventually, slowly, she begins to let herself luxuriate in Joseph Carter telling her he's not going anywhere.

Technically they're only supposed to be seeing each other the first

Friday of the month—it's still hers, still marked out in his diary—but she comes down to London every week of January, on some pretense or other, or simply because he asks her. Flights are so cheap anyway, why would she not?

At the end of the month, she finishes a day of one-to-ones in her home office and walks out into the living room to find Fiona waiting expectantly, keys in hand, shoes on.

"Umm, hi?" says Siobhan.

"Finally!" Fiona says, already leading her toward the door. "Shoes! Shoes!"

"What?"

"Put some shoes on!"

"Why?"

"We're going out, obviously."

"Where?"

"Shoes!" Fiona insists, passing Siobhan the nearest pair of boots by the door.

Siobhan looks scathing and immediately swaps them for a pair that coordinates with her outfit. She may not know where she's going, but she knows whether to wear brown or black boots with a blue dress.

Fiona jams Siobhan's arms into a coat as soon as her boots are on.

"Where are you taking me, woman!" Siobhan protests as the flat door closes behind them.

Fiona has an overnight bag slung across her body; there's a cab waiting for them outside the building, and she chucks the bag into the boot before they jump in the back. The taxi driver apparently already knows the plan, because he starts driving right away, no questions asked.

"Is this a kidnap?" Siobhan asks.

Fiona laughs. "Yes," she says fondly, reaching for Siobhan's hand, "I, your flatmate, am kidnapping you so that I can . . . have you all to myself? But somewhere else?"

"You're not going to tell me where we're going, are you?" Siobhan says, crossing her legs, holding Fiona's hand in hers. She'd have shucked off the gesture of reassurance not too long ago, but she's getting better at that sort of thing these days.

"Nope," Fiona says, with a cheerful smile. "And it's a long drive, so we'd better find something else to talk about."

She's right: it *is* a long drive, almost an hour and a half, and by the time the cab pulls to a stop it's so dark outside Siobhan still doesn't have a clue where they are. She knows they've gone south of Dublin, but that's pretty much it. When she climbs out of the taxi, the first thing that hits her is the smell: the air is fresh, the kind of fresh you only find somewhere in the depths of the countryside. Her heeled boots sink slightly in the mud; they're on a lane lined with dark trees.

"Okay, this is still fairly kidnappy," Siobhan says, looking around for Fiona, who is pulling the bag out of the boot. "Hey, what are you doing?"

Fiona is climbing back in the cab.

"Are we not there yet?"

"You are," Fiona says, blowing Siobhan a kiss. "Have a fantastic night."

And with that she pulls the cab door closed. Siobhan blinks, turning around, looking for some sort of clue as to what the hell's going on, and it's then she notices the glow of lights in the trees across the road. She frowns, stepping closer, then lets out a shriek as a large man steps out of the woods.

"Surprise!" the large man says.

Siobhan clutches her chest. It's Joseph; he comes toward her, wearing a rather worried expression on his face.

"Oh, are you okay?"

"What are you doing here? What am I doing here? Where is here?" Siobhan says, but she's already in his arms, and she lifts her chin to kiss him.

"I wanted to do something romantic for you, because we're always rushing and squeezing in time," Joseph says, pressing light, teasing kisses to her lips. "So we're going camping."

Siobhan goes still.

"Pardon?" she says. "Have you met me?"

Joseph bursts out laughing, pulling her in against his chest. "Don't worry," he says. "Follow me."

He leads her through the trees—there's a narrow track here, graveled and well trodden. When it opens out, Siobhan breathes in sharply, eyes widening.

There's a beautiful tent in the clearing, its flaps pulled back to reveal a gorgeous cozy interior complete with a gigantic bed covered in throws and cushions. There's a large decking area out front, with a fire pit and low seats; Siobhan lets out an involuntary squeal when she sees a wood-fired hot tub on the other side of the tent.

"Glamping," Joseph says, his voice full of laughter. "Camping Siobhan style."

"I love you," Siobhan says, launching herself at him. She feels giddy, filled with an unbridled, unfamiliar sort of joy.

"So, what do you want to do first?" he says, beaming down at her. "There's a pizza oven, and they've left us ingredients for that, if you're ready for dinner—or we could jump in the hot tub?"

"Bed," Siobhan says, already tugging on his hands. "We're starting with bed."

SIOBHAN'S PHONE WAKES HER EARLY THE NEXT morning—it's on silent, but the flash of a new call on the screen cuts through the darkness of the tent and catches her eye. She squints. It's Richard. Again. Siobhan frowns at the phone, uneasy. This is the fifth time he's called her since December, and he's sent a few messages, trying to get back in her favor. **Siobhan, I'm sorry, you were quite right to give me a dressing down.** That sort of thing.

She's got a one-to-one booked in with him in mid-February, but she's already spoken to the Bray & Kembrey HR team about not feeling she's the right coach for him; they were blessedly sensitive to the issue and will soon be informing Richard that they'll assign him someone else.

"You okay?" Joseph whispers, snuggling in behind her.

"Mm," Siobhan says, swiping the missed call away. He'll get the picture soon—Siobhan has had plenty of experience at ghosting men, and it always works eventually. The last thing she wants to think about this morning is Richard. Siobhan is far too much of a realist to describe anything as *perfect*, but last night with Joseph had been pretty close. They'd had champagne in the hot tub, eaten gooey vegan cheese by the handful after their homemade pizzas fell apart in the pizza oven, and all that was *after* they'd had the sort of sex Siobhan hadn't really known was possible until she'd met him. Joseph makes her genuinely weak with desire—she feels languid now, loose limbed, as if she spent yesterday running a race and then headed straight to a spa. Somewhere in between exhausted and relaxed.

"Is that Richard again?" Joseph says.

She hadn't realized he could see the screen over her shoulder. He shouldn't even know Richard is one of her clients, but he'd pieced it together pretty quickly when he'd seen a *Richard (B&K)* popping up on her phone a few weeks before.

"Don't worry," she says. "I'm not going to reply to him. I never do—promise."

She nuzzles back against him, spooning close into the heat of his body. It's warm in the tent, despite the January chill. Joseph kisses her ear.

"I know. But he shouldn't be calling."

Siobhan is awake now, too awake to go back to sleep. She checks the time—half six—and then turns over so she's face-to-face with a dozy, muss-haired Joseph. She wonders if she'll ever get over the luxury of waking up beside him like this, knowing he's all hers; it feels too good to be true. There's that impulse again, pulling at the corners of her, telling her that the moment she lets him in, he'll disappear.

"You're thinking about me running off, aren't you?" Joseph says without opening his eyes, kissing her fingers and knotting them between his own.

"Yes," she says. It's disarming being so honest with him. Every time she does it and he stays, every time she shows him a little more of herself and he doesn't run away . . . it's as if that scar across her heart grows paler.

"Will it help if I tell you I won't?"

"Run off?"

"Mm." He shifts closer, dropping his lips to her hands again, tracing kisses along each finger in turn. They're weighed down under so many throws, deliciously cozy.

"You'd have to say it so many times you'd get sick of it, honestly. It's like water into sand." She tries for a rueful smile, but Joseph's kissed her lips before it's quite formed.

"I don't mind," he says, lips still against hers. "I want to keep saying it. I want to say it over and over until you know it's true."

She smiles and kisses him more deeply. "What about you?" she asks eventually, settling back against the pillow. "I mean . . . I *did* run off, really, when I stopped talking to you last year. Do you worry about that happening again?"

"Oh, all the time," Joseph says, and he pulls her body flush against his.

Siobhan's stomach tightens at the contact, but there's guilt there, too.

"I'm not quite as good at reassurance as you are, am I?" she says penitently, pressing her lips to his collarbone.

"Well, how about . . ." Joseph trails off.

Siobhan pulls back slightly. There's something new in his voice. He ducks his head and kisses his way along her shoulder; she gets the feeling he's avoiding eye contact.

"How about you just tell me once, and really mean it, and I'll believe you," he says.

Siobhan waits it out as the panic comes—he wants more of her, she can't give it, she can't let him in like that—and then passes. She's come so far already this year. It feels almost miraculous to know even as the fear comes that it will go again.

She lifts a hand to his cheek and shifts so she's meeting his gaze squarely. He's a little tense around the eyes, a bit nervous, even.

"I'm yours," Siobhan says. "I love you. There will be no more disappearing. I'm here to stay."

Jane

JANE? PLEASE CALL ME WHEN YOU CAN. I'M SO SORRY FOR BE-
ing such a twat at New Year's. If you let me explain . . . I don't want
to make excuses, but I'd really love the chance to talk to you. Xx

Jane swallows, turning her phone facedown on the coffee table.

"Joseph?" Aggie calls from the kitchen, where she's cooking them
risotto for dinner.

After New Year's Eve, Jane came back to her beautiful white-
walled flat. She couldn't afford to keep renting the place in Wales
anyway, and she missed Winchester more than she'd ever imagined a
person could miss a place. Since her return, she and Aggie have got in
the habit of having dinner at Aggie's place.

"How could you tell?" Jane asks, stretching her legs out on the sofa,
luxuriating in how at home she feels here. Her shoes are on the shoe
rack by the door, her cardigan slung over the back of a chair.

"Your face does this thing when Joseph messages you, a sort of . . ."
Aggie leans back so Jane can see her through the kitchen door and
makes a wincing face, bottom lip wobbling.

Jane laughs. "Oh, thank you, very flattering." She sobers. "It's just . . . it's becoming so hard to ignore his messages."

In truth it's almost impossible. They gnaw at her, tug at her, eat into every moment when her brain doesn't have something else to keep it busy.

"Still not ready to talk to him, though?" Aggie says, back at the stove.

"Still not ready," Jane says with a sigh.

Her phone buzzes on the table—Jane turns the phone over and frowns. It's Colin. He's never called her before. They have each other's numbers in case of charity shop emergencies. She hesitates before answering, but then is struck by the chilling thought that perhaps something might have happened to Mortimer.

"Hello?" she says.

"Jane?"

"Yes, hi? Is everything okay, Colin?"

"I've killed Bluebell!" Colin roars down the phone at her.

Jane holds the phone away from her ear slightly.

"You've . . . killed . . . Bluebell?"

"Killed her off!" Colin shouts cheerfully. "Just told Mum she's really a seventy-one-year-old man called Mortimer, and do you know what she said?"

Jane feels a smile growing. Aggie is leaning back to see her through the kitchen door again, curious.

"What did she say?" Jane asks.

"She said, *I'm ninety-six, Colin. When you get to my age you don't give enough of a shit about anything to have 'objections.'*"

Jane laughs. "Well that's . . . nice?"

"It's very my mother," Colin says, and he's laughing, too. "But I just wanted to tell you. I wouldn't have done it if we hadn't had that chat. I think I'd stopped noticing how much it bothered Mortimer. You can stop seeing a person when you've loved them for this long and you know they're not going anywhere. But Mortimer is a man worth moving mountains for, and he deserves the sort of wedding he wants."

"So are you going to propose?"

"Lord, no!" Colin yells. "That's his job! I've done my bit! I've killed Bluebell!"

Jane laughs. "And you've told him?"

Colin's voice softens. "He cried a bit," he confesses. "It was all rather lovely."

"Then you just have to wait, now, until he decides the time is right to propose?"

"That's it. Back to the waiting game. But I've said it before and I'll say it again, Jane Miller. Some things are worth waiting for."

A WEEK LATER, JANE HEADS TO AGGIE'S STUDIO AFTER A visit to the Job Center, where an enthusiastic young woman with pink hair said lots of encouraging things about her very scant CV; Jane is now clutching a handful of job ads and feeling alive with possibility. *So much choice, eh?* the pink-haired woman had said as she'd hit print on the adverts, and Jane had been surprised to notice that the idea of making choices didn't frighten her any longer. It felt exciting.

Aggie's studio is housed in an old mill that's full of all sorts of businesses, everything from therapists to marketing start-ups. The building is ramshackle and rambling—Jane can never quite remember the route from the front door to Aggie's studio, and usually ends up turning a corner into some sort of open-plan meeting area full of young, fashionable people drinking coffee from bamboo cups.

Aggie looks up when Jane finally makes her way into the right room, and beams at her.

"Now, there's the woman I need!" she says. "Hold that, would you?"

Jane dutifully holds the other end of a roll of wallpaper. Aggie tilts her head one way, then the other.

"Too red?" she says. "Red photographs so badly."

"A bit red, but more pink," Jane says, and Aggie *tsk*s between her teeth, rolling it up again.

"How are you feeling about lunch, are you ready for this?" Aggie asks, stuffing her pencil into her bun as she turns to the next wallpaper sample roll.

Jane's stomach lurches. "I'm not . . . looking forward to it," she says. "But I think I'm ready. What about you? How are you feeling about your secret weekend away?"

"It's not a secret, exactly," Aggie says, busying herself with the wallpaper. "I'm going to visit an old friend who I ought to see more of. Kasima. You reminded me that . . . I don't know. You just made me want to see her, is all." She gives a brisk smile. "She was my neighbor when I first came to Winchester. She helped me."

After Jane had told her what had happened in London, Aggie had given Jane a glimpse of her own past. She'd told Jane about the life she had left behind in Cornwall when she'd first fled to Winchester five years ago. She'd had a design studio there, much bigger and more prestigious than this one. When her mental health had deteriorated, she'd hidden it so well that nobody had noticed, and it wasn't until Aggie had burned down her own studio that her friends and colleagues realized there was anything wrong with her at all.

"Helped you, as in, helped you settle in?" Jane asks, moving to pin down the edges of another sheet of wallpaper.

Aggie huffs a laugh. "You could say that. She got me a cleaning job at her office. She encouraged me to try therapy, and when the NHS waiting list was so long, she loaned me the money to go private." Aggie isn't meeting Jane's eye; she usually seems so at ease, but she's visibly biting back her emotions now. "She had no obligation to help me, nobody telling her to do it. She just helped me because she saw I needed help."

"Sounds familiar," Jane says, looking up at Aggie through her eyelashes.

Aggie smiles. "Eh, well. That sort of kindness, it gets into your bones. Once you've felt it, you can't help but look for ways to pass the feeling on." She sniffs, pulling herself together. "Anyway, I'm seeing her tomorrow, then I'm off to Falmouth to visit one of my old colleagues. I left a lot of people in the lurch when I came here. You being so brave, you reminded me I'm not done dealing with my past, either."

"Oh," Jane says, lifting a hand to her chest. The idea that Jane could be brave enough to inspire anybody is new and strange, and a little lovely.

"But—you first," Aggie says, pointing another pencil at her before jamming it in her bun alongside the others. "Are you ready for this?"

Jane swallows and nods. "I'm ready."

JANE'S STOMACH FLIPS WHEN THEY APPROACH THE CAFÉ. Lou is already there; Jane called her a few days ago. Since New Year's, since seeing Richard, she's thought a lot about the words that Lou said when she came to see Jane in the charity shop. *You could come to London? Face him on your own terms? I'd have your back, you know, if that helps.*

That sentence. *I'd have your back.* It was small, but it had meant so much, and it made it a lot easier to be brave.

"Hi," Lou says shyly as Jane introduces her to Aggie. They head on inside together, a strange threesome, with Lou in her smart work clothes, Aggie with four pencils in her bun and walking boots under her corduroys, Jane in her pale-pink Friday jumper and jeans.

Everything at Cafemonde feels as if it is on a slight slant—viewed from outside, the building is gently, charmingly subsiding into Winchester's cobbled streets, and whether or not the floor inside is really level, once you're in there you can't shake the feel of quirky wonkiness. Their food comes quickly, great steaming plates of fried breakfast for Jane and Aggie, an avocado salad for Lou.

"Oh, wow, that looks good," she says, eyeing Jane's fry-up enviously. "I can't remember the last time I ate anything that looked that delicious."

Jane pushes the plate her way. "Let's share," she says.

Lou hesitates and then pulls a face. "Oh, go on then," she says, with a smile. "Thanks."

They eat in silence for a while. Eventually Lou looks sideways at Jane, gaze curious.

"You said on the phone that Richard found you?" she says.

Jane's pulse begins to flutter, tapping insistently at the base of her throat, but she tries to keep her breathing steady. It's just habit, this fearful feeling. She has done the frightening thing—she's faced Richard. She shouldn't be afraid anymore.

"Yes, he found me. He said someone from Brays might approach me with some questions about our relationship. He offered me money to keep quiet."

Lou's eyes widen. "Wow," she says.

"We wondered if you might know exactly what he's under investigation for?" Aggie says through a mouthful of baked beans.

Lou nods. "The rumor is, a staff member has accused him of sending her inappropriate messages," she says. "And I heard that someone else came out saying he'd bullied them into not speaking up about something back in 2016—you remember Effie, who has the office next door to Richard's?" Lou asks Jane, who nods. "She said she heard an altercation, but when she asked Richard about it, he strong-armed her into never mentioning it to anyone, and she needed his support if she wanted to go for partner, so she went along with it. There's a new head of HR at Brays these days, and she takes stuff like this really seriously. She's been doing some real digging on Richard."

"Do you remember when exactly it was that Effie heard that altercation?" Jane asks, fork hovering halfway to her mouth. "I left midway through 2016. I might still have been there."

"Yeah, actually—February fourteenth. I remember because it was Valentine's Day. It made me think it might have been something romantic, if he was rowing with someone on that day, and . . . I hope you don't mind me saying, Jane, I wondered if it was you?"

Jane shakes her head slowly, lowering her fork to her plate. Her heartbeat isn't just fluttering now, it's hammering, thudding in her chest like a warning. She looks at Aggie.

"That was just a few months before I left the firm. And . . . that's when I first saw Joseph," she whispers.

Aggie breathes in sharply. "Joseph Carter?"

"Who, sorry?" Lou says.

"A friend," Jane says after a moment. "He worked in IT at Bray & Kembrey at the time."

Lou squints in thought. "Tall, good-looking, little professor-ish glasses?" she says.

Jane smiles slightly. "That's him. He rowed with Richard in 2016, on Valentine's Day. I remember that Richard made me clear something out of his diary from that morning, and said I wasn't to tell anyone about what had happened. At the time it didn't seem all that strange—he often asked me to clear things out of his diary retrospectively if they didn't happen as planned, because he liked it to be an accurate reflection of what he did and when, in case he needed to refer back to it. And I figured he just didn't want anyone to know about the altercation because he was embarrassed, or perhaps saving face for Joseph, who was obviously distraught about something." Jane closes her eyes for a moment. "*Just an old friend holding grudges*, Richard said."

"Oh, wow," Lou says, eyes even wider. "What was it you deleted from his diary?"

Jane chews her lip and closes her eyes again. She tries to remember it. Joseph had barged straight past her into Richard's office, the door slamming shut behind him. She hadn't heard everything that had happened in the office, just muffled raised voices and the odd phrase—

Your fault, nothing to do with me. And then Joseph had come flying out of the room again, his face tearstained and twisted, and stumbled his way out into the corridor. She remembers the sight of his hand gripping the doorframe for a moment, knuckles red and white and scuffed.

Then Richard had emerged. He'd smoothed down his hair and said to her, *Ignore that nonsense, please. Just an old friend holding grudges. Not to be mentioned to anyone else, understood?*

Jane had jumped up to check he was all right—was he injured? He'd brushed her off, and she'd retreated behind her desk again. By then she had learned that if he wasn't in the mood to be touched, it was best to remain professional.

"And then he said, *Delete the one-to-one that was in my diary for this morning,*" Jane says, opening her eyes.

"Just the one-to-one? That's all?" Lou says.

"Yes," Jane says regretfully. It could be almost anything—a meeting with a colleague, a client . . . "But I do remember it was a female name." She swallows, looking down at her plate. "I checked because . . . by then I wasn't at all sure he was being faithful to me."

Lou shoots her a sympathetic look. "Well. That's certainly interesting," she says. "I'm sure it would help back up what Effie's saying. Are you thinking . . . well . . . what *are* you thinking, Jane?"

Jane swallows. This has occupied her thoughts almost as much as Joseph has: The question of what to do. How brave to be. How brave she *can* be, after all this time, after spending Richard's money.

"I'm trying to make my mind up," she says carefully. "But I'm thinking I might like to take Richard Wilson down."

Siobhan

READY FOR V-DAY 2.0? XX

Siobhan grins down at the message, weaving her way through the crowds as she heads toward Leicester Square station. She's in ridiculous shoes—they pinch her toes like pincers, and the heel is razor thin, but they make her legs look phenomenal, and she wants to walk into that café and see Joseph's face light up.

She's wearing the red dress she wore last year, to the fateful Valentine's Day when Joseph didn't turn up—the first time she tried to ghost him. Her least effectual attempt.

This year when he said they should go for breakfast and actually both turn up this time, she decided to let him see exactly what he missed in 2015.

You better not be late xx

She hits send, and the reply is there when she next glances down at her phone.

I know better than that now xx

For a very sentimental moment, which Siobhan would never confess to anybody, she presses the phone to her chest and holds it tightly.

She loves this man. She loves the journey they've been on, with all its mess, its ups and downs. She loves the person she's become since she first met him. As she makes her way down the steps into the station, clinging tightly to the handrail, she feels lighter and happier than she has felt for as long as she can remember.

The snag in her morning appears once she's settled in her seat on the tube, handbag on her lap. It's Richard Wilson, sitting opposite her and to the left.

"Shit," she mutters, looking down at her bag and fiddling with the chain strap.

Today was the day they were meant to have their one-to-one, now canceled because she said he should see a different life coach. He's still not stopped calling and messaging. She blocked him, but he's found other ways to get through to her: on the contact form on her website, then on her newly reactivated Instagram. It could be a coincidence that he's here, but London is a large city, and Siobhan is not naïve enough to believe that their paths have crossed serendipitously, though Richard is trying very hard to emulate the posture of a man who didn't get on this train specifically in order to sit opposite her. He presumably knew she'd be in London because they'd had the one-to-one booked in, but how did he find her here?

Joseph may be right. She should do something about this. She sighs inwardly as Richard looks up, catches her eye, and feigns surprise.

"Siobhan!" he says, smiling.

"Richard," she says, and there's a warning in her voice—surely he can hear it. But he just keeps smiling. "I'm getting off at the next stop," she says as the train begins to slow.

"Oh, me too," he says, standing with her.

She grits her teeth. "Richard, I don't want to talk to you. I think I've made that pretty clear."

The train stops. A few people are glancing their way with curiosity; Siobhan lifts her chin slightly as she moves toward the doors.

Richard follows her along the platform, so close his arm brushes her shoulder. For the first time she feels something more than irritation— not quite fear, but unease, maybe. He's bigger than she remembered, and though the station is full of people, this is London, and she's not convinced anyone would help her if she asked them.

"Why are you still trying, Richard?" she says as they wait in the queue for the escalator. She faces forward, glancing over her shoulder at him. He seems perfectly at ease, which raises her hackles even further. "I don't want anything to do with you."

"Whoa, hey," he says, as if she's a feisty horse. "I just want to talk, Siobhan, the way we used to talk."

"You're not my client now, Richard," she says curtly. "I don't have to listen to you."

They're on the escalator now, making their way up through the station; she glances back at him again. He smiles, one of those warm, engaging smiles that she can't help feeling he's learned from a TED Talk, and all of a sudden she's *angry*. She's going to be late for Joseph now—she's had to get off a stop early, and it'll be at least a fifteen-minute walk from here.

"What do you want from me, Richard?" They come to the top of the escalator; people jostle past them, and he reaches out a hand to steady her as someone knocks into her shoulder. "Don't touch me," she says, shrugging him off and walking to the gates. "Leave me alone."

"All right, Shiv," he says. Her nickname in his mouth makes her want to lash out—it feels intimate, as if he's touched her.

The gates hold him up; she's through before he's got his card out of his pocket, and then she begins to run. It's a good job she's a woman who knows how to move fast in heels. She ducks under arms, pushes through the middle of conversations, ignores the tuts and exclamations.

It's better once she's out in the open air. There was something about the close stuffiness of the station that made Richard feel more threatening—his nearness was so unavoidable. Now that she's out in the sleeting, icy rain of Piccadilly Circus, with a hunched man in a wooly hat trying to pass her a copy of the *Metro*, and a busker singing out their own version of Hozier's "Take Me to Church," she feels free again.

Still, she moves fast. She's late, and Joseph will definitely tease her about it, given how much stick she gave him for standing her up last year. By the time she reaches the Strand, her back is damp with sweat under her giant fur coat and the rain has probably ruined her hair. But all thought of Richard is gone; she smiles as she catches sight of Joseph across the road, sitting in the window of the café, his eyes turned down to the menu. Around him there are endless sets of couples stretching to either side, and she bites her lip, remembering how it felt to sit alone at a table like that on Valentine's Day.

The traffic is stationary, as always on the Strand. She begins to make her way between the idling cars, and as if he feels her gaze, Joseph lifts his head and meets her eyes through the window. He beams, and she smiles back at him, swinging her hips a little more, dropping her shoulders back as he watches her cross the road toward him. *I'm late, but of course he's waited for me*, she thinks, her smile growing.

"Siobhan!"

She turns in surprise toward the sound of Richard's voice behind her; she was so sure he hadn't followed her, certainly not all the way here. She's mid-step. Distracted. Unsteady on her feet.

In the moment when the motorbike speeds its way between the waiting queues of cars, when it glances off her body and throws her spinning to the ground, when her head cracks sickeningly against the tarmac, Siobhan is still halfway through her thought about Joseph. *I'm late, but of course he's waited for me*, she's thinking, as her body begins to crumple. *He's always waited for me.*

There is a sudden roaring silence. Then white noise, coursing through her, as if her pain is audible and she's vibrating with its single, awful note. And just like that, in an instant, as if the universe doesn't care that her story is really just starting, Siobhan Kelly has less than one minute left to live.

There's no acceptance. She doesn't have time for that. There's only anger, and pain, and loss.

Joseph is coming to her; though she can't see, she knows he's coming. Pushing through the café. Shoving against the door, forging through the traffic, hands slamming against the bonnet of a car as it almost knocks him down.

As her last seconds bleed away, it's not Siobhan's life that passes before her eyes, it's the life she has finally let herself begin to imagine. Quick kisses first thing in the morning as Joseph passes her a coffee. Slow walks down shorefronts as they talk about their future. Wedding dress shopping with Fiona as Siobhan abandons her scruples about marriage because she *loves* him, because she knows it's forever even if her head still says forever is too good to be true. And the children. The children. All the children she has ached for, the children she already knows, deep in her belly, and loves with every scrap of her being.

It hurts. There is no hurt like it. But because she is Siobhan Kelly, and a fighter to her core, as those last few seconds are passing, it's not despair she's feeling. It's something fiercer than that. She's bargaining with her body, the way she always has. Pushing it harder than it wants to be pushed. *Just give me a few more moments*, she thinks. *Long enough for him to get to me, and look me in the eyes, so I can tell him—*

Miranda

BANG.

"Miranda!" Jamie barks down at her. "It's fucking raining timber! What the fuck are you doing standing there like a melon!"

"Lemon," AJ corrects him mildly, but he's frowning down at Miranda with concern as he spins in his harness, kicking away from the tree trunk.

She scurries out of range. She's been doing this job way too long to stand under a tree daydreaming while the men are working up there. It strikes her that Carter did the very same thing a year ago, on the day when AJ had to rescue her from the oak. She and Carter were so good then. Everything about him had seemed so completely perfect.

And now it's Valentine's Day once again and everything is *crap*. It really is. She can't stop thinking about AJ now that he's seeing someone else—to her shame, since he's been off-limits he seems to have become exponentially sexier, and he was pretty sexy to begin with. And she thinks about Carter a lot, too. She misses his ease, his big smile, the way they made each other laugh.

More than all of that, though—she wants answers from him. It's the unsolved mysteries that are keeping him in her mind like this, she's sure of it. That breakfast in Central London that he never explained. The date he missed on Valentine's Day. It makes her itch to think that she'll never know the *why* behind it all. Miranda is just one of those people: she picks the label off her beer bottle, she itches mosquito bites. She can't leave things alone.

And Carter's story doesn't feel done. There's something more to it. Until she knows what it is, she's starting to worry that she just won't be able to put the whole thing to bed.

"Are you all right?" Spikes says, showing an astonishing and unprecedented level of interest in her life. Usually the most she gets out of Spikes is a *What's up*, and he rarely waits for an answer before plodding off or talking about football.

She blinks at him. "Did someone ask you to ask me that?"

Spikes doesn't look offended. "AJ," he says. "He thinks you're moping."

The fact that AJ cares both pleases and irritates her in equal measure. She turns back to gathering up branches, relishing the ache in her muscles; she's worked every job Jamie's had this last month, desperate for the distraction. Her body is the fittest it's ever been, and she's got so many scratches on her limbs that the scabs on her knees have scabs now.

"Rosso?" Spikes prompts her, clearly not planning to let up until he's finished his assignment.

She sighs, glancing over her shoulder at him. "I think . . . I've made a bad decision. I just can't work out which one it was."

"Right," Spikes says, starting to look a little nervous, the way he always does when things get complicated.

"This year has been crap so far, and that's completely my fault. I'm stuck in limbo. But life's too short for that, right?" She straightens up as the thought sinks in. "Yeah. Life is *totally* too short for that. I mean, you never know when you're just going to . . ." She waves an arm. "Fall out of a tree or something."

"Yes?" Spikes says, glancing longingly toward the chipper.

"I need to decide what I want and go get it. Don't I?"

"Yeah?" Spikes is blinking too much, a sure sign of discomfort, should any further signs be required for Miranda to clock that her audience is not enjoying himself.

Unfortunately for Spikes, he asked. And Miranda needs to talk.

"Because if I really think there's a chance of my one big love here, and I've screwed it up, then no wonder I'm feeling so mopey and useless. I don't *do* waiting around. I'm a person who tackles things head-on, aren't I?"

Spikes seems to have realized his verbal input is not required.

"Yeah. Yeah," Miranda says, suddenly feeling better than she has in weeks. "Today is the day of love, isn't it, and so you know what—I'm going to do something about it." She beams at him. "Thanks, Spikes. You're so great."

Spikes brightens. "Oh, right, thanks," he says. "No problem."

On impulse, she stands on tiptoe and kisses him on the cheek. His mouth drops open. Miranda has always suspected that Spikes has only managed to be friends with her by pretending she's not a woman at all; perhaps it was a little unkind to kiss him. But she felt such a surge of fondness for him, with his big, spade-like hands and his kind eyes darting to and fro as he tried desperately to work out what he ought to say.

"What are you doing for Valentine's Day, Spikes?"

"Me and Trey are going to the pub," Spikes says, jamming his hands into his pockets. "Blind dates," he adds miserably.

Miranda's eyes widen. "Oh, no way!"

"Trey's idea," Spikes says, looking everywhere except at Miranda.

"His sister's been trying to set him up with someone for ages and he wanted me to go with him in case it's awful." Spikes scuffs a foot in the wet grass. "We'll probably just get stood up."

Miranda smiles and pats him on the arm. "Some pretty great romances have started that way, you know," she tells him.

Jane

WHEN JANE FINALLY MUSTERS THE COURAGE TO TAKE
down Richard Wilson, it is Valentine's Day. This feels right, somehow.

She has Lou on one side of her and Aggie on the other as she makes
her way through the city of London, all its sleek glass and metal shining
silver in the rain. Aggie is wearing a large orange anorak and wellies;
Lou is in a sleek gray trench coat; Jane's in her pale-pink jumper again,
because it's a Friday, and—as Aggie reminded her this morning—being
brave doesn't have to mean she changes everything all at once.

Jane hasn't been inside the Bray & Kembrey offices since 2016.
They are so unchanged it unnerves her: they've not even switched out
the old fake flowers in the large vase by the reception desk. Blessedly
she doesn't recognize the receptionist; she signs in as a guest and takes
her lanyard in shaking fingers.

Jane turns and looks at Aggie and Lou, who are both standing in
the waiting area, watching her, a picture of concern. She smiles.

"I'll be fine," Jane says, answering the question on their faces. She
swallows. "I'm ready."

SHE TALKS ABOUT FEBRUARY 14, 2016, FIRST. THE MYSTERI-
ous one-to-one with a woman that she removed from Richard's diary,
the man who had barged into the office and tried to fight with Richard. She doesn't tell them Joseph's name, but perhaps they already
know it; she sees two of the women from HR glance sharply at each
other when she mentions the fight.

Jane goes through every item on the list she has clutched in her
sweating palms. The harassment claim she saw on the desk. The money
Richard paid her. And the truth about her relationship with him, all
its shame and ugliness, its intensity.

They ask a lot about this, largely around consent, a line of questioning Jane perhaps should have expected but hadn't—it makes her very
uncomfortable. She took Richard's money; she obeyed him quite will-
ingly; she loved him. To talk about the *imbalance of power* between
them seems to diminish her culpability, and she's not quite ready to let
herself off for the part she played in allowing Richard to rule her life.
It'll take more thought, all this. The conversation makes her feel a
little nauseous, as if the horizon is shifting on a changing tide.

They are kind to her. Professional but gentle at the same time. She
looks at their serious, inquisitive faces and thinks suddenly of Aggie's
painting in her flat, the one that says, *Most people are shit, what are you
going to do about it?* And she thinks, *I'm going to notice all the ones who
are doing their very best not to be.*

"Thank you, Jane. Let me walk you down," says the head of HR,
rising from her seat. She's in a black pencil skirt and jacket; there's a
little snag in her tights, on the side of her calf, and her hair is coming
loose from its careful bun.

"Can you . . . Are you able to tell me what happened on that Valentine's Day in 2016? I've always wondered," Jane says, once they've
said their good-byes and the door has swung shut behind them.

"I shouldn't, I'm afraid," the head of HR says as they step into the lift. She bites her lip. "Awful, though. He got himself mixed up in some really unpleasant business. But everything you've told us has been extremely helpful." She inhales between her teeth. "He won't be long for this firm, that's for sure—or any other. I shouldn't say so, but I think you deserve to hear that."

"Thank you," Jane says, feeling a flash of quiet victory. She doesn't want to wish harm on anybody, but *oh*, she does wish just a little harm on Richard.

Lou and Aggie are waiting for Jane in the downstairs seating area. Aggie stands out like a traffic cone in the muted grays of the office. They jump to their feet as Jane says good-bye to the head of HR, and by the time she turns back to them, they're both doing the very specific hover that she recognizes as the action of people who would like to go in for a hug but aren't sure if they should.

She smiles at them both. Their wide, caring eyes. The very fact of them being here, two women who were relative strangers to her just a few months ago, going out of their way to be kind. It's almost overwhelming how grateful she feels to have them, and how much lighter she is for having come back here and faced the truth.

"Let's go have tea and cake," Jane says, her smile widening. "I want a cinnamon bun."

Miranda

IN THE END, A DAY OF THINKING LEAVES MIRANDA NO closer to knowing what it is she wants—except that she wants *something* from Carter, and she can't leave him alone until she gets it. Eventually she remembers that she hates thinking, and so here she is, dressed in jeans and the flannel shirt she grabbed off the radiator after her post-work shower, with wet hair and insufficient layers for a February evening. And she's knocking on the door to Carter's mother's house.

Mary Carter answers. They blink at each other for a moment. Mary has a shawl clutched to her chest; her clothes are buttoned up wrong, and Miranda's heart softens. Poor woman. Poor Carter, seeing his mother like this every day, trying to juggle caring for her with everything else he does.

"Siobhan?" Mary says. "Is this her? Joseph? Joseph, don't cry, she's come back!"

Carter steps into the hallway and stops stock-still when he sees Miranda in the doorway. He's disheveled, dressed in tracksuit bottoms and a T-shirt—no wonder, the house is boiling, she can feel the heat even from the doorstep. His hair is half-standing-on-end and there are bags under his eyes.

"This is Miranda," Joseph says flatly. "Come in, Mir, close the door behind you."

"Thanks," Miranda says, stepping into the hall and feeling foolish. What's she doing here, barging in on Carter and his mother like this? She doesn't even have a plan. She taps her hand against her thigh, fingers fidgeting.

"He's not doing very well," Mary whispers to her in the silence. "He's ever so sad."

Miranda swallows. The house always has this air of disturbed stillness, as if it's waiting for someone to move in. She'd always thought that strange atmosphere was because of Mary, but perhaps it was Carter all along. The way he looks now is certainly completely different from the man who tickled her until she cried with laughter, who would bend her over backward when he kissed her hello. Perhaps this crushed, crumpled man is the real Joseph Carter. She would very much like to meet him.

"Come on through," he says eventually. "Mum, we'll just be in the kitchen if you need me."

"Of course," Mary says, stepping aside and watching them go.

The kitchen is much cleaner than the first time Miranda saw it—Carter's never let it get that way again—but it's messy, and the washing-up needs doing. Carter moves to the fridge and stares inside, his tracksuit bottoms sagging at his hips.

"Are you all right?" Miranda asks before she can think about whether it's appropriate. As flattering as it would be to think that Carter is this disheveled because of their breakup, she can tell it's not that. He barely seems to register her presence—if he was upset with her, or hurt that they'd parted, wouldn't he be shocked to see her?

"Fine," Carter says. "What would you like to drink?"

She glances at the table and her eyebrows shoot up when she sees he's drinking whisky. He's never been a big drinker—it was a running joke that she could always sink more pints than he could if they went to the pub. But a third of the bottle is missing already, and he's just staring into the fridge as if it might hold all the answers.

"A tea would be great," Miranda says.

Carter doesn't move. Miranda heads to the kettle.

"Why are you here?" Carter asks abruptly. "It's not really a good time. To be honest."

Miranda frowns as she fills the kettle. "I'm sorry," she says, biting her lip. "But now I'm here I sort of . . . I feel like you're not okay, and maybe you shouldn't be on your own?"

"I'm not on my own. Mum's here."

"Carter," Miranda begins, then stops again, because what *does* she want to say? She grits her teeth in frustration at herself. "Carter, I want to know what happened with Siobhan."

"I know you do," Carter says after a long silence. His voice is hollow. "You made that pretty clear at New Year's. Isn't that why we broke up?"

"Is it? I'm really not sure."

She turns to look at him as the kettle rises to a boil behind her.

"Have you *ever* talked about this? With anyone?" she asks.

He's finally closed the fridge; he has his back to it now, and his eyes are on the bottle of whisky.

"No," he says. "No, I haven't."

"Why not?"

"Because." He swallows, Adam's apple bobbing. "It hurts."

Miranda moves tentatively toward him. "Maybe that's a reason to talk about it all the more. Carter. Come on. We're done, you and me, I think that's—I mean, now I'm here, I don't know about you, but it feels . . . obvious."

She flounders, stopping a few feet from him. It's the truth: now that she's looking at him, bruised and broken, she feels tenderness and friendship and certainly love of a sort, but she isn't in love with him. She's starting to wonder if the man she dated was a figment of both of their imaginations. Carter never once showed her this side to himself, but he seems more real now than ever.

"I hope that's not hurtful," she says, pulling a face.

Carter gives her the ghost of a smile. "It's not hurtful. You're right. It does feel obvious. I'd never be—I'd never let myself be in this much of a state in front of you if I was in love with you."

"So I'm here as a friend, then. And you look like you need one."

What a relief to discover that Miranda does actually know what she wants, now she's here. She wants honesty, and authenticity, and she wants to help.

Miranda pours water into the mug, remembering that first time she met Mary, how on edge she'd felt. Even then she'd not been herself around Carter—always trying to hold herself in, to say the right thing. She turns toward him as the tea brews.

"I know what guys are like. They don't ask each other how they are as much as they should. And I know most of your friends are guys, right? So has anyone actually pushed you on this before? Has anyone actually said, *Are you all right, Carter, because you don't seem all right?*"

He turns his face away, and she reaches for his arm, holding it firmly. "If you want to cry, just cry. I hate seeing you get all twisted up like this. There's nothing wrong with crying. I think I told you that once before, actually."

"If I start now," Carter chokes out, "I won't stop."

Miranda glances at the clock above the door. It's almost six.

"I've got nowhere else to be," she says. "So you don't have to stop. You can just keep crying."

IT'S AWFUL. GUT-WRENCHING. HE GETS THE STORY OUT piecemeal, between sobs, as Miranda moves around the kitchen, tidying, and then eventually beginning to cook them something to eat, mainly because she can't possibly sit still while listening to the story of how Siobhan Kelly died.

"Carter, *no*," she says, hand to her mouth. "Did you get to her in time? Did you speak to her before she . . ."

His head is in his hands. He shakes it without lifting his gaze. "No. She was . . . she was . . . It was too late, she couldn't speak. But she gripped my hand." He takes an unsteady breath. "She . . . This is going to sound mad."

"Go on. It won't sound mad to me."

"She used to do this thing when she was beating herself up about something. When she was stressed or anxious. She'd dig her nails into her palms, like this." He lifts his head and clenches his fists, looking down at them on the table. "And it left these marks on her palms. And as I held her hand, she just moved her thumb across my palm right where my nails would dig if I did it, you know, right here." He points to the center of his hand, tracing a line. "And I've always felt like . . . maybe she was saying . . . don't beat myself up." He shrugs, dropping his head into his hands again. "I dunno. I dunno what it meant."

Miranda can hardly keep herself from crying. "I bet she did mean that," she says fiercely. "I bet she was telling you to be happy, and not to suffer. Oh, Carter, it must have been . . . I can't . . . To have *seen* it . . ."

"I can't forget it. I sometimes feel like I've never stopped seeing it—her head turning, the motorbike, her body spinning like a rag doll . . ."

He descends into wrenching sobs again. Miranda has never seen someone so emotional. He's held his grief inside himself for years, and this is the result—she can't bear to see his shoulders leap with each ragged sob. It's as if his body can hardly hold it.

"I wanted to kill him. The man who followed her. In the end I couldn't do anything. Not enough evidence to prove he was harassing her. So he's still living his nice plush life, still working at Bray & Kembrey . . ." Carter slams a fist into the table and Miranda jumps; he doesn't seem to notice. "Shiv was the love of my life." He lays his head down on the table, cheek to the wood, shoulders shaking. "I can still hardly believe she's gone, and it's been *years*. She only came to this house once, you know, just once, but it's still full of memories of her. I know she's gone, but I can't . . . believe it. What's wrong with me?"

Miranda turns back to the stove, stirring the pasta sauce she rustled up from the contents of the fridge. She takes a deep, shaky breath. It's no use worrying what to say now—if she doesn't get it quite right, at least she's trying. And it seems like nobody has ever tried with Carter before.

"For what it's worth, she's not gone," Miranda says. "She's still a huge part of your life, and she always will be. And I don't believe in one great love."

She feels rather than sees Carter flinch at that.

"I don't," she says firmly. "I believe you have more love in that heart. I think you've got more to give, and maybe one day a woman will come along who you want to give that to. But not for a while. You need to stop dating, Carter. You're not ready."

"It's been *three years*," he chokes out again. "I must be ready. I have to be ready."

He sits up slightly. His eyes are blurred and puffy. She should have taken the whisky away from him; she bites her lip, examining the almost empty bottle by his hand.

"I was good to you, wasn't I? I was good to you?"

"You were good to me," Miranda says slowly. "But you couldn't give me everything, and I could tell. You weren't ready. And you weren't honest with me. You need to be able to go into a relationship being open about what you've been through, Carter. You deserve that."

He shakes his head. "Nobody would want me if they knew how broken I am."

His words are slurring.

"That's nonsense. One day a woman will love every inch of the real, proper you—maybe she'll be a woman who's had struggles of her own, and she'll be glad that you understand what that feels like."

She checks the pasta. It's odd how easy it feels to talk like this, about Carter meeting someone else. She's actually a little proud of herself—it's good to know, after months of jealousy and paranoia, that she has that sort of generosity of spirit after all.

"Can you tell me where you were last Valentine's Day?" she asks. "I'm guessing . . . you not showing up . . . It has something to do with Siobhan?"

Carter's quiet for so long she wonders if he's gone to sleep, but eventually he speaks.

"I passed out," he says, voice gruff. "I just had a drink to—you know—I just wanted something to get me through the day, and I never allow myself that usually, but on . . . on this day . . . And then I didn't stop."

Miranda eyes the whisky bottle again with growing concern. "Mm," she says.

"Then when I woke up it was half two in the morning. I felt terrible. I didn't know what to do. I cleaned myself up the next morning and bought you flowers, and I came straight to see you. Oh, and, and that breakfast you were always asking about? That breakfast after Scott's, in April last year?"

"Yes?" Miranda says. She doesn't want to be insensitive, but this mystery has eaten at her for *months*. "Where were you then?"

"Siobhan had bags of friends, but there were two she was especially close to, like sisters. They'd been trying to arrange a get-together between the three of us ever since the funeral. They'd set aside some of Shiv's things that they thought I should have. I met with them that morning. I said yes to it the night before, when I was drunk, with Scott, and talking about Siobhan a little bit, and I finally thought, *Maybe I'm ready*. But it was awful. They talked about her like—they were so comfortable. They cried, but they laughed, too. Like, remembering her, sharing stories. I couldn't do it. I couldn't. It's like—it's like saying she's really gone, and I don't want to say it, Miranda, I don't want to let her go, because I said I never would, I said I'd never leave her, and she was so afraid I would and I don't want to. I can't. I can't let her go."

Miranda frowns, trying to follow—his words are now so slurred she can barely understand him.

"Here, Carter, the food's ready," she says gently.

In truth the pasta is still pretty hard in the middle, but he needs to eat something *now*—he's dangerously drunk.

Miranda serves up and then takes a bowl through to Mary, who is parked in front of some sort of car chase on the television, but who accepts the food with polite gratitude and seems perfectly able to manage eating it on her lap, to Miranda's relief. But by the time she returns to the kitchen, Carter is passed out, fork still in hand, pasta barely touched beside his head.

"Oh, crap," Miranda mutters, shoving his shoulder. Nothing. He looks completely broken, folded over on the kitchen table, his face smoothed clear of emotion but still reddened and wet with tears.

Miranda's phone trills in her pocket; she fumbles to answer. It's Frannie.

"Hey, you okay?" Miranda says, trying another prod at Carter's shoulder.

"Yeah, so, like, where are you?" Frannie says. Her tone makes Miranda sit up.

"I'm . . . I'm at Carter's. Why?"

"You're at—*what?*" Frannie says, voice rising. "What have you gone there for?"

A voice murmurs in the background. Miranda frowns.

"Who's that?"

"So, umm. It's AJ," Frannie says. "He came here to do some big romantic gesture on Valentine's Day? But, like, you're at your ex-boyfriend's, so . . . Shall I tell him to go?"

"Oh my God," Miranda says, pressing a hand to her chest. "Oh my God."

That voice in the background again. Miranda jumps up out of her chair.

"No!" she says. "No, no, don't tell him to go! Tell him . . ." She looks back at Carter, his puffy, sad face, his uneaten dinner. "Argh. Can you put him on?"

"Sure. He really is yummy, Mir, don't screw this up," Frannie says, before handing over the phone.

"Hello?"

Miranda closes her eyes at the sound of AJ's voice. Things are suddenly feeling very clear and very obvious. She takes a deep, shaky breath.

"Hey," she says. "Listen, I'm having a weird evening."

"Me too," AJ says, and there's that characteristic amusement in his voice. "I was at dinner with Abigail . . ."

Ugh, Abigail. Miranda has made a point of trying very hard not to think about we-stayed-up-all-night-at-New-Year's Abigail.

"And out of nowhere I thought, Abigail would never climb a tree with me in the dark. And I thought, what the hell am I doing? Miranda Rosso's single now." He pauses. "You are still single, right?"

"Yes! Yes. I am. I'm just . . . at Carter's place right now." She cringes. "But I'm here as a friend! And he's actually just passed out on the table and I'm not sure I can leave him without being a totally terrible person. But I *really* want to see you. And hear whatever you have to say." Her words come in a rush. "And climb a tree in the dark with you, or whatever you want to do, because AJ, God, I've tried like mad not to fancy you, but I really *do*, you know?"

"I *thought* you did," AJ says. His voice is so warm and close on the phone. "Though you did test my ego a little for a while there."

"Ah, can't have done you any harm," Miranda says, grinning. Her expression sobers when she looks back at Carter. "Listen . . . you're a man who drinks heavily from time to time, right?"

"Err, is there a correct answer to that question?" AJ says.

"How can I wake Carter up if he's passed out? Should I?"

"Is he going to drown in something?"

"No?"

"Breathing all right?"

Miranda puts a hand in front of Carter's nose. "Yeah, I think so."

"Leave the man be, then. Get yourself over here. I've got a speech to make, and if you don't get here soon, your sisters are going to get it out of me and hear it first. They want me to do a test run before you get back."

Miranda rubs her forehead, unable to hold back her growing smile. "Oh God, I'm sorry about those two. So you think I should just . . . leave him here? Passed out? There's only his mum here with him, and she has dementia, I'm not sure she could help him if he needed help. He's been in a really bad way today. He told me—some stuff . . . His last girlfriend, she died on Valentine's Day. In *front* of him," Miranda whispers. "He literally saw her get run over on her way to meet him for a date."

There is a long silence on the end of the line.

"Hello?" Miranda says after a moment.

"I'm just wondering whether I'm enough of a jealous prick to tell you to leave your traumatized ex-boyfriend passed out with his elderly mother and get over here so I can kiss you," he says. "And I'm surprised to find I am actually *not* that much of a prick."

Miranda grins. "I'm proud of you."

"Text me the address," he says, and she can hear he's smiling. "I'll come to you."

AJ BRINGS THE SMELL OF COOL WINTER AIR WITH HIM AS he steps inside Mary Carter's house. He's dressed in his usual ripped jeans and hoodie, bearded and scruffy and so gorgeous it makes her shiver. Miranda feels as if her whole body is beaming at the sight of him. What a relief it is to let that feeling in.

"Hi," she says a little shyly as she closes the front door.

"Hey." There's his well-practiced seducer's smile, the cocky tilt of the head—but she doesn't care now, because she *knows* him, and she knows he's not the guy he was when she first heard rumors of the womanizing Aaron Jameson.

"So you went to my flat," she says.

"And you went to Carter's house," AJ says.

Miranda fidgets. "I'm sorry. It's just . . . It's been nagging at me so much, what happened with him. I never got the answers I wanted. But I swear there's nothing romantic between us now. I'm so glad you— I'm really . . . It's . . ."

AJ waits for her to trail off, and then, slowly, deliberately, he reaches across and lays a hand against her cheek. He smooths his thumb across the line of her cheekbone, and she feels as if he's drawn something there in fire.

"Miranda Rosso," he says. "I'd like to take you on a date."

"Okay," she says weakly.

His eyebrows inch up, and there's a smile playing at his lips. "I'm going to need a hard yes," he says. "I've waited a good long time for this."

"Yes, yes," she says hurriedly, lifting her hand to his wrist and taking a step toward him. Her heartbeat seems to be beating through her whole body and she thinks, *Oh, this must be what it's like to want to rip someone's clothes off.*

"Oh no," he says, smile growing as she lifts her chin, eyes on his mouth. "You're not getting your first kiss now."

"No?" Miranda says, and it comes out a bit poutier than she'd intended.

AJ turns his head to the left. Miranda follows his gaze. Carter's mother is standing in the doorway to the living room, watching them, perplexed.

"Mary," Miranda says. "This is my—my—this is my friend AJ."

She winces. Mary continues to stare at them both until, eventually, she says, "How lovely. Do come in. Would you like a cup of tea?"

She sweeps them through to the kitchen, the quintessential hostess all of a sudden—and then stops short when she sees her son passed out beside a bowl of pasta at the table.

"Oh," she says in a small voice.

Miranda moves toward her and takes her arm. "He's absolutely fine, Mary," she says in her most grown-up tone—an imitation of her mother, if she's honest. "He's just had a long day and dropped off. Let's get you back to the sofa and we'll find something good on the telly."

Once Mary is settled, Miranda returns to the kitchen to find AJ examining the unconscious Carter while tucking into the unfinished bowl of pasta. At a look from Miranda, he says, "Waste not, want not?"

She *tsk*s and heads for her own plateful, bringing it over to the table. After a momentary dither she sits down next to AJ; her feet tangle with his under the table, and she inhales sharply at the feel of his legs against hers. He smiles slowly.

"Do you know what feels really good?" he says. "You *letting* yourself do that. I've spent a year watching you dodging me."

"Well, yeah. You were . . . It was . . . difficult," she finishes lamely, spearing a mouthful of pasta. She's always taking the piss out of this man—why is she suddenly so completely tongue-tied? It's hard to swallow her mouthful; it feels as if her heart is beating in her throat.

"You mean I'm irresistible," AJ says, leaning back in his chair and stretching.

"Wasn't there a speech?" she says. "Is the speech *I'm irresistible*?"

AJ sobers a little. "No," he says. "You want to hear it?"

"Yes! Of course I do."

"All right." He clears his throat, wiping his mouth with the back of his hand. "Miranda Rosso," he says. "I'd like to take you on a date."

She blinks at him. "That was it? That was the speech?"

AJ wavers slightly. "You seemed to like it in the doorway. Anyway, I'm not finished."

"Oh good," Miranda says, beginning to feel their usual dynamic return. She waves her fork at him. "Go on, then."

He shoots her a look but continues. "You came into my life at a moment when I was working on being a better man. I'd started the year with a resolution: no more hookups, and more self-respect."

He's looking down at the table now. Miranda's heart squeezes.

"I had this idea that maybe there would be a woman worth settling down with out there somewhere, and I wasn't going to find her unless I stopped, you know, sleeping around."

"Right," Miranda says, trying not to think about that sentence too hard.

"But you've always been with someone else. And I gave up waiting."

Miranda bites her lip, pressing her foot a little closer to his under the table.

"I couldn't believe it when Spikes told me you and he had broken up." He jerks his head toward the sleeping Carter. "It was the worst timing. Abigail was sweet and kind, she was up-front and easy, there was no trouble. I'd waited for you for almost a year. I figured I deserved someone who wanted me back. And then there you were. Single again. And *looking* at me."

"I wasn't looking at you!" Miranda says, blushing.

AJ raises an eyebrow. She flounders.

"I mean, definitely not more than usual."

"More than usual," he says steadily, holding her gaze. "Don't tell me otherwise, Rosso, I know you too well for that. I spent the best part of a year watching you keep your distance—I saw how you'd shift so we were never too close and how your eyes would always slide away from mine. When you were single, you didn't look away quite so often. I think you wanted me looking at you again."

Miranda is beginning to feel a little ashamed of herself. "I would never . . . I didn't mean to . . ."

"So I got hopeful. More hopeful than a man should be when he's with someone else. But things were going well with Abigail, and I thought you had your chance, you could have left Carter anytime you wanted for me, and you never did. In fact, you made it pretty clear you never would have."

This speech is not turning out quite the way Miranda had hoped it would. She stares down at her plate of pasta.

"I thought, the ball's in your court. But then, you know, tonight, just out of the blue when I was thinking about the sort of woman you are, and the sort of woman I want . . . it struck me that you never would, would you? You can't even bear me talking about you *looking* at me when I'm with someone else. You're too good a woman to try to steal someone else's man. I let you know I was there, didn't I, all year? I let you know you could have me if you wanted me, even though you had a boyfriend? But you'd never do that. You'd never do that to Abigail.

"And I was thinking all this, and I looked at the woman sitting across from me, and she was perfectly nice, but all I could think was, *She's not Rosso.*"

Miranda is breathing fast, eyes still fixed on her plate. Nobody has ever talked to her like this before. Nobody has ever seen her the way AJ sees her—as somebody worth waiting for.

"I may not be the sensible choice for you—I'm not Carter, with his suits and his compliments and his whole grown-up life, you know. But I'm pretty sure I'm the *right* choice. I think you're my woman worth settling down for, Miranda Rosso. I think you're my one."

"Can I kiss you now?" Miranda asks, looking up at him at last. "Please?"

"Come here," he says, pushing his chair back.

Miranda gets up and moves toward him shyly, coming to stand between his thighs. He puts his hand on her hip, shifting her to sit on his lap. He's warm beneath the hoodie, and solid, all muscle. Her skin feels different, as if every inch of her is on high alert, hyper-aware of the slight hitch in his breathing, the color in his cheeks.

"Do you remember that day you cut your ropes?" he whispers, lips an inch from hers.

"I remember."

He smiles. "That whole journey down with you pressed against me tight, like this," he says, cinching her body even closer to his.

Her heart hammers.

"I wanted you so badly then. I've wanted you ever since. I just knew how it would feel between us. You can't make up chemistry like that, you can't fake it or force it. Your body and my body," he says, smoothing a hand up and down, from her hip to her waist. "They just line up right, don't they?"

Miranda shifts to kiss him, but he's pulling back just a fraction every time, making her wait. Each time her desire seems to ramp up until she's burning with it, and their lips haven't even touched yet.

She lifts her hands to his chest, sliding them under his hoodie to the warmth of his T-shirt. She can feel the hair beneath the fabric, the hard planes of muscle. She runs one hand up to his throat, tracing a thumb along his bearded jaw, and his eyes turn glazed as she shifts her hand into his hair. Their lips are so close to touching.

"Miranda?"

She jumps. It's not that she's *forgotten* Carter is there, it's more just that the sudden intrusion of her ex-boyfriend's voice when she's sitting in AJ's lap is a bit peculiar. AJ tightens his grip on her as she moves as if to stand, and she relaxes back against him as Carter stares at them, bleary-eyed.

"Hi," she says, a bit apologetically. "AJ came to . . . help . . . you?"

AJ snorts. "I came to tell Miranda I'm in love with her," he tells Carter. "Hope that's all right with you, mate."

Miranda stares at AJ. *Love*. Aaron Jameson really just said he loves her. Her heart is thundering double time, and her skin still tingles with his closeness, and all she wants to do is press her lips to his.

But. Sometimes real life gets in the way of these things. She looks back at Carter; there are red creases on the side of his face from sleeping on the table.

"Shit," Carter says, and her heart sinks.

"Oh, Carter, I'm sorry," she says, disentangling herself from AJ's arms. "This was really insensitive of us—we just—I'm sorry . . ."

"What time is it?" Carter says, stumbling to stand.

"What?" Miranda says.

"Time? Is it?" Carter manages.

They all check the clock.

"Ten," Miranda says with surprise. "When did it get so late?"

"*Ten*," Carter says, face dropping in horror. "No! No!"

He begins scrabbling around on the sideboard, grabbing his keys and wallet.

"Whoa, whoa," AJ says, rising in his chair. "Slow down, mate."

"I have to go!" Carter says, and then he trips over a chair and goes flying. He lands hard, only just getting his hands out in time to stop himself crashing face-first into the floor tiles.

"Joseph?" Mary calls querulously from the living room. "Is everything all right in there?"

"All fine, Mum," Carter manages, pushing himself up onto his elbows. There's a bruise already blooming on his left eyebrow; he inspects his red palms, wincing.

Miranda ducks down beside him. "Carter. You're absolutely wasted.

You can't go anywhere. Come on, sit back up at the table and tell us where you're trying to get to."

Carter manages to get back into a chair with help from Miranda; he's shaking. AJ hands him a pint glass of water and sits down opposite, his face unreadable.

"There's this woman," Carter manages to say, taking a few gulps of the water. He stares down at the table. "A friend."

"A friend," Miranda echoes, exchanging a glance with AJ. "Who you said you'd see on Valentine's Day?"

"Yeah. We got . . . She goes to the Hoxton Bakehouse. She's beautiful, and a bit strange, but in the best way, you know? Sort of fascinating. I said to myself, I'm not going to date anyone, not so soon, I'm clearly not ready. I mean, me and you had only just broken up. I'm not going to try to talk to her or anything. But she said she had a boyfriend, so I thought, oh, that's safe, right? Just friends!"

"Right . . . ?" says Miranda.

"But I should have known that just-friends thing never works. I should have known. Because then it turns out she *doesn't* have a boyfriend after all."

"I hear you, mate," AJ says to that.

"And now we're . . . *friends*. And she's so beautiful and smart and lovely. But we're just friends. She's asked me to be her date because she doesn't have one, and it's a big engagement party that she's dread—dread . . ."

"Dreading," Miranda finishes for him. "So you were supposed to be a friend-date?" She winces. "And you never showed up?"

"Oh God," says Carter, lowering his face to the table.

"No, no, not that again," Miranda says, hauling him up. "Right, I'm sure this is fixable."

She looks at him, then at AJ, whose expression is very dubious.

"No way that man is sobering up enough to be seen in public tonight," AJ says.

Miranda pulls a face. "Okay," she says. "Carter, where's your phone?"

"Hmm?" says Carter.

"Your phone?"

"Threw it at the wall," he mumbles, sagging in his chair. "My bedroom."

AJ and Miranda exchange another glance, then, as one, they head for the stairs. Carter's bedroom is messier than Miranda has ever seen it: she stares at the piles of clothes and queues of half-drunk water glasses for a moment and thinks of all the times she hastily tidied her own bedroom before Carter came around. They'd been so keen to impress each other. Now all that tidying just seems like an exhausting waste of time.

"Here," AJ says, ducking down and picking up a cracked phone from the carpet. "Hmm," he says, holding down the power button. The screen flickers and then lights up, strangely purple, with a jagged line running across it.

"Well, there goes that plan," Miranda says, heading back downstairs. "I don't suppose you stored this woman's number anywhere else?" she asks as she walks back into the kitchen. "Oh, bloody hell. Carter!"

Carter's passed out again. She shakes him awake and repeats the question. He shakes his head mournfully.

"I'm fucked it up," he says, which, though it doesn't make sense, does seem to Miranda to be a very good summary of the situation.

"Okay, what about tomorrow? Why don't you go and see her first thing? I mean, I forgave you for standing me up, didn't I, and I was actually dating you," Miranda points out.

"She's got work at the shop. With the party people. The people from the engagement party."

Miranda perks up. "*Perfect*. You sober up tonight and then go along to her shop first thing tomorrow and make it up to her! But," she says, raising a cautionary finger, "you are *not* going to date this woman, Carter."

AJ frowns. "Easy, Mir," he says warningly.

She scowls. "Not because I care!" she says. "Because look at him, he's not ready!"

AJ inspects Carter. "Hmm. Fair."

"I'm not ready," Carter repeats mournfully. He's slumping further and further in his chair; eventually AJ grabs him by the scruff of his shirt and hauls him upright again. "Thanks," Carter says, eyes briefly focusing on AJ. "Oh, it's the big tattooed one," he says in surprise.

AJ's eyes twinkle. "Hi."

"You and Miranda?" Carter says.

Miranda squirms.

"Yeah," AJ says. "Me and Miranda."

"Oh," Carter says. He nods slowly. "Yeah, that makes sense, doesn't it, really?" He pauses. "And I can't date Jane?"

"Do you want to?" Miranda asks.

"Yes," Carter says immediately. "I think she's lovely."

"Have you told her about Siobhan?"

"No," Carter says after a long moment. "No. I've never told anyone else. Scott knows, obviously. Mum can't ever get it straight in her head. But I can't . . . be talking about it. Going around talking about it. Not yet. Oh, Miranda," he says, dropping his head to his forearms on the table. "I'm not ready. I'll only hurt her. I'm such a mess."

"More water, mate," AJ says, giving him a firm pat on the shoulder and shifting the pint glass closer to him.

"How about you give it one year," Miranda says. She feels a new sort of confidence, one she's never felt around Carter before: a genuine belief that she might know what's best. "One year being single. One year focusing on sorting yourself out. This time next year, if you're ready to fall in love—and maybe that'll even be with this Jane of yours—then you go out there and get your woman. But until then:

friends only. You owe that to yourself. You need to start healing, Carter."

Carter takes a long drink of water and then looks at Miranda. He stretches out a hand. For a moment he looks more like himself: earnest, boyish, charming. "One year," he says. "I'll shake on it."

They shake hands.

"Now," AJ says, turning to Miranda, "we are putting your ex-boyfriend to bed."

This takes much longer than AJ and Miranda would like. As Miranda corrals Carter up the stairs, into his room and under the covers, she's very aware of the heat of AJ's gaze, his steadiness, the way he leans in the doorway and watches her with those enormous arms folded across his chest and a slight smile on his lips. By the time they've turned out Carter's light and crept from the room, her skin is buzzing again, and all AJ has done is look at her.

"Thank Christ for that," AJ says, and he doesn't wait another moment. There in the hallway of Carter's mum's house, at the top of the stairs, in the darkness, he gathers Miranda into his arms and kisses her.

She *melts*. It's that sort of kiss, the sort that leaves you boneless and giddy, the sort that makes you lose any sense of time and place. AJ pulls her closer. His hands run down her back, to her waist, her hips, then one snakes up to tangle in her hair; it's as if he just can't get enough of touching her, and she's the same, running her palms across the contoured muscle of his shoulders, gripping the back of his neck. His tongue flicks against hers. She imagines his hands moving over her like this when she's wearing nothing at all, and lets out a moan against his lips.

"I was going to take you to the tree we climbed at night," AJ says, voice hoarse, as they take a breath. "This isn't exactly the most romantic spot, but I just couldn't wait."

Miranda turns her head, looking at where they're standing. She remembers something Carter told her earlier, about how this house was full of memories of Siobhan. And Miranda feels a sort of awareness—nothing ghostly, nothing like that, but perhaps a kinship with this woman whose absence has defined Miranda's last year, though she hadn't even known it.

Siobhan's story was cut short so soon. Miranda tightens her arms around AJ and leans her head against his chest, and she feels impossibly fortunate. No more prevaricating or overthinking. From now on, when good things come, Miranda Rosso will grab hold of them and not let go.

Jane

ON FEBRUARY 15, 2020, JANE IS WOKEN BY THE SOUND OF someone knocking on the door to her flat in Winchester. She sits bolt upright, heart thundering.

"Jane?"

Oh my God.

"Joseph?" she says, clutching the duvet to her chest. She's wearing a nightie, threadbare and vaguely Victorian, one of those saggy long white things that can often be found in charity shops (exactly where Jane found this one). As she reaches to check the time, her phone opens on the message she sent to Joseph last night, sitting on Aggie's ochre sofa, drinking decaf coffee with cream.

I'm sorry for ignoring your messages. It's been very hard trying to get over you, and I was hurting after the way you looked at me on New Year's Eve when I told you the truth about why I left London. But if you would still like to talk, I think I'm ready now. Perhaps we could meet. x

She hadn't meant . . . She squints at her phone. Seven in the morning.

"Sorry!" Joseph calls through the door. "Is it too early? It is, isn't it?"

Jane needs to put something else on. This nightie is hideously unattractive, not to mention dangerously threadbare. She rummages desperately through her wardrobe, suddenly extremely awake. Joseph is here. Joseph is *here*.

Joseph is here.

By the time she opens the door, Jane is flustered, and the blue poncho she has thrown over her nightie has definitely only made her look stranger. She's just lifting her hand to her hair—why didn't she think to check her hair before this point?—when their eyes meet.

"Hello," he says, and there's the smile, the Joseph smile, the one that makes her feel as though she's stepped into the sunlight. "I really, really hoped I'd find you here."

"Hi," she says a little breathlessly. "Would you like to come in?"

The smile widens and his shoulders sag with relief. "Absolutely," he says.

She closes her eyes for a moment as he moves past her. Just the smell of him makes her heart tighten with longing. It's no different from three months ago: she's not an inch closer to letting him go.

"Let me put the kettle on," Jane says, moving to the kitchen and lifting it from the hob.

"Jane," Joseph says, and then his hand touches her upper arm. Just lightly, but it's enough: she feels something like a crackle, like the moment when static sparks. Her breath catches. "Jane, I'm so sorry about New Year's Eve. I really want to explain, if you'll let me?"

She swallows. "You don't have to explain. I'm sure it was a shock finding out I was *that* Jane."

In the weeks before Richard got rid of her, she'd heard plenty of people in the office call her *Richard's sexy little secretary*; one woman had referred to her casually as *Richard's whore* in the queue for coffee. And that was all said within her hearing. God knows what Joseph would have heard.

"It wasn't that at *all*," Joseph says. "I promise, Jane. I promise. I heard Richard had a relationship with his secretary back in 2015, but . . . that wasn't why I was shocked."

The exactness with which he remembers the year startles her; she glances over her shoulder at him. He's pulled a chair out from the table and sat down, but he gets up again immediately, walking to lean on the fridge, then pushing away to fetch her mugs from the cupboard. He's so unsettled he's making Jane even more nervous; her hands shake as she reaches for the coffee granules.

"I don't know if you remember, or if you were even there—I can't recall, though I've really tried—but back in February 2016 . . ."

Joseph takes a shaky breath. Jane glances at him again: he's pale and serious.

"I remember," she says quietly. "You came into the office and had a fight with Richard. I'm sorry. I remembered around this time last year, and by then I'd already begun to fall for you, and I couldn't bear to tell you who I was. Everyone at Bray & Kembrey thought I was—just—trash. Well"—she pauses, thinking of Lou—"that's how it's always felt to me."

The kettle whistles.

"But I'm done hiding from all that now," Jane goes on, her back to Joseph as she takes the kettle off the hob. "Yesterday I went into the Bray & Kembrey offices to tell them everything Richard didn't want me to tell. They think what I've said about him, along with the new evidence they have of inappropriate behavior, will be enough to get him fired."

Joseph is silent for so long she turns to look at him. He's sitting down again and has one hand raised to his mouth; his eyes are wide.

"Richard Wilson's lost his job?" he says.

"He will, I think," Jane says, a little unnerved by his reaction. "Joseph?"

He shakes his head slowly. "I'm sorry. It's just . . . God. I can't tell you how many times I've wanted to take that man down. And you're telling me it's done? *You've* done it?"

"Well, I mean . . . yes? I suppose?" She brings the coffees to the table and sits down opposite him, trying to read his expression. "Joseph?" she says tentatively. "Why did you fight with Richard that day?"

Joseph takes a deep breath and wraps his hands around his mug of coffee. "On the fourteenth of February, 2016, my girlfriend— Siobhan—she died," he says, his words so rushed it takes Jane a moment to realize what he's said.

"Oh, Joseph, oh my God," she says, reaching compulsively to touch his arm. Whatever she'd expected, it certainly hadn't been this.

He looks down at her hand for a moment in a wondering sort of way, then covers it with one of his own, hot from the mug of coffee.

"Richard had been following her. He'd got a bit obsessed with her, I think—she turned him down and he didn't like it."

Jane winces. She remembers how persistent Richard was when he wanted something.

"He was there when she died." Joseph's voice is quavering slightly and his cheeks are pale. "She was hit by a motorbike, but she was looking the wrong way because he'd followed her there. I felt—I was . . . I felt it was his fault. I blamed him completely, I left the firm because I couldn't bear to be in the same building as him . . . I'd never despised anyone before, but I *hated* him. I've wished awful things on that man, Jane."

Jane grips his arm. "You were grieving."

He shoots her a grateful look. "Still, letting go of that anger has been a big part of moving forward. The first couple of years after Siobhan died, I . . . I didn't cope very well. Especially on Valentine's Day." He swallows, still looking down at his hand over hers. "After last year, when I was too drunk to come to that engagement party with you, I made a pact with a friend. I said I wouldn't date for a year." He looks up then, his expression rueful. "You can imagine how many times in the last few months I've regretted that promise, but it was important for my—I guess my recovery, really. I'd been trying so hard to meet someone new, but I was still so utterly in love with Siobhan, I couldn't really let anyone else in."

Jane's heart is beginning to beat faster. "So you . . . you didn't have a girlfriend? At Constance's wedding?"

He looks pained. "I'm sorry for letting you think that. It was cowardly. It was easier than telling you the truth. I still . . . I'm still a bit of a mess now, to be honest. It's taken me years to get to a point where I can even talk about this—it's 2020, for God's sake." He lets out a gruff laugh, but there are tears in his eyes. "And I'm still so broken."

Jane shakes her head. "Joseph. It takes as long as it takes. And . . . I don't know, you have such high expectations of yourself. You can be broken. That's okay. Lots of us are. It doesn't mean you're not a wonderful man. It doesn't mean you can't ever be happy."

His face twists; he's struggling to hold back tears. Suddenly the table between them is too much—Jane pulls away to stand, then reaches for his hand again and leads him to the sofa.

"Anyway," Joseph says shakily as they settle side by side. Jane moves to pull her hand away, but he holds it tighter, and something *zings* through her, a sort of painful tenderness, or perhaps it's hope. "All this year, with you, the book clubs, the dinners, being *friends* . . . it's been a kind of torture." He's looking down at her hand in his, cradled in his lap. "At first I thought it was just a challenge because you're, you know." He waves his free hand at her, with a quick glance. She catches the vulnerability in his eyes and her heart tightens in her chest. "So stunning. But then I got to know you, and you're just . . ." He closes his eyes. "You're so kind and smart and you like all the same books as me," he says, and Jane smiles at the tortured tone of his voice. "Every time I made you laugh I felt like I was flying. I can't tell you how many times I've almost kissed you. Then at the wedding I was just . . . I just lost it, and I thought, *If I kiss her once maybe it'll make things easier*, but it was like a spark on kindling. I haven't . . . I haven't had that sort of . . . I didn't know I could feel like this about someone again, Jane. So then as well as feeling like I shouldn't get too close to you because of the promise I'd made, I was feeling all sorts of guilt about betraying Siobhan's memory, and I've just . . . Yeah. A mess," he says, pointing to his chest.

He's still avoiding her eyes. Jane squeezes his hand.

"Look at me?" she says. "Please?" Her voice cracks slightly. Hearing him say these things about her, it's too good, and there's a bright, fierce joy growing in her chest.

He looks at her. Another shock goes through her as their eyes meet, and she realizes she's holding her breath, heart racing, her fingers clutching his so tightly it must surely hurt.

"I love you, Jane," Joseph Carter says. "I am so completely in love with you."

Jane's head goes fuzzy; she genuinely feels as if she might faint. She has become so used to working in worst-case scenarios—she is accustomed to depriving herself, to never expecting anything from anyone. But here is Joseph Carter, the man she loves with all her heart, sitting across from her, holding her hands, telling her he loves her, too, and it's so enormous and so wonderful she has to clutch his hands tighter to remind herself it's real.

"I won't be perfect," Joseph says, and there are tears in his eyes now.

"Joseph, stop," Jane says, and suddenly they're closer, thigh to thigh, both hands twining together. "I don't want you to be perfect. Why would I want that? I want *you*. I want all the parts of you, the broken ones, the ones you've kept hidden away." She untangles one hand from his and lifts it to his cheek, and his eyes snap to hers, full of hope. "That's love, isn't it?" she whispers. "Or that's how I love you, anyway. I'm greedy. I want all of you."

He rests his forehead against hers.

"I want to make you so happy, Jane," he says, voice choked. "I want to bring you coffee with cream in bed every morning, and I want to make you laugh, really belly-laugh the way you hardly ever do, and I want to read books and eat cinnamon buns and know what outfit you like to wear on a Sunday. I want to be part of your routine. I want to stand next to you in a crowded party and hold your hand tight and make you feel safe. I want to *know* you, all your habits, all the secrets you've held in. You're not on your own now, Jane. You've got me. Always."

Their lips touch on *always*. It's a kiss that should have happened a thousand times already, but could only ever happen here, now, with so many truths between them. It's not glamorous: the kiss is damp with tears, and they're both trembling. But it's pure. It's absolute. It's a kiss that says *always*.

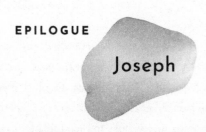

Joseph

AS THEY UNRAVEL THEIR SCARVES AND SHRUG OUT OF
their coats in the warmth of the house, Jane turns and sends Joseph
one of those smiles that make him feel like he's unfolding: a proper,
happy Jane smile. They were rare at first—he tended to get the wary
ones, the ones that disappeared before they'd really formed. Now every
time she gives him a proper smile he feels as if he's been handed something precious.

It still seems miraculous to Joseph that 365 days have passed since
he told Jane he loved her, and nobody has come along and asked him
to give all those precious moments back.

They've been out for a long walk—the February wind was bitterly
cold and fierce, snapping at their faces as they walked hand in hand,
and for a moment Joseph thinks fleetingly—an old habit—of how red
his cheeks will go. The first time he told Jane how much he hates the
way he flushes in the heat, she'd just leaned across and kissed the color
on his cheeks. *Do you know how much I love it when your cheeks get
flushed?* she'd said, at which point he'd gone even redder.

"Ready?" she asks him gently.

"I think so," Joseph says, reaching for her hand, and it's the truth—he's a little nervous, but he's ready. "Let me just check on Val and Mum."

His aunt and his mother are happily nattering together at the kitchen table with tea and biscuits; his shoulders relax when he sees them, and Val shoots him a look that says *all good*. His mother is happier lately—she remembers less, but the frustration and sadness that accompanied those first couple of years after her diagnosis have eased. She doesn't know what she's forgotten these days, and that's a blessing.

By the time he heads up to his home office, Jane's already there, setting up a second chair at the desk. For a moment, he just watches her. Her long, dark hair swings over her face; she's wearing jeans that are worn at the knees, and one of the baggy jumpers she loves so much. Jane may have chosen to stop wearing the same clothes every week, but she's still such an endearing creature of habit; he loves finding her in one of her favorite at-home jumpers, the ones only he gets to see.

Watching her now, he wants to kiss her, to slip his hands under that baggy jumper and find her soft curves. She glances up at him and gives a quick, wicked smile that says she knows exactly what he's thinking, and his breath hitches. Maybe *that* sort of Jane smile is his favorite, on reflection.

As they settle side by side and hit the Zoom link, it strikes Joseph that he doesn't feel guilty for how much he wants her, not even today. He thought learning to be happy again, after Siobhan, would be a Herculean effort, but actually it is a string of small victories like this, moments he hardly notices happening until they've passed. He laces his fingers with Jane's as the chat loads and everyone appears on-screen.

"Happy Valentine's Day!" someone yells.

They're all there—Joseph and Jane are last to join. There's Marlena, looking glamorous despite constantly complaining that lockdown means she can never get her hair cut; there's Kit, Vikesh, a few of Siobhan's drama school friends, and a sight Joseph will never tire of seeing: Scott and Fiona, in the same video box.

Scott had always harbored a soft spot for Fiona, ever since that horseback ride at New Year's all those years ago; he'd ask after her whenever he saw Joseph, as if one day Joseph would say, *She's well, mate, and asked if you wanted to go out with her?* It was a running joke, until the day when Fiona took Joseph shopping for a costume one Halloween—of all Siobhan's friends, Fiona's been the one most determined to stay in touch with Joseph. As they tried on hats, she confessed she'd always had a bit of a crush on Scott. It took the two of them another year to actually call it official once Joseph put them in touch, partly because Fiona was whisked off to LA for a new TV role, but now they are firmly settled together in Dublin.

Joseph beams at them both, then his grin widens as he glances to their left, where Miranda is perched on AJ's knee in a room he recognizes as the bedroom of their new flat in Erstead. Fiona had been delighted at Joseph's suggestion of asking Mir and AJ along; in a strange way they seemed like part of Siobhan's story, though they'd never met her.

"So," Fiona says, "obviously I wish we could have done this in person, the way we planned, but basically the principle is the same—I just wanted us to get together and . . . I guess, sort of keep Shiv here with us by remembering all the great times. And all the times she wasn't so great and lost her temper when someone undertook her on the motorway or dared to point out that she *always* burned anything she tried to cook."

That gets everyone laughing. Joseph feels his shoulders relax a little more. He can do this. It still surprises him, but he *wants* to do this. Jane's fingers tighten on his.

"Gone but never forgotten, right?" Fiona says.

"Absolutely," Joseph says, because that's important—always important when you lose someone, but especially for Siobhan. It had always seemed cruel that a woman who was so afraid of being left behind had to be consigned to the past. Siobhan had so badly wanted to *live*; she'd wanted to be seen and felt and heard. And now she was gone.

But never forgotten.

The Zoom is only scheduled to last for an hour, but they end up talking for almost two. There are tears, some from Joseph; Jane cries, too, and he loves her for it, the way she can weep for this woman she never knew. From the very start, Jane didn't just accept Siobhan's memory into their life but welcomed her. It was only when he met Jane's father that Joseph began to understand Jane's insistence that the people we'd loved and lost shouldn't just be left behind.

Though Jane has reconnected with her dad, though she's finally told him the truth about leaving London, she still struggles to speak to him about her mother. It seems so obvious to Joseph that Jane *longs* for connection with her mum—coming to Winchester and working for the Count Langley Trust is surely proof enough of that. But Jane seems hardly aware of it, or perhaps can't quite articulate that need yet.

But it's there. When Joseph suggested to Jane's father that he might put Jane in touch with some of her mother's relatives, the expression on her face had been almost painful to see. Aching hope, longing, all quickly repressed. Jane grew up in a home where her mother was a topic too painful to discuss; her father is a shadow of a man, still grief-stricken decades on. As Joseph had watched Bill Miller trudge back out to his car after his visit, shoulders bowed, he'd thought, *Thank God for Miranda for making me talk. Thank God for Jane, for showing me how to love again.*

"Hey, Joseph?" Marlena calls through the screen.

"Yeah?"

"You know what Siobhan would be saying to you right now?"

He feels a smile growing. "What?"

"She'd say you better have some fucking *great* Valentine's Day plans for that woman of yours, because from what we've heard, you have a lot of making up to do for the year you stood her up."

Joseph turns to look at Jane, who is rather shamefaced.

"It came up when we went to the pub in the summer," she protests as the others laugh. "Marlena is very easy to talk to."

"I know all sorts about you now, Carter," Marlena yells. "Now get going, everyone, I've got a Zoom date to prepare for! Love you all!"

They hang up in a chorus of waves and good-byes; Joseph's cheeks hurt from smiling and are still a little damp with tears. He wipes his glasses on his shirt, swallowing hard.

"Don't listen to Marlena," Jane says as they stand. "We absolutely don't have to do a date. Today's Siobhan's day."

Joseph shakes his head. He's been looking forward to this for months. His plans are perfectly in place, which is really saying something (Joseph's plans rarely fall into place, no matter how hard he tries). But with some help from his aunt Val, who they formed a support bubble with last year, he is pretty confident he's about to give Jane Miller the best Valentine's Day date of her life.

"Come on," he says, leading her downstairs by the hand. "Surprise time."

"Oh!" Jane says when she realizes where he's leading her. "Am I going to be allowed in the basement at last?"

He's banned her from the basement for almost two months now. This has not been an easy project to undertake in secret while both working from home—thankfully Jane's new job in HR for the Count Langley Trust requires her to go into headquarters from time to time, so Joseph ordered the biggest deliveries to arrive when Jane was out. Still, he has had to be very sneaky, which is really not his forte.

"Okay," Joseph says, turning to Jane as they reach the stairs down to the basement. "Close your eyes."

She blinks those enormous, mesmerizing eyes at him, lined with their impossibly long lashes, then obediently closes them. Joseph leans in to kiss her—he can't help himself—and then turns to lead her carefully down the steps.

"Open your eyes."

She gasps. That sound—the wonder in it, the childlike joy . . . it's exactly what he'd hoped for over the last six weeks of work.

"Oh, Joseph," she says. "A library!"

Deep-cleaning the basement had been top of their list when they first moved into this house last autumn; Joseph had decided not just to deep-clean it but to transform it. He'd scrubbed and painted, he'd lined the walls with shelves, he'd ripped out the ugly old carpet and laid higgledy secondhand rugs everywhere. And then he'd chosen a reading sofa, with two arching lamps, where he and Jane can curl up together.

"This is incredible."

Joseph watches as tears bead in Jane's eyes; she's wandering the shelves, running her fingers along the spines.

"Where did you *get* all these books?" she asks, staring wonderingly over her shoulder at him.

He can't stay away any longer—he moves behind her, sliding his hands around her waist, tucking her head under his chin as she strokes the books in turn.

"Lots of them are Mum's and Val's. Some are secondhand—Mortimer and Colin helped a lot, though obviously wedding planning is still their number one priority . . ." He coughs and Jane laughs. Mortimer and Colin are taking their wedding planning *extremely* seriously. Last Joseph heard there was talk of live swans being involved. "And I did a huge order from P&G Wells," he adds.

Jane turns in his arms. "Your bonus?" she says, voice hushed.

He kisses her. "What better way to spend it?"

At the very first book club he'd arranged with Jane, he'd told her books were his happy place, and he'd seen her face transform. She relaxed, she smiled; she gave him a hint of the woman under that guarded exterior. *Books are my happy place, too*, she'd told him, and Joseph has often wondered whether that was the moment he fell in love with her.

When Joseph thought of 2020, he wouldn't think of the fear and anxiety, the stress, the isolation. He'd remember the nights when Jane lay in his arms and they talked about places they'd never been, but which felt as real to them as the bed where they lay, and people they'd never met who seemed like old friends. He'd remember the stories they'd shared.

"Here," he says, directing her toward the picnic set up on the coffee table. "Happy Valentine's Day, Jane."

He shifts so he can catch her expression when she spots all the food laid out on the table. Watching Jane's expressions is one of Joseph's greatest joys—she'd always hidden so much of herself, but she's getting out of the habit, and seeing her unfurl is endlessly delightful.

"Oh, look!" She laughs. "All my favorite things!"

"So, there's a rule in this library," he says as she lifts the lid on the pot of clotted cream and sniffs the jam, breaking into a smile when she clocks that it's cherry. "You can only enjoy yourself here. One hundred percent unadulterated enjoyment only. Hence . . . all your favorite foods for dinner."

"What order do we eat it all?" she says, pinching a slice of mango out of a bowl. "Cinnamon buns to start, then Chilli Heatwave Doritos for main and scones for pudding?"

"There's no order, Jane," Joseph says, laughing, bundling her into his arms. "You choose."

"Decadent," she says, with one of those mischievous smiles. She kisses him, a slow, luxurious kiss, the kiss of two people who are starting to truly believe they have all the time in the world together. "Thank you," she says, voice low. "This is so wonderful."

"Well, Jane Miller," Joseph says, dipping his head for another kiss. "It's about time you got the Valentine's Day you deserve."

ACKNOWLEDGMENTS

First up, I want to thank my agent, Tanera Simons, who is always an invaluable support to me, but never more so than with this book. Thank you for being custodian of the book four manuscript when that was needed, and thank you for all the bewildering brainstorms about how to manage dates, both in the book and in my real life . . .

Secondly, I'd like to thank Gilly, who gave me an idea that became the key to unlocking this story, and who is a truly rare and wonderful friend. I hope when we are old and gray, we are still sending each other voice notes about our dogs and/or characters misbehaving.

Thank you to my editors, Cassie, Emma and Cindy, for trusting me to pull this book off and for all your incredible creative input. Thank you to Hannah, Ella, Hannah, Bethan, Ellie, Aje, Kat and everyone at Quercus, who are brilliant, and thank you to Brittanie, Fareeda, Angela, Jessica and everyone at Berkley, who are also brilliant—I am so lucky to work with you all.

This book involved some fairly unusual research, and I'm particularly grateful to Tom of Tom Fisher Tree Care for showing me how to climb an oak, fielding weird phone calls about boom lifts, and sharing his stories with me. Thanks also to Anna Wright of ACW Arb for giving up your time to speak to me about being a female tree surgeon, and to all who contribute to Arbtalk, which has been an invaluable resource! All tree-related errors are of course my own.

I'm very grateful to Lisa Burdett and Maggie Marsland for chatting to me about the world of life coaching—again, all errors are my own (and Siobhan's errors are very much her own too . . .). And thank you to Jack, who gave a very generous donation to CLIC Sargent so that his girlfriend, Lou, could have her name in this book.

There are a few extra-special people who endured the confusing experience of discussing this novel while it was in progress. To my parents: thank you for all the phone calls, for keeping up with the plot twists and for generally being wonderful. To Pooja: thank you for the lockdown walks and for not minding all the spoilers! To Paddy: your acknowledgment really belongs in the next book, but I should probably also thank you for climbing way too high up a tree during our research session with Tom so that I could witness him yelling "Eke yourself down slowly!" with borderline panic—all very good for authenticity. Finally, thank you to Sam, the love of my life and the most patient brainstormer of all: after all these years I still can't quite believe you're mine. Surely that's too good?

I'd like to finish by thanking the key workers who strode out into a terrifying world in order to keep us all safe in 2020 and 2021. Every single one of you is absolutely amazing, and I hope you never forget that—the rest of us certainly won't. Thank you for your bravery.

The
No-Show

BETH O'LEARY

DISCUSSION QUESTIONS

1. The three women at the heart of this book all have quite different personalities. Who did you relate to the most—Jane, Siobhan or Miranda?

2. When Jane first comes to Winchester, she is completely overwhelmed, and she creates some systems to help her manage her new life. Do you think these routines of hers are a positive step, or was this a mistake?

3. Siobhan is also hurt by a previous relationship, but her trauma manifests quite differently. How is she changed by the experiences she had with Cillian?

4. At various points, Miranda struggles with her feelings for both Carter and AJ. Did you feel she was better suited to one than the other? What would you have done in her place—would you have stuck by Carter if you had all the information she had?

5. New Year's Eve is a pivotal moment in the novel. Were you surprised by the revelations that came out at the party? What had you expected to happen?

6. Several of the characters in *The No-Show* struggle with their mental health. How do their friends, family and support networks help them? What more could be done for people in their shoes?

7. What was your perception of Joseph Carter? Did your view of him change as the novel progressed?

8. Siobhan's friend Kit says, "I'm sure people didn't use to get ghosted in Victorian times, did they?" How has being ghosted and stood up changed with the advent of mobile phones and dating apps? Do you think it happens more often now, or does it just happen in a different way?

9. Each of the women brings out a slightly different side to Joseph Carter. Do you think you're consistent no matter who you're hanging out with, or are you a little different when you're with different people?

10. What did you think of Richard? How did his character make you feel? To what extent would you say he was responsible for what happened to Siobhan?

Photo © Ellen O'Leary

Beth O'Leary is a *Sunday Times* bestselling author whose novels have been translated into more than thirty languages. Her debut, *The Flatshare*, sold over half a million copies and changed her life completely. Her second novel, *The Switch*, has been optioned for film by Amblin Partners, Steven Spielberg's production company. Beth writes her books in the English countryside with a very badly behaved golden retriever for company. If she's not at her desk, you'll usually find her curled up somewhere with a book, a cup of tea and several woolly jumpers (whatever the weather).

CONNECT ONLINE

BethOLearyAuthor.com

BethOLearyAuthor

BethOLearyAuthor

Ready to find
your next great read?

Let us help.

Visit prh.com/nextread

Penguin
Random
House